THE CURE

K.J. KALIS

Copyright ©2019 K.J. Kalis
eISBN 978-1-7334480-1-7
ISBN 978-1-7334480-2-4
All rights reserved

Published by:
BDM, LLC

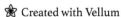 Created with Vellum

1

Kat Beckman pulled the blankets up under Jack's chin as she sat on the edge of his bed. It was a mother's reflex. "I've got to go to the hospital now, buddy," Kat said, staring at his little face highlighted by the dim light from the lamp with the trucks on it that he insisted stayed on all night.

"I know. You have to see Gramma."

"That's right. But Dad will be here and I'll be back before you even stop dreaming."

Jack turned away from her as she pulled the blanket up over his back, the sleeve of her sweater sliding down her arm. She quickly pulled it back into place so she didn't have to look at the scar. Kat's husband, Steve, silhouetted in the light from the hallway watched her cover up her arm, but she was never sure what he thought. Kat pushed those thoughts out of her mind.

Getting up from the bed, she walked out of the room as quietly as possible. Steve followed her down the steps to the front door where her bag was waiting.

"I'll be back," she said, Steve standing behind her.

"Kiss mom for me."

"I will." Steve gave her a peck on the cheek and Kat stepped out onto the front porch. The night air was cool and damp. Rain had come to the city of Aldham earlier in the day and the moisture was still lingering. It likely wouldn't dry up until the sun came out the next day.

Kat got into her car and pulled out of the driveway, checking to make sure her overnight bag was stowed on the passenger seat. Jack's toys clanked off of the back seat and onto the floor as she took one of the turns to get to Mercy Memorial Hospital. The noise of Jack's toy truck careening off of the back seat reminded Kat that she was spending yet another night away from her family. The nights away from Steve and Jack had become more and more frequent as Laura's cancer progressed. It had started in her stomach and had moved to her liver from there. The newest treatment was supposed to be working, but an immune system compromised by harsh medication after harsh medication had put Laura in the hospital with an infection and dehydration. Steve couldn't bear having his mom spend the night alone and Kat couldn't bear to have Steve gone from Jack every night, so they had been switching off.

Not that she'd been doing it willingly. Like most families who had a loved one with cancer, costs were paid all around. The stress, interruptions, monetary cost and emotional cost had taken a toll on the whole family and her marriage. It wasn't that she didn't love Laura. She did.

Kat took the final turn into the hospital and tried to remember how their life had been before Laura had been diagnosed. She had work that she liked as a freelance journalist. Steve had his own consulting firm and they both had plenty of time to spend with four-year-old Jack. Time to go to the park, play in the sandbox and roll his beloved trucks up and down the driveway.

Kat pulled the car into the closest parking spot she could find to the hospital entrance. She was so absorbed thinking about what she was missing at home that she nearly overshot the parking spot and nearly hit the guardrail. "Stupid cancer," she muttered under her breath as she walked into the hospital.

Kat walked inside the doors, smelling the now-familiar faint odor of germicide. She heard a floor waxing machines running somewhere down the hallway and around the corner where she couldn't see it. As the elevator doors opened in the lobby, Kat tried to decide if she should go down to the cafeteria for a cup of tea to take up to Laura's room, but checking her phone, she saw that the cafeteria just closed. No tea tonight.

A couple of medical residents walked out of the elevator as the doors opened, black circles under their eyes, evidence of sleep they hadn't had during their shift. Kat shrugged her bag back up on her shoulder and pressed four for Laura's floor.

When the doors opened Kat walked under the sign that said, "Enter Here." She put down her overnight bag and walked over to the sink. With so many cancer patients on one floor, hand washing wasn't something that's optional. The water was so hot that it stung. Kat dried her hands off and then walked onto the floor.

"Hey Emily," Kat said to one of the nurses heading in the opposite direction as she walked towards Laura's room. Emily smiled and waved. With how frequently Laura had been in the hospital, Kat and Steve had gotten to know pretty much everyone on the floor. Kat slowed down just enough to not miss Laura's door -- room 415.

Inside the room, the lights were already dim. Laura was almost never awake when Kat got there. Kat waited until the last second to leave Jack, so evening rounds and medications were already done. Kat glanced at the monitors, Laura's heartbeat showing up as little blips on the screen and the IV pumps humming quietly as they pushed fluids and antibiotics into Laura as quickly as she could absorb them.

Luckily, the rooms at Mercy Memorial were single rooms

with a little sitting area for family. It wasn't as comfortable as being at home, but it would do for the few hours that Kat would be there. As she sat down in the vinyl-covered chair that would convert to something like a bed, she felt a little angry at having to be at the hospital again. She shook it off and told herself that she was being selfish. Before she had a chance to get too angry, a nurse came in with a steaming hot cup in her hands.

"I brought you some tea," the nurse said.

"Oh, that's so nice. I was going to stop at the cafeteria, but I was too late. It was closed," Kat said, reaching for the mug, breathing in the scent of the tea. One of the regular nurses, Sarah, always brought her tea when she stayed over. It was a special honey chamomile blend that she kept stashed at the nurses' station. "Sarah isn't working tonight?"

"No, she's off. I'm Carrie. I'll be here all night."

"It's nice to meet you."

The fob around Carrie's neck chirped. "I've got to go," she said.

"No problem," Kat said. "See you in a few hours."

"Yup. Let me know if you or Laura need anything." With that, Carrie left the room and Kat was back with her thoughts.

Kat grabbed the TV remote and turned it on low, no sound. She took a couple of sips of the tea. Holding the warm mug in her hands was somehow comforting, even though it wasn't really cold outside or even in the hospital, for that matter. Kat leaned back in the chair, putting her feet up. She started to feel really tired and set the mug down on the table next to the chair. She felt her eyes begin to close and she drifted off to sleep.

A hand on her shoulder roused her out of sleep. Kat felt strangely groggy like she had too much to drink. She opened her eyes, but they felt heavy. She looked up to see a man wearing scrubs and a surgical hat standing in front of her. A surgical mask partially obscured his face. Kat glances towards Laura.

"She's okay," the man said.

Kat tried to ask who he was, but her mouth wouldn't form words.

"Laura's cancer is really bad. There's a cure, but you can't get it here," the man says. "If you are interested in saving her, there's a way." He pulled what looked to be a gold medallion out of his pocket and put it on the tray next to Kat's now-cold cup of tea.

Kat's eyes closed again and the man took the cup of tea, pulled up his surgical mask and pushed the cart he brought onto the floor down the hall, waving to the nurses and whistling quietly as he went.

2

Kat woke up still on the hospital chair, her head pounding and her eyes bleary. She slept soundly -- more soundly than she had in months. The recliner that the hospital offered as a guest bed squeaked as she turned towards Laura. Laura was still sleeping. She did that a lot. The monitors had kept their nightly vigil. The only thing that had changed was the new IV bags and the light coming into the window from outside.

Laura's day nurse, Diane, came into the room. "Hey," she whispered. "How are you? You slept right through a shift change."

Kat blinked a couple of times and sat up in the chair, feeling cold as soon as the blanket fell off. "I'm okay. I slept really hard. I dreamt there was a cure for cancer."

Diane walked over to Laura and injected something into her IV. Laura never stirred. "That happens. You get worn out from caring from your family. You just crash. I've got lots of families that dream there is a cure. I wish! I'd be happy to be out of a job."

"Yeah, I must have been overtired," said Kat. "I've been

researching a story, taking care of Jack and coming here. It's a bit much."

Diane walked over to Kat and patted her on the shoulder. "Just go home. She's probably going to sleep today. We will call if there is a change."

Kat nodded and picked up her bag. She never even opened it the night before. The side table where her tea had been had her cell phone and keys on it. She scooped those into her hand. Laura didn't look like she was going to wake anytime soon. Kat grabbed Laura's hand and gave it a gentle squeeze. She headed home.

THE SMELL of frying bacon was the first thing Kat smelled when she walked in the door. Jack came running over to her, still in his favorite truck pajamas with the footies attached. "Hi, pal!" she said.

"Hi, mama. You back?"

"Yes, little bear, I'm back."

"I have to go. Red truck needs bacon."

Kat smiled. "Well, okay then. You go eat."

Jack frowned, "No, red truck needs food."

"Of course, sweetie." Kat watched him scamper off as she set her bag down just inside the door. She'd unpack it later. Walking towards the kitchen, she leaned in to say good morning to Steve. He leaned over and gave her a kiss on the cheek. "How did things go?"

"She slept the whole time."

Steve leaned over and looked Kat square in the face, wrinkling his brow. "Looks like you actually slept too."

"I did," Kat said, snagging a piece of bacon. "Some nurse brought me the tea that Sarah usually makes for me. I took a couple of sips and it knocked me out. Who knew chamomile could do that to you?" Kat finished chewing the bacon. "I'm going to go take a shower. I've got to get the hospital smell off of me."

Kat walked up the stairs, taking her bag with her. A good, hot shower would help her to wake up, she was sure of it. She tossed her bag on the bed and walked through the doorway to their bathroom.

She started the shower and turned the knob all the way over to hot. The steam started to curl out of the shower. Kat waited for a moment to get undressed. She stuck her hand in and felt the water temperature, cooling it off just a bit. As she pulled off her sweater, she heard a clang on the tile, like something metal had hit the floor. Wondering, Kat looked down, instantly thinking maybe it had been an earring and then remembering she hadn't worn any. As she looked under the edge of the cabinet, she saw something that glinted in the light. She picked it up and a chill ran down her spine. It was a gold medallion. Immediately, Kat slumped to the floor, the water in the shower still running. She looked at the medallion. The reality of the night before just starting to sink in.

Kat closed her eyes, taking a deep breath, thinking she was just imagining things. Even with her eyes closed, the medallion was still in her hand. She stood up, stuck the medallion back in her sweater pocket and folded it carefully so that it didn't fall out.

Kat tried to let the hot water wash away the night before, but questions came up in her mind faster than she could process her thoughts. What had happened? Who was that man in the scrubs? What did he want? Kat got out of the shower and toweled off, putting on jeans and a sweatshirt. Her chin-length blonde hair still wet from the shower, she fished the medallion out of her sweater pocket, threw all of the clothes into the hamper and pushed the medallion down deep in the front pocket of her jeans. She'd deal with that later.

· · ·

KAT DIDN'T HAVE time to tell him what had happened. She let him go. No need for both of them to be worrying and wondering. And, even if Steve had the time, what would she tell him? She tried to imagine that conversation. "Honey, I drank some tea and thought I had a dream about a cure for Laura's cancer and a gold medallion, except that it might not be a dream at all?" Kat shook her head. She needed answers.

3

Kat needed to think. As a journalist, she knew that working with the facts was the best course of action. The timing hadn't been right to tell Steve anyway.

The noise of Jack rolling his trucks along the floor and talking to himself was soothing in a way. Kat leaned on the counter, trying to gather herself. She opened the cabinet above the coffeemaker, pulled out her favorite blend and filled the carafe with water.

The coffee would take a minute to brew. Kat decided to get her laptop. Padding in bare feet into the next room, across hardwood floors that were spanned by rugs, Kat unplugged her laptop from the small desk in the home office that she and Steve shared. He mostly worked out of his office down the street, but she preferred working at home. Her editor didn't mind. It allowed her to be where she could spend time with Jack. She felt safe at home, or at least she used to.

Kat took her laptop back into the kitchen and set it down. The kitchen was supposed to be the center of the home. For Kat, it literally was. Not only did they spend the most time there as a family, but it was one of the best places she could keep an eye on Jack. She liked the feeling of knowing where he was.

She opened the laptop and gave it a minute while it woke up, rolling her wrist and getting the kinks out. She poured herself a cup of hot coffee and quickly scrolled through her emails to see if there was anything she needed to respond to. Her editor, Van Peck, had sent her back some comments on two stories she had been working on.

Kat had worked with Van for a couple of years -- ever since she and Steve settled in the area. Kat had been an embedded journalist with the Army in the Middle East. Van had done time in the Marines and had done two tours in what service members affectionately called "the sandbox" so he understood Kat's experience working that far from home, almost always in danger. Kat had ended up coming home on a medical furlough. Although that had been seven years ago, she still hadn't fully recovered.

Kat thought back to when she and Van had first met. She went to his office to pitch him on a story. She had dressed up in what she considered work clothes. Jacket, blouse, nice shoes. She wanted to make a good impression. Van was working behind his desk and came out from behind wearing an old black American flag t-shirt that looked like it hadn't seen the washer in a long time, ripped jeans -- not the stylish kind, but actually ripped from years of wear -- and flip flops. Van smiled at Kat, "Either you are dressed up or I need to work on my wardrobe." Kat liked him from that first meeting.

Since then, Kat and Van had worked on a bunch of stories together. Van liked her style. Kat liked his easy way of editing. She never felt pressure from him, which was what she needed after her experience in the Middle East.

The work she'd done in the sandbox was what she considered serious journalism. She had been in the middle of the action. She had seen the impact of the military on stabilizing the region. She saw kids who had previously been afraid to play soccer start to poke their heads out of their homes and eventually come out onto the streets in their villages to enjoy their lives again.

And, she had seen trauma. Lots of it. The cost to everyone in the region -- both native and military -- had been high. Loss of life, loss of limb, loss of innocence.

Kat took a couple of sips of coffee and got up to refill her cup, poking her head down the hallway to see what Jack was doing. He was still scuffing along on the floor, pushing two trucks, a beam of sunlight hitting his hair as he moved across the floor. He was happy, Kat thought. At least one of them was.

Things had been different since Laura got sick. Laura's sickness had come on them in the blink of an eye. One day, everything was fine. Steve was working, Jack was at a friend's house and Kat was on her way to meet a source for an interview on a vaping piece she was working on for Van. Steve called while she was driving.

"What's up," she said, clicking on the blinker to make the last right turn to meet her source.

"Mom is at the hospital," Steve sounded upset.

"What happened? Why?" Kat asked.

"I'm not sure. She said that she had a stomachache that she just couldn't shake. She saw her regular doctor this morning and he sent her over to the hospital for testing. I'm heading over there now to see what is going on."

"Okay. Do you need me to come? Jack is at Beth's house."

"No, no. I'm sure it'll be fine. Probably just reflux or something." With that, Steve hung up and Kat finished her day, not realizing that they were embarking on a journey none of them wanted to take, most importantly, one that Laura didn't want.

Laura had been a single mom for a long time. She was a strong woman. Kat loved that about her especially since Kat's own family wasn't part of the picture. Right after Kat finished college, her parents had died in a car crash. It was devastating. Her brother was so sad about losing their parents that he and Kat had lost touch. Kat had been left on her own. Once she met Steve, Laura took Kat under her wing. Kat loved having a mom, even if it wasn't her own.

That one phone call from Steve started them on days in the hospital with more tests than Laura thought she could bear. Four days later, they finally found out the news. Laura had stomach cancer. What caused it, like every cancer, the doctors didn't know. What they could do was to give her strong chemo-therapy to try to beat it. Kat and Steve had offered to have her move in with them, but Laura didn't want Jack to see her sick, so she stubbornly refused. "I've lived on my own for decades. I'm not about to change that now," she said, turning her head away from them when they offered.

It had been eight months of treatment. There was some progress, but not a lot. Laura's cancer had spread to her liver and the doctors were doing whatever they could for her, but there was no cure. Laura had gotten weaker, lost her hair and about twenty pounds. She was still a fighter, even with her current infection and stay in the hospital.

KAT FOUND herself staring out of the kitchen window, the one right above the sink. She had been doing that a lot lately. The stress of Laura's illness and her challenges with Steve didn't help. In the backyard, she could see a little sapling that she and Jack had hung birdseed and peanut butter covered pinecones on the week before. Spring was just arriving, and the birds were hungry. She and Jack had spent an afternoon with their pinecone project, peanut butter and birdseed all over the kitchen, in Jack's hair and on his face. They had gone out into the yard, Jack wearing his green rain boots and jumping in every puddle he could find. They hung the pinecones in the tree. As the first birds found them, the branches swayed under the weight as they landed and left.

Kat caught herself staring and felt frustrated. Laura's illness had taken a toll on all of them. The social worker told them it was inevitable. "All of my families go through this," she said, shaking her head. "I wish there was an easier way."

The thought brought Kat back to the night before, but she shook it off. Fear crept into the back of her throat. Questions started to filter back in. Kat refocused on her computer. She had emails to deal with. Things that needed attention, not just some ravings of a crazy guy at the hospital. She'd have to remember to call Laura's floor later and tell them to talk to security.

Kat rolled her wrist to get the ache out as she started to type replies to her emails. She kept it covered most of the time because it reminded her of what she wanted to forget. Kat quickly sent an update to Van to let him know how she was coming on her stories.

Her work since her accident hadn't been anything that serious. It was enough to keep her in the journalism game, but it wouldn't win her a Pulitzer. Local political pieces, profile pieces on the new K9 for the police department and an expose on mishandled funds by the local park board were topics that Kat was happy to take on. Nothing too heavy, but not actually puff pieces either.

Kat finished her emails and went into their laundry room to turn on the dryer. The clothes she had started yesterday needed to be warmed up before she could fold them. The routine of watching Jack, working and doing chores had been a salve to Kat's soul for the last four years. She liked the pace of the day. She liked their life the way it was -- the way it used to be before Laura got sick.

Kat followed the noise of trucks to see what Jack was doing. He had taken up residence under the dining room table and brought his blocks out to build a ramp for his trucks, something that Steve had taught him to do. "Vroom, vroom," he hummed under his breath. "Hi mama," he said absent-mindedly.

"Hi, pal. Whatcha doing?"

"I'm building a ramp so the trucks can launch into space!"

"That's great, buddy. Let me know how that works out."

"Okay, mama."

As Kat walked back into the kitchen, she realized that her family would have never let her play under the dining room table. When she grew up, there were rooms that were sacrosanct. They were only used on special occasions, and then very rarely. She and Steve had no such rules in their house. They had bought it with the intention of using every inch for fun. And, they had succeeded... mostly.

Kat rubbed her wrist as she heard her cell phone ring. She picked it up and answered. It was Van.

"Hey. How are you?"

"I'm good," Kat said, hearing the uncertainty in her own voice.

"Are you sure?" Van was one of those people who had a radar for knowing when something was wrong. He never pushed her, but he did make sure Kat knew when he thought she wasn't telling him something.

"Yeah, just a long night at the hospital." For the first time since she got dressed, Kat reached into her pocket and felt for the medallion, trying to make sure she wasn't imagining its presence. It was still there, warm from her body heat. She pulled her hand out without looking at it.

"I can imagine. Just wanted to check in on the follow up about the fire at the industrial park?"

"It's almost done. I'll have it to you this afternoon."

"Great," Van paused. "You sure you are okay?"

"Yeah, I'm good. Thanks, though," Kat lied.

"Okay. Talk soon." Van hung up before she could reply.

There had been a fire in the local industrial park the week before, just on the outskirts of town. Over the last ten years or so, the city had converted its tax base from manufacturing to professional services and retail. It helped that Mercy Memorial, the hospital where Laura was being treated, had gotten an enormous endowment and had built a whole new wing that brought in patients regionally and created jobs.

Kat pulled up her notes on the fire. The fire in the industrial park -- one of two different complexes about five miles outside of town -- wasn't a surprise. Many of the buildings had been abandoned for years. While there wasn't a big homeless population in the area, a few people had broken into the buildings. There were also kids who were just looking for a good time and used the buildings for a place to hang out, practice their tagging skills or smoke joints. The fire itself wasn't a surprise because of the fact that the buildings had been abandoned. What was a surprise is that it looked like someone had tried to piggyback pirated electrical service into one of the buildings and it had shorted out. No one knew why.

Kat pulled up the email from the fire chief, John Norlan. She read it through, "Hi Kat. Glad you are working on this story. I've attached our report. Looks like someone was trying to access electrical service and shorted something out. Strange thing is that it looks like they were trying to get a lot of volts -- more like a 220 line than typical 110 electrical service. Looking forward to your piece. John"

Kat had developed a good relationship with the local police and fire departments. After being embedded in the Middle East and reporting on the local activities of the military she knew that people that were called to the service, police or fire were generally folks that were just trying to help. There were some who were in it for the power, sure. There were some that made bad decisions. That happened in every profession. But, for the most part, the people that Kat had met wanted to help. That was all. Having a good relationship with the people serving in the area made her job easier.

Kat leaned back on the stool wondering why someone would want to pull high voltage power into the building. A 220 line would be used for something like a dryer or a furnace, not your typical lamp or television. It seemed like a question that had no answer unless the police could identify who had broken in. That would be nearly impossible as the security cameras had gone offline long ago.

Kat shrugged off her thoughts. Unlike many journalists, her job wasn't to interpret. It was to report. That's what Van kept telling her, at least. Kat looked back at the email that Chief John had sent to her. She forwarded it to Van to get his reaction and closed her laptop.

Kat rubbed her wrist. The change in temperature always seemed to bother it. She remembered a time when she used to laugh off people who complained about their joints in the weather. Kat stuck her hand back in her pocket and fished out the medallion that she found in her sweater. A flush of frustration and fear followed her. She walked over to the window that was over the sink to look at it under the bright morning sunshine. There seemed to be a logo on it, the picture of a pyramid with some other details that she couldn't quite make out. On the backside was a medical cross. There didn't seem to be any other information. Frustrated, Kat shoved it back in her pocket. Mysteries like this unnerved her. Maybe it was because of her job, maybe it was her need for control, but either way, she wanted to know what exactly had happened the night before. Who was the man that approached her? How did the medallion get in her pocket? Had he drugged her? Most importantly, was he for real? Did he really have a cure for cancer? The questions crashed over her like a wave. She felt like she was drowning.

Kat shrugged her shoulders up near her ears, trying to relieve some of the tension that lived there. She saw a few dishes left in the sink from breakfast, a crust from Jack's toast, a half a cup of coffee that Steve had left. Kat loaded the dishes in the dishwasher. It was no good to try to write at the moment. She was too consumed by trying to figure out the solution to the night before.

Finding solutions had gotten her in a lot of trouble in her life. Kat dried her hands on a towel, closed the dishwasher and found memories from the Middle East creeping up on her again. They did that. It was something that her therapist had told her would happen, but she fought it every time it happened. Kat slid down and sat on the kitchen floor just below the sink, hoping this flashback wouldn't last too long. In moments like these, she felt like she was back in the sandbox again.

4

As she sat on the floor in the kitchen, Kat thought about the day she had gotten the nod to go to the Middle East. It had been an assignment she desperately wanted. One that she used every connection she had to get. The day came when her editor had called her into the office and said, "Kat, I've got good news. Pack a bag. You leave in four hours."

The idea of being an embedded journalist with the Army in the Middle East seemed like real journalism to her. Being in the center of the action, there to get the details as they happened and to tell the stories, was a dream come true.

Or so she thought.

On the plane ride over, she sat alone at one end of the plane with a group of grim-faced, newly deployed service members. Some of them slept. Some of them talked quietly, but most of them had the same hardened look to their faces. It was one she'd never forget.

Landing in "the sandbox," she was immediately taken to the General's office. She hadn't expected that. General Barton was a tall, thin man, with arms and legs that reminded her of a praying mantis. He was the base commander. Later, she'd learn that his officers called him "General Arms." His reach was everywhere, literally and figuratively.

"Sit down, young lady," he said to Kat from his seat behind his desk when she went into the trailer that served as his office. Kat sat, but didn't say a word.

"You are here to serve as an embedded journalist."

"Yes, sir." Kat didn't know what else to say, so that seemed appropriate.

He looked up at her over his glasses. "You understand that much of what you see here can't be reported."

"Yes."

"This isn't a playground. We have serious and dangerous work to do here."

"Of course."

"And your classified status and your presence here depends on you doing what needs to be done, the way we expect it."

Kat was surprised by what he said. General Barton must have sensed her hesitation. He said, "You aren't in America anymore. You might have free rein as a press member there, but that does not apply here. Are we clear?"

"Yes."

"Dismissed."

With that, Kat got up and left his office. She was sure he didn't even look up when she left.

Kat stepped out into the blazingly bright light and heat of midday to find a Sergeant waiting for her. "Are you the journalist?"

Kat nodded. "Yes."

"Great. Come this way."

After a bit of silence, Kat learned that his name was TJ Weiss. He was originally from Oklahoma and was there with his team to run special operations. "You aren't with the Army?" Kat asked.

"Those guys? No," TJ laughed. "I'm a SEAL. We just got here and they told me I had to play nice with you."

Kat felt a lump in her throat form, "Does that mean I'm going with you on missions?"

TJ stopped and raised his eyebrows. "You think that's a good idea?"

Kat looked at her feet and mumbled, "I'm not sure."

TJ kept walking, "Well, the fact that you aren't sure is probably your first good decision since you hit the ground."

OVER TIME, TJ and Kat became close. Looking back, she knew it was probably a little too close. The longer that Kat was on the base, the more they were attracted to each other. They were both single and far from home. Their relationship didn't develop further than a couple of quick hookups, but the bond they had developed was real.

Until things changed.

They were headed out on a routine drive to do a little bit of reconnaissance. Kat was allowed to go with teams when the mission wasn't top secret, or when they weren't anticipating trouble from any of the locals. September 17th was one of those days. It was a routine look at one of the towns near the base. They liked to drive out to check on routes in case there had been movements they didn't know about. The team was just about to turn around when Kat spotted some smoke on the horizon. "TJ, what's that?"

TJ squinted and pulled out his binoculars. "Not sure."

Nothing much had been going on at the base, so Kat was eager to have something to report on. "Are we going to check it out?"

TJ smiled, "You looking for some action?"

Kat just looked down at her Army issued boots. "Maybe?"

"What is going on?" TJ took another look through the

binoculars and radioed in their position to the base, telling them they were going to go up the road another mile to get a look before they turned around. They got the okay and the caravan crept forward, the tires grinding on the sand and gravel. They made it about half a mile to a place where the road had eroded on one of the sides from the last torrential rain that came through the desert. It was still passable, but the caravan had to move to one side of the road to get through it. From where she was sitting, she could see the Humvee in front of them shift to the right, tilting slightly as they moved off of the main road. As soon as the tires turned and touched the berm, the Humvee in front of them was enveloped in a fiery explosion. Before they could even react, their own Humvee was engulfed in flames.

Time sped ahead and stopped at the same time. Kat didn't remember the actual explosion. Whether she blacked out or was unconscious, she never could figure out. The smoke and the smell was overwhelming. She remembered feeling confused about where she was and seeing Charlie, the driver, laying on his side, blood coming from his head. He wasn't moving. The soldiers around her were moving or yelling, whatever they could do to get away from the Humvee and take cover.

Kat couldn't. She remembered being completely frozen in place, unable to move. Panic started to rise in her, but before she could think, she felt strong hands grabbing her Kevlar vest and hauling her out of the vehicle, her legs hitting the road with a thump. TJ dragged her across the road and behind a group of rocks just as the whistle of a rocket launcher finished off their Humvee. The tap-tap of gunfire rattled as the soldiers took aim at the ridge where the rocket came from, others yelling into their radios, marshaling help.

It felt like forever until she was safe.

TJ had later told her that they had only waited for three minutes for helicopters to cover the area with air support.

Within seven minutes, there were more Humvees on the scene to rush them back to the base.

Kat didn't make it back to her position as a journalist on the base. Her left wrist had been shattered in the explosion. She needed immediate surgery and was shipped back to the U. S. to recuperate. TJ was sidelined with a concussion for two weeks -- but what happened to them seemed small compared to the four Army members who had lost their lives in the first Humvee plus the loss of Charlie from theirs.

Sitting on the floor of the kitchen, Kat took a couple of deep breaths. The memories of that day had taken a long time and a lot of therapy to get over. When she first got back, she would hyperventilate so badly that she'd nearly pass out. After doing that one time, Kat decided that hyperventilating on the floor was a better plan than falling off a chair.

"You okay, mama?" Jack said, padding his way into the kitchen, still in his pajamas although they were closer to lunchtime than breakfast.

"Yup, buddy, just taking a break." Kat stood up and smoothed her jeans down over her thighs. "Maybe you could go brush your teeth? I'll come in and help with clothes in a minute. That okay?"

Jack scrunched his nose at her, not wanting to interrupt his latest truck game. "I can do my own clothes."

Kat nodded. "Maybe we could take a truck to the park this afternoon if you get ready?"

With the promise of trucks and a trip to the park, Jack scampered off to get ready.

Knowing that she had a few minutes before Jack would come looking for her, Kat decided to write a few paragraphs on her story for Van. The fire in the industrial area still had questions that needed to be answered. So did the medallion that was in her pocket. Kat pulled it out and looked at it again. The front and back of it still looked the same to her. The cross on the back was something she'd recognize as a medical insignia, but the triangle on the front -- that was a mystery.

Kat tapped on her mousepad to wake her laptop up. She started a search for cancer treatments. All of the typical treatments came up, as they always did. The search showed doctors and cancer hospitals all over the globe. Kat changed her search to cancer cure. Not much came up. Angry at the thought that she was being duped, Kat slammed the lid on the laptop and went to go find Jack.

5

Edgar Cahill circled the block to make sure he wasn't being tailed. The chances of it were slim in this area of town. The industrial buildings that had been bustling just a few years before were nearly all boarded up and abandoned. Of the many places he had traveled, this was one area that he just wasn't too worried about. The only snafu they had was when they first got into town. They had found a warehouse that was perfect, but one of his guys hadn't done the electrical right and it caused a fire. That was the kind of attention they didn't want. While Edgar thought they should move on, his bosses felt otherwise.

Edgar pulled his car, a nondescript gray Honda car, near one of the loading docks behind a block wall. It was one of the best places for him to park. He had easy access to the building and unless someone was looking for him or his car, they wouldn't see it. He eased open the creaky door to the car -- it was one he bought for cash a few towns over using a fake ID -- and stepped out into the darkness. He never used a flashlight or the light on his phone. There was no reason to take a chance in case someone was driving by. Padding over to a door in the same scrubs he had worn to the hospital, Edgar pulled out a key fob and passed it over a pad that looked like an old utility covering attached to the building. The door gave a slight click. It was a new technology that Edgar's bosses liked. Quiet, difficult to penetrate and easy to remove.

Edgar quickly closed the door to the building, giving his eyes a moment to adjust. When they first found the building, he was surprised that someone had left industrial machines there. As he walked by, the cover on one of them flapped slightly. The H & M Tool Company had been one of the first to close in the area, more because the owners were tired of the work and could see the writing on the wall than anything else. They still owned the building and used it to take tax write-offs while they ran other profitable businesses elsewhere. With the building so far outside of the city limits, no one cared if the lawn was mowed or what happened to the machines inside. Edgar chuckled to himself. For all he knew, H & M Tool Company was still paying salaries to workers who hadn't walked in the door for years. There were more ways than ever to scam the system. The more he knew, the more skeptical he became of how the world works.

"It's a dog eat dog world, right buddy?" Edgar stopped in the middle of the room and leaned down to pet his dog Woof, who didn't get up but managed to wag his tail anyways. Woof traveled wherever Edgar did. It was part of the deal. The bosses wanted him to travel more, but he'd only go where Woof could. Edgar had found Woof in one of the cities he worked three years ago, shivering by a trash dumpster, clearly abandoned by someone that didn't care. Edgar had scooped him up and taken him wherever he had gone ever since, even taking the time to make sure that Woof saw a vet for shots and checkups. Woof was the only family Edgar had. Wherever Edgar went, Woof went too.

Standing up, Edgar walked over to a woman who was holding a tablet. He couldn't ever remember her name. Mary? Meredith? "How are we looking?" he asked.

She nodded and said, "Pretty good. We are almost done here."

"Did a new location come in yet?"

"No. I'm still waiting."

Edgar frowned. His bosses tended to think that he and his team could move from place to place with a moment's notice. Although they were faster than they used to be, it still took time and energy to find the right place to house their operation when they were moving so much. A few weeks here, a few weeks there. Edgar almost had to send out a scout team as soon as they landed in one place. It never worked that way, though. The bosses tended to keep him in the dark until he absolutely had to know.

"Jackasses," he muttered.

MOVING into a new city not only meant new targets, but they needed to find a place to stay. It wasn't like Edgar could rent a storefront in the center of a city and work from there. They needed to find outlying areas that were abandoned, or nearly so, that also had close access to hospitals, clinics and patients. Their hub had to be large enough to house them and their operation, it had to have a place for Woof to roam around and they needed a way to leave quickly, in case they were detected, or quietly, in case they weren't.

Edgar frowned and pulled up the back of his scrub pants. He hated the way that they fit. On his average frame, he looked very much the part of a surgical technician or nurse. That was the goal. He usually kept his dark hair trimmed but had lately been growing it out a bit to match the beard he had. Beard, mustache, goatee -- they were all part of his transition from city to city.

"Let me know as soon as they tell us something. I'm going to swap out my phone." He held up the one he currently had. "Keep an eye on this one while we wrap things up."

The nurse looked at him and said okay.

Edgar went into what had been the H & M office and sat down in a desk chair they had found there. Abandoned buildings with leftover furniture were a bonus in his business. The team had converted the office into a makeshift bunk room. There were four cots with blankets and pillows on them. There was a hot plate, small refrigerator, microwave and some other basic necessities that the team brought from city to city. Edgar flipped open his laptop to watch some local television. He put his feet up on the desk and balanced his computer on his belly, watching clips from a football game.

The team set up much of the equipment before Edgar and Woof arrived in a city. They'd rent a U-Haul and fill it with their equipment and head out, sticking to back roads. They'd only gotten pulled over once and luckily the trooper didn't ask to look in the back of their truck. Even if he had, Edgar always had his guys put the household goods near the door. Cots and chairs would be the first thing the cops would see. They'd just assume their cover story about moving was correct and let them move on. They'd never find the scientific equipment they moved unless they unloaded the whole truck. That was more of a hassle than most cops wanted to deal with.

Back roads had become some of Edgar's favorite. Highways were too densely populated. And, if they broke down, it would attract too much attention. People in smaller cities were far more trusting. Their trust made it easy to move from place to place. While Edgar didn't love driving, he hated flying even more. Because of that, the bosses usually kept Edgar in North America. He'd been as far south as Chile and as far north as

Alaska. Boats got him and Woof to outlying regions. The Apex bosses had put another team in Europe to handle that market. They were currently expanding into Asia, Australia and New Zealand. There was no counting the amount of time he'd spend in cars and even the occasional boat to get the job done. The work was okay, but the pay was great.

Edgar got up and opened the refrigerator door. He'd been up all night dealing with the Beckman's. Trying to get people to understand what he was offering was the hardest part of the job. There wasn't a lot in the refrigerator to eat. A couple cans of pop, three beers, grape jelly and some oranges. In the back was a half-eaten jar of marinated herring, the kind swimming in mayonnaise. Edgar pulled the jar out and grabbed a sleeve of saltines from the counter. Sitting back down, he balanced the laptop on his stomach while he dipped saltines into the jar, scooping glops of fish and onions out onto the crackers.

When the game highlights were over and he saw that the Cowboys had won, he stood up, wiped his hands on his scrub pants and headed out of the office. The nurse was sitting at one of the old machines, using an industrial-sized table saw as an improvised desk, checking her tablet again. The job used to be much harder before we were able to get Internet access, he thought, nodding at her. Mary? Meredith? Why couldn't he remember her name? Edgar walked down the hallway behind the office to a room that had a sliver of light coming out from under the door. Pulling the fob he used to get into the building out of his pocket, he swiped it across another panel and the door popped open. Inside, John was reading a newspaper, sitting on a chair. Edgar nodded to him and walked further into the room. He and his team didn't talk too much. They were always concerned about listening devices even though no one knew where they were hiding out.

The room was lit by blue bulbs that cast a harsh glow over the machinery in the room. Two lab tables had been set up parallel to each other, their stainless surfaces reflecting the blue bulbs. A microscope, centrifuge and a couple of plastic utility containers, the kind that nurses bring into the room when they take blood, were filled with syringes, needles, blue stretchy tourniquets and bandages. At the far end of the room, a generator hummed quietly. The prep team had done a good job of drilling through the building's outer wall to install an exhaust pipe for the equipment, ending it near some tall weeds that no one would see unless they looked too carefully. Next to the generator were two full-sized refrigerators. The one on the right had a blue cord tied to it. The refrigerator on the left had a red cord on it. Edgar took a look inside the refrigerators. They had been equipped with a special locked keypad that only Edgar and one of his nurses could open. The only other people that knew the codes were the Apex bosses.

The thought of someone attacking their operation made the hair on Edgar's neck stand up as he opened the door to the blue refrigerator to check their vials. He never understood why they needed such big refrigerators, but sometimes they had to house other items for the bosses -- other vials, human organs, other medications. Recently, they had added red vials to the inventory that had proved to be quite successful. The bosses called them the killing vials. One dose and the patient would die within the hour. The yellow vials, the ones they used to either give someone cancer or make the case they had worse, were in the same refrigerator with the red ones. Edgar much preferred using the blue ones. It brought complete healing within hours. He pulled one of the blue vials out of the tray and walked over to John, who pushed a tablet toward him without looking up. Edgar entered the number printed on the side of it into the tablet and authenticated it with his finger-print. The bosses would know instantly he had checked out a vial of serum and was on his way to complete another transaction.

The door clicked on his way out of the room, leaving John to finish reading the paper until the end of his shift.

Edgar started to head out the door, the vial in his pocket, until the Mary/Meredith the nurse stopped him. "You might want to change your pants," she said, pointing to the oily herring stains on his legs. "That's memorable."

Edgar sneered at her as she turned away. He walked back into the office and opened a cardboard box that had scrubs in them, pulled out a pair marked large and put them on. The herring stained pair went right into the trash. They never bothered washing scrubs. They just put on new ones that the bosses had ordered. The old ones would be burned when they left. The bosses had a separate crew for that.

On his way out the door, Edgar stopped to pet Woof again, giving him a dog treat that he had gotten in the kitchen when he changed his pants. "Be a good boy," Edgar said, letting Woof lick his face, "I'll be back in a bit."

Edgar went out into the darkness, getting into the car and pulling away without any lights on. He had gotten used to walking and driving in the darkness. He kept the lights on the little car off until he got out of the industrial park and started to head into town. It wasn't a long drive to Mercy Memorial. Long enough that he didn't have to worry that anyone would stumble upon their group in the industrial park, but not too long to be inconvenient. He'd had several patients there over the last couple of weeks.

As Edgar drove, he hummed along to Johnny Cash music. He wasn't sure what he liked about it, but it seemed to keep him focused on what he needed to do. Johnny's voice was serious and gravelly. Edgar liked that. He turned the wheel into the parking garage and chose a spot in the basement where the employees parked.

Before he had arrived in the city, his team had done a sweep of the hospital, giving him information on which doors required key cards and where the security cameras were. Edgar was adept at walking right by them without anyone ever seeing his face. With no tattoos and frequent changes in his hair, he would be hard to discern from any of the other medical staff that came in and out. Edgar parked in a spot that always seemed to be open. There was a light out above the spot, so the whole side of the garage was darker than usual. He was sure no woman in their right mind would park in that darkness. "Their loss is my gain," he muttered. Edgar pulled the vial with the blue serum out of his pocket and a syringe. He punctured the blue vial with the needle and drew it into the syringe, capping it and sticking it in his pocket.

Edgar used the fake badge he had to go in the employee entrance. He didn't stop in the locker room or bother to try to pretend to login. He walked down a brightly lit hallway, pretending to look down at his phone whenever there was a camera nearby. He went around the corner and down a hallway where he had stashed a medical cart in a storage closet. He grabbed a surgical hat and mask from the bins on the shelves, put the hat on, just a few wisps of his hair hanging out. The mask he put on halfway, to help shield his face. He pushed the cart into the hallway. With the equipment he was using, he looked like he could be from pathology or surgery. The more people made assumptions, the better, he thought. The mask half hanging off his face obscured his look without drawing attention to him.

He got into the elevator with a couple of nurses who were busy checking their phones. The popularity of social media and smartphones had made his job so much easier. People were always checking their feed. They very rarely noticed what was right in front of them. With a beep, the elevator door opened. Edgar nodded to the nurses as he pushed the cart out onto the floor where Roger Baker was. The nurses didn't even look up.

With the late hour, the nursing staff was down to a skeleton crew. The halls had been dimmed to allow the patients to rest as best they could. A faint beeping could be heard from some of the rooms. As Edgar pushed the cart down the hallway, he saw signs for infectious precautions -- patients who couldn't be seen without a gown, gloves and a mask on. He saw other signs that read "oxygen in use." Cancer patients developed lots of other issues than just their cancer. The cancer was a gateway to more disease than Edgar liked to think about. What Edgar did for patients and their families was a simple transaction. It was an opportunity for them to start again. In his time with Apex, almost all did. Very few turned down his offer. It didn't matter to him. It only mattered to his bosses that he made the offer and followed through on instructions. The result -- life or death -- wasn't important.

Edgar pushed the cart against the wall just outside of room 414, the room of Roger Baker. Roger had been in the hospital for three months, suffering from lung cancer. "Smokes will get you every time," Edgar muttered as he stepped inside the room. The only glow came from a small light right over Roger's bed. There were eight different IV's all running into Roger's body at the same time. Some to keep him hydrated, some to keep him fed, some to kill the cancer, some to keep the cancer treatment from killing him. A monitor kept track of Roger's heart rate and blood pressure, lending an eerie light over Roger's sunken face.

Edgar stayed back in the shadows for a moment looking at Roger. The poor man was skin and bones, all of the muscle in his body having atrophied during his treatment. Roger knew he couldn't walk or stand up easily by the portable toilet right next to the bed. The smell in the room was one that Edgar would never forget, no matter how long he did the job. It was a combination of latex, germicide and a sweet smell he just couldn't place. He wasn't sure he wanted to know what it was.

It was time. Edgar walked closer to Roger's bed, making

sure he was asleep. The sedative that the doctor had ordered had worked it's magic. On his first visit, Edgar had noticed that Roger was a light sleeper and had called in a sedative for him before his visit tonight. The nursing staff had done their job without ever wondering who called in the medicine. Walking over to the side of the bed, Edgar pulled the syringe out of his pocket and injected it into a port on Roger's IV. The blue serum disappeared into Roger's body and Edgar dropped the syringe into a red hazardous medical waste disposal box.

"Do you need some help?" he heard someone whisper.

Edgar turned around. A nurse had come into the room.

"No, I'm okay, I think," he said.

"I saw your cart in the hall. This guy has flimsy veins. Were you trying to pull a sample to get a level?"

"Yeah," Edgar lied, using the nurse's story as his own. "I gave it one go, but I can't seem to get enough."

She nodded, "Let me help." She quickly inserted a needle into his arm and filled the vial, handing it to Edgar.

"Thanks," Edgar said. "I'll get this down to the lab."

"Great," the nurse said, while she was checking Roger's IV's. "I don't think we've met before. I'm Kathy," she whispered.

"I'm Mike. Nice to meet you." Not wanting to get involved in what could be a memorable conversation, Edgar quickly took the vial and pushed the cart back down to the elevators, the wheels vibrating and clattering.

As soon as the elevator doors opened, Edgar ducked into a janitor's closet with the cart and left it there, dumping the blood sample from Roger in a red hazardous material bin.

Humming, Edgar pretended to play with his phone while he walked down the hallway and pushed open the door to the parking garage. Taking a quick look behind him, he made his way back to the car he had stashed in the dark parking space, careful to duck away from any of the cameras. He walked quickly and quietly, his rubber-soled shoes making virtually no noise on the pavement, even though parking garages bounced sounds around more than a rubber ball.

Edgar started the old car and pulled out of the parking place, again looking for the security cameras and turning away from them. His goal was always to blend in. To be utterly forgettable. That's what made him so dangerous.

6

As the sun rose, Roger Baker woke expecting to feel exactly the same way that he had for the last few months. Tired, sick, nauseous. He hated the metal taste that he always had in his mouth from the chemo and the sores and lesions from the radiation. He had said to his wife, Amber, who was the CEO of a multinational real estate firm, "The only good part of cancer is that I can fit into my pants from high school again." Roger rolled over in his bed. As the cloudiness from the sleep medication wore off, he realized that the funny taste in his mouth was gone. He licked his lips. He was thirsty, but there was no metallic taste. He stretched in his bed, at least as well as he could be hooked up to IVs, oxygen and other equipment. There was no ache in his bones.

Roger touched the controls on his bed to put it up to a sitting position. He looked around and realized that he was starved. That, in itself, was a miracle. He touched the nurse's call button. One of them came in within a minute or so, "How are you, Roger?" he asked.

"I'm good. Can I have some breakfast?"

The nurse checked his chart and said, "Sure. You haven't

had much to eat in about three weeks, so we can definitely get you something. What do you want?"

"Three scrambled eggs, four pieces of bacon and two pieces of rye toast with strawberry jelly and coffee. Can you make sure the bacon is crisp?"

The nurse looked at Roger and raised his eyebrows -- the whole floor had known how sick he was and didn't expect him to make it through the week -- "Roger, with that menu, I'll go down and get it myself. Give me ten minutes."

Roger chuckled, feeling the energy moving through his bones, "I'll give you five. Hurry up!"

The nurse laughed and headed out of Roger's sight. As promised, he was back in just a few minutes with a meal for Roger. He pulled over the hospital tray, angling it right over Roger's legs. He lifted the plastic cover that was keeping the food warm, "Now, you haven't had much to eat, so try to take it slow." Roger could tell by the nurse's expression that he didn't think Roger would eat any of it.

"Sure."

The nurse stepped away from the bed, but Roger stopped him, "On your way out, could you turn on the television for me? There's a financial channel, right?" The nurse raised his eyebrows again but did as Roger requested.

Roger took a deep breath and let the smell of the bacon fill his nostrils. The oxygen cannula was in the way, so Roger took it off, expecting to see his nurse come charging into his room because his blood oxygen level bottomed out. He didn't. Roger took a sip of the coffee, which was surprisingly still hot. The bitterness hitting his tongue was a welcome relief. Roger took his fork and stabbed at the eggs, wondering if they would taste metallic. They didn't. After a moment of experimentation, tasting and trying each of the foods, Roger downed the entire plate full of food and drank all of the coffee. Relaxing after his first big meal in weeks, Roger felt awake enough to watch the stock market reports, something he hadn't felt like doing in more than two months. He turned the volume up and noticed that the commentator had changed her hair. It was lighter now and shorter. Roger shook his head, unable to believe how much better he felt.

The nurse came back into his room. "How did you do with the breakfast?" he asked.

"Honestly, I probably could have had another egg or two," Roger said, watching the look of shock on the nurse's face when he realized that Roger had eaten everything on his plate.

"You ate all of this?" the nurse said, stunned. "Where's your oxygen? I told you to keep that on."

"I would if I needed it," Roger said, suddenly feeling more like himself than he had in years.

The nurse glanced at his oxygen levels, and reached for Roger's sensor, taking it on and off of his finger. He even tested it on his own. "Looks like the sensor is working fine. Are you feeling okay? How long ago did you take the oxygen off?"

Roger smiled, victory on his face, "About a half-hour ago. So, my levels are okay?"

The nurse replied, leaning over Roger to listen to his chest with the stethoscope that he kept looped around his neck, "Your levels are better than mine." He stood up, "Your chest sounds completely clear." The nurse frowned, clearly not sure how to handle the rapid change in Roger's status. "I'm thinking I'm going to grab a blood sample for the lab and call your doctor. You aren't planning on heading out to run a marathon right now, are you?"

Roger laughed, "No, but I would like a shower."

The nurse nodded and grabbed a needle and syringe. Roger hated being stuck, so he stopped the nurse, "I think that someone was supposed to take a level last night. What happened to that one?"

The nurse checked the laptop that was stationed in Roger's

room to track his stats and his medications and said, "It's not showing here. Maybe there's been a mess up at the lab. I'll just take another one and get it processed. I'm sure Dr. Meyers would want a fresh look anyway."

"Just as long as she doesn't get on me for my cholesterol levels after all those eggs and bacon," Roger said.

The nurse drew the sample and unhooked Roger from enough of the equipment that he could take a shower, though he was still tethered to the IV pumps. Roger took off the hospital gown he had been wearing for the last two days and stood under the warm water and began to scrub his skin. He wanted to get the hospital smell off of him and use the citrus soap that his wife bought for him. It had some funny name, like "uplifted" or "energize" or something like that. Roger couldn't remember, but that didn't bother him. He washed every inch of his body, at least the parts that he could reach without disturbing the needle still stuck in his hand. Toweling off, Roger put on clothes. Not a suit, but not a hospital gown, either. Before he got sick, he always complained about having to put on a suit for work. It was pretty much the outfit du jour as an attorney, but now he couldn't wait to put another one. "Too bad I don't have a case today," he muttered to himself. With the energy he had, he knew he'd win anything put in front of him, prepared or not.

Roger pulled on a UCLA t-shirt and a pair of sweatpants. He even used his own socks and slippers, not the hospital socks that had non-slip rubber on the bottom of them. He pushed the IV pole back into his room and decided to sit down on the chair next to the bed instead of getting back in bed. If they wanted him to get back up there, they'd have to tell him that, he decided.

He was just watching the half-hour report on the Dow Jones when his wife, Amber, walked in the room. As usual, she was dressed for work, wearing a green skirt, a matching jacket and a shimmering silver blouse. Her job as the CEO of Stanton Real Estate Holdings kept her busy and gave them enough money to do what they wanted. Most of the time, what Amber wanted was new clothes. Roger used to object, but looking at his wife now, her beautiful face staring at him in surprise, he didn't really care how much money she spent on clothes or if they had to build a bigger house just to hang them all up.

"How are you feeling today?" she asked, laying a hand on his arm.

"Great," Roger said, smiling at her with a twinkle in his eye.

"What does that mean?" Amber asked, her eyes narrowing, "And where is your oxygen? You need that. Roger, you have to do what the doctors tell you!"

"I don't need it. Look at my levels."

Like most cancer families, Amber and Roger had gotten a crash course in medicine, knowing more than they ever wanted to. Amber looked at the monitor and quickly took the finger fitting off of his hand, sliding it onto her own.

"The nurse already did that."

She looked at her own number and then put it back on Roger, watching carefully. The number stayed in the high nineties -- exactly where it should be. "You smell good. You showered?"

"Yup. And there's something else."

Amber sat down on the edge of the bed, close to her husband. "What's that?"

"I ate." While eating might not seem like a big deal to someone who is healthy, Amber knew that getting a cancer patient to eat was like trying to roll a three-ton boulder uphill. It had been one of the most difficult parts of Roger's treatment.

Roger quickly told her about how he woke up feeling better than he had in years, had eaten a big breakfast, had watched the opening of the stock market and had taken a shower. "I had no idea that the Dow hit a new high."

Before Amber could comment, Dr. Meyers came into the room, her heels clicking on the floor, a tablet in her hand and her white coat swishing around the hem of her skirt. "How are you feeling today, Roger?"

"Pretty good, doc."

She pulled up a wheeled stool and started swiping through screens on the tablet. "The nursing staff called me. They said you've had a spike in your oxygenation and were able to eat. I'm happy to see that. I just need to see if your blood test results have come back in." Roger saw her blink at the screen a couple of times and swipe left and right. "I'll be right back," she said.

Roger and Amber looked at each other. They waited quietly, not sure what to say to each other. They had been in a lot of meetings just like these and it was never good.

Dr. Myers came back with the morning nurse in tow. "Lou said that you ate your entire breakfast and you took a shower."

"That's right."

"If you don't mind, I'm just going to do a quick exam, okay?"

"Sure enough, doc."

Dr. Myers listened to Roger's chest both front and back and checked a few more screens on her tablet.

Roger waited, the knot in his throat growing while he waited. "Did the blood test come back?

Dr. Meyers nodded, "Yes," she frowned and then smiled, "it looks like the immunotherapy that we've been giving you has been working. I've never seen it work quite so fast or so completely, but you have no more blood markers for cancer."

Roger and Amber blinked at the doctor and at each other. Roger said, "Are you saying I'm cured? I get to go home?"

Dr. Myers stood up. "I'm thinking that maybe you should stay for observation today."

"But, if I'm cured, why? I want to get out of here."

Roger saw Dr. Myers look at him and then at Amber. "Will

you stay home with him today? I just need to know that he's stable."

Roger saw Amber nod. Dr. Myers tapped a few more screens on her tablet. "If you can agree to that, I'll send you home. You have to promise that you'll call immediately if there are any changes. I'd like to see you in my office in about two weeks for some follow up blood work, but other than that, go enjoy your life."

As Dr. Myers left the room, Amber started to cry. "I can't believe this," she whispered. Lou unhooked the IVs and pulled the needle out of Roger's arm and another one from the port in his chest. "I don't know what happened, man, but enjoy it. Dr. Myers will probably take that port out at your next visit if your next labs come back clean." He pushed the IV pumps off to the side of the room, leaving Roger unhooked from all of the equipment for the first time in a long time. "I'll be back in a minute with your paperwork. I'm sure you are eager to breathe some fresh air."

As Lou walked away, Amber leaned in close to Roger, speaking barely above a whisper, "Could it be true? Could what that man said really have worked?"

Roger grabbed her hand and smiled, tears in his eyes, "I know that you had to take a risk to get the information, but I think it saved my life...

7

On his way home from the hospital, still driving in the darkness, Edgar made a stop at Mercy Memorial and walked into a room. He didn't push a cart this time. He pulled a yellow vial out of this pocket and injected a sleeping patient -- a woman -- with it. Within a minute, he could see that her blood pressure started to drop and her breathing started to labor. He disposed of the syringe and went back to his car. He hated to use the yellow serum. It always speeded things up, but sometimes it was necessary.

Once back at the warehouse, Edgar pulled an encrypted flash drive out of his pocket and stuck it into his laptop computer. He ran the encryption key and saw a spreadsheet of nearly five hundred properties all over the world that were currently abandoned or unoccupied properties of Stanton Real Estate Holdings. Although he had checked the data before he administered the blue cure serum to Roger, Edgar rechecked the data Amber Baker gave him against search information he had already acquired. There were dire consequences for clients who gave him bogus information. The information looked legit and so he sent it over to the bosses. They would like this trade. They now had a list of ideal sites to run their operations and a grateful CEO who would happily turn the other way if they left a bit of a mess at one of her properties.

8

J ack held Kat's hand tightly as they went up the elevator
to see Laura. Jack didn't like elevators, he never had.
Kat didn't know why, but she always felt a strong
squeeze from his little hand cupped in hers while they
stood waiting for the doors to open. She squeezed back.

As soon as the doors opened, Jack ran down the hallway to
see Laura. Although he complained that Laura couldn't play
and he didn't like the smell, he loved the ice cream cones from
the cafeteria. As Jack scampered off, Steve grabbed Kat's hand.
"He's not the only one that might need a little squeeze." Steve
smiled at Kat. She could tell he was putting on his best brave
face. This journey hadn't been easy on any of them or their
marriage. "Love you," he said as they got close to Laura's room.

Sarah, the nurse that normally worked overnights with
Laura, happened to be there and waved hello and then came
over to greet them. "The doctor wants to see you. I'll page him
to let him know you are here. I was just about to call you."

Kat took a couple of steps to the side to keep an eye on Jack
who was already standing on a chair to see Laura. He was a
focused child. If he wanted something, nothing would stop

him, Kat thought. Turning back to Steve, she said, "Jack's already in there bothering your mom. Do you want me to go in and get to him?"

"No," Steve said. "Mom loves it. It's a great distraction."

While they waited in the hallway, Kat's phone vibrated in the back pocket of her jeans. She pulled it out, looked at it and Steve nodded. She stepped away from the nurse's station, seeing Steve walk into his mom's room and pull Jack off of the bed rail. "Hello?"

"Hey there." It was Van. "Just checking in. How are things?"

It always amazed Kat that Van seemed to know when something was going on. If she believed in psychics, she'd think he was one. "We are at the hospital. The doctor wants to see us for some reason. Listen," she said ducking down the hallway and whispering into the phone away from earshot, "The other night something weird happened. It might be the basis for a story, but I'm not sure."

Thinking about it, Kat wasn't sure that there even was a story about the other night. That was, except for the medallion. Without the medallion, which was pushed into the corner of a drawer in her bedroom, she might have just brushed the whole incident off as just a bad dream.

"What happened?"

"Kat quickly told Van the story about being at the hospital, the nurse she didn't recognize bringing her the tea and how she thought it was all a dream until she found the medallion in her pocket when she got home."

"Are you okay?" Van asked.

Kat paused, not understanding what he was asking, then it occurred to her that she had been drugged. "Yes, yes -- of course."

As an editor, one of the things that Kat liked about Van was that he was always measured. Not much got him excited. She knew that wasn't his editorial training showing up, it was his background as a Marine. "Good. Now, do you think this is a real offer or do you think it is a hoax?"

Kat took a breath and turned around to see if Steve or the doctor had come to the nurses' station yet. No one was there, except Sarah, who was typing something on the computer stationed in front of Laura's room. Kat knew she only had another minute or two before she had to go. "I don't know. I haven't told Steve. I'm not sure what happened."

"Why didn't you tell Steve?"

It was an obvious question, but one she had avoided thinking about. "He would have freaked out at the idea that I got drugged if that's what it was. It just would have put more pressure on us. And I don't even know if this guy is legit or not. He could have just been crazy that wandered in off the street."

Kat looked again down the hallway and saw Steve walk out of the room and Dr. Jeffers, Laura's oncologist, walk over to the nurses' station. Steve motioned to Laura to join them. "Sorry, I gotta go," she said to Van. Van nodded. She'd catch up with him another time, once she'd sorted all of this out a little bit.

By the time Kat walked down the hall, Jack's little face had appeared at the door or Laura's room and he had charged her, running and jumping into her arms. At four years old, he was all or nothing, either running and climbing and playing trucks, or fast asleep wherever they happened to be.

Kat made it over to Steve and Dr. Jeffers, Jack's arms wrapped around her neck, his legs clinging to her waist. "Hey, Dr. Jeffers, how are you?" Kat asked.

"I'm fine. Thanks for asking." He looked at Kat and Steve. "I'm glad that you are both here." Kat watched his face and wondered why he wanted the in-person visit. He had stubble on his chin that he normally didn't have and circles under his eyes that his glasses didn't quite cover. "I came in early this morning. Sarah called because she was concerned about Laura." He tapped the tablet screen he was holding in his hands, typed in his passcode and looked at her stats. "For some reason, overnight she's taken a turn. I'm not sure that she can tolerate any more treatments."

Kat looked at Steve, who immediately became angry, "What do you mean? She was doing fine. You said the new treatments were working and that she could go home in a day or so!"

Kat put her hand on Steve's arm. "Doc, can you tell us what happened? What do you mean she can't have any more treatments?"

Doctor Jeffers set the tablet down on the counter of the nurses' station. "Sometimes we see cancer patients that, for no reason, take a turn for the worse. They might be fine one day, but then they aren't the next. We don't know why. There are limits to the treatments that we have for cancer. I have to admit, this one is a mystery."

Steve interrupted, "People have had cancer for generations. Why can't you fix this?"

Doctor Jeffers sighed, "Listen, Steve, I understand. I know how frustrating this is. I see it every day." He stopped and looked towards Laura's room. "I wish I had better news. Her blood pressure is dropping and her heart is weak. There's fluid in her lungs. It's time for you to make peace with her illness and say your goodbyes. I'll have Sarah talk to you about hospice options. I'm sorry." With that Doctor Jeffers left. Kat could tell by the look on his face that he didn't understand what had happened to Laura, but that he didn't have any other options to offer her. More questions wouldn't give them more answers. Dr. Jeffers simply didn't have them.

Jack, who was still clinging to Kat like a bear cub in a tree, lifted his head off of her shoulder and said, "Mama, why do we have to say goodbye to Gramma? Are we going home?"

"Yup, in a little bit. Why don't you go back in and show her your red truck? Maybe you can tell her a story."

Jack wiggled, signaling that he wanted to get down. "She saw it already."

Kat leaned over and tapped his nose with her finger, "But did you tell her a story about it? Gramma loves trucks almost as much as you do."

"Okay," with that Jack scampered off to see Laura, who had barely lifted her head since they got to the hospital.

Steve ran his hand through his hair. It had once been jet black, but now flecks of gray speckled it. "What happened?" he said, looking at Laura and then at Kat. "I was just here yesterday, and she seemed fine. How do you go from being fine one day and become terminal the next? That's what Doctor Jeffers was saying, wasn't he?"

Kat nodded, unhappy that she had to agree with him. She didn't want to use the word terminal. She was afraid of how Steve would react. He needed some time to come to terms with the new information they had. "He did say hospice." She looked down the hall past Laura's room. There were more rooms just like hers, where people lay dying from cancer. Kat realized that Steve was right. People had been suffering for generations with the disease. So many other diseases had been cured or were easily treatable. Why not cancer?

Out of one of the rooms at the end of the hall, Sarah emerged, pushing a rolling table that had a laptop on it. Kat saw her push it against the wall in front of the room and start to type. "Let me go talk to Sarah," she said to Steve, "Maybe she can help us understand what happened." He nodded. Kat started to walk down the hall and pointed to Laura's room where Jack was rolling his red truck on the floor. Steve nodded.

Sarah had just finished typing on the screen of the laptop, the image switching from patient records to a login screen with Mercy Memorial's logo on it when Kat walked up to her. "Hey, Sarah."

"Hey, Kat. I'm so sorry. Doctor Jeffers told me about Laura. She's so sweet."

"Thanks. Can you tell me what happened?" The journalist in Kat came out, or at least it sounded that way. "She seemed fine to Steve yesterday. There was even talk of her going home today or tomorrow. I don't understand..."

Sarah started to walk down the hall, motioning for Kat to follow her. "I wish I had an explanation for you. I've only seen turns like that a few times in my career. Some good, some bad. But we will get her great hospice care and she will be comfortable and..."

"Wait," Kat said, putting her hand on Sarah's arm. They both stopped walking. "You've seen turns for the good and the bad?"

"Yeah, well, the turns for the bad seem to happen more often." Sarah wrinkled her brow. "I am surprised about Laura, though. She really seemed to be getting better." She shook her head as if dismissing a thought. "Yeah, we have had a good one that was strange. Last year, I had this woman and her daughter. The daughter was the patient and the woman was a microbiology professor, I think. The daughter had glioblastoma, you know, the brain tumor?"

Kat nodded. Glioblastoma was almost always fatal.

"Anyway, it was really bad. The little girl was stage 4B and there was nothing we could

do for her. One night she went to bed on a ton of pain meds. We thought she only had a couple of days left. She had lost her sight and was having trouble swallowing. We had prepared the family for the worst. But then the morning shift came in and she was a totally different child. She was playing games on her tablet and came out to the nurses' station because she was so hungry. I remember she ate two bowls of Fruit Loops. The doctors reran all of her scans and just like that she was fine. No more glio."

Kat took a moment to soak that in. "What happened after that morning?"

Sarah looked like she was thinking. "Last I heard, she's completely recovered. Never seen her on the floor again. The docs were really weirded out by it. They'd never seen anything like it before." A light flashed down the hallway. "Sorry, I gotta go."

"No problem," Kat managed to say before Sarah ran off.

Alone in the hallway, Kat decided to go check on Steve and Jack. A lump formed in her throat as she walked into Laura's room. Laura's color was decidedly paler than just a couple of days before and there was a rasp in her throat that was new. More IV bags had been crowded onto the pump stand by her bed. Laura rolled her head to the side and opened her eyes as Kat stood to one side of her bed. Jack and Steve were playing trucks on the floor. Kat frowned, thinking they would both need showers when they got home to get the hospital smell out of them.

"Hi, Gramma." Kat had called her that since the day that Jack was born.

"Hi," Laura whispered.

"How are you feeling today?"

"Like two trucks hit me coming from different directions."

Kat smiled. At least Laura hadn't lost her sense of humor. Kat and Laura hadn't always been close. Laura had been protective of Steve when they first met, but after she saw how quickly Kat and Steve fell in love, she softened towards Kat. Kat grabbed her hand, "Did Steve talk to you?" Laura nodded. "I'm sure the doctors will figure out something soon."

Laura looked straight at Kat, locking eyes with her. "It'll be okay either way. Know that," she whispered.

Tears formed in Kat's eyes, but she didn't let them fall. It was so hard to see Laura suffer this way. Laura had become a mentor to her, especially since her own parents hadn't been in the picture for so long. Killed in a car crash just after Kat graduated from college, Kat hadn't had any mother figures in her life until Laura came along. It was like losing her own mother again.

Kat took a deep breath, trying to send the tears back where they came from. It didn't work, but at least she was able to keep the tears from taking over. "Don't worry about anyone but you, okay?" she said to Laura. "I'll take care of the boys. They will be okay."

Laura managed a weak smile, her eyes closing, "Let's not say goodbye just yet."

With that, Laura seemed to fall asleep, though it was hard to tell if she was sleeping or unconscious. Kat looked at the heart monitor that was just over her bed. There was still a heartbeat, so they still had time to figure out what to do.

As soon as Laura fell asleep, Steve scooped up Jack from the floor and they walked out of the room and back to the car. The drive home was quiet, both Kat and Steve lost in thought and sadness and grief.

When Steve stopped the car at an intersection near their house, he said, "How did this happen? I just don't understand how she goes from feeling better to doing badly so fast. I mean, it was overnight!"

Kat sighed, the lump in her stomach growing bigger by the minute. "Maybe there is another treatment option that we don't know about. Sarah was saying that a girl on the floor recovered overnight from glioblastoma."

Jack muttered, "Glee-o, glee-o." Unfortunately, Jack had learned a lot of words that a normal four-year-old simply didn't have in their vocabulary because of his time visiting Laura.

Kat shot a glance at Steve and pulled a pair of earbuds out of the glove compartment. "Here, buddy," Kat said, handing Jack her cell phone and earphones, "Put these on. We have a little bit of a drive left. It's your favorite truck program."

Jack smiled, "I love trucks," and pulled the earphones over his head.

Kat and Steve had been careful around Jack. They hadn't wanted to upset him with Laura's illness -- Laura wouldn't have wanted that either. Jack plugged in the earbuds and Kat looked at his face. He looked like Steve's childhood pictures, but blonde like her. His cheeks had a bit of pink in them and he had full lips, like Steve.

They drove along in silence for a minute or two. "Maybe I can find out a bit more about the girl that was healed," Kat said, thinking again about the medallion and wondering if there was a connection.

"Why bother?" Steve said. "It was probably some treatment my mom doesn't qualify for or some crazy miracle." He sighed. "I think we are out of options."

The road stretched out in front of them, houses along the side of the road. Kat wondered about the families that lived inside. Did they have problems like her family did? Did they have memories they fought against? Kat gripped the car seat as she felt a wave of nausea wash over her. She took a deep breath and tried to relax.

Steve glanced over to her, "Smoke?" he said.

"Yes." That was their code for her slipping into old memories from the Middle East. Her therapist had suggested they come up with a code word so that Steve would know if she was sliding into the trauma of her past. He didn't say anything more than that.

9

Pulling into their driveway, Kat and Jack got out of the car and went into the house ahead of Steve. Jack ran off to play and Kat started a cup of tea in the kitchen, setting the teakettle on the stove, needing one after the news of Laura's condition and her own flashback. She liked the process of making tea. Though she didn't buy fancy teas, the time between when she put the kettle on and waiting for it to boil was somehow soothing to her. With everything going on, that's what she needed.

Kat's thoughts started to swirl in her head. Laura's change in status had shocked Kat's system. Laura might only have days or weeks to live. According to the doctor, there was nothing they could do. While she was waiting for the water to boil, Kat went into the bedroom and pulled the medallion out of the drawer. At that moment, Kat wasn't sure what she wanted to do with it or even why she went and got it. She felt confused. The whistle on the tea kettle broke into her thoughts. She turned off the stove, pulled a mug out of the cabinet next to the sink and dangled a tea bag into the bottom of the cup. The hot water danced over the teabag, creating little bubbles as the tea began to steep. Kat tugged on the string as Steve came into the house from the garage. He said, "I think I'm gonna go for a run. I need to think." He walked away before Kat could say anything.

That was how Steve was. He processed things on his own. Late one night, sitting out on their porch, Steve told Kat that running was his way of pounding through things. He didn't really like it, but he felt so much better after he ran that it didn't matter.

Within a minute or two, Steve came out of their bedroom, having changed from jeans into running shorts and a t-shirt. He sat down at the kitchen table, putting on his shoes when Kat finally spoke. "There's something I need to tell you," she said.

"What's that?" Steve didn't even look up from tying his shoes.

"Remember the other night when I stayed at the hospital?"

"Yes."

"I think I was drugged."

Steve stopped tying his shoes and looked at her. "What? You were drugged?"

Kat walked over to the kitchen table and slid into a chair, setting her tea on a flowered placemat. "I went to the floor as usual, but Sarah wasn't there. Some nurse I didn't recognize brought me tea. She said Sarah had left a note to make it for me. So, I drank it."

Steve furrowed his brow, looking like he was getting impatient. "And then?"

"I think I took a couple of sips of it -- I don't really remember -- and then I woke up. When I did there was a man in scrubs right in front of me."

"Maybe he was there to check on Mom," Steve said.

"Let me finish," Kat said, laying a hand on Steve's arm. "He looked at me and said something like, 'There's a cure if you want to save Laura, but it will cost you. If you are interested, take this.' He left me some sort of a gold coin or medallion. I think he left because I don't remember anything else."

"Kat... "Steve started to say. She knew he was thinking that she had dreamt the whole thing or that it was stress or her PTSD kicking into high gear.

"Wait, let me finish. I came home. I didn't even remember what had happened. I felt a little funny in the morning and totally forgot about the visit and the medallion. Remember how I came in to take a shower?"

"Yeah."

"Well, as I was getting undressed something fell out of my pocket and clanked on the tile." Kat pulled the medallion out of her pocket and set it on the table in front of Steve.

Steve stiffened, "Is that...?"

Kat nodded. "I think it is the medallion that the man in the scrubs was talking about." Kat looked directly into Steve's eyes. "I didn't dream this. This is real. You can touch it and you can hold it. See?"

Steve picked the medallion off of the table and turned it over in his hand as he leaned back in the chair. "Why didn't you tell me about this?"

"Honestly, I didn't know what to make of it. I thought I was imagining things. I didn't even know if what I remembered had been real or a dream until the thing hit the floor in the bathroom."

"How did it get into your pocket?" Steve asked.

"I have no idea. If I remember right, the man in the scrubs put it on the little table next to the chair we sleep in. I think it was there next to my cell phone, but it wasn't there in the morning."

Steve set the coin down on the table, "When you got home and found it, why didn't you tell me then?"

Kat knew where he was going and he was right. She tended to want to figure things out herself. She wasn't always good at letting people in. That very fact had led them to marriage counseling more than once. She was working on it, but trust didn't come easily to her. She'd been hurt too many times. She took a deep breath and said, "I'm sorry. I really didn't know what to do with it. I didn't want to get your hopes up and really, when it happened, Laura was getting better."

Steve stiffened, but seemed satisfied with her answer, "And now she's not..."

"And that's why I'm showing it to you. It could be a total hoax, though. I can't figure out what to do with it even if we wanted to try."

Steve picked up the medallion and walked over to the window, holding the coin in the bright sunlight. Kat watched him turn it over. "Did you take a close look at this?" he asked.

"Yeah, but I couldn't figure it out. I bet the guy is a con artist."

Steve brought the coin back to Kat and set it on the table. "Maybe..." He shrugged his shoulders.

Kat picked up the medallion and stuck it in a cup in the cabinet. "I'm going to put this away for now. I'm not sure what to do with this, but I don't want to lose it."

Steve frowned. "Not sure I understand what's going on. I'll be back in five miles," he said, not even giving her a kiss on the cheek. As Kat watched him walk out the door, she knew he wasn't mad. It felt that way, though. There wasn't really anything to be mad about. Maybe a run would do him some good.

There was nothing to do now but wait. "Jack?" she called. "How about some playtime in the yard?"

Jack came scampering into the kitchen, oblivious to the discussion that Kat and Steve had just finished. He had a truck in each hand. "Where daddy?"

"He went for a run. How about if you and I go play on the swings?"

"Can trucks come?"

"Yup. Let's go."

Jack was out the door before Kat had even finished getting the words out of her mouth. She slipped her feet into some green rubber garden shoes and was opening the back door when her phone rang. Looking at the screen, she could see it was Van again. She let it go to voicemail, stuck the phone in her pocket and went outside.

Kat walked across their backyard. It was a haven for their family. Almost an acre, there was plenty of grass and a tall solid wood fence that surrounded the whole property. The yard was the reason they had bought the house. In the evenings, Kat and Steve liked to sit outside in front of a fire and watch the stars. As Jack had gotten a bit older, Steve had added a big swing set to the play area, complete with a sandbox for Jack to play trucks in. The mature trees provided shade from the sun and color in the fall. Kat always felt safe and relaxed and free in the backyard.

"Mama, swing time!" Jack giggled happily as he pulled himself up onto a swing with a blue seat. He took one hand off of the chains that held the swing, "Hold the trucks?" Kat nodded and put them in her pocket. She stepped behind Jack and gave him a push. "Harder, harder," he called until he was swinging as high as Kat felt like she could let him.

Her thoughts turned to Laura and the medallion. What had happened? Laura seemed to be doing better and then all of a sudden, she wasn't. The doctors at Mercy Memorial had done a good job with her. Stomach cancer was a difficult diagnosis. The treatments had improved over time, but there was still no sure cure. There was no sure cure for any cancer. Kat felt a surge of anger and pushed Jack a little harder. She caught herself when she heard Jack laughing. He thought it was fun, but the last thing she needed was to have him end up in the emergency room with Laura already in the hospital.

She grabbed the back of the chains and stopped the swing, "Hey buddy, the trucks want to play too."

"Okay trucks. Your turn!" Jack took the trucks from her hand. He ran over to the sandbox, dropped to his knees and pushed the trucks up and down hills he had made a few days before.

Kat sat on the bottom of the slide to stay near. She didn't like leaving him outside by himself even with the fenced-in yard. There was just no way of knowing what could happen, even in their safe neighborhood. It made her nervous.

Nervous was something that Kat had grown accustomed to when she came back from the Middle East. Her therapist had said that her body had gone into shock, not just from the physical damage, but from the emotional damage as well. She warned Kat that any new emotional upset could bring back the same shock symptoms -- feeling lightheaded, nauseated, disconnected and not being able to think clearly. They had worked on techniques for Kat to use. Much of it was a lot of deep breathing. She told herself that she and Jack were safe in the backyard. In a minute or so, the numbness subsided a bit and she realized that Jack had moved over to the far edge of the sandbox. It was a big sandbox, much bigger than a traditional one you could buy at any superstore. Steve wanted it that way.

As Kat sat outside with Jack, she remembered the day that they built the sandbox. One Saturday when Jack was three, Steve came out of the bedroom wearing a hard hat. It was bright yellow and sat up high on his head. He had put on a plaid shirt, jeans and work boots. Jack was at the table, rolling a red truck next to his bowl of Cheerios and looked at him, his face wrinkled, "Daddy? Why are you dressed like that?"

"We have a project today, buddy. Are you ready to help?" With that, Steve had produced a small pair of work boots and a matching construction hat. Jack jumped off of the chair, "Thanks you!" he said, still wrestling with his words.

Kat smiled and said, "And what are you building today?"

Steve looked at her, looked at Jack and said, "It's a surprise. You will see it when it is done. C'mon Jack, we've got work to do."

"That's right, mama." Jack put the hat on and followed Steve down the hall in his sock feet, carrying his new work boots.

Kat heard the truck start and saw Steve and Jack pull out of the driveway. A few hours later, they were back with a bunch of twelve by eight boards that Steve set up into a square. Steve used their wheelbarrow and began to fill the square with bags of sand. Kat remember walking out into the yard and saying, "Wow! What's this?" Jack was using a play rake to move the sand around.

He looked up proudly and said, "I'm helping Daddy make a sand place."

Kat smiled, "Do you mean a sandbox?"

"Yes!" he said and went back to work raking the sand.

Those were the happy memories that Kat wanted filling her head. She didn't want the ones from her time in her own sandbox. She didn't even want the ones of Laura being sick. She'd had enough sadness to last a lifetime. Absentmindedly, she rolled her wrist and refocused on Jack, her memories sliding back into the place they had come from.

Jack had set up two of his trucks to crash into each other and was making his version of engine noises when Steve came back into the yard.

His color was better after his run. He pulled his earbuds out of his ears and Kat could see the sweat on his forehead. He seemed calmer and more relaxed. "How is going, Jack?" he asked.

"Mama and I have been playing this whole time." He abandoned the trucks for a moment and ran over to Steve, wrapping his arms around his dad's legs. "I glad you back."

"Me too, buddy."

Jack hopped back into the sand and said, "You smell." Steve and Kat both started to laugh. That was the first laugh they shared in a long time.

Kat stood up, brushed the sand off of her jeans and scruffed his hair, saying, "I'm sure he does. Daddy needs a shower."

Jack didn't look up from what he was doing. "Yes."

Kat looked at him and said, "I'll be right back. I'm just going to walk with Daddy back to the house."

Kat and Steve started to walk back to the house. Kat asked, "Did the run make you feel better?"

"A little. It's hard, given the circumstances."

"I get it," Kat said, pulling the back door open. She stood in the doorway while Steve went into the house. She stayed outside she could keep an eye on Jack.

Steve walked over to the refrigerator and pulled out a bottle of water. "I haven't done a good job asking you how you are doing. I realized that while I was running. This has got to be hard for you. Are you feeling okay after the other night?"

Kat smiled a little. She knew that Steve loved her, but he sometimes got so caught up in what he was doing that he didn't remember that she was going through some version of the same thing he was. "Yeah. I'm okay. I've had a few episodes, especially after the night at the hospital, but I'm feeling alright. Like you said, given the circumstances." There was a tension between them, but Kat didn't know what to do about it.

Steve took a long drink of water out of the bottle and put the cap back on. "I'm going to go take a shower. Why don't I join you in the backyard as soon as I'm done? We can try to figure something out."

Kat nodded and Steve walked away. Kat went back outside and sat in her favorite chair under a tree that had layers of thick leaves. Getting out of the bright sunlight made it much easier to see Jack, who was now at the top of the slide, sending his trucks down one by one. They'd careen down to the bottom, flip over and crash, and Jack would go down the ladder, rung by rung, retrieve the trucks, stuff his pockets with them and do it all over again. Kat shook her head. He'd probably play like this for at least another hour.

Steve came outside and sat down next to Kat. He smelled like soap and clean clothes. It was much better than the sweat and hospital smell that he had before. He had grabbed an orange sports drink, turned the cap and took a sip. Kat said, "Nothing feels very normal right now. It might look normal, but it doesn't seem normal."

"You can say that again," Steve said. He turned and looked at Kat. "What do you make of the guy in the scrubs? Do you think he was legit or just crazy?"

Kat raised her eyebrows, "I don't know. My first reaction would be to say he's just a scam artist. I mean, if there was a cure for cancer, how come our doctors don't know about it? On the other hand, what if it is legit? He took quite a risk to get in front of me, and he left that medallion or whatever it is. That's evidence."

Steve looked down, a shadow of sadness passing over his face. "I just want to feel like we've done everything we can to help mom," he said. "I don't know if this guy is for real, but it might be worth trying."

Kat felt a knot in her stomach form. Trying to figure out who this man was meant they'd have to take a risk. After what happened to her, the risk didn't sound all that good. For a while after she'd come home, she didn't even want to go out in public. It all seemed too scary. Kat took a deep breath... again.

"Another episode?" Steve asked.

"Yeah. I feel like crawling in the bed and never getting out. All of this, it's just too much." Kat felt a tear slide down her face.

"Laura getting sick, now there's nothing they can do. The weird man in the scrubs..." She pointed to Jack, "And I worry about him. How is he going to deal with Laura's death?"

Steve reached out and grabbed her hand. The warmth steadied her. Steve said, "All we can do is take it one day at a time and explore every option."

10

Jack had come in from playing... finally. Steve was sitting at the kitchen table working on a presentation for one of his consulting clients. Kat was sitting next to him with her own computer, working on a story for Van. Steve's phone rang.

Kat looked up to see his reaction. He quickly got up from the table and went into the other room where she couldn't see him. She could only hear muffled voices. Kat typed the response to a couple of emails and waited for Steve to come back into the room.

"That was the hospital," he said, looking paler than before. "Mom has taken another turn. They wanted to know if we have a DNR for her." Kat knew was a DNR was, a do not resuscitate order.

Steve pounded his fist on the counter. "This is not happening," he yelled. "She can't die." He looked at Kat with pleading eyes. "We have to do something. We cannot just sit here while she suffers."

Kat looked at him, "What choice do we have?"

Steve's eyes hardened. "I know that you don't want to face

what happened to you the other night. I know it brings up a lot of bad feelings, but it may be the only shot we have. Where is it?"

"Where is what?"

"Kat, you know exactly what I'm asking you for. Where is the medallion?"

Stung, Kat got up and walked over to the cabinet where she had stuck it in a mug and handed it to Steve.

"What do we do with this?" Steve said, looking at it more closely under the bright light from the kitchen window. She watched him turn it over in his hands, "I'm just not seeing anything that lets us know what to do next."

Kat felt paralyzed. She knew that Laura needed help, but there was something in her that felt terrified down to her core. She took the medallion from Steve, her hands shaking. She was trying to help, but all she could think about was the smoke and the hands and how much she hurt and the body in the Humvee...

"Kat, come back," Steve said. "We are here. You are safe. I just want you to look at this with me." He bent over to look at her almost nose to nose, "I am here. Just talk to me."

Steve's voice helped to pull her out of the episode even though he sounded impatient. She came back to the kitchen with the pretty window into the backyard, with the soft rug under her bare feet. She felt the medallion in her hand. She closed her eyes for a moment, trying to gather herself. "Can you get the magnifier? Maybe we missed something."

Kat sat back down at the kitchen table while Steve rooted through their junk drawer. He walked over and handed it to her. "Here you go."

Kat used the magnifier to look at the medallion. If the man in the scrubs wanted her to contact him, there had to be a way. The medallion was the only piece of information she had to work with. She looked up at Steve, who was standing over her,

"Can you go check my bag and my sweater and see if there's anything else in there?" Steve nodded, knowing that sending him away gave her a minute to get herself together.

Kat rolled the medallion in her hands, letting it sit flat on her palm. On one side, the medallion had a pyramid and a few other symbols that Kat had a hard time seeing. On the opposite side, there was a cross, like the kind that medical professionals wear. There were literally no other instructions on the medallion. Kat hoped that Steve had better luck.

While she was waiting, Kat started to wonder why the man would give her a medallion and ask her to contact them, but he'd make it so hard? The whole thing didn't make any sense, but Kat realized that at least following through on looking would make Steve feel better.

Steve came back into the kitchen with her sweater and her bag. The contents of her bag were all rumpled and disorganized. Steve had clearly been thorough in his examination of the bag. "Sorry," he mumbled. "I was just trying to look."

Kat took the bag from him and set it down next to her chair. "It's no problem. The clothes had to be washed anyway," she lied, not wanting to make a big deal out of nothing. Kat stood up, still looking at the medallion. "There has to be something here. You sure there's nothing in my bag?"

Steve said, "No. I went through the whole thing."

Kat realized that they had both looked at the top and bottom of the medallion, but that wasn't the only surface. There were edges too. Looking more closely, she realized that they weren't ridged, like so many coins, but completely smooth. Running her finger across the edge, she started to feel a few little bumps. "What's this?" she asked, handing the coin over to Steve. "Look at the edge. The whole thing is smooth except for a couple of little bumps. Do you see that?"

Steve had grabbed the coin from her and sat down at the table. "Can you bring a flashlight?" he asked. Kat fumbled in the drawer and found one that worked from a giveaway at a parade they had been to a few months before with Jack. "How about this one?"

"That works. Can you hold it so I can use the magnifier?"

"Sure," Kat did her best to point the light where Steve needed it.

"There are definitely little bumps there. I can feel them." Steve leaned his head closer to the magnifier, "Wait! It says something."

"What? What do you mean?" Kat said, surprised that they had found anything on the medallion at all.

"Do we have some paper?" Steve asked.

"Sure." Kat grabbed a legal pad from her work bag and a pen and set it next to Steve. "Can you hold the magnifier too?" he asked.

Kat pinched the magnifier between her fingers, hoping she could hold it steady enough so that he could see.

"That's good," he said, scrawling some words down on the paper. "I think it's a URL." Kat waited as Steve looked at the medallion for another minute. It looked like he was checking to make sure that he got all the information. "I don't know what this is. This is a weird website address." He handed the pad of paper to Kat.

On the yellow pages, Steve had written apexsolution-szq1437jpqmm44.onion.

"Who uses a dot onion extension?" Steve said, standing up and running his hands through his hair. "That can't be real."

Kat sat down at her laptop and brought up her browser, opening an incognito tab. She muttered, "It might not be as crazy as you think."

"What do you mean?"

She leaned back in her chair, "Dot onion is on the dark web. It's part of the Tor network. It's short for "the onion router." It was originally developed by the Navy so they could research

privacy. We used this extension all the time when I was away."
She opened her own copy of the Tor browser, typed in the
website address and waited, wondering if anything would
happen. If it didn't what would Steve say? If it did, what were
they opening themselves up to?

"What's taking so long?" Steve asked.

"This is normal. The dark web doesn't work the same as the
white web. It takes a little longer." A moment later, a website
came up. It was a single page with a black background. On the
upper left-hand side of the page was the medical cross that was
on the medallion. On the upper right side of the page was the
pyramid that was on the other side of the medallion. There was
a white box in the middle of the page with greyed out lettering
that read, "enter patient name here." There were no other boxes
on the page.

Steve leaned over her to see the page. "What are we
supposed to do with this? There's no explanation. Just a box.
This doesn't seem right."

Kat knew from her work as a journalist that dark web pages
looked and behaved a lot differently than the white web. She
never knew if the "white web" was the right word for it. She and
her colleagues just used that term because it was like light and
dark. Most people assumed that the dark web was full of criminals and thieves. It was. What they also didn't realize was that
in many countries where free speech and freedom of religion
weren't part of everyday life, the dark web was one of the only
ways to communicate outside of their own villages, towns and
cities. Journalists used the dark web to talk to people anony-
mously all the time. In fact, Kat had used the dark web when
she was in the Middle East to gather background, data and
information from her sources. That was, until the day of the
accident. This was the first time she'd been on the dark web
since.

"This is pretty typical. I used this a lot when I was over

there," Kat said, looking at the page. "So, what do you want me to do? Clearly, they want Laura's name." Another lump formed in Kat's body, this time in her throat. She knew that entering her name on the dark web would mean they would have to move forward. There would be no going back.

Steve was clearly shaken and unsure, "I mean, if we do this and we don't like what they have to say, we can just walk away, right?"

"We don't know that," Kat replied, staring at the cursor blinking on the screen. "We don't know anything about these people. Are they scam artists? Are they the real deal?"

"Maybe we should do some research," Steve said.

Kat looked at him, struggling to explain and keep her own fear from taking over. "What exactly are you going to research? Listen, if these people wanted to be found they wouldn't be on the dark web. They wouldn't have drugged me. They wouldn't have come in the dark of night to give me the medallion. These aren't the typical rules of your corporate partners." As soon as she said it, she was sorry. She knew the words would sting Steve. He knew about the risk that she had taken as an embedded journalist.

Fortunately, Steve ignored her comment -- at least the last part -- and said, "What do we do?"

Kat said, "I don't know. If we don't try, Laura is going to die. But I'm afraid of what they might ask. I don't know anything about these people. Neither do you. And we have no way of knowing."

Steve looked at her. "And we are running out of time."

11

Sarah pulled the flash drive out of the hospital's computer and looked around. There was no one else on the floor to see her, so she didn't even know why she looked. Nerves, probably.

Sarah put the flash drive in her pocket and walked towards the staff bathrooms. Swinging between night shift and day shift had been hard the last few weeks and they had lost several people on the floor. Sarah shook her head as if she was arguing with herself. Cancer was hard to cure. It was even harder to be a nurse for cancer patients.

And then there were cases like Anna Bryan, the twelve-year-old that had been miraculously healed of glioblastoma. The nurses on the floor called her "fruit loop" after she woke up one morning feeling better and ate four bowls of cereal. There had been no explanation for her rapid healing. Sarah remembered seeing Anna's team of doctors, plus the hospital president and the chair of oncology using the conference room to discuss her case. There simply was no explanation. How could a patient go from being terminal one day to completely cured the next?

Sarah felt the flash drive in her pocket as she made her way down the hallway, her shoes quiet on the floor. She only had an hour left in her shift and she was excited to go home and get some rest.

After Kat asked all the questions about treatments, Sarah did a little research. She couldn't see anything that was different about Anna Bryan's case, and neither did any of the doctors. After their meeting, they had just filed Anna's information and left it at that. Sarah wasn't satisfied. There had to be an explanation. While the doctors came in to see the patients, the nurses were the ones that took care of them when they hurt, felt sick or couldn't stop throwing up. She had held people who had just discovered their hair was falling out. She had hugged family members who didn't know what to do after a diagnosis. She had sat with patients who had no family as they took their final breaths.

There had to be something to Anna's cure. Sarah just felt it in her bones. If she could just get the flash drive to Kat, maybe with Kat's journalism connections she'd discover something that they'd missed. Maybe it needed fresh eyes outside of the hospital.

Sarah pushed open the heavy door to the restroom and walked inside. She walked over to the sink and looked at herself in the mirror. The circles under her eyes were the payment for too many hours at the hospital. As she looked down to turn on the water, a hand came around from behind her stuffing a washcloth over her nose and mouth. The room started to go fuzzy and Sarah thought she smelled something sweet.

As Sarah slumped to the floor, a woman dressed in surgical scrubs and wearing gloves stuffed the washcloth into her pocket. She grabbed Sarah under her armpits and dragged her into the handicapped stall at the back of the restroom, propping her up against the wall next to the toilet. From out of her other shirt pocket, the woman pulled a tourniquet, syringe and vial of fentanyl. She tied the tourniquet around Sarah's arm, drew the fentanyl into the syringe and injected it into Sarah's arm, watching it disappear into one of Sarah's veins. There was nothing now that anyone could do. She'd given Sarah more fentanyl than any human could handle. The woman didn't even bother to pull the needle out. She dropped the vial in between Sarah's splayed legs and stood up, watching. A blue tinge started to form on Sarah's lips.

Satisfied that Sarah was dead, the woman felt in Sarah's pockets and found the flash drive that had Anna Bryan's medical information on it. She pocketed it and the gloves she had been wearing. Leaving the washroom, she walked down the hall and logged into one of the staff computers. No one, save Sarah, was on the floor, so she was alone. Pulling up the medical records for Anna Bryan, the nurse found the option to delete all of her records and clicked on it. For all intents and purposes, Anna Bryan had never been a patient at Mercy Memorial. No one would remember Anna Bryan's miracle or Sarah, the nurse that had overdosed on her floor's bathroom.

The nurse used a hand wipe to clean the desk and the keyboard of any prints and started walking down the hallway to the stairs. The next shift of nurses and doctors would be arriving any minute. Using the stairwell was a more deserted option with fewer cameras. Down four flights of stairs and out into the night, the nurse walked around the corner and got into a grey car driven by a man. They pulled away from the curb, slowly, watching for traffic.

An hour later, a doctor who had just started her shift walked into the ladies' room and saw Sarah's feet. Yelling for help, she checked Sarah's pulse. There was none. Her body was already cold.

Nurses and a few other doctors came running down the hall. "It's Sarah. She's gone," the doctor said. The staff looked at her in disbelief. "Sarah?" one of the custodians asked, "What happened?"

"Looks like an overdose," the doctor said. "Someone call 911. We need the police."

12

Kat stared at the screen for a moment longer. "Steve, what do you want me to do?" Her stomach was churning. There was no telling where the simple act of putting information into the computer could lead them. Kat's gut told her that it wouldn't be a simple journey.

Steve got up from the kitchen table where Kat's laptop was still logged into the Tor browser on the dark web. She waited. He needed to make this decision. It was his mom after all. Kat saw him run his hand through his hair as if clearing his hair away from his face would clear the thoughts in his head. He sighed, "Okay, do it."

Kat shook her head and typed in Laura's name on the landing page. She clicked the green box that said enter.

Kat expected to see something happen. An acknowledgment, instructions, something, but nothing happened. There was absolutely nothing. The page seemed to log them out of the network. It pulled up a news service where the headline was, "Top Movie Exec Arrested After Stealing Area 51 Secrets."

Steve leaned over her shoulder, "Wait, what happened?"

Kat looked at the screen, wondering the same thing, "I don't know. You'd think we'd get some sort of response, wouldn't you?"

Steve said, "Try it again."

Kat typed in the website address that was printed on the medallion again. A page came up that said, "404 Error" and redirected her back to the news site again. "Maybe I typed in the wrong address," she muttered and tried it a third time. Again, no luck.

Steve slammed his hand on the counter again. "This is all a hoax. There is nothing we can do."

Kat looked at the screen and looked at him, a surge of feelings rising. Fear, sadness, anger -- they were all there. "I typed it in correctly. I don't know what to tell you."

"Maybe you just made the whole thing up," Steve said.

Kat froze in place, anger taking a front seat. "Really? Why would I do that? I'd go as far as having a medallion made and drugging myself? Are you crazy?"

Steve blinked as if Kat had thrown cold water on his face. "No... I'm sorry." Steve hung his head. "I don't know what to say. That was wrong. You wouldn't do that."

"No, I wouldn't."

Just then, Jack and his trucks came into the kitchen for a snack. "Truckies want pretzels, please!" he said, climbing up onto one of the chairs.

Kat refocused on Jack, burying the anger that was choking her. How could he say that she made it up? That didn't even make sense. She'd like to blame it all on Laura's sickness, but her gut told her there was something more. Something she couldn't place. She opened the door to the cabinet and fished out Jack's favorite pretzels and put a bowl of them out. Normally, hand washing happened before snacks, but Kat was too tense to worry about that.

Steve sat at the table, his head in his hands. Jack crunched on a pretzel and looked at Steve, "Whatsa matter, Daddy?"

"Buddy, I'm fine. Just tired from my run."

Kat scowled at him, knowing that he could do a better job talking to Jack. She realized that was a discussion for later.

They sat quietly together as a family while Jack finished his snack. Jack hopped up and ran off as soon as he was done. Kat started to put the pretzels away. The doorbell rang, "I'll get it," Steve said, standing up from the table.

Kat rinsed her hands to get the pretzel salt off of them as Steve walked back into the kitchen. He was carrying a box. "This just came," he said. He set it down on the table and looked more closely at it, "Did you order something?" he said.

"Probably," Kat said, turning back towards the sink. Just as she did, she heard a phone ring, but it wasn't one of their phones. "What's that? Where's that coming from?" she asked Steve.

Steve didn't answer, but Jack did. "The box is ringing," Steve said, starting to pull at the flaps to get the box open.

Steve and Kat immediately began looking inside. Kat's mind was racing. A moment later, they heard the phone again, this time with a single chirp. Steve dug his hand into the packing at the bottom of the box. "Wait, I feel something," he said. Out of the box, wrapped in a plastic bag, was a cell phone. "Is this for us?"

Kat just looked at him and then realized that Jack had come back into the kitchen and was watching all of this unfold. "Hey Jack, I think it's time for you to go watch a truck video."

"I want more pretzels."

Kat quickly poured a few more in a small plastic bowl. "You can take them with you."

"But you always say I'm not allowed."

"Well, today you are."

"Cool!"

While Kat scurried Jack out of the kitchen, Steve pulled the phone out of the bag. He handed it to Kat. It looked like a typical burner phone. Kat's mind started to race. Was it the man in the scrubs? Was this real? Was he just a con man?

She opened the phone and the screen lit up. The history showed one call to the phone and a text. Kat tapped on the screen and went to the text app.

"What does it say?" Steve asked, his face pale.

Kat read it to herself, her body quickly feeling like it wasn't her own. She was numb. "It says, 'The cure costs. Bluebird roster. Text when you have it. 24 hours."

Kat's hands shook, but she didn't say anything.

"What does it say?" Steve repeated, taking the phone out of her hands. Kat sat down while he looked at the text. "What's Bluebird?" A flash of recognition fell across his face. "Wait, they want information from your military days, don't they?"

Kat could do nothing but take long, deep breaths. The smoke was coming, and coming fast.

"KAT, KAT," Kat heard Steve's voice through the fog. She found herself on the floor, a cold washcloth on her head. She struggled to sit up. Steve's put his hand under her elbow and helped her.

"What happened?" she said, still waiting for the last bit of fog to disappear. "We had the phone and all of a sudden all I could smell..." She let the words evaporate in the air. Steve knew where she had gone. "How did I end up here?"

Steve slid down and sat next to her on the floor. "We were looking at the phone and you kept staring at the text. Next thing, you passed out."

"Sorry about that. It just took me back."

"Yeah, I kinda figured that." Steve reached over and smoothed a hair away from Kat's face. "What is Bluebird? What's the Bluebird roster?"

Kat looked at Steve blankly. Since she had left her position as an embedded journalist, the military let her keep her clearance. She wasn't sure exactly why or if it had just been overlooked. She had always been very careful about using it. She only had it because once in a while they called her in to do a project for them. Every couple of years. The projects were pretty basic -- editing, writing, some basic analysis. That was why she was allowed to keep it. She always wondered if having it meant that the military could keep a better eye on her after what she had seen. She'd always suspected they were watching her to see if she would compromise her security status. She hadn't. "I can't really say," she said to Steve.

Steve sighed. "We have a problem. These people offering the cure want something that apparently only you can give them. I don't know what Bluebird is, so this isn't on me."

He suddenly sounded like her enemy and not her husband again. Kat turned and looked at him, "You know what you are asking, don't you? I'd have to compromise my clearance. I could go to jail."

"I know, but Mom is going to die."

"You'd rather have your mom alive and me in jail? Thanks." Kat struggled to her feet, another wave of nausea came over her.

Steve stood up too. "That's not what I meant, and you know it. I don't want Mom to die and I don't want you to end up in jail." She felt Steve touch her shoulder, "But what if there is something to this cure they are offering? I mean, how did they know that you would know about Bluebird or whatever it is called? Maybe it is the real deal."

Kat took a moment to think. She didn't want to get into an argument with Steve. He was trying to smooth things over. They were both stressed. "This is an impossible situation. Your mom is dying. I get that. These people drugged me and clearly have access to information, but what they are asking me to do could get me in big trouble. And, how do we even know they will come through? How do we know that they have some cure that would work?"

"Didn't you tell me that there was a girl who had been miraculously cured of cancer a while back?"

"We have no idea if her recovery had anything to do with these guys." Kat chewed on her lip and remembered the conversation she had with Sarah. She'd have to check in with her to see if she had any luck learning more about the girl and what happened to her. Kat opened the phone again and looked at the text. These clearly were people who had resources. They knew she had been in the Middle East. How she wasn't sure. They knew about her clearance. They had drugged her. They were active on the dark web. And, they were offering something that she and Steve desperately wanted, a cure for Laura.

Kat fought back a wave of anxiety. She took a couple of deep breaths, hoping to push it back into the cave it came out of. No luck. The lightheadedness grew as she thought more about the path ahead.

Kat went back to her laptop. She could feel Steve watching her, giving her space. She heard the refrigerator door open. She knew he was wondering what she would be willing to do. Giving up classified information could get her charged with treason. She needed more information. Kat exited out of the screens she had been working on and went to a search engine that featured local news to try to find out how they knew so much about her. Before she started the search, a story caught her eye, "Local Nurse Overdoses at Work." Kat leaned forward to get a better look at the image. "Steve," she whispered.

Steve closed the refrigerator door and walked over to her carrying two bottles of water. "Oh my God. Is that?"

Kat's throat tightened, "It's Sarah."

"What happened to her?"

Kat clicked on the text of the article. "She OD'd on fentanyl. It says they found her in the bathroom."

Steve sat down at the table. "I had no idea that she had a drug problem. I guess it is pretty common at hospitals, though."

Kat was surprised. Steve's cynicism bothered her. She stared at him until he caught her eye. Sarah was the last person she had talked to about a cure for cancer. He said, "You don't think...?"

Kat felt a surge of fear ride through her. "You don't?"

Steve looked at her and shook his head. She could tell he was on overload. They both were. What had started off as a difficult diagnosis of cancer had turned into something more. Something much more. Kat looked back at her screen, the arrow pointing to the title of the article about Sarah. From behind her, she heard Steve say, "I'm gonna check on Jack." Kat nodded and rubbed her brow knowing they both needed a moment to gather themselves. Kat tried to understand what had happened to Sarah. Her gut told her they were all pawns in a bigger story. It was a feeling she was familiar with. She'd written tons of stories that started out one way and ended another once all the pieces were in place. The trouble with this story was that she just didn't have all of the pieces yet.

Clearly, the man in the scrubs wasn't just any run-of-the-mill con artist. He knew her past. He knew that she had a classified clearance. How she didn't know. And, Kat's interaction with Sarah may have been what caused her death. Why it did or what Sarah had stumbled on, Kat wasn't sure.

Kat shut the lid of her laptop and did the few dishes that were in the sink. She went into the laundry room and picked up a few pieces of clothes that had been left on the floor and put them into the washing machine. It was a nervous habit she had developed working at home. When she couldn't make sense of something, she cleaned. She needed to feel normal. And yet, she couldn't shake the feeling that there were forces at work that she didn't understand and couldn't control.

Kat looked out the small window out of the laundry room

and wondered how the box got to them so quickly. Neither she nor Steve had considered that. She realized that the man in the scrubs not only knew about Laura and her clearance, but he knew exactly where she and Steve lived. The hair on the back of Kat's neck stood up. She took a step toward the window in the laundry room. It faced the street. She looked both ways, trying not to disturb the curtain that covered the view. There was a landscaping crew mowing a lawn a few doors down across the street, the sound of their mowers and blowers bouncing off all of the houses. There was also a plumber's truck at her neighbor's house a couple of doors down. Nothing seemed suspicious, but she still had an eerie feeling that they were being watched.

Concerned about Jack, she quickly left the laundry room and walked to their family room where Jack was supposed to be watching a television show. Steve was sitting on an upholstered chair, his favorite spot in the room, working on his computer. She saw him stop every few seconds, his gaze unfocused. He was clearly thinking about what had happened to them.

"Steve," she said quietly, trying not to attract Jack's attention. "Come here for a minute."

Steve got up from the chair and stepped out into the hallway.

"How do they know where we live?" she asked. Steve didn't say a word.

Kat looked at him and said, "They got that box to us. How would they have gotten our address? They might be watching the house."

The realization took a moment to sink in. Kat knew that Steve was struggling. He didn't have the same training that she had, but he also didn't have the same memories that she wrestled with every day. "Do you think that Angela is home?" Angela was one of the other moms in the neighborhood. She had a bunch of kids and always loved to have him over. Jack kept her son, Vito, from fighting with his sister.

"She texted this morning and said that if Jack wanted to come over to play, he could."

"I'm going to get him out of here," Steve said. "I think I'll stop at the hospital while I'm out to check on Mom. Is that okay? Want me to come right back?"

Taking Jack to Vito's house was a smart idea. It would give Kat some time to think. She needed a little space to process everything that had happened in the last few hours. "Naw, I'm good. Go ahead." She called Jack, "Hey buddy, how about going to Vito's house for a little bit?"

Jack turned away from his program and looked from Steve to Kat, "But, I'm in the middle."

Kat clicked off the television. Normally she wasn't so abrupt with him, but they needed to get him somewhere away from the house until they could figure things out. "Mrs. D'Amato wants you to come over and play. She said Vito is being bad."

"What? Vito isn't bad," Jack smiled, knowing Kat was playing with him.

"I heard he is. He is eating ice cream for lunch."

Jack's eyes got really big. Ice cream was his favorite. "Could I have ice cream for lunch if I go to Vito's?"

Kat pretended to think hard about the question when all she really wanted to do was scoop him up and get him in the car. "I bet. Now, let's get moving! The first one to the car gets an extra scoop." She looked at Steve, "You'd better hurry up, Dad. Jack is super-fast!"

Steve nodded. He already had keys for the car in his hand. "I'm getting ready to run. I'm all warmed up. You'd better hurry." As Jack scampered off to get his shoes on, Kat felt Steve grab her arm. "Are you sure you are okay here by yourself?"

"Yeah, I'm fine. I just need to figure some things out."

She felt the scruff of Steve's beard on her cheek as he gave her a peck. "I'll be back soon. I'll have my phone on me if you need me." With that, he headed out the door. Kat knew that if she did need help, if someone meant to harm her, Steve would not be able to get back in time. She was on her own.

Kat watched from the front door as Steve and Jack pulled away in Steve's car. She waved and smiled, pretending to be excited for Jack to go to Vito's house. If the man in the scrubs was watching the house, she needed to pretend that she didn't know. She glanced down the street, trying to decide if anyone was watching the house. The landscapers were gone and the plumbers seemed to be sitting in the cab of their truck eating lunch. She didn't see anything that was obvious, but it was clear from the box delivery that these people knew what they were doing.

Kat closed the door and locked it, turning the deadbolt until she heard a click in the doorframe. She walked straight to their bedroom at the back of the house. She opened a cabinet door on her nightstand and saw the face of her gun safe. While it might have looked like any other piece of furniture, the night-stand wasn't a typical piece of furniture. It had been specially designed to house a fingerprint enabled safe where she could keep her pistol. Kat pressed her finger on the keypad and the door immediately clicked open. She pulled out a Sig Sauer P320. She had trained with it for the last several years, part of her classes in self-defense.

When Kat first told Steve that she wanted to get a pistol, he balked. She had come back from the Middle East with so many bad memories that he was, frankly, concerned she'd have a bad day and kill herself. Kat saw it differently. Knowing how to use her pistol gave her back some of the power that had been taken from her by the enemy she had never seen. After months of talking and arguing, Kat finally suggested that they see her therapist together. On their way home from that session, convinced Kat was on solid footing, they stopped at the gun store to get Kat what she wanted.

The customized nightstand had been a gift from Steve on her next birthday, a few months later. One of the sticking points about Kat getting a gun was not only her memories but Jack. Steve had grown up with hunting guns but was worried about Jack at so young an age. On her birthday, Steve had called her out to his truck to show her a box with a bow on it.

"What's this?" she asked.

"Your birthday present," he said, smiling. He lowered the tailgate. "Here, open it."

"Right here in the driveway?" Kat asked, reaching for the cardboard.

"Yup. I'll carry it in for you. It's heavy."

Kat pulled at the cardboard flaps and saw the nightstand. "What's this?"

"It's something to keep us out of court."

Kat wrinkled her nose at him.

Steve laughed. "I'm just kidding. Here, look at this."

He proceeded to show her that the lower cabinet door had a safe in it where she could keep her guns. The drawer above had a false bottom to it, where she could store magazines and extra ammo if she needed it.

Kat remembered that he looked at her sheepishly. "Like it?"

At that moment, Kat wrapped her arms around his neck and gave him a kiss. "I love it," "Can you carry it in for me?"

REACHING INTO THE SAFE, she pulled out the Sig, cleared it, gave it a quick dry fire to make sure the trigger was operating normally and then loaded it, racking one into the chamber. She opened the drawer above and grabbed a stretchy holster with a hard-plastic insert. She secured the band around her waist, inserted the gun, and pulled her shirt down over top. No one would ever know that she was carrying. She closed the safe door and stood up, hearing her phone in the other room. Walking quickly, worried it was Steve, she looked at the screen. She almost didn't answer. It was Van.

Normally, she and Van would talk at least once a day. Over the last few years, they had grown close. Their love of reporting, facts, honesty and his military background combined with her experience in the Middle East gave them a bond that only people who had been serving overseas would understand. Van didn't love fluff stories and he also didn't love micromanaging. Those were two factors that helped him and Kat to get along even when they disagreed. And when they disagreed, it could be heated. They only talked so much because they had become colleagues and friends. She trusted his judgment and he clearly trusted hers.

"Hey," he said as soon as she picked up the phone. "I've been trying to get you."

Kat balanced her cell phone on her shoulder as she walked around the house closing the blinds. No need to give anyone extra views of the interior they didn't have to work for. "Yeah, things have been a little crazy," she said.

Kat went into the laundry room and started both the washer and the dryer, hoping the noise would buffer her call. Knowing that the man in the scrubs, whatever his name was, knew where she lived had put Kat into full evasion mode. She didn't want to be overheard. Shaking off the thought, but still walking outdoors, "Steve's mom isn't doing well."

"I'm sorry to hear that," Van said.

"That's not all. One of her nurses OD'd this morning. Fentanyl."

"That's awful. Did she have a drug problem?" Van asked.

"Not that we know of. I just talked to her a day ago. She seemed fine to me."

"You never know about people," Van said. "She was probably hiding it. Those nurses have access to all sorts of drugs. On other topics, I wanted to check in on your stories. I'm guessing you haven't gotten too far with everything going on?"

Kat let him move on. She wasn't sure how much she wanted to tell him about her being drugged, the medallion and the information that the man in the scrubs wanted. "You guessed right. Sorry about that."

"No problem. Just wanted to see if I should hold space for you in layout this week."

"I think you'd better go on without me," Kat said, feeling a lie form in her mouth, "There's just so much going on. We're hoping to bring Laura home in the next couple of days."

"I thought you said she wasn't doing well?" Van asked.

Kat had to double back on what she said. She tried to clear her thoughts, knowing she needed to be able to cover her tracks. She didn't want to give anyone outside she and Steve the information that she had about the medallion. No one else needed to be in danger -- if she was in danger. Kat stammered, "Yeah, sorry. I didn't sleep well last night. Laura wasn't doing well last night, but the hospital said she is doing better this morning. You know, things change from moment to moment." She tried to laugh off her mistake... and her lie.

She could hear Van's tone soften, "You sound tired. Call me after you get some rest. Say hello to Steve and the little man for me."

"Will do." With that Kat pushed the end button on her phone and breathed in the fresh air. The backyard seemed exactly the same as it was yesterday, the day before, the month before. And yet, Kat's life felt like it was swirling out of control. "Deep breaths," she whispered to herself, feeling the smoke start to rise in her nostrils. "One step at a time."

Kat walked to the back of their yard where she and Jack had been playing trucks in the sand earlier. The red truck was still in the sand, abandoned for a snack or another toy. Kat couldn't remember which. She picked it up and held it in her hand, gripping it tightly. She remembered complaining about cleaning up after Jack and how he was distracting her from her writing. Tears started to well up in her eyes. She chased them back down with a swallow. What she'd give now to just clean up trucks and pretzel bits all day long.

Kat sat down on the edge of the slide, smoothing her jeans over her legs. It was her favorite perch when Jack was in the backyard. Sitting on the edge put her eye level with him and kept him close. That's all she wanted, to keep her boys close. Having Laura sick had made all of their lives more complicated. The appointments, time at the hospital, questions from the doctors -- it was almost too much. Kat used her toe to draw a circle in some sand that had escaped the sandbox. She knew that it wasn't Laura's fault, but Kat, selfishly she knew, was angry that Laura's stomach cancer had upset the delicate balance that she had built to keep herself sane.

As she stood up, she could feel the cracks in the emotional foundation she had built splinter some more. She wanted peace and she wasn't sure she'd ever have it again.

13

V an put his feet up on his desk in the only spot that wasn't covered in piles of papers and stacks of files. His office always looked that way. The rest of the office was neat and tidy. Alyssa's desk was right by the front door. She faced anyone who came in. Her desk, a secondhand work desk that had been left by one of the other tenants in the building, had been a little beaten up when he moved into the place, but the landlord was just glad that someone wanted to move the furniture. Van's desk and both of their chairs had been reclaimed from the same abandoned office suite down the hall.

No one touched Van's desk. Although the piles of paper were seemingly chaotic, to Van they weren't. When he hired Alyssa to be his assistant, he told her that he had to fire his last assistant because she kept trying to clean his office. Alyssa promptly told him that she hated to clean and wasn't his mother, so he wouldn't have that problem with her. She got the job on the spot.

Van had started *The Hot Sheet* just over three years before, when he retired from the Marines. He liked the work that he did. With his eye for timely stories, the online readership had grown to just over two hundred thousand people. Van had eyes on getting to half a million.

Van's cell phone was on the edge of the desk. He had just hung up the phone with Kat Beckman. Over the last year, Kat had become his most important journalist. She had a sharp eye for detail and an innate sense of when something didn't seem right about a story. Several times Van had told her that a story was ready to be posted and she told him to wait, coming back to him with a new twist that either completely changed the story or facts that couldn't be argued. Either way, Van had learned to trust Kat's judgment and not push her. She seemed to do better on her own.

That was the case now. Kat told him her story wasn't ready. That was okay. What wasn't okay is that he knew there was more going on than she had told him. His gut told him so. Sure, Kat's mother-in-law was sick and that could throw a wrench in the works for anybody, but it was more than that. Kat seemed nervous and cagey. It wasn't a Kat that he had seen before.

Van took his feet off the desk and tapped the touchpad on his laptop. Entering his password, he opened a browser window and typed in the name of the hospital where Kat's mother-in-law was hospitalized -- Mercy Memorial. Why every hospital had a name like that, he'd never know, although he supposed that having mercy at a hospital was probably a good thing. Typing quickly, he did a search for recent news items about the hospital. A few stories came up, one on a drug trial, one on a double arm amputee getting new arms and a small story at the bottom of the page about a nurse that had OD'd on fentanyl in the hospital's bathroom the night before. He scanned the article quickly and saw that the police had ruled it an overdose.

Three things caught Van's eye in the reporting. The article

was buried low on the page. Someone didn't want it to be found. Van understood why -- no hospital wants patients thinking that they have an issue with drug abuse among their staff. Two other things grabbed Van's attention. The death had been on the oncology floor. He knew that Laura, Kat's mother-in-law was being treated for cancer. Although he didn't know offhand, she could have been on the same floor as the OD. There was a quote in the article from a colleague who knew Sarah well. "I'm just so surprised," the quote in the article read, "Sarah was a fitness nut. She was always taking supplements. She was even training for a Tough Mudder next month. I've never even seen her eat a potato chip!" Van had heard of Tough Mudders. They were Spartan-style races where competitors had to climb obstacles and even jump barriers that were on fire. Sure, there could be people addicted to drugs who were training for a physical competition, but something about the article didn't really ring true. Who was this Sarah? Why did the hospital want the article buried so deep?

Van stood up from his desk and paced behind it. Along the back wall of his office were three bookshelves. They weren't fancy, just some that he had purchased from the local office supply store when he started. There was nothing about Van that was fancy. He got a five-dollar haircut from the barber down the street, keeping his hair short and cropped. He wore a button-down shirt over his jeans, but it wasn't tucked in. He wore ratty cowboy boots, the toes scuffed and nicked from years of wear.

Kat had pushed him off the phone faster than normal this morning. He was trying to square that with the fact that her family was going through something tough. Cancer was a grind. It was a battle, in many cases a worse battle than the ones he had seen overseas as a Marine. At least overseas you could see your enemy. It wasn't inside of you, eating away at you moment by moment. He shook off the thought. He stopped for a moment, staring at the computer screen where the article about the nurse was still showing. Shutting the computer screen, he grabbed his phone and his keys.

"Going out for a bit," he said to Alyssa, who barely nodded as he walked out the door of the small office.

14

With Steve dropping off Jack at Vito's house and then stopping at the hospital for a few minutes, Kat had a little time to think. That's what she needed. Her best work always happened in the quiet. She decided that was how she was going to approach what was in front of her.

Kat walked inside the house from the backyard and closed the door, turning the lock. She couldn't remember the last time she had been so vigilant about securing the doors, except when she first came back from the Middle East. In some ways, it surprised her. She hadn't even noticed the change.

The road to her healing had been a bumpy one. Her therapist had told her it would resemble something closer to a stock market graph, ups and downs, a few ups and then a down before a bigger up. Healing never had a smooth, pretty upward arc. Not watching the locks was something she hadn't even noticed she had stopped doing. Kat frowned, feeling like she was off track. She needed to concentrate.

On the kitchen counter, she found what she was looking for, the phone that had been in the box. She opened the phone again and reread the text. Time was ticking. She needed to decide what to do about the Bluebird roster. She put the phone down and leaned her hands on the counter, wondering what would happen if she didn't do anything...

That's what she wanted. She wanted to go back to a time when she and Steve were happy. She wanted to go back to the time when Laura was healthy and could come over and play with Jack. No more appointments, nights at the hospital and certainly no more medallions and the feeling of fear and uncertainty chipping away at her.

There was a choice to make. It would have to be made sooner rather than later. Kat found the medallion on the kitchen table. She picked it up and turned it over and over in her hand. The reality was that she was out of choices. She couldn't go back. She couldn't turn back time and erase the parts of her life that she didn't want. That just wasn't possible.

If she did nothing, Laura would die. If she did what the text asked, Laura might live and Kat might go to jail. And, she didn't have a lot of time to figure it out, one way or the other. Time was ticking. If she did what they asked, she had no idea if she could pull it off or if they would actually help Laura.

Kat sat down at her laptop already and searched for the Bluebird mission using a standard Internet browser. She knew nothing would come up, but she wanted to see what information -- if any -- was available. There was nothing. Just thousands of articles about birds. The information that the man in the scrubs wanted wasn't about wildlife. It was only something that someone with a clearance could provide.

It wasn't an issue of not knowing what Bluebird was. She knew that already. It was an issue of what to do with the information. She took a deep breath, hoping that would clear her head. It didn't. If she got the information they wanted, what would they do with it? If she got caught getting it, would she get arrested? Kat stared at a corner of the floor, almost frozen. She felt trapped. There was no good answer. If she got the information, she'd open herself up to prosecution. If she didn't, her family could be arranging a funeral sooner rather than later. A prickly feeling started to cover her body. She couldn't afford to have an episode. It would cloud her thinking and she needed to be clear right now.

Her mind drifted back to the Middle East. Bluebird was an operation that she had witnessed in Afghanistan. She had begged and pleaded with the base commander to let her go observe an actual mission, not just reconnaissance. He had put her off for a month, but her daily nagging finally wore him down. She had to sign a special release in order to go and they had assigned an extra person to the mission team to watch her. That was his only job.

That day, Kat got to attend the mission brief before they left. Their target was a Taliban leader called Ahmed Al-Shah. He was one of the most powerful tribal leaders in the area. He was aptly named Bluebird because of the light blue headscarf that he wore everywhere. It wasn't traditional Afghani garb, but Al-Shah didn't seem to mind.

He had come to the attention of the base commander because intelligence reported that he was planning on attacking one of the American bases in the Middle East and pairing it with an attack at the same time on US soil. If successful, it would be a devastating blow to the Americans in the region and at home both physically and emotionally. It had to be stopped. While the commanders had been aware of Bluebird in the past and had left him under observation, his escalation meant that they had to deal with the threat. The time was now.

At the briefing, the base commander sat in, which he normally didn't do. He had stared at Kat the entire time. She knew that General Barton didn't want her to go, and he would do what he needed to in order to make sure she felt his ire.

The briefing included what they called "the roster." It was the names of all of the operators going on the mission. It was a small team, only five guys, plus Kat and her escort. The men going on the mission were all SEALs. It wasn't TJ's team, but her brief time at the base told her that they were ready for combat.

Kat hadn't been allowed to make notes of who went on that mission. She couldn't bring a cell phone in the room or even a pencil. The General had made sure of it. The men going had been specifically brought in for the event. They didn't introduce themselves by name, so she really didn't know who had gone on the mission that day. It was mission security. Although she had a clearance, she clearly wasn't part of the club.

THE PRICKLY FEELING had left Kat's body for the moment. She needed to think about something else. She decided to check on Jack. She sent a quick text to her friend Angela. Angela texted back that Jack and Vito were drawing pictures. While she was texting, Steve checked in. He said he was just pulling into the hospital parking garage. She had time.

Kat went into the garage and around behind the back of her car. There was a trap door in the floor, which she pulled open. A dusky bulb turned on and revealed a short ladder. Kat turned around and went carefully down the steps, holding onto the wooden handrails. Three rungs later and her shoes hit the dirt floor.

Their home was an older one with a root cellar. They didn't really use it for anything. When they had bought the house, Steve had the idea to either can some of their own food or to use it as a storm shelter. They went down in the cellar once when there was a tornado warning. Other than that, the cellar was just a place for a little bit of storage.

Kat used the flashlight feature on her phone to better illuminate the area. It was small, maybe eight feet by eight feet, with a dirt floor. The trapdoor had likely been outside at some point in the past, with the previous owners just including it in the attached garage when they built it. There were some wooden shelves on the walls and an old broom, rake and shovel in the corner. A couple of empty, filthy glass jars sat on the shelves. Kat noticed that the old patio furniture Steve had promised to get rid of was still down there. That was a fight for another day. Turning back towards the ladder, she inched her body around it. There was an additional space behind the ladder that was one of the darkest parts of the house. She had found it when they first moved it. Someone had left a wooden storage box back there. She was sure it had been there for decades. She tugged on the wooden box and moved it to the side, pulling out a metal storage box. She replaced the wooden box and moved out into the main area of the cellar where there was a little more light. Balancing the metal box on a rung of the ladder, Kat pulled out a plastic bag that had papers in it. She sat on one of the old patio chairs, the plastic rungs sagging beneath her weight with their age and opened the bag.

The box held a few things that she wanted nearby, but not ones she wanted to find. Her old passport, a few Afghani currency notes and coins, her military id, a few papers and several small black notebooks. She pulled a gray scarf out of the bag. It smelled like the cellar but was still intact. It was the one that she wore while in country to honor the headscarf traditions. It was also the one that she had with her on the day that she was injured.

She put everything back except for two of the small black notebooks. She had carried the same type of notebook throughout her career as a journalist. She even carried them now that she was at home. Pocket-sized with lined paper and black covers were her favorite. An elastic strap kept the pages together. Some journalists tried to bring technology in country.

She learned that paper and pen worked better with so much dust and grime floating through the air.

She pulled one of the elastic straps around the backside of the notebook and looked at the pages. They were filled with symbols and letters that meant something only to her. Lots of journalists had their own code to protect their information. Kat was no different. No one could read her story notes except for her.

Some journalists wrote in longhand, some wrote in shorthand and some had their own codes. Not only did Kat have a special code, in a few of the notebooks she had actually started in the back of the book first. Instead of reading left to right, she wrote her notes right to left. Journalists with big stories or stories that had potential consequences kept their notes close to the vest. Writing in code had a side benefit. If she ever got called into court she could easily avoid answering questions about her notes and sources. No one except for her would know what she had written. It would be nearly impossible for any attorney to ask questions about documents they simply couldn't read. It was the First Amendment at its best.

Kat quickly looked through a few of the notebooks and found the one she was looking for, sticking it in the back pocket of her jeans. She put the rest of the notebooks back in the plastic bag, sealed it and put them back. She hid the metal box back behind the ladder and climbed back up the rungs of the ladder. Stepping out into the garage, she felt her skin prickle. She didn't like the cellar, but she didn't want those memories where she -- or others -- could find them. Quickly, she turned off the light and closed the trapdoor, putting an old tarp over the top of it to make it look like it wasn't even there. She felt her way back into the house through the dark garage. Even though it was daytime, she didn't want anyone to know she'd been in the garage if they were watching the house.

Now in the kitchen, Kat took a minute to thumb through

the notebook. She found the notes from her time in Afghanistan and set a pencil in the binding to keep the book open. Her notes were faded from the moisture in the cellar, but they were still readable, at least to her. She walked over to a kitchen drawer and pulled out two prepaid cell phones. They had been sitting in the drawer for a couple of years. Steve had bought them just in case of an emergency. Kat decided today was an emergency.

She opened the box, powered up the phone and plugged it in to charge. She looked in the notebook and found two phone numbers. She chose the second one and sent a text that read "I need glue."

Now she had to wait. Kat put on a pot of water to boil and looked out into the backyard through the window above the sink wishing that Jack was outside playing with Steve, but also glad that neither of them were home both for Jack's safety and her own peace of mind. Kat's hand drifted down to the butt of the Sig on her hip. She felt it through her shirt. Knowing it was there helped. She hoped she didn't have to use it.

The water in the pot began to whistle and she poured hot water over a teabag in a mug. As she watched it steep, the burner phone vibrated.

"What kind of glue do you need?" the text read.

Kat quickly typed in, "Wood glue for my sandbox."

Within a few seconds, the phone vibrated again, "Sander's has that. They are open until 8 pm."

KAT TOOK her tea into the family room where Jack had been playing. Trucks were strewn all over the floor and the television was still tuned to Jack's favorite program. He had left in such a hurry that he hadn't turned it off. Neither had Steve. On days when there wasn't much going on, Kat felt like she spent all day long just putting away toys and picking up after Jack. She wished that was the only kind of chaos that she was facing today. It wasn't. Options raced through her mind as she put the trucks back into the basket that was nestled into the corner of the room. She shut off the television and at the same time realized she could pull the plug on the whole operation. She could just let what might happen, happen on its own. She didn't have to get the Bluebird mission files for the man in the scrubs. She didn't have to do any of it. It wasn't her fault that Laura got cancer.

Kat fluffed a few of the pillows on the couch. She needed to think and did it better when she was moving. No one cared if her pillows were fluffed and trucks put away. She didn't really care either.

From the family room, she could hear her phone ringing. It stopped before she got there, but when she looked, she saw that Steve had called three times. She'd been so absorbed in thought that she didn't even hear the first two attempts. Kat picked up the phone and hit the redial.

"Where have you been?" Steve asked, sounding breathless.

"I've been here. I was just in the other room and didn't hear the phone."

"You okay?

"Yes, of course. I'm fine. What's going on?"

There was a pause, like Steve didn't know how to tell her what was on his mind. "I'm just outside Mom's room. She's taken a turn."

Kat felt the breath go out from her. "What do you mean a turn?"

"The nurses said that her heart rate has slowed and her blood pressure has dropped some. They were going to move her to hospice, but she is too fragile."

Kat sighed, "How is that possible? I was just there. She was fine! Do they know how much time she has?"

Kat heard Steve's voice break as he answered her question, "They don't know. A few days at most."

There was a pause. Kat didn't say anything and neither did Steve. Kat wished he was home or that she was at the hospital.

Steve broke the silence. "Did you get what they wanted?"

The breath caught in her throat. "I don't know that we should..."

Steve interrupted her, "I need to know if there is any hope or if I should just get ready to say goodbye to my mom. Can you get what they want?"

His response punched her in the stomach. Kat whispered, "I don't know."

Steve suddenly sounded angry. "You have to. Kat, it's my mom. You are the only person who can do this."

"I know that. But do you understand the consequences? I could go to jail. I wouldn't be able to see you or Jack. Do you understand what you are asking me?"

There was silence on the line. Steve said, "I guess... I guess I didn't really think about that part. I don't want to lose you, but mom is dying. The doctors said there is literally nothing else they can do."

Kat didn't say anything for a moment. She knew they were at a stage where one wrong comment from either of them could land them in a huge fight. It wasn't what they needed. "I'm trying to think it through. I'm trying to do something."

"What are you doing exactly?" Steve said. Kat knew he was trying to be gentle, but she could hear the impatience and fear in his voice.

"I can't talk about it." Kat started to pace around the house. "I have to go out in a little bit," she said, realizing that they were close to dinnertime already. "Why don't you stay with your mom's and then pick up Jack on your way home."

"Okay," Steve said, seemingly relieved to have someone else decide, Kat thought. Maybe it was just that she was trying.

"I'll talk to you later," Steve said. "Text me if you need anything."

Kat ended the call and realized that she was hungry. She hadn't eaten all day and her stomach was reminding her of it. She didn't have a lot of time so she made a quick sandwich and ate an orange, hoping the fruit would help keep her from feeling run down, which she was. She finished her sandwich, tossed away the napkin she had eaten it on and grabbed her car keys. It was time to go.

15

Van had left the office with not much of a goodbye to Alyssa, his assistant. That was pretty much par for the course. It wasn't something that he even worried about. Van did his own thing. People that couldn't deal with it, he didn't keep in his life.

Van went down the narrow staircase that led out onto the street from his office. He had chosen a low-key building not only because of the low rent but because people who wanted to come and give him tips didn't necessarily want to meet him in a building filled with fancy glass and chrome. It wasn't his personality anyway. Van was more of a jeans kind of guy. There was really nothing fancy about him. Except for his boots, maybe, which reminded him that he was due for a new pair.

What did matter was the story. When Van was in the military, he always wanted to know why they were going after a target. He wanted the briefers to tell him not only about the geography and the city they were going to, but also about the people. He wanted the why behind what they were doing. He was always concerned about consequences and ultimately, the people that were behind the story. What Van knew is that without the people, there wasn't much of a story.

That was one of the reasons that he and Kat worked so well together. She understood story better than nearly every other journalist he had ever worked with. He didn't have to tell her to go back and learn more about the people. She already knew about them. She had a way of immersing herself in the circumstances and personalities in a way that he'd never seen before. He respected that.

As Van walked to his truck, he knew he might be poking his head in where it wasn't wanted, but he had heard something in Kat's voice that didn't ring true. It didn't sound like her. He had to follow up. It was his job as his editor. He wanted to protect all of his journalists.

What Van did know is that Kat was preoccupied with Laura's illness. Van had met Laura at Jack's last birthday party. Van had been over a few times for dinner when they had to work on a story. Kat could watch Jack, she and Van could work and Steve was always game to throw a few steaks on the grill and talk sports.

Van opened the door to his truck and got in, giving the engine a moment to warm up while he put on his seatbelt and found a place for his phone. He pulled out of the spot in the lot behind the building next to his and found his way into traffic.

Van took one of the main roads out to Mercy Memorial. There weren't a lot of cars on the road. It was the middle of the day and the people that had to be at work were there, lunchtime having already passed. Driving over the hill just outside the hospital proper, it struck Van how much land they must have. While they didn't live in a particularly rural area, it wasn't completely urban either. Mercy Memorial must have purchased a big tract of land before any development had really started. The grass was green and had been recently mowed. The shrubs were manicured. For a hospital, they kept it up pretty nice. Must be a good way to get donors, Van thought. There was a main parking garage that serviced employees, patients and families, but Van preferred one of the open lots.

Van found a parking spot and pulled in. It was at the end of the row where no one else had parked. Everyone he knew that had come back from the Middle East had their idiosyncrasies. He was no different. Open spaces kept him calm and happy. The fewer people to crowd him, the better.

Van walked toward the main entrance of the building and went past the emergency room, which was positioned right by the front doors. Right in front was an ambulance with the lights still flashing. The paramedics had the doors open and were pulling out a patient, one of them doing CPR as they went. It was an older fellow, looking pale and slightly blue. They managed to unload him without missing a beat of CPR. Van stepped aside so they could get the gurney through the doors. He heard the hiss of the doors slide open. The gurney rolled past him, a trauma nurse already getting information from the medics as they kept on working.

Van had seen a lot of people come in on gurneys when he was in the Middle East. Not that he worked in the medical bay, he would just see them as the Humvees came back with injured in them. It wasn't something he'd ever forget.

Injuries were unfortunately common for military members in the Middle East. The people at home only thought about IED's -- Improvised Explosive Devices -- and insurgents. What they didn't realize was that there were also friendly fire incidents, training injuries and just stupid accidents. Van walked down the hallway and saw a guy hobbling along on a pair of crutches. It reminded him of when a friend of his ended up getting sent home because he tore his Achilles tendon playing basketball. There was no glory in that, Van thought, but then getting hurt playing basketball might be better than going home with a war injury and the mental and emotional baggage that came with it.

Van had been one of the lucky ones. His dad had always told people, "It's like Van's been dipped in gold," because of his crazy good luck. He had spent his time overseas and had gotten into some scrapes, but he had come home with all of his parts and much less mental scarring than many of his friends. When he first came home, a friend of his had suggested that he attend a support group for military members that were trying to assimilate. One meeting of lukewarm coffee, stale cookies and men and women who had lost legs, arms, eyes and their ability to speak kept Van from ever going back. He wasn't in that boat and had no intention of picking up an oar. It wasn't that he didn't feel for his military brothers and sisters. It was just that the spots in groups like those were for people who really needed them. That wasn't him.

Van made his way down to the end of the hallway at the opposite end of the hospital from the emergency room. He pushed open the door to the stairwell and trotted down one flight, pushing open the fire door that was at the bottom of the stairs.

Few people went to the basement of any hospital and yet that's where Van often found his best information. Basements were the holding place for people who knew everything that happened in all types of businesses, not just hospitals.

When Van stepped into the basement, he felt a little bad for stepping on the shiny, fresh waxed linoleum tile. They were flanked by murky beige painted walls. While the hospital was clearly updated upstairs, apparently the management had forgotten there was a lower level to contend with.

only offices in the basement were the morgue, the control room with all of the mechanicals of the hospital and the security office. Van walked down the hall and opened the first door that he saw.

"Hey Benny," Van said, "Things quiet today?"

Benny, whose real name was Benjamin Franklin, wasn't a typical hospital security guard. In fact, Benny was way too qualified for his job. A past police chief, Benny wanted something to do after he retired where he could use his skills. Running the hospital security team was the perfect fit. There was certainly no lack of action, but Van knew from their conversations at O'Henry's that there were less politics too. The hospital staff had enough on their hands.

Benny leaned back in the office chair that he was sitting in, the top button of his collared shirt undone, the tie and jacket flung over a chair nearby and grimaced at Van. "Not as quiet as I'd like. I've got a nurse and a doctor couple engaged in a domestic, a family that freaked out and smashed a glass window and a kid on the pediatric floor trying to steal meds." He shook his head. "It's always something."

Van had met Benny a few years beforehand when he was researching a story on painkiller abuse in hospitals. Although Van was the online editor, he wanted to keep writing and so he did feature articles every quarter or so. He and Benny had struck up a friendship and met for beers at O'Henry's Bar once in a while, trading stories and laughing. Van liked that Benny not only knew what he was doing, but he was willing to do the extra detective work to expose problems in the hospital, or wherever he found them. He and Benny had even detained a couple of teenagers who tried to rob the bar a few months back. Benny held the suspect until the police arrived. Benny was the real deal.

"What kind of trouble are you into now?" Benny asked.

"You don't want to know," Van replied, sitting down in a chair on the other side of Benny's desk. Van was sure that the chair had been in the hospital for twenty years, the faded fuchsia floral upholstery held together with duct tape. At least the chrome armrests still looked okay, he thought. "Why don't you get some real chairs in here? Don't they have a budget for basement dwellers?"

Benny grunted. "Because I don't want anyone in here. If they get too comfortable, they won't want to leave." Benny stared at the screen in front of him and clicked his laptop to get a different video feed view up on the monitors. Van saw him reach for his radio and key it up. "Linda, the thief in peds is back at it." Van heard the radio crackle with Linda's reply. "I've got it. The parents are coming to help."

Benny turned and looked at Van. "So, why are you taking up space in my office?"

"I think you know why."

"Ahhh, yep. The nurse that OD'd. It's a good follow up to your story from a couple of years ago. That what you're after?"

Van nodded. "What floor did that happen on?"

Benny pulled a folder out of the stack on his desk and flipped it open. "This is a copy of the file. Thought you might be coming by. Four. Oncology."

Van reached for the folder that Benny extended over the desk. Knowing that it was oncology made him wonder. It seemed strange to him that Kat had clammed up at the same time that the nurse described in the folder had died. Coincidence? Maybe. The only thing was that Van didn't really believe in coincidences. Kat had clammed up before, but nothing like this. His gut told him that there was more going on. He'd like to believe that it was just because of the troubles with her mother-in-law, but something didn't feel right. When things didn't feel right, he started to ask questions. It was just his way.

Van looked at the file that Benny had compiled. For a hospital security team, Benny ran a tight ship. Most of his team were former police or military. Linda, the woman handling the pediatric thief, was a former FBI agent. Van had met her on other trips to the hospital.

In the file were reports that Benny had printed off about

what had happened. There were reference numbers to the formal police reports and copies included in the hospital file. On the left-hand side of the file were images of Sarah. Van looked at them carefully. Sarah was slumped on the floor, her eyes open and lips blue. There was a trickle of foam coming out of the right corner of her mouth. Her right arm was across her lap, her legs at a funny angle. In her left arm was a needle. It looked like she OD'd before she even had a chance to take the tourniquet off.

"Anything interesting about this incident that I should know?" Van asked.

Benny pulled up a digital copy of the file on his screen. "Not too much. It's a shame really. From all of our interviews, Sarah seemed to be the last person that would OD. She was training for some race..."

"A Tough Mudder..." Van interjected.

"Yeah, that's it. Some race where you get all muddy and jump over fire." Benny scowled, looking at Van. "Not for me."

Van nodded. "Anything else that seemed interesting?"

"One thing, maybe, though we are still trying to sort it out. When we found the vial of the fentanyl we did an inventory on the floor. The drugs were the same brand that we use here, but that lot number wasn't one that we ordered."

Van thought about that for a minute. "It was hospital grade stuff?"

"Yup. I'm thinking that it came from a different floor. We are checking the hospital-wide inventory now."

"Did Sarah work on any other floors?"

Benny shook his head, "Naw. She was always on oncology. You know, oncology is pretty specialized with all of the drugs and the treatments the nurses have to know about."

Van nodded. From working with Benny, he knew that there were some doctors and nurses that floated from department to department. They handled general issues. The more specialized areas, obstetrics, critical care and oncology had their own staff. "Could she have known someone who got her the drugs?"

"I guess."

Van thought for a moment, considering his last question. He knew that while Benny was cooperative and someone that he considered a friend, Benny's patience would run out soon. "One last thing. Did anything show up on the security feed?"

"Naw. We don't have coverage at that end of the hallway on oncology." Benny clicked a couple of keys on the laptop and pulled up the feed from that night.

Van watched the video. Apparently, the cameras they had on the oncology floor only covered the elevator and the nurses' station. Benny played the video at one and a half times. It moved along at a pretty good clip, but there wasn't much to watch. There were a few doctors and nurses that came up onto the floor, but not many. Sarah had been working the night shift that day. The last few frames showed Sarah at the nurses' station, typing into the computer, leaving the computer and walking away.

"Based on the timeline, she OD'd right after," Benny said.

Van stood up to leave, knowing he was about to overstay his welcome. "Can I take this copy with me?"

"I shouldn't let you, but yeah," Benny said. Benny bent the rules for Van, knowing that he wasn't going to get drawn into anything. That was their deal.

"Thanks," Van said, "I'll get it back to you tomorrow."

Van pushed open the door to the security office, glancing back at Benny, who was already staring at the multiple views of the security cameras in the hospital. Van didn't go back the same way he came in. Instead, he continued down the hallway and out the back stairwell, giving the security camera a little salute as he passed by. He knew Benny would see.

Van walked around the back of the hospital where the phys-ical plant was on his way back to his truck. The smell of garbage hung in the air but dissipated as soon as he walked around the corner.

Van started to think about the information that Benny shared with him. As soon as he got back to his truck, he flipped open the file again. Sarah had been pretty. She looked to be small, maybe only five feet or so, with brown eyes and a brown bob. Witness statements had nothing but glowing things to say about her. She had been pleasant, always on time and easy to work with. No one had anything negative to say about her. That could be a warning sign, Van thought, but he put that idea aside when he saw the close-up image of the vial of fentanyl that had been found in her pocket.

It was strange that the vial wasn't from oncology. Van stared at the image of it. Where had this vial come from? Mercy Memorial, like most hospitals, was nothing short of militant about their stores of painkillers. They knew exactly how much they had at any one time and who it had been administered to. New technology gave all doctors and nurses access to barcode scanners for drug tracking. Van had seen it before. Whenever a patient needed a drug, especially addictive painkillers, the nurse would use her passcode to get the drugs out of the locker, scan the vial, go to the patient's room, scan the vial again, scan the patient's armband and administer the drug. It was a lot of work for nurses.

Van knew that all the technology was just a serious cover of liability for the hospital, not to mention cost control. Drugs used to be able to walk out of hospitals in pockets and purses at the end of a shift, but that is no more. The tight controls used not only saved hospitals millions of dollars in theft, but they made sure that the most addictive drugs were kept under tight control. Though the efforts took labor hours, it was a win-win for the most part.

The origin of the drugs was the only thing that hung Van up on Sarah's story. It would be natural for her to snag fentanyl from the hospital. She worked there. She had access to the meds. But it was strange that the vial that was found with her wasn't from the floor. Would she have gone to another floor to get the drugs? Van wondered about this but decided to get moving. Alyssa would be looking for him at some point and he needed to get back to the office. Van put the truck into gear and headed back out the long driveway of Mercy Memorial, the file sitting on the front seat of his truck.

On the way back to the office, he started thinking about Kat again and tried her cell. There was no answer. He hoped she was okay. Van turned the truck into traffic and back into town, headed to work. He clicked on the radio, listening to some pundits talking about immigration issues. Large, macro issues never interested him that much. He wanted to know the story about the people. Sarah's story was one of the people he'd like to learn more about. What people said about her and how she died just didn't match. That didn't necessarily mean anything, though. His original story about painkiller deaths took a lot of lives that seemed just fine on the outside. An overdose wasn't necessarily a suicide. Sometimes it was just a mistake. Maybe Sarah's was just that. A mistake.

Van parked the truck back in the small lot behind the building next to his office. She grabbed the file and locked up the truck, heading back to the office. He pushed the building door open and took the stairs two at a time. When he walked in, he saw Alyssa in virtually the same position he left her, hunched over her desk.

"Still here?" he asked.

"Waiting on you," she mumbled.

"I hope it's for something good?"

"Not really." With that, Alyssa looked up. "You have some checks to sign and a couple of the writers need to talk to you about their stories. Lana is going to miss her deadline again."

"She'd going to be lucky if we keep holding her spot," Van said. Alyssa nodded.

Van looked at her. Alyssa was pretty in a natural sort of way. She never dressed up and frequently came to the office with her hair wet and without makeup after her morning workout. She had been a college softball player. Van liked that she was a no-fuss, no-muss type of girl.

"Could you track down this lot number for me?" he asked, pointing to the picture of the vial in Benny's folder. "I need to know what hospital it was sold to. As much information as you can find."

"Uh-huh. Where will you be?" she asked.

"In my office. Got some work to do, but I need this as soon as you can get it."

16

The drive to Sander's Diner was a close one, just about twenty minutes. Kat circled the block a couple of times when she left the house and took a route she didn't normally use, using some counter-surveillance moves she had learned. When she got about a mile out from the diner, she pulled over on a side street to see if anyone else pulled down to watch her. They didn't. For the first time all day, Kat felt a little bit calmer. Getting out of the house was helping.

Out of her bag, Kat fished two phones. She had the burner phone she had powered up to meet her contact. She also had the one that the man in the scrubs had sent to her. She shoved both phones back in her bag and pulled back out into traffic, settling on a parking space in an alley just behind the diner. She could use the back entrance and not risk being seen if she was being tailed.

She got out of the car, a slight drizzle hitting her face and hands. She locked her car and walked into the diner, the bag on her shoulder helping to cover up the butt of the Sig she still had on her hip.

The diner was one of the oldest in the area. While many

diners had popped up and were as much a part of the history of the area as the newest mall, Sander's had been built in the 1940's. It still had some of the old charm and a lot of the dirt and grease to go along with it. Kat didn't mind. As she walked in the back door, a bell rang, announcing her arrival. She nodded to the waitress, a young girl wearing a red t-shirt that said Sander's on the back in white lettering. "Sit anywhere," she called over her shoulder. "I'll be there in a minute."

With that, Kat chose a booth in the back of the diner where she could watch the front door. There were only a few people in the diner. A couple sitting in the window, eating burgers and fries. There was a man with his back to her. She could see over his shoulder every time he turned a page of his newspaper. There was a family with a couple of kids and two older ladies eating pie. Kat looked to her right and saw two cooks in the kitchen and only one waitress walking around offering hot coffee. She approached Kat. "Coffee?" she said.

"Please," Kat answered, turning over her mug, which had been upside down on her placemat. The waitress poured her a cup and Kat got a good look at her. In addition to her Sander's red t-shirt, the waitress had on skinny jeans, Converse tennis shoes and a couple of rope bracelets on her wrist. She wore glasses and her dark, bobbed hair looked like she had just let it dry on the way to work.

"Are you meeting someone?" the waitress asked.

"Yes."

The waitress nodded. "I'll come back."

Kat took a deep breath and put both hands on the edge of the table, steadying herself. Using the burner phone had been a desperate move. He had responded, but she wasn't sure if he would show. Kat reached into her purse, checked her phone and the two burners. Nothing. She sent a quick text to Angela to check on Jack. Angela sent back a picture of him with chocolate ice cream on his face. He was clearly having a good time.

Kat let her know that Steve would be picking Jack up in a little bit.

As she put the phone away, the front door opened, chiming just like when she walked into the diner. A man stopped in the doorway and looked her way. Kat saw him start to move toward her.

He slipped into the booth, taking off his leather jacket. "Hey," he said, almost whispering.

Kat looked at him, surprised by how little he had changed. "I wasn't sure you would come." Even though they lived close by, they hadn't really kept in touch. Their past had made things sticky between Kat and Steve.

"You sent up the bat signal. What did you think would happen?"

Kat looked at TJ, all of a sudden remembering how close they had been. She fumbled with her spoon, "I guess I wasn't sure."

TJ smiled, the skin around the edges of his eyes wrinkling up. "You knew I'd come," he said.

"Yeah, I guess I did. It's just been a long day." After Kat had returned to the U.S. after the accident, she cut ties with all of the men that were on the mission that day. Part of it was trauma, part of it was for their protection and part of it was because of how close she and TJ had gotten. It had been at least four or five years since she had heard from any of them. And, when they did reach out, she didn't reply.

TJ nodded, his square hands resting on the table, "How's the wrist."

She pulled her sleeve up and rolled it for him, "Pretty good."

"I'm thinking we aren't here to talk about your wrist, are we?"

Before Kat could answer, the waitress came back and

offered TJ something to drink. Kat waited to answer him until he'd asked for a cup of coffee and a piece of rhubarb pie.

The waitress looked at Kat, "Can I get you anything?"

"Just more coffee," Kat said.

The waitress nodded, "I'll be right back with that."

Kat went back to TJ's question about why they were meeting. "No, we aren't. This isn't about my wrist," Kat said. "I've got a problem. It's not the kind I can solve by myself."

"Tell me," said TJ, his demeanor changing.

Kat had noticed that whenever there was a perceived threat or problem, team guys -- that's what SEALs called themselves -- had a way of changing their personality. It was like their armor came up. They became superhuman. Kat always wondered what part of their training allowed them to do that. "It's my mother-in-law," she said. "She has cancer."

TJ looked at her, "That's awful. Is she doing okay?"

"Not really."

Kat began to tell him about how Laura had been diagnosed and all of the appointments and the testing. She told him about the treatments and the stress to their family and how she and Steve had fought and how they were trying to protect Jack.

"That's not why you reached out, though, is it?" TJ asked.

"No, it's not. If this was just about Laura's cancer, I never would have called."

"You could have."

There was a pause. Kat absorbed the comment, but let it go. "Something else happened. I was drugged."

The color of TJ's face changed as he realized what she said. He looked angry. "What? What do you mean?"

Kat began to relay to him the story of the last day. She told him about leaving Jack at home with Steve, how her favorite nurse Sarah always brought her hot tea when she stayed with Laura and how someone else brought the tea. She told him about the man in the scrubs and how she had found the medallion in her pocket when she got home. She told him about how Laura was terminal just a few hours later and about Sarah's death. "The man said that there is a cure."

TJ looked at her with more questions than answers written all over his face. "A cure for cancer?"

Kat nodded. "Yes." Kat shared with TJ how she had come home feeling foggy after her night at the hospital, sure that what she had remembered was a dream. "Steve and I took a hard look at the medallion and found a website on it. It was a dark web site."

TJ raised his eyebrows. Kat continued, "We got online."

"Your computer was protected, right?"

Kat frowned, "Protected enough."

TJ nodded. "You should have had a secured interface."

"I know, but we were just trying to figure it out."

"Okay. Keep going."

Kat said, "We went to the website and it asked for Laura's name. We typed it in and submitted it. The site disappeared. We weren't able to get back to it. Steve and I thought that it was a hoax until we got a delivery about twenty minutes later."

"A delivery?"

"It was a box, actually. We found a burner in it."

"A burner?" Kat saw TJ's fists clench, but she decided to keep going. "A text came on the burner as soon as we got the box. It said that there was a cure, but that we'd have to pay. They don't want money. They want information."

Kat wasn't sure what to expect next. She didn't know how TJ would respond. Not that she'd been around a lot of SEALs, but the ones she had been around had a way of processing information without giving you any idea how they would respond. Kat remembered a quote that her dad used to say, "Still waters run deep." That's how the team guys she had met worked. You were never quite sure what they were going to do until they did it.

"Do you have the burner with you?" TJ asked.

Kat fished it out of her bag and handed it to him. "Here you go."

TJ read it and closed it, passing it back to Kat. "I'm assuming they are asking for the list of operators on an op from when you were embedded?"

Kat's chest clutched. "Yes. It was a mission that General Barton sent me on to observe." She dropped her voice to a whisper. "It was to take care of a Taliban leader."

"And these people with the supposed cure, whoever they are, want to know who was on the mission? Do you know why?"

Kat nodded no. "I have no idea. This is all of the information that I have. And, I'm on a timeline." Kat pointed to the front of the phone. "They installed a timer on the front of the phone."

TJ looked at it and then looked at Kat. "Supposing you can get the information, what happens if you don't get it to them in time?"

Kat felt a wave of nausea come over her. TJ was right. There were a lot of unanswered questions. She didn't have any more information than she had given him. Her hands started to shake. She clenched her hands together and set them on the table. "I don't know."

TJ was silent for a moment, rubbing his beard and looked at the phone one more time. He handed it back to Kat and set his hand on top of hers. The warmth steadied her. "It's okay. This is a problem like any other. You just have to work it one step at a time." He lifted his hand off of hers as the waitress brought his pie and coffee. She refilled Kat's cup and nodded as she walked away.

Kat watched TJ as he leaned back against the seat. He hadn't changed much since she had seen him last. Still the same short hair and beard. He still walked like someone who hit the gym on a regular basis. She could tell from the way his sleeves fit that he did. He was one of those guys that were always prepared for anything.

"Let's go through some options, okay?" TJ said.

Kat nodded.

"Let's say that you buy that these guys have a cure for cancer. You'd have to access the mission list and get it to them. Do you still have your access?"

Again, Kat nodded, knowing that TJ wouldn't want to be interrupted while he was running the scenario. It was something she had experienced many times when she was embedded. The first time someone had been running scenarios and she had asked a question before they were done, she got kicked out of a briefing.

"You have your access. That gives you options. You understand that you'd be compromising your clearance?"

She nodded again.

TJ continued. "And if you handed off that information it would be a crime."

Kat didn't answer. She knew that even considering giving up the information was crazy. She let TJ run the rest of the scenario. "On the other hand, if you don't give them the information, we don't know what will happen. Clearly, they know where you live. They know about Laura. We just don't know what a no answer would do. Does that seem to be about the size of it?" TJ asked.

"Yes," Kat said, trying to keep herself calm. She looked past TJ to the rest of the diners. A couple of them had already left. A new couple had come in and sat down, menus up, trying to decide what to eat. Kat envied them. They weren't hiding in the back of a diner trying to decide what to do.

Frustrated, Kat looked at TJ. "I don't know what to do. If I give them the information, I'm a criminal. If I don't, Laura will die. They have me stuck between a rock and a hard place."

TJ picked up his cup of coffee and took a sip. "I think that's the point."

Kat let that sink in for a moment. She had been so busy reacting that she hadn't taken the time to really look at the strategy that the man in the scrubs had used. He had them cornered. There was no way out. She had to do something. Even doing nothing was something. There were consequences no matter which road she took. Kat's hands began to shake again. This time, she pushed them down into her lap. Tears started to well up in her eyes. Kat looked down at her hands, trying not to let the tears spill down her face.

TJ didn't move. She almost wished that he had told her that everything would be all right. He didn't. TJ wasn't that way. If she wanted sympathy, she'd have to get it elsewhere. Kat felt like time was standing still. She was boxed in. There was nowhere to go. It wasn't a question of if someone would get hurt, it was just who. Would Laura die or would Kat have to take the fall and go to jail? Kat felt like she sat there for hours, but it was only a few minutes.

When Kat looked up, TJ still hadn't moved. He didn't reach out to comfort her. He looked at her, seeming to search her face. "I'm not sure what you should do. You don't have a lot of options here."

"I know."

"It's a hard decision."

"What would you do?" Kat hoped his answer would shed some light on how to move forward.

"That's an impossible question to answer. You know the whole, 'God, family, country' thing? You're stuck smack dab in the middle. I don't know what I'd do."

The conversation turned back to more normal things. Kat's work. TJ's life. They didn't get back to the decision Kat needed to make, both of them skirting the issue.

TJ looked at his watch. "I've gotta go. If you need to talk

more, let me know." With that, he pulled some cash out of his wallet, set it under his coffee cup and slipped out of the booth, walking out the back door, leaving out the same door that Kat had come in. Kat waited for a few minutes and then left. She wanted to give him the opportunity to get out of the area in case she had been followed. TJ would expect that much. While Kat wasn't in the military, she had learned enough from the people that she had lived and worked with in the Middle East that she knew what was important to them.

Kat stood up and slid out of the booth, checking to make sure that she had her bags with all of the phones. She pushed down on the butt of her Sig to make sure it was seated in the holster. Slinging her bag over her shoulder, she walked out the back door of the diner and turned toward her car. She watched carefully to see if anyone seemed to be watching her, looking at every single parked car to see if there were any passengers just sitting and watching. There weren't. She found her car and immediately locked the doors before she started it.

On the drive home, she felt numb. TJ was right. There weren't any good solutions. Whether she acted or didn't, something would happen. Either Laura would die or Kat would go to jail trying to save her. That much she was sure of. She considered the man in the scrubs as she made a turn onto the freeway, taking a different route home. She would have liked to think that he was a good person, just offering the cure to people who needed it. The fact that he wanted classified information meant something totally different. He had an agenda. She realized that if she gave him the information, there was no way to control what was done with it. He could target the people that were on the mission. They could lose their lives. National security could be at risk. Kat's throat tightened as she pushed past traffic to get to her exit.

As Kat's car got closer to her neighborhood, she drove to the office building where Jack's pediatrician's office was and circled the block a couple of times, looking for tails. There weren't any. Kat quickly turned towards home.

Driving down her street, she realized that the lights had all come on in her neighborhood as the sun had started to set. She pulled up into the driveway and opened the garage door remotely. Steve's car was home. It would be nice to see her boys.

17

K at pulled her car into the garage after she met with TJ. She shut it off and pushed the button to close the garage door, but she didn't get out. She felt tired. There was no part of her body that didn't feel achy. She remembered a time when she had more energy than she knew what to do with. That wasn't now. All she wanted to do was sleep. She had done nothing but think and talk to TJ, trying to wrestle the right decision out of the situation. She had been left with nothing but more questions, more suspicions and a gnawing sensation in her gut that there was no good decision. No outcome would work.

The door to the garage opened, Steve's form silhouetted in the light from the hallway. "You planning on coming in?"

Kat opened the door to the car, pulled her bag over the driver's seat and got out. "Yeah. I'm coming." She walked up the two wooden steps into the house. The lights were on, but Steve had left the blinds closed. She could hear Jack in the family room playing with his trucks. His voice comforted her a bit.

Steve gave her a hug. "I didn't know you were going out."

"I needed some air."

"Where did you go?" Steve's brow furrowed.

"I met with TJ. I needed advice."

The furrow on Steve's brow pulled a little deeper on his face. "Really? Why would you do that?"

Although she and Steve hadn't even met when she was in the Middle East, for some reason TJ's very name brought out the competitive, jealous husband in Steve. They hadn't even met. That was what was strange, Kat thought. Steve wasn't the jealous type.

"I don't want to go there with you right now. I needed advice. I think you know why I'd go to him," Kat replied, walking away and into the kitchen. She set her bag down on the seat of one of the kitchen chairs and went over to the stove to start some tea.

Steve followed. In a way, she wished he wouldn't have, but she knew that he would want more answers. He probably wouldn't leave her alone until he got them. "Did you get what you needed?"

"I'm not sure. I need to think." Kat walked over to the sink, teapot in hand. She turned on the water and started to fill the pot. She decided to change the subject. "How's your mom doing?"

Steve sat down at the table and sighed. "She's weak and barely conscious. I was going to stay there tonight, but I didn't know where you were. Then I decided it probably didn't matter since she wouldn't know I was there."

"Steve, you can go if you want. I'm here. I'll take care of Jack."

"But what about the phone and the man that drugged you? What are we going to do about that?"

"I don't know. I love your mom and I don't want her to die. I also don't want to spend the rest of my life in jail."

She saw Steve look at his hands. "Could you get the information if you wanted to?"

"I'm not sure." She continued, setting the pot on the stove, "Even if I had it, I'd have to log in to the secure portal and see if it is still listed. They track all of that. There would be questions about why I logged in and what I did with the information."

Steve stood up and said, "If you can't get the information, why'd this guy ask you? Maybe he thinks you can?"

"I don't know."

"Is there anyone you can call to get the information?"

He was like a dog with a bone. "Steve, I don't know." Her words came out more sharply than she intended.

Steve looked at her and got up. "I guess it's your call. I'm going to go see what Jack is doing." Steve walked out of the room.

Anger boiled up in Kat's gut just as the tea kettle began to whistle. Steve clearly didn't understand what she was up against. Accessing that information might save Laura's life, but it could endanger others, not to mention put her in jail. He didn't seem to care about that. He just wanted to give the man in the scrubs the information he wanted and hope for the best. His hope was based on someone who was blackmailing them.

Kat turned the stove off and slid down to the floor, ending up on the mat that was in front of the kitchen sink. She pulled her knees into her chest and curled up in as tight of a ball as she could. Fear gripped her. It was too much pressure. The smell of smoke was in her nostrils. She could hear the voices and feel hands pulling her out of the wreckage. Deep breaths, Kat, she said to herself.

She didn't know how long she sat there. At some point, she heard Steve take Jack up to bed, his little voice calling, "Night, Mama!" as he went up the steps. She responded in a cheerful voice so he wouldn't come looking for her. Steve never came back down.

Having lost her own parents at such a young age, she understood what Steve was facing, but could she really do what she was being asked? Every move she made brought back more and more memories of the accident. They kept surging up like waves whipped by a storm. The more stress she was under, the more viciously her mind and body attacked itself.

Kat got up and walked to the living room and laid down on the couch. There was a blanket folded across the back. She pulled it down and covered herself, not even making the effort to change clothes or go upstairs. Hours were ticking by and she still didn't know what to do.

It was the middle of the night and Edgar was at the warehouse. He had just gotten back from another hospital visit. Another patient, another day. He checked his phone. There had been no message from Kat Beckman.

He was frustrated. He had nearly a one hundred percent closing rate. He was thorough and nearly always got the bosses the information they needed. The one time that he had failed, the client was misdiagnosed and released from the hospital with an infection, not cancer. The bosses had found the information they wanted another way. Apex did exactly what they promised. They provided solutions for challenging information problems.

Beckman had been difficult so far. He hadn't heard from her the way he expected, and by the looks of the reports from people he had watching the house, she and her husband were going about their business like nothing had ever happened. The bosses wanted the Bluebird mission roster. That's what they needed. She could get it if she wanted to.

Edgar started to pace through the warehouse. That's what he did when he needed to think. His assistant just watched him. They weren't a very communicative group. It was better that way.

As he walked past one of the abandoned machines left behind on the main floor of the shop, Woof rolled over for a belly rub. Edgar squatted down and gave Woof what he wanted. No matter how frustrated Edgar got, Woof made him feel better.

Unfortunately, it wasn't better enough for Edgar. He walked to the secure room and nodded at the guard. He pulled open the door of one of the refrigerators and grabbed a vial of red serum. He walked it over to the guard who pushed a tablet toward him without looking up. Edgar entered the numbers and hit enter. The screen went blank.

Edgar walked out of the secure room and headed for the warehouse door. It was time for him to give the Beckman's a little incentive.

The night was calm and quiet. Edgar rode with the windows down, humming a Johnny Cash tune. He couldn't remember the name of it or any of the words, but he could remember a few bars of the melody. He headed to Mercy Memorial and found his favorite parking spot. The light was still broken. Their maintenance people weren't exactly on the ball. Edgar shook his head at no one in particular, thinking that fixing simple things like broken lights should be a given. Either way, it made his job a bit easier.

He went in through the same employee entrance that he had been using, making a mental note that he needed to change that on his next trip to Mercy. It was getting a bit too routine. Someone would eventually notice him, although it would be difficult to figure out who he was with his scrubs on. Edgar walked down the hall and opened the janitor's closet where he had stashed his medical cart. It surprised him a little that no one else had found it and moved it. The security at this hospital was particularly lax. In his initial briefing, the bosses had told him that security was run by a guy who was actually named Benjamin Franklin, a former police chief. After a good laugh, Edgar had been a bit concerned, not by the guy's name but because the hospital's security chief was a former police chief. After making a couple of visits he knew that the chief was certainly looking in all the wrong places.

Edgar pushed the cart down the hallway, his surgical mask hanging on this face by just one loop over his ear. He would prefer to wear it over his entire face, but that would be a sure hint that he was trying to not be found. He looked down at the cart at all of the right times to miss the security cameras. He went to the elevators, taking it to the fourth floor.

Over time, Edgar had discovered that oncology floors had their own strange smell. Not quite sweet, not quite antiseptic. It was a strange smell that he couldn't really describe. The odor hit him as soon as the doors to the elevator opened. If he ever got out of the business, he wouldn't miss the smell, that was for sure. He walked down the hallway, pushing the cart, the wheels rattling a little bit.

WHEN HE FIRST STARTED WORKING FOR the bosses, he had just been fired from a hospital in Houston. He was an underpaid surgical nurse who just wanted to make a little extra money by selling a few vials of painkillers. He was sitting in a holding cell all by himself, waiting for a court-appointed attorney. Instead, a fancy attorney came and took him to a conference room.

"I can get rid of this for you, but you'll have to do some work for a few people I know. Interested?"

"Heck, yeah," Edgar had replied, knowing that with no job he'd be stuck with a two-bit hack who couldn't get a job in a real law firm. This guy was going to get him off and give him a job. It sounded like a good deal.

The attorney left the room and came back a few minutes later. "We are all set. Let's go."

Edgar was surprised. The detectives that had been in just before the attorney said he was going downtown and then to be arraigned. "No court?"

"Nope. You are a free man with a new job."

Edgar was suspicious, but the idea of having work to do instead of jail time seemed better. The attorney walked out the back door of the police station with him, the detectives nodding as he walked out. He thought it was strange. He followed the attorney out to his car. "Get in. We need to talk about your job."

Edgar got into the attorney's Lexus and they drove off, ending up at a quiet burger joint a few miles from the police station. They walked in and took a booth at the back of the restaurant, the attorney loosening his tie as they sat down. He and Edgar ordered lunch, a wrap sandwich for the attorney and a burger and fries for Edgar. Edgar ate like a man who hadn't eaten in a long time. In reality, he'd only missed one meal.

Neither of them said much until their food was finished. The attorney, Edgar couldn't remember his name, put his napkin down on the table and said, "We have some business to do."

"Yeah," Edgar said, finishing up the last bite of his burger. "Thanks for getting me out. I don't have to go to court, then?"

"No. That's all taken care of. I squared it up with the detectives. They understand your financial situation."

Edgar wondered what that meant, but he didn't ask any questions. The attorney continued. "In return for getting you out of this scrape, we'd like for you to help us with a job. It will become permanent and pays very well if you can get it done."

"What's the job?" Edgar asked.

"We need someone with your skills to administer serums to patients that we identify for you."

Giving injections was part of Edgar's everyday job. He could do that in his sleep. "I can do that. What's this for? Plastic surgery, maybe?"

"Cancer patients."

Edgar nodded. "No problem. Do you run a private hospital or something?"

The attorney put cash on the table to cover the check and slid out of the booth. "No, not a private hospital. It's something you have to keep quiet, though. You can't tell anyone what you are doing."

Edgar stood up to follow the attorney out of the restaurant. Not telling anyone wasn't a problem. He didn't have any family and his friends were pretty non-existent. "Okay. How much is the pay?"

Based on the attorney's body language, Edgar could tell the meeting was over. It didn't even look like he was getting a ride home. The attorney looked at him and said, "The first job is fifty thousand dollars. We will be in touch." The attorney got in his car and pulled away before Edgar could ask any more questions.

It was a nice day, so Edgar walked back to his apartment, thinking the entire time about what a strange turn his life had taken in just a few hours. From desperately needing money to being offered fifty grand to just inject a couple of people -- you couldn't get any better than that.

Nothing happened for a few weeks. Edgar used up nearly all of the money in his checking account on rent, food and beer when one night he got a text on his phone. The message told him to go to the local drugstore and purchase a prepaid phone. He'd need it for work. Happy to have something to do and relieved they hadn't forgotten about him, he went right then.

Once he got the phone, he texted the number that he'd been given. He was told to go to the airport. There was a ticket waiting for him. He should pack for three days. He had an hour to get to the airport.

That night, he boarded a flight to Florida. He was given a confirmation number for a rental car and the address to a hotel. He followed the instructions and was at the hotel by ten o'clock that night. In the lobby, he was met by the person that would train him. Jake. At least that's what he called himself.

After a few days of following Jake as he made his rounds to the local hospital, he was sent to the airport and flown home. He was told payment would be waiting. It was. In his apartment, there was an envelope on the kitchen counter with a cool fifty thousand dollars in cash and a note to keep his cell phone on. There was another job in forty-eight hours.

EDGAR STOPPED the rattling cart that he used during his travels around the hospital outside a door on the fourth floor of Mercy Memorial. It was two down and on the opposite side of the wide linoleum floored hallway from Laura Beckham's room. There was a lone nurse at the nurse's station, wearing headphones. He didn't even look up. Edgar had a lot of experience with the night staff. They were just there to administer meds and make sure everyone was alive for the morning shift. Edgar slid the glass door open just enough to enter the room. He had to push the curtain aside to actually see the person in the bed.

A woman was sleeping soundly. Sally Redmond had the pallor of someone who had been through chemo recently. Around her head was a flowered headscarf. Edgar didn't need to look at her chart. He knew all about her. She had stage three metastatic breast cancer. She was doing well. Her treatment was working. She was due to go home in the morning to her husband and her son that was just home from his junior year in college. Edgar stepped closer to her bed. Her breathing was calm and deep. Her color wasn't too bad for someone undergoing treatments. She even had pictures of her family and her two Persian cats next to her bed. Anything to make staying in the hospital a little more normal.

Sometimes Edgar wished he had more time to just sit and watch the patients in the hospital. He knew a lot of their personal information -- their type of cancer, their family members, where they lived, what they did -- but he never got to see them when they were awake, to see their mannerisms, to hear their sense of humor.

Though Edgar could have easily lingered in Sally's room, he had work to do. He didn't want to risk her waking up and seeing him staring at her. Out of the pocket of his scrubs, he pulled the vial with the red serum and a syringe already attached to a needle. He inserted the needed into the rubber stopper and drew the red serum into the needle, putting the vial back in his pocket. He'd dispose of the vial and needle on his way out of the hospital.

The bosses had made it easy for him. Three different serums in three different colors, all with different effects. Blue healed, yellow made patients terminal and red killed. No measuring or calculating for body weight. One dose worked for every patient. The only time he had ever used more than one vial was for a guy with colon cancer who weighed 400 pounds. He'd gotten two blue doses.

Back to work. With the syringe loaded, Edgar stepped close to Sally's bed and injected the red serum into her IV line. It disappeared into her body. He recapped the syringe and put it in his pocket with the empty vial. It was time to go.

He stepped out of Sally's room, making sure that the curtain and glass door were exactly as he found it. As he pushed the cart down the hallway, the nurse finally looked up. Edgar gave him a wave and kept moving, pushing the cart to the elevator.

Edgar made his way down to the basement and pushed the cart back into the janitor's closet where he had been keeping it. He stopped in the men's bathroom and put the vial and syringe in one of the hazardous materials needle disposal boxes that were by the sinks. As he saw the vial and needle drop in, he thought about how many of those boxes there were in every hospital. Hundreds, could be thousands, he realized. They were in every patient room, bay, surgical area, testing area and every single bathroom. Finding any single vial or needle would literally be like finding a needle in a haystack.

Edgar washed his hands and slipped out of the bathroom, heading for the little grey car that was waiting for him. Pushing the door open to the parking garage, he could hear rain coming down outside the levels above. He started the engine and slowly pulled out, heading for the warehouse. At the first stop sign, he checked the time. He'd have a text to send soon.

J ason Sikorsky tapped his fingers like drums on the desk of the nurses' station. He'd worked for Mercy Memorial for three years, starting in post-op and then moving to oncology two years before. He chose the night shift intentionally. He didn't want to be bothered with family members who asked too many questions, tears or too many doctors. He liked the clinical part of nursing and the nights were just that.

Mercy was more laid back then his last hospital. At his previous job, they watched you like a hawk. It was no fun. There was no freedom and God-forbid you spent too much time with a patient -- he got yelled at by a supervisor because he sat with the daughter of a man who had just had heart surgery while he slept for ten minutes, helping her color the unicorn in her coloring book.

There were usually three nurses on duty at night and a doctor on call. For the last couple of weeks, everyone had been on vacation, so they were short-staffed. He was alone on the floor that night. It wasn't a problem. The floor wasn't full and everyone was sleeping. He could just watch monitors and do reports while he listened to his music.

Jason got up to stretch. He'd been sitting for what felt like hours. He slipped his headphones off and heard beeping and saw a red light flashing above the door of a room down the hall. An alert went off on the monitor in front of him. He took off at a run, hitting his automatic pager to get help from the floor above since he was alone in oncology.

It was Sally Redmond. Jason found her laying on her side, her cardiac monitor flatlining. Jason quickly turned her on her back and started compressions, pushing the call button that hung around his neck with his hospital id. "Room 403. Cardiac code. I need some extra hands."

Jason kept the compressions going for the long thirty seconds that it took for the house doctor and another nurse to come up from the floor below. He could tell that they had taken the steps two at a time. They were both breathing hard. "What'd we got?" the doctor asked.

"Nothing remarkable. She was supposed to go home tomorrow."

"Charge to 200," he told the other nurse. "And get the bag on her right now." The other nurse charged the defibrillator and waited for a second. "Clear!" They shocked Sally three times, adding doses of epinephrine between. Nothing.

The doctor looked at Jason after a few minutes. He reached for Sally's neck to check for a pulse. Jason and the other nurse were still doing compressions and bagging her. "How long has she been down?"

Jason looked up at the clock and said, "Ten minutes, maybe a little longer."

The doctor took his hand off of Sally's neck. "Okay. I'm going to call it. Time of death, three fourteen. Thanks, everyone."

With that, the doctor walked out of the room. The other

nurse, someone Jason didn't know, put her hand on his arm. "Sorry. Do you need help with this?"

Jason shook his head as he stepped to the side of the bed to turn off the monitors. The room was suddenly silent after a flurry of activity. "No, I'm okay. I'll call it in and make the notes."

The other nurse nodded and walked out of the room heading back to her floor, leaving Jason alone. He stayed for a minute, removing IV lines and EKG pads from her chest. He pulled the sheet over Sally's face and left the room, walking slowly to the nurse's station. It was time to make a call. "Hi," he said when the night attendant in the morgue answered, "I've got a body."

20

When Edgar reached the warehouse, he pulled up near the loading dock again, the night pitch black with just enough light from the moon that he could see. His body felt tired. He always did by the time they finished in a city. Working pretty much every single night took a toll. Not to mention that he wasn't sleeping in his own bed. The bosses had promised him a month off after this city was done. He needed it.

Before he went into the warehouse, he needed to send a text. He picked up his burner and pulled up Kat Beckham's number. She hadn't even replied to his original text. The bosses were concerned she wasn't taking them seriously. He was too. Edgar started a reply to the text he had sent to Kat earlier. It didn't say much. A simple, "Sorry about Sally," was all he wrote. He closed the phone, shut off the car and went into the warehouse a smug smile on his face. All he could do at this point was wait.

21

K at had finally fallen asleep. It wasn't a deep sleep. It was the kind of sleep that you hoped would keep you going the next day. Memories from the Middle East and thoughts of Steve, Jack and Laura took up the place where there should have been rest. It didn't help that she was sleeping on the couch instead of the bed where she should have been curled up next to Steve.

A quiet beep woke her up out of her sleep. It was the burner phone. She reached for it, still laying under the covers. There was a new text that had come in from the man in the scrubs. It simply said, "Sorry about Sally." Kat sat straight up, trying to clear her head. What did that mean? Maybe the text wasn't even for her? Was the man in the scrubs so inept that he had sent the wrong text to the wrong person? If that was the case, she thought, the decision was made. She wouldn't need to do anything. The guy was clearly a joker, some crazy person who preyed on families.

Kat immediately felt better. She pushed the blanket off onto the couch and stood up, taking a long stretch. She felt the tightness in her body and decided that a hot shower would do her good. Leaving the burner phone where it was, she walked to the staircase and went quietly upstairs, trying not to wake Jack.

She went through their bedroom, seeing Steve in the moonlight. He had fallen asleep working on his computer. She could tell. It was sitting in the spot where she would normally lay, the blue charging light blinking on and off. He was a good man, she thought. It would be good to get their marriage back on track once all of this was over. Her heart ached a little bit. She just wanted to keep Steve and Jack safe. Maybe they'd even get a dog. Jack had been wanting one.

Kat went into the bathroom and turned on the water, letting it run while she got undressed. She stood under the hot water, turning the knob to make it as hot as it would go. She saw her skin redden under the heat, but it warmed her body up and felt good against her achy body.

Getting out of the shower, she brushed her teeth, put on some body lotion and slipped into leggings and a t-shirt. She stood staring in the mirror, noticing how pale her face was, her blonde hair hanging near her face in loose waves, wet from the shower. She combed it quickly and turned the light off before she ever opened the door. She didn't want to wake Steve. At least one of them needed a good night's sleep. She opened the door, feeling the cool night air that had been blowing in through the window press at the heat of her skin from the shower. She looked toward the bed and Steve wasn't there. His laptop was, but he wasn't.

Kat instantly felt bad. She hadn't meant to wake him. She padded down the steps and went to the kitchen. Even though it wasn't even morning, she was famished and really wanted a sandwich.

The lights were already on in the kitchen. She could hear Steve's voice, but she couldn't make out what had happened. It sounded like he was talking to someone, but Kat couldn't figure out who it could be at four o'clock in the morning.

Coming into the kitchen, the light hurt Kat's eyes. Steve was pacing, talking to someone. "It's okay. I'm sorry that it happened. Do you want me to come to the hospital?"

Kat couldn't figure out what was going on.

Steve stopped and looked at her in the doorway. "Hold on for a minute." He covered the microphone on his cell phone and mouthed, "It's mom."

"I thought she was sleeping a lot?"

"The commotion down the hallway must have woken her. She's upset."

Kat felt another small flicker of hope in her chest. It added to the one that she felt just before her shower. Maybe there was a way to get back to normal, she thought. Kat mouthed to Steve, "Why is she upset? Is she okay?"

"Her friend died overnight. You know, the one she has been through chemo with? She had metastatic breast cancer."

Kat felt like she had been punched in the stomach. "What was her name?" Kat asked Steve, fear crawling up into her belly.

"Hey mom, what was your friend's name?" Steve asked. He nodded as Laura told him. "Mom said her name was Sally."

Kat slumped down into one of the kitchen chairs, having lost all of the strength in her legs. Her head was spinning and she was starting to feel lightheaded. She had gone from feeling grounded to feeling lost in just moments. It was as if all hope had been drained out of her.

Kat wasn't looking at anything. All she could do was stare. Kat didn't even know Sally, but her heart was heavy. Steve must have seen her with a blank look on her face because the next thing she heard was, "Honey, are you okay?"

She couldn't even answer. Words wouldn't come out of her mouth. She knew she was entering a stage of shock. All she could do was go get the phone from the family room, putting one foot in front of the other. She had left it on the table before she went to go and take her shower. She walked back and handed it to Steve without saying a word. He opened it, the timer still running on the front display.

"Oh, my God," he said. "You don't think they..." The sentence didn't get finished.

They both sat there in silence for a minute, each in their own worlds, trying to process what had happened. Steve finally broke the quiet. "They killed Sally."

Kat nodded. It certainly looked that way. Terror rose in her throat in a way that she'd never experienced before. It curled up her legs, crossed her chest and had her by the throat. She could barely breathe. She wanted to run. Run anywhere. But all she could do was sit. She felt frozen, just trying to get the next breath into her body.

Steve's voice called to her, "Kat... just breathe. We will get through this." She felt his hand on her shoulder. She realized that he must have gotten up from his chair. She hadn't even seen him. She heard him, somewhere deep inside, but that didn't stop the grip that her feelings had on her.

22

Outside of Kat and Steve's house, Victor sat in a white van that was labeled for the local cable company. The prep team had done a good job on the van. It had tools and clipboards -- all of the things that anyone would need to convince local law enforcement that he was just there doing his job. He even had a hard hat and a safety vest. Those were nice touches, Victor thought.

He had been sitting on the Beckman's house for hours. They only watched a target overnight if they were squirrely. The Beckman's were. Victor wasn't sure why the bosses had chosen them. It didn't matter. That was above his pay grade and he got a big stack of cash to sit in a truck and do nothing but play on his phone.

Victor reached into the brown paper bag that was next to him on the seat. There was a deli down the street that was open twenty-four hours a day and had great pastrami sandwiches. Not everyone wanted to eat pastrami in the middle of the night, but he didn't mind. He unwrapped the sandwich, the smell of garlic and meat filling the truck cab. Just as he took a bite, lights hit the back of his van. It wasn't just a passing car, it was a cop.

Victor straightened up in his seat and grabbed his clipboard. He watched the cop with a level of amusement as he approached the van. He was a young guy, clearly new to the job. This will be fun, Victor thought, rolling down the window.

"Evening, officer."

"Hello, sir. Can I see your identification?"

"Sure." Victor fumbled for his wallet, which was jammed into one of the crevices of the seat. "Did I do something wrong?"

The cop ignored his question, shining the light from his face to his ID. "Taking your lunch break at four in the morning?" the cop asked.

"Yup. Pulled the late shift. Gotta get everyone's television working before breakfast."

"Smells like a pastrami from Madeline's."

"That would be right. I have an extra if you'd like one," Victor offered.

"No, thanks. Just get moving off this block when you are done."

Victor nodded. "Thank you, officer."

With that, the officer shut off his light and walked back to his cruiser.

Victor knew that he would need to get moving in the next hour or so. Based on the look on the cop's face, he knew he'd be back. Hopefully, that's all the time he'd need to wrap this up. The pastrami was doing a number on his stomach. He nodded to the cop as he drove by, giving him a little salute with the remainder of his sandwich.

Victor checked his phone for the time. As he did, a light went on at the Beckman's. He picked up the binoculars he had stashed under the seat and focused on the house. Earlier in the day, they had drawn the blinds, but with the darkness he could see silhouettes backlit in the house. First a male and then a female. Bingo. That's all he needed.

Victor swallowed the last bite of his sandwich, crumpled up the paper and tossed it into the bag. He turned on the van's engine, letting it warm up a bit, leaving the lights off. He grabbed his cell phone and typed a quick text, hitting send. He put the phone back on the seat next to him, gently put the van in gear and eased off the brake, the van rolling silently down the street with no lights on. His job for the night was over.

EDGAR'S PHONE BUZZED. It wasn't Kat, but it was something almost as good. The text simply read, "The eagle has landed."

Apparently, Victor had seen movement. They must know about Sally by now. That's what he was counting on.

23

The shaking in Kat's hands stopped after a few minutes. Steve had brought her water. She took a couple of sips.

As she stood up, the reality of the situation hit her in a whole new way. She could feel Steve's eyes on her, "Are you okay?"

"Yeah, I just need a minute."

"Okay." She watched him sit back down on the chair, still holding the phone in his hand, his other hand empty, but the fist clenched so tight his knuckles were white.

Kat walked up the steps to their bathroom. She turned the light on and leaned her hands on the sink, looking in the mirror. She didn't like what she saw. It was more than the smudge of black circles under her eyes. It was more than the faint white tinge to her lips. She was ashamed of herself. She wanted to be the strong woman that Steve needed as a wife and that Jack needed as a mom.

Kat pushed her blonde hair behind each ear and turned on the cold water. Her hair had dried into a wavy mess. She leaned over and splashed it on her face, over and over again, the rhythm of the water and her breathing helping her to focus. After a minute or so, she reached for a towel and dried her face. Still pale, but with a bit of pink coming back into her cheeks from the sting of the cold water.

She knew, looking at herself in the mirror, that the pain of the past held her captive. The circumstances she was in held her captive now. But it was worse than that. It was one thing when she had to manage her own pain. It was something else when she had to watch her own family suffer.

And they were.

Laura's illness. Sally's death. There was little doubt in her mind that whoever the man in the scrubs was, whoever he represented, they wanted what they wanted, and they wanted her to help them. It didn't matter the consequences. She knew they'd keep coming until they got what they wanted or Laura died. They might even keep coming if she gave them what they wanted. TJ had been right. There were no good answers.

Kat dabbed at the final drops of water lingering on her neck. The fringe of her blonde hair was wet again. She pushed it away and pulled her hair into a low ponytail to get it off of her face. As she did, a memory came flooding back of her father from when she was very little. It was one of the few that she had. He used to say, "The only way around is through." As much as she would like to go around this -- around Laura's cancer, around the night she was drugged, around the terminal diagnosis, around Sally's death and the demands of the man in the scrubs -- her dad was right. The only way around this was through.

KAT QUICKLY CHANGED her clothes and went back down into the kitchen, putting the Sig back into the holster on her belt. Steve was standing in front of the coffeemaker, his hair still mussed from the sleep that had been interrupted. She saw him look at her, "You seem better," he said, pouring a cup from the pot.

"It's enough. I've had enough. We need to get this under control," Kat said, reaching for a mug.

"I know, honey. Do you want me to make you some tea?" Steve answered.

Kat could tell from his response that the stress and lack of sleep had blunted his thinking. He didn't know what she meant. Kat grabbed the handle of the coffeepot and poured a cup.

"You don't want tea?" Steve asked.

"It's not going to be a tea kind of day." The words came out more sternly than she wanted. She paused, waiting to see how Steve reacted.

She watched him for a minute, seeing the stubble on his face, his brown eyes looking at her with more questions than answers.

24

By the time Steve showered, it was almost daybreak. Kat had already thrown in a load of laundry and was working on clearing her email when he came down. Steve was dressed in jeans, boots and a t-shirt. "So, what's the plan for today?"

"How about if you come outside and we will have some coffee?" Kat said, using her head to motion that she needed him to follow her. They both went out the back door.

The sunrise was beautiful. The sky was lit up with orange and pink against a blue sky with just a few wisps of clouds. There was no rain coming, at least for the next few hours. The early morning hours meant the birds were chirping, having a conversation in the big tree outside the back of their house about the day. Their friendliness didn't even begin to distract Kat from her mood.

"Why are we outside?" Steve said as she closed the patio door behind them.

"Do you have your phone with you?" Kat asked.

"No, I left it inside."

"Okay, good. Listen, I think they might have bugged the

house. I can't be sure, but I don't want to say anything inside about what is going on right now."

"Why do you think they bugged the house?" Steve's furrowed brow meant that he hadn't even considered the possibility that the man in the scrubs had done more to them than drug Kat and kill Sally. It still hadn't fully hit him yet.

"Why wouldn't they?" Kat sighed. "Think about it, Steve. They've gone to a lot of trouble to contact us. They seem to know what is going on. They know about Laura, about her condition, about her relationship with Sally. Why wouldn't they bug the house?"

Steve's eyes got big, the reality of the situation hitting him even more deeply. "Jack is in there."

Kat held up her hands. "I'm sure Jack is fine. They won't hurt him. It doesn't help them. Just let him sleep. While he does, we need a plan."

"Are you going to give them the information? I mean, how would you get it?"

Kat weighed her options. Steve knew that she still had clearance. She might be able to get a secured computer and get the information. She might not. It depended on if the files were still available.

Steve rubbed his hands through his hair. "Maybe the thing to do is to talk to Van. He was in the military, right? Maybe he could help?"

Luckily, Steve had come up with the same solution that Kat had. It was time to loop in someone who could be trusted. Kat said, "Yeah. That's what I was thinking. Let me text him and see if he can meet us."

"What about Jack? I don't want him to be here without us if you think the house is bugged."

Steve was right. It was better to just take him along. "Let's see if we can meet Van at the park. Jack can play on the swings while we talk."

Steve put his hand on the doorknob to get back in the house. Kat put her hand on his arm, "Remember, not a word of this once you are inside. Just tell Jack that we have a surprise for him. We don't want to tip them off about where we are going."

Kat went back in the house and got her phone. She sent a quick text to Van asking if they could meet at the park in an hour.

25

Van's phone buzzed with an incoming text. It wasn't even seven o'clock and it was already starting, he thought, rolling over in bed, the sheets twisting over his hips as he tried to reach for his phone.

The night before had been a long one. He had worked for hours on the data that Alyssa had sent over about the vial of fentanyl that had killed the nurse at Mercy Memorial. Hours of looking at strings of numbers trying to figure out if there were any from the lot number that killed Sarah in the hospital. It looked like the vial may have come from a batch out of state, but he couldn't be sure. Some of the numbers were close, but that lot had never entered the hospital doors. Where it had come from, he didn't know. He had sent an email to someone who might be able to help, but there was no reply yet.

He'd also tried to track down a patient that Kat had mentioned to him – a young girl who had recovered miraculously from glioblastoma. Sarah seemed tied to that case, but the hospital couldn't seem to find the records. Van had texted Benny, but even after talking to the doctor, they couldn't find her information. It seemed to have disappeared from the database. Benny was furious and nearly hung up on Van in his hurry to bellow at whoever was working in the IT department at the minute.

At one point during the night, he had gotten so frustrated trying to put the pieces of the puzzle together that he went out for a late run. Putting another five miles on his newest pair of running shoes cleared his head and helped him to solve problems. His headphones, now laying on the nightstand, had pumped out a steady diet of everything from a little hip hop to some country music. Van didn't care what he listened to, just that it could keep up with his pace.

The run helped, but it didn't solve the problem of the lot number. Where had that vial come from? Where had it been shipped to? While he was running, he realized that he'd probably have to contact the company directly. Knowing they likely wouldn't be too cooperative, worrying a lawsuit or expose coming, Van wasn't sure he could get the information from them.

After his run, Van went back to his apartment and took a shower, putting on a fresh pair of shorts, but leaving his shirt off. He didn't realize it before his run, but his apartment smelled like a combination of sweat and old take-out food. He opened windows and let the fresh night air in. He grabbed his laptop, a bottle of sports drink, flipped on the television and propped himself up with pillows to see what other information he could find on the vial and the company that made the drug.

Apparently, he had fallen asleep that way. When his cell phone chirped with a text, the television was off -- it had timed out -- and his laptop was on the bed next to him.

"Holy God, who is texting this early?" he asked.

Everyone knew that Van wasn't an early bird. Even his assistant and writers knew that texting before ten o'clock in the morning wouldn't make you the favorite of the day.

Van grabbed his phone and grunted, "This better be good."

His finger unlocked the phone and he saw that it was Kat. She needed to meet in an hour at the park. He replied back, "911?"

He waited a moment, wondering if this was an actual emergency or if Jack had just gotten her up too early."

The text came back in seconds. "Yes."

Early or not, Van knew if Kat was asking for a meeting this early and it was a 911, then he needed to go. The park was only about fifteen minutes away, so he had a little time. Pushups, sit-ups and another shower got him awake and ready to move right on time.

Van drove to the park and left his truck on a side street right on the edge of the playground area. There weren't very many people in the park yet -- a few joggers and a few people walking their dogs. There was a coffee cart across the street, hoping to snag workers as they went into an office building. Van walked over and got three coffees, a chocolate milk and a chocolate chip cookie from the vendor. He took them across the street and sat on a picnic table near the slide.

"Hi Uncle Van," Jack said, practically running right by him on his way to the swings. "I get playtime first today!" Jack's sing-song voice brought a smile to Van's face.

"Hey pal, where're your folks?" he asked. Jack darted back to him.

"They're coming." He pointed and Van turned to see Kat and Steve walking across the park.

"I see them," Van said. "Hey, before you take off, I've got something for you."

"What's that?" Jack asked.

"Breakfast of champions." Van handed him the chocolate milk. It already had a straw in it. Van passed him the bag with the cookie in it. He was hoping Kat wouldn't be mad. The cookie was the size of a dinner plate. "Don't tell your mom, okay?"

Jack giggled, "Okay. She'd want me to eat cereal."

Van wrinkled his nose. "Cookies are better for breakfast."

Jack smiled and ran right to Kat, as Van knew he would, "Look, mama! Uncle Van brought me breakfast. It's a cookie!"

Van watched Kat nod and smile and send Jack off to the play area with his cookie and his milk. He managed to sit on the bottom of the slide and eat on his own.

Kat and Steve approached the picnic table where Van was sitting. "Morning," Van said. "Coffee?" He held out a cup to Steve.

Steve took it, looking grateful. "Thanks."

"Kind of an early meeting. What's the 911 about?" Van said, handing Kat a coffee.

"Remember how I told you about how I thought I was drugged at the hospital?"

Van nodded, thinking about their conversation. "Yep. Did something else happen? Are you guys okay?"

Kat said, "Yeah, we are okay for right now. But I think there is more to the story and we didn't want you to come to the house."

"Why?"

"I'm worried that it is bugged."

Van paused. This was clearly more serious than he thought. He watched Kat intently as she explained what had been going on. He knew that she had ghosts in her past, but her voice and hand movements made him think this wasn't her imagination.

"We got a call last night that one of Laura's friends had died."

Van said, "I'm sorry to hear that. What happened?"

Kat looked at him and said, "We think she was murdered."

26

K at stared at Van. She knew that he would quickly put all of the parts of the story together. "I don't think I got a chance to tell you much more than I thought I was drugged, right?"

Van nodded, "Yeah."

"Well, there's more. The medallion they gave us had the name of a company, Apex Solutions, and a dark web URL on it, so we went online and put Laura's name in the box. That's what it wanted. We thought nothing had happened -- that it was a total hoax, but then a few minutes later, a box was delivered. We thought it was for Laura, but it wasn't. There was a burner buried in there. A text came through just as we got it saying that there is a cure for cancer but that it costs. The cost is a mission roster from when I was in the sandbox."

Van's face froze. Kat could see he was calculating now. He knew that she had her clearance. "They want information in return for some possible cure for cancer? Is that what you are saying? There's a black-market cure for it?"

"I guess. I think this guy is going around manipulating people for information in return for the drugs they have."

"Hold on a sec. I'm still trying to wrap my brain around the fact that there is a black-market cure for cancer. All those big pharma thugs couldn't be bothered to share it with the rest of us, huh?" Kat could tell that Van was getting angry. "And, they want a mission roster from you?"

Kat nodded.

Van whistled, the air pushing through his teeth. "You have got to be kidding me. Not good."

"I know."

"You could go to jail for that."

"I know."

"Do you even have access to that information anymore?"

"I'm not sure," Kat lied. "I might have to try to dig it up with some help."

Van held up his hand, telling her to stop. Kat knew he was processing all of the information. "What you are saying is that these people, whoever they are, have a cure for cancer and are going around basically blackmailing people so they can save their loved ones. Do you have any idea how many millions of people have died from cancer over the years? That number has to be astronomical."

Kat nodded.

"If this is true, it's quite the story." Kat saw Van stop and scratch his ear. "Wait, why do they want that mission roster? That doesn't make any sense."

"I have no idea. It happened a long time ago, but that's what they wanted. They even had the mission name."

"How is that possible?"

Honestly, Kat didn't know and she didn't feel like they had time to figure that part out. Every second that went by was a moment closer to Laura losing her life. She needed Van to stay focused on where they were now. There would be time for more investigation and reporting later.

"There is more." She watched as Steve walked away to

check on Jack. It gave her a minute to talk to Van alone. "As soon as this all started, all of a sudden Laura was terminal. She had been doing better. It doesn't make any sense. Then last night we got a text in the middle of the night saying that they -- whoever they are -- were sorry about Sally."

"Who's Sally?"

"She was a friend of Laura's. They had gone through chemo together. She was supposed to go home this morning."

Van scowled, "Wait. She was supposed to go home this morning?"

"Yup. We got a text saying they were sorry about her. A couple of minutes later Laura called, hysterical because she had woken up to all of the commotion. We knew before she did. I think they killed her as a message to us."

Van sat down on the picnic table again. He took a sip of his coffee. The quiet that she had seen in TJ had fallen over Van. It was something that was common to military men and women. They got very quiet and very still the more challenging the situation was. Kat wondered how they learned this. They all did it. While she was waiting, she Kat absentmindedly reached for her Sig, which was hidden underneath a light jacket. It was secure. She saw Van glance at her.

Van asked, "What about the change in Laura's condition? Didn't you tell me she was getting better?"

Kat remembered that she hadn't shared that part of the story with Van. "Yeah, just a couple hours after we got the burner, the hospital called and said out of the blue that Laura was terminal. Three days ago, she was responding to treatment. Doesn't seem possible that she turned that fast."

Van gave a quick nod. "Did you hear about the nurse on the same floor that died?"

"Sarah. Yes, we knew her. She was the one that usually made me tea," Kat said, turning away from Van a little bit so she could see Jack and Steve. Steve caught her eye and gave her a little half-smile as if he was telling her to do what she needed to do. He was pushing Jack on the swings, Jack's small hands wrapped tightly around the chains and his hair blowing back and forth in the wind. On any other day, it would have been a pleasure to watch. Today, Kat was consumed with fear and confusion.

Van's words broke her concentration. "The nurse -- Sarah -- I don't think she was an addict."

"What?" Kat wondered why Van thought that. "The hospital said it was an OD, but I have my questions. She didn't seem like the type, if there is one..."

"It was an OD, but I don't think it was because she was an addict. Turns out that Sarah was preparing for a Tough Mudder."

Kat knew about those races. She and Steve had often joked that if they didn't have Jack they might travel around the country going to race after race just as an excuse to be down in the dirt and see new places. Kat also knew that you had to be in really good shape to run over all of the obstacles.

"Did she have an injury? Maybe she just overdid it?"

Van said, "That part I don't know. This is where it gets strange. The lot number of the fentanyl wasn't from Mercy Memorial. Before I left this morning, I found some information that would suggest that the vial came from somewhere out of state. Not nearby either. I don't have anything definitive on that yet. I'm waiting to hear from a contact. I should know more in a few hours."

Kat felt Van's warm hand on her arm, which made her look his way. He sighed, "One more thing... right before Sarah died, she had pulled up some patient records on a girl that had a glioblastoma."

Kat felt like the air had been knocked out of her stomach. She was the one that asked Sarah about the girl that had been healed. Now Sarah was dead. Were they connected?

"Kat, the thing is that those patient records are no longer there. It's like they never existed in the system."

"What? How? Wait -- how do you know all of this?"

Van smiled at her. It was a lot to take in. He said, "Remember, I know the security chief at the hospital. I texted him and asked him to run a quick check. They were in the middle of it anyway with her case being open."

Kat looked at him, "So what you are saying is that she was pulling up patient records on a case I had asked about and died right after?" Van nodded. Kat said, "That can't be a coincidence."

Van looked at her. It was probably the most intense stare she had ever felt. "Kat, you know we have to get this story out. We have to get that cure from these people and get it to a lab so everyone can have access. These guys running around blackmailing people -- that's just sadistic."

"A lab?"

"Yeah. I know a guy. He's got his Ph.D. in Biochemistry. I met him a few years back. He runs a secure facility about ten miles from here. He'd replicate it for sure."

They both stood there in silence for a few minutes, the pieces to a gigantic puzzle they couldn't understand starting to fall into place.

Kat watched as Steve walked back over to them. "You make any progress?"

Kat tried to feign a smile. "Maybe a little. Van thinks that Sarah's OD is connected to all of this."

Van quickly explained to Steve what he had found out about the vial and the files that she had been accessing right before her death. Steve said, "This gets worse by the minute."

Kat knew that Steve was right. There was not much more they could do other than play along. They were in a zero-sum game and if they didn't do something, they would be out of time and out of any options. Laura would be dead. At least now they had the option to try to get the information and let it play out. Maybe they'd even be able to get the cure to the lab.

Kat looked at Steve. "We need to go home so I can get something. I'm going to try to get the information."

"Sure, but how?"

"I think I can access it myself."

"Your clearance will do that?" Steve frowned at her.

"I don't know," she sighed. "I've got to try..." Steve started to say something, but Kat interrupted him. She saw him look down at his boots and then he grinned back at her, the first time either of them had smiled since this all started, "Thanks."

Kat and Steve said a quick goodbye to Van and corralled Jack back into the car. All of the early morning running made him tired, so Jack was quiet. They all were. As Steve drove the car home, Kat kept checking their mirrors to see if anyone was following them. No one was.

Turning down their street, they saw the same cable van that had been there for the last day or so. Kat started to wonder about them and then realized she needed to focus on getting the Bluebird roster information. Steve pulled the car straight into the garage. Jack managed to unbuckle his booster seat and hop out as soon as Steve shut the engine off. He ran in the back door before Kat or Steve even got out.

As she reached for the door handle, Kat felt the warmth of Steve's hand on top of hers, I'm sorry about this," he said. "If mom had never gotten cancer, we wouldn't be in this position."

Kat softened for just a moment. They had had good times and bad in their marriage, like any she supposed. At that moment, Steve's acknowledgment of what she was going through was exactly what she needed in order to keep going. "That's nothing you could actually control, now is it?" she chided. "Unless you are God and I didn't know that."

"I'm not..." he said, smiling.

"I'm well aware." With a smile of her own, Kat got out of the car and headed into the house, her smile fading as quickly as it had come.

Inside, Kat listened for Jack, who seemed to be playing trucks in the other room. She went upstairs to their bedroom and opened the safe. Inside was one thing that she hadn't taken out earlier when she retrieved her Sig. It was a small encrypted flash drive. It would allow her to access the information that she needed at the secure site. She went down the steps and back into the kitchen, where Steve was waiting. "Did you do it yet?" he asked.

"It's not quite that fast," she said. "I have to actually go get it." She grabbed her purse and the flash drive and said, "I'll be back."

"Where are you going?" Steve asked.

"This isn't information that I can access from here. I'll be back in an hour." She gave him a kiss. "Hold down the fort, will you?"

Kat went back into the garage and got in her car without actually answering his question. She couldn't. Knowing where the secure site was wasn't something she could share with anyone. She pulled out of the garage and headed down the street. The cable guy was still there. It looked like he was eating a sandwich. He gave her a little wave as she passed. Ballsy, she thought. If he was watching their house, he certainly wasn't being too coy about it.

Kat watched her mirrors to make sure that he wasn't following her. She turned a corner and pulled over to wait. No cable van. She couldn't risk him, or anyone, knowing where she was going.

Driving into town, she made a couple of loops around the same block just outside of the shopping district. She pulled into a parking area that was behind an old restaurant that was getting ready for the day's service. She walked into the screened back door of the restaurant, just off of an alley and immediately took the stairs down. The smell of beef cooking hit her nostrils and she realized that she was starved, but she didn't have time to eat. When she got to the bottom of the stairs, she stopped in front of a door that said Employees Only. A key from her keyring got her through that door. Once she was through that door, she entered a hallway that was neat and tidy, freshly painted off-white walls and clean tile welcomed her. It was a far cry from the restaurant upstairs. It was meant to be. At the end of the short hallway was a steel door with no window. There was a keypad in front of the door. She punched in a code and touched her palm to the screen. The door unlocked.

Inside, there was no smell of beef cooking. It looked more like an office than anything else. There were eight cubicles in the center of the room, flocked with gray material. A few larger offices were against the wall and there was a conference room in the back that could hold about ten people. None of the cubicles had any identifiable features to them. No family pictures. No paper calendars. No books or paper. There were about five people in the office at the moment. On her way in, she passed the security guard that was always stationed at the door. He was sitting on a stool next to a small table that held a metal detecting wand, the kind that you'd find at the airport, a flashlight and a walkie talkie. Kat tried to remember his name as she walked in but ended up just nodding and saying a quick hello. She wanted to get in and out as quickly as possible.

The cubicles weren't meant to be permanent workspaces. They were a place to work for a few hours and then disappear back into the community. The room was an access hub for the military. There were hundreds of them throughout the country, in back rooms of restaurants, like this one and basement office buildings, in industrial parks and in hospitals. This was the one that Kat had been assigned to and she came in semi-regularly to get information. Her work wasn't considered top secret, so she could do some of it from home, but for the Bluebird mission roster, she'd have to be in the office.

In each cubicle, there was a terminal. They were set up to only connect to the internal military intranet. She sat down at the one near the end. No one would walk by, she thought, since the other offices were mostly dark except for the one far in the back. She was on the opposite side of where people would go to get coffee or use the bathroom. It didn't matter too much. Each computer had been fitted with a screen filter that made it difficult, if not impossible, to read over someone's shoulder. The privacy screens had annoyed her at first, but she quickly learned how to work with them. For her purposes today, they seemed like a good idea.

Sitting down, Kat pushed her hair behind her ear and wobbled the mouse. The computer lit up. She plugged in the flash drive that allowed her to use the computer and waited a moment for the encryption key to load. It took her right to the military access panel that she was looking for. She typed in her login information -- a username and password that she had committed to memory. Once she was in, she started the search, wondering if she'd even have access to the information anymore.

"I don't know if... "she mumbled as she typed. Kat went to the mission search files. The database held missions that hadn't been declassified, but that had been "retired." Once a mission had been over for five years, there was less need to keep it secret according to Army thinking. Kat found the files for the correct year, then the correct command and then finally the base where the mission had begun. Kat clicked on the link to see the mission list. She scrolled past other missions that she had heard mentioned in passing while she was in Afghanistan. Seeing the names of the missions brought up a wave of feelings that Kat simply didn't have time to deal with. She kept scrolling and forced herself to look right at the screen and not think about the smell of smoke that was filling her nose.

Down toward the bottom of the screen, she found the Bluebird file. She clicked on it. Multiple pages tiled neatly on her display. She clicked through the documents. Some of them were maps, and some covered the basics of the trip including how much gas had been used in the vehicles. Kat was surprised there wasn't a list of how much toilet paper they used. The military kept records of it all. Some of it was redacted. Some of it wasn't. Kat felt her breath catch in her throat. She was hoping the roster wasn't blacked out.

Toward the back of the stack was the information that she was looking for. It was a one-page document from the commander assigning people to the mission. She knew that it was a SEAL team. It wasn't TJ's team, but she knew that he was friends with a few people in that group. On the page was the list of the SEAL team members, her escort and at the bottom, her name. Ahmed Al-Shah had long been gone off the face of the planet, but the memories of that day would be with her forever. She guessed that any of the team members would say the same.

Kat couldn't risk printing the file. That would end her up in jail before she even made it to the door. She looked around to make sure no one was watching and she quickly pulled another flash drive out of her bag. It was blank. The problem was that she didn't know if the drives at the site would accept a regular flash drive. She had only used her encryption key in the past. She inserted it into the drive hoping it would fit. It did. She did a quick screenshot of the page. It took just seconds. She quickly put the flash drive back in her bag and hid it in a pocket that slid down to the bottom of her bag.

So she wouldn't attract any attention, Kat spent another minute just closing out the files and erasing her history. The computers were programmed to do that anyway, but she didn't want to take any chances. She pulled her encryption key out of the drive and held onto it.

As she stood up to leave, the computer screen went blank and her heart started to beat furiously. It wasn't in Kat's nature to do things that weren't on the up and up. Sure, she was a risk-taker, but her risks didn't usually involve jail or espionage. She slung her bag over her shoulder and walked toward the door. The security guard was still sitting on his stool by the door.

"Ready to go?" he asked, picking up the wand.

"Yes, sir."

"Can I check your bag?" he asked.

All of a sudden Kat remembered his name was Thomas. Why she couldn't remember that earlier, she didn't know. "How's the family, Thomas?"

"All good, Miss Kat. All good. My boy is about to graduate from high school." Thomas had a big smile on his face. Kat was hoping it was enough to keep him from finding the other flash drive. She watched Thomas open up her bag and shine his flashlight inside. He quickly shut it off, using his hands to feel around the outside pockets.

"That's great," she answered with what she was worried would be an unnatural level of friendliness. "What's he gonna do after graduation?"

"He is off to the Army. Wants to be a medic."

"You have to be so proud. That's great."

Thomas quickly wanded her and the device went off as it passed over her pocket. When Thomas wasn't looking, Kat had stowed her encryption key in the same pocket as her keys.

"Whatcha got in your pocket?" he asked.

Kat pulled her keys out of her pocket. "Just these," she said. "Sorry, I forgot I put them in there. I should have put them in my bag."

"No problem," Thomas said, setting the wand back in its place and handing her bag back to her. "You are good to go."

"Thanks." Kat started to walk out, hoping that Thomas couldn't see her nervousness.

"Hey, Kat, you have your encryption key, right?" Thomas called after her.

"Yup. I do. Thanks for reminding me though." She patted her bag to show him where it

was. Kat retraced her steps, through the handprint secured door, down the hallway and through the door that said employees only. She went up the small flight of steps, passing a guy with glasses and a briefcase on the way in. Probably an analyst, she thought.

Kat made it to her car, her heart still thumping in her chest. She pulled away from the parking lot and drove around the corner to a small park where she could stop the car for a moment. She pulled out the flash drive from the bottom of her bag and looked at it. It was hard to believe that a little piece of plastic and metal could do so much. With it, she had the chance to save Laura, or even eliminate cancer altogether.

It didn't take Kat long to drive home. She was less concerned about tails leaving the office than she was going there. As Kat got close to her house, she saw the cable guy again. He gave her the same look and little wave. He didn't even try to look like he was busy or doing work. She was sure he was watching their house. At this point, she wasn't sure if she should be furious or indifferent. She didn't have the energy to try to figure it out.

In the garage, Kat shut off the engine and went into the house. Steve was in the kitchen working on his computer. Jack was sitting on the floor, a plate of crackers between him and his trucks. "Where's the phone?" Kat asked. As soon as she said it, she realized she didn't even bother to say hello.

"Hi mama," Jack said, his mouth full of food.

"Hi, pal."

Steve stopped what he was doing and took off his glasses,

setting them down on the table. He pulled the burner phone out of a drawer. Kat didn't know that he had put it away. "Didn't want any little hands carrying this off."

"Good thinking," Kat said, seeing that there wasn't too much time left on the timer running on the phone's display screen. She pulled up the string of texts and sent one of her own. "I have it. Now what?"

All she could do was wait.

27

E dgar's phone chirped. "Finally," he breathed. Staying in one place for too long always made him feel a bit claustrophobic. He was feeling like it was time to get out Aldham. Too many complications, especially with this last target. Killing the friend, killing the nurse -- all things he didn't really want to do. Ultimately, he wanted to save lives. If that meant sharing a little information to cure a loved one of cancer, why was that a bad thing?

Edgar sat in the warehouse office watching the local sports news, staring at the blonde with too much makeup on. He had his feet up on a box that he had turned into a footrest. It was still pretty early, so there was little to do. Normally, he would have been sleeping, but he was waiting on Kat. Again. The drone of the newscaster and the hum of the little refrigerator were normally enough to put him to sleep even in the most uncomfortable chairs, but not today.

Edgar dropped his feet to the floor and opened up his phone to see what they had said. Kat's message was simple. "I have it. Now what?"

Edgar had been planning for this, but he wanted to take a

minute to think about it one more time. He had discovered that more mistakes were made when he acted too fast than when he took a moment to consider his next move. What was that old adage, the one about measuring, he wondered, staring at the phone. "Measure twice and cut once," he remembered. It was something his grandfather used to say while they were out fishing. What it had to do with fishing, he couldn't remember.

Before he texted Kat back, he wanted to make sure he knew where she was. He pulled up another number from his phone, the one for Victor, who was sitting on the house. He typed quickly, "Is she home?"

The message came back almost instantly. "Yes. I've been made."

The fact that the Beckman's had figured out Victor was watching the house didn't worry him. Victor was good at what he did, but not as good as the other guy they used to have. Stokes -- Edgar never knew the guy's first name. He could blend in better than anyone he'd ever met. Victor had gotten a bit cocky if Kat found him. Edgar would have to talk to the bosses about that.

"Stay until she leaves and then get out of there. The bosses want you to help the set-up team."

Victor replied. "Roger that."

Getting Victor out of the city before the rest of them made sense. If anyone was going to mess things up it would be him. Edgar looked back at the phone. It was time to message Kat back. He started to type, "Go to the Cedar Street Park on the north side. There's a wooden bench by the duck pond on the north side. Tape the information under the seat."

The phone chirped back. "No."

Edgar hissed under his breath. No? How could she tell him no? He had the cure. Who did she think she was?

Most of the time, when someone had the information that Edgar needed for the bosses, they were more than eager to hand it over. It wouldn't matter if Edgar told them to strap the information to a stick of dynamite, hold it in their teeth and light it while they waited for him. They wanted the cure that badly. Most of the time, they'd do anything he asked, knowing he had the life, or death, of their loved one in his hands. They were usually like putty, completely willing and completely malleable.

But not this time.

His phone chirped again. "I want to meet in person. You can hand me the cure yourself."

Man, this girl had balls, Edgar thought. She didn't know anything about him. Maybe she was up to something?

Edgar wasn't sure what to do. He couldn't go back to the bosses and tell them that he didn't get the information. At the same time, it was forbidden for anyone else to handle the serum except his team. He wasn't ever to hand it off to anyone else. Never.

He wasn't sure what options he had. He needed the information from Kat so he could get out of this horrible city. And, if Kat wasn't going to cooperate, what choice did he have? Edgar took a deep breath and sighed. He didn't have a lot of choices now. He needed the information. He'd have to make it work.

He tapped on the screen to reply to her text. "We don't do it this way. Put the drive under the bench."

Kat's reply came back faster than he could process what was happening. "No. Meet me or no info."

28

K at looked at her phone, watching for the man in the scrubs to reply. He wanted her to just leave the information out in the open and trust that he'd do the right thing and give the serum to Laura. There was no way Kat was going to risk jail time for something so sketchy. She didn't know him. She didn't trust him.

The last text she had sent to the man in the scrubs was that she wanted to meet in person. He said he didn't work that way. That part didn't matter to her. What did matter to her was that she got the cure for Laura. She wanted to see the man in the scrub's face when she gave him the information, to look him in the eye. Why she wasn't exactly sure. She knew that if she told Steve that she was pushing this guy, he'd probably freak out. All Steve could see was the finish line of his mom getting cured.

Kat could see a bigger picture. Spurred on by her meeting with Van, she knew that letting someone run around the world blackmailing people for a cure to cancer was not only evil, but it was like playing God. Why did the man in the scrubs and this company, Apex Solutions, get to decide who lives and who dies? The man in the scrubs and whoever he represented at

Apex Solutions, had to be brought into account. They couldn't be allowed to blackmail people for a cure. Kat wasn't sure she had the strength to do it, but she had to try. As much as she loved Laura, she was also a journalist. It was her job to watch out for the people around her.

She sat down at the kitchen table, straightening the placemat that was in front of her, waiting for the man in the scrubs to text back. She didn't have to wait too long. The phone chirped. "9 pm, Old Fort Dock, Pier 3."

That was all that the text said. When Kat closed the phone, she noticed that the timer was still running, but it had reset to allow for a few more hours. Maybe the man in the scrubs was human after all.

29

A fter leaving Steve, Kat and Jack in the park, Van went to the office. There was a lot more to the story than Kat had told him initially. Why she hadn't told him the whole thing, he wasn't sure.

He unlocked the door and flipped on the lights. Alyssa wasn't in yet. Van walked to the coffee maker and started an entire pot. They had bought one of those fancy one-cup-at-a-time brewers, but at the rate that Van drank coffee, it didn't make sense. Besides the fact that it annoyed him that he got one measly cup of coffee and had to take the time to make another one. That didn't make any sense to him when he could just refill his cup and microwave it. The coffee pot started to gurgle as the water began to heat. The smell of the coffee would start to fill the office in a minute or two. Although Van didn't like mornings, he did like his version of mornings, which involved brunch and lots of coffee.

While he was waiting for the coffee to fill the pot, he went into this office and opened up his laptop, scanning his email. He had to look past an email requesting a review on a pair of pants he had bought online and a few emails from writers with questions and drafts. At the bottom, between an email from one of his writers and another from his gym, was the email he had been waiting for. It was from a contact that he had at the FDA.

Over the years, Van had built up contacts in pretty much every industry. Pharmaceuticals were no exception. While they didn't all necessarily want to be quoted, they were willing to give him information that would help, especially if it was for a good cause. The guy he had reached out to, Brad Yates, had been with the FDA long enough that he had credibility and access, but not so long that he had become jaded.

The email from Brad was pretty short. "Call when you get a chance. I have information you might want."

Van waited the short amount of time that it took for the coffee to finish perking and to pour himself a cup before calling Brad. "Hey, it's Van," he said when Brad answered the phone.

"Hey man. I can't talk long. I'm about to walk into work, but I looked up the lot number you sent me last night. Here's the thing. It doesn't exist."

It took Van a second for it to register. "I'm sorry, say again?"

"The vial -- that image that you sent me? -- that lot number doesn't exist. I'm not even sure that the company, Medicus, is the one that made it."

"Wait, is Medicus legit?" Van asked, grabbing a pad of paper to make notes.

"Yeah, Medicus is legit. They work in all fifty states. We see them and their products a lot." Brad paused. "Hold on a sec. Let me walk down the block a bit."

Van waited while Brad got into a position where he could talk. He scribbled on his pad the name of the company, Medicus, and the vial number with a question mark next to it.

"You there?" Brad asked.

"Yeah, go ahead."

"Here's the thing. The vial number doesn't exist with any

batch number I could find. While the name on the vial says Medicus, I'm not sure it's theirs. The typeface or something doesn't seem right. I have to look at it again, but it almost looks like a forgery. It's like someone made the drugs and then labeled them to look like Medicus but didn't take the time to double-check the lot numbers."

Van scowled, "Why would someone go to that length to make drugs look like they belong to a company when they don't?"

"No idea. I'm going to take this to our investigative unit this morning and have them do an eval."

Van wasn't sure that was a good idea. Kat was still in play. Laura's life was still in the balance. Starting an FDA investigation might spook whoever was behind the supposed cure that Laura was being offered. "Dude, can you hold off on that for a day or so and let me do some looking? There's a bigger story here."

Van could hear Brad pause at his end of the phone. "I gotta get this to our investigators ASAP. If I don't, it's my head on the chopping block."

"I get that. Can you give me twenty-four hours? Might even be less. I just want to check a couple of things and make sure no one is in harm's way." Van held his breath. He was hoping that Brad would give him the time to do what he needed to.

"Okay. You've got until tomorrow. If you find out anything else, will you let me know?"

"Yeah. Talk soon." With that, Van hung up the phone. He set it down on his desk and made a few more notes with questions that he had. Who would dupe fentanyl? If you were just going to sell it on the street to druggies, why bother with the fake labeling? And who is manufacturing this? For what purpose? The questions swirled in his head.

Van knew that fentanyl use was an epidemic. A dangerous one at that. Unlike heroin and other drugs, fentanyl and its cousin carfentanil were lethal a high percentage of the time. There had even been cases of police officers on a traffic stop who had overdosed without ever taking it themselves. One of Van's writers had done a story on a police officer who stopped someone who had been snorting fentanyl powder in their car. When they opened their car window, just the amount that blew out of the car was enough to almost kill the officer.

Van also knew was it had become the drug of choice for murders that were meant to look like overdoses. Someone upsets you, your drug dealer substitutes fentanyl for your normal heroin. You take your normal dose and you OD before you know what happened.

It had become a problem in hospitals as well. Traditional drugs used to revive addicts weren't always effective with fentanyl. Three, four or five doses might be needed in order to bring someone back if the police or paramedics got to them in time. That was a big if. Sometimes it took ten doses. Fentanyl was flooding the shores from China, making its way through the Mexico and United States border.

Van sat back in his chair for a minute, taking in what Brad had told him. He didn't have all the pieces yet, but he knew there was a big story lurking in the shadows. Somehow it inter-sected with the man that had drugged Kat. Just thinking about it made Van angry. Kat had been through enough. She had seen more than she was trained to deal with and yet she came home, met Steve and had a beautiful child. She didn't deserve to be caught up in the mess that she was in. That didn't even begin to account for the rage that was beginning to grow deep inside of him knowing that either someone had a cure for cancer they were holding onto or they didn't and were simply taking advan-tage of vulnerable families.

Van knew he had to help. He just wasn't sure how. More than anything, he wanted to protect Kat. One night, facing a deadline, she had shared her experience in Afghanistan over

Indian food from the corner restaurant. He had known Marines, well-trained professional soldiers, that weren't able to piece life together after their tour even with all of the training and mindset work. Kat came to the Middle East with nothing but her courage and a desire to tell the truth. Van respected that.

Van tapped on the mouse pad of his computer, waiting for it to light up. He opened a new search tab and typed in Medicus Pharmaceuticals. The computer loaded an expectedly sophisticated home page with images of smiling, happy people in medical settings. He didn't know anyone that looked that delighted in a hospital. This was the best place for him to start his search.

Van spent a couple of hours on the Medicus website, looking at all of the information the company had that was public-facing. As he paged through their site, he could see that they manufactured drugs for a lot of different conditions -- everything from diabetes to painkillers. Everything on their site said that they were cutting edge, worried about the health of their patients and totally compliant. Van frowned. Maybe they were, maybe they weren't. He didn't know. What Van couldn't figure out was why someone would want to create a dupe of a drug vial. That was a lot of work and precision in order to move drugs.

What Van knew from his research was that the drug business was big business. Every disease and disorder promoted another customer. He wondered if the drug companies hoped they were customers for life. Chronic diseases were the best. It was a sure form of cash flow that allowed the company to research and line their pockets with the promise of a cure... someday. And, if a patient happened to have a side effect, all the better. The drug company would come up with another drug for that, ensuring more sales.

Van knew he was overly cynical about big pharma. He had

seen too many people get hooked on drugs or have well-meaning physicians prescribe pill after pill to deal with one condition after another, when all someone needed was a life-style change. Maybe walk a little or stop eating salami sand-wiches for every meal. Sure, there were people who really needed medicines. Van was okay with that. What he didn't like was the idea that someone could end up on five or six drugs for something that could be taken care of by getting rid of fast food.

Typing on his keyboard, Van visited the FDA website. Generally, there wasn't a lot to find there. All of their good information was kept tightly under control until they needed to make a public splash. The agency's position was that if they could handle things in-house, they would. They wanted to partner with big pharma, not embarrass them if it could be avoided. Public scandals weren't good for consumers.

Van stood up from his desk, stretching some of the stiffness out of his muscles. Sitting for too long always did that to him. He looked out the small window that had a view out of the back of his office. There was a parking lot, a side street and the lot where he parked his truck. A fence surrounded the parking lot and a few cars passed by. There wasn't a lot of traffic at this time of the day. People were either already at work or they weren't going to work. Van watched a couple of kids walking down the sidewalk with someone that looked to be their mom. They both had backpacks on and she was leading the way with a determined stride. Van wondered if they were late to school.

Turning away from the window, Van sat down at his desk and opened a new search browser. He started a dark web search for the company that Kat had mentioned -- Apex Solu-tions. Companies on the dark web didn't usually have a website. If they had something to sell, maybe. Mostly they didn't. Scrolling through the results, Van didn't find a website for the company. He hadn't expected to. Criminals didn't like to advertise. What he did find was some mention on a few forums of people looking for more of what Apex had to offer. Van found that curious and read more. He found a story from someone in Ghana who had posted an anonymous message tagging Apex Solutions, telling them that they had more information to offer. "My uncle now has cancer. I have information on weapons in the area. Need the cure. Will trade." Another post from Italy said, "My daughter has Ewing's Sarcoma. Have info on potential coup in EU."

There weren't a lot of posts, but just seeing a few verified for Van that this was a global organization. If they weren't peddling a cure for cancer, people believed they were. It was anecdotal evidence, but evidence nonetheless.

30

E dgar went into the secured room and got a vial of blue serum, checking it out on the tablet before he left the room. John, who was still stationed in the room, was reading the sports section of the paper. "Anything good in there?"

"Yeah, it looks like the Browns finally have themselves a quarterback."

Edgar knew that John was a big football fan. That's really all he knew about him. Edgar wasn't even sure that John was the guy's real name. When you worked for someone like Apex, the truth and lies tended to mix together until you weren't sure what was real anymore.

"That's good news, I guess," Edgar said, closing the tablet.

"It's about time," John said, folding the paper neatly so he could read the next page. "It's only been like twenty years."

"Yeah, they are like the bad news bears."

"Don't even get me started on the Bears," John said.

Edgar walked to the door, opened it and heard it click behind him. He didn't know how John could sit there for hours and hours inside the room with basically nothing to do. He smiled to himself. Where else could you get paid to read about football? Only at Apex. As Edgar headed for the door, he started to think about what he'd do with his time off. Maybe being outdoors was the way to go. Maybe some sunshine, too. All this working in the dark really wore him out.

As he got into the gray car, he started to think about hiking. That might be a good vacation. He hated vacations where you just sat. There was a lot of sitting in his job. He didn't like beach vacations much either. More sitting around. He paused for a minute. At least with beach vacations there were some girls to look at. He pushed the thoughts out of his mind as he pulled away from the warehouse. He had other things to think about. There would be no vacation if he didn't finish what the bosses had sent him to do.

Edgar chose the pier intentionally. It was isolated and there were plenty of places to hide. He ran through what he hoped would happen as he drove. With any luck, Kat Beckman would show up, he'd give her the serum, she'd give him the flash drive and he'd be on his way. Edgar reached for the radio and turned it on. There was a station that was playing old country-western music. A little Johnny Cash would help him get ready for the meet.

Kat had been a particularly difficult client. The information the bosses asked for wasn't that big of a deal, Edgar thought. They had demanded for more difficult information from clients in the past, everything from locations of secret military installations to malware code that could shut down half of the U.S. if it was used. A list of names didn't seem that challenging, especially if they wanted Laura to live.

Edgar pulled into the gravel-covered driveway that led to the pier, the tires of his car crunching on the bumpy road. It was unsecured except for a chain-link fence with barbed wire. The gate was always open, according to Edgar's team. Why they had a fence if it was never closed made Edgar wonder. Maybe it was because the pier itself hadn't been in use much in the last ten years. The little car bumped along the driveway out to the docks. It was filled with potholes that simply had been neglected. As he got closer to the water, the night air chilled a bit. The warm weather was coming, Edgar could feel it, but for the time being, the cooler water held off the heat and the summer humidity.

Edgar's car crept around the pier a little bit as he tried to decide where to park. At dock three, there was a boat moored. The lights were off and Edgar doubted anyone was on board. Down further, at what Edgar guessed to be dock seven, there was a fishing boat loading supplies. The boat was probably about sixty feet long and had seen better days. It was far enough away that he could see the fishermen working, but he wasn't sure they could see much more than his car rolling through. He knew there was enough transient traffic at the pier that they wouldn't give him a second thought. The water was to his left. On the right, there was a steel warehouse, about fifty yards from the docks, and metal shipping containers stacked nearby. Edgar pulled the car behind a stack of shipping containers, turned off the lights and put the keys in his pocket. Out of the trunk, he pulled a pair of black surgical gloves and a surgical mask. He pulled his hood up and held the mask and gloves in his hands. He'd put them on when he saw Kat come in. He did not want her to see his face.

It was time to move. He walked around the shipping containers where he could keep a better watch on the driveway and docks. The only noise was a little bit of gravel moving under his feet as he found a spot to watch. There was still no movement at dock three from either Kat or the people who owned the boat. The dockworkers at dock seven had finished loading and were now standing on the dock smoking. The lit ends of their cigarettes glowed in the darkness.

Edgar took a couple of steps forward, still in the shadows of the warehouse and the shipping containers. If he didn't like what he saw, he could slip away virtually unnoticed. It seemed like a good place for a meet. Humming under his breath, there wasn't much more for him to do, other than wait. He ducked farther into the shadows, hoping Kat would be on time.

A few minutes passed. He checked his phone and saw that she should be arriving at any time. He put his gloves on and pulled the vial out of his pocket. Using his handkerchief, he wiped his prints off of it. No reason to take a chance if Kat got fancy and wanted to try to run his prints.

The fishermen down at dock seven had started up their boat. Edgar could hear the diesel engines idling. He could smell the exhaust. When they turned on their running lights, he stepped back into a blacker shadow, not wanting anyone to spot him, especially with his gloves on. The voices of the fishermen carried over the water. He could hear laughing and then yelling. The captain, Edgar figured. Peering around the corner, Edgar saw all of them get on board except for one man, who untied the lines from the cleats bolted onto the sea wall. He stepped on board just as the boat pushed off from the dock. As the bow of the boat nosed away from land, Edgar's last view of it was the fishermen pulling on their yellow fishing gear, suspenders up over shoulders, disappearing out onto the water.

The quiet had become somewhere between deafening and soothing. Edgar wasn't sure which. All he could do now was wait.

31

K
at could tell Steve was worried. He kept pacing around the house and asking her if she was sure that she wanted to go alone. "I'm sure," she said for what felt like the thousandth time. "I need to go alone. We don't want to spook him." Kat put her hand on Steve's arm. "I've got my gun and my cell phone. I know what to do."

"He probably has a gun too. It's just not safe," Steve said.

"I know you are worried. I'll be fine. I'll text when I get there and as soon as I get back to the car. I'll go straight to the hospital, okay?"

"Okay. I'll bring Jack and we will meet you there."

Kat found herself frowning a little bit. As a mom, she wanted Jack home and in bed. She also wanted Jack safe. One late night wouldn't hurt Jack, she thought, trying to soothe the mom nerves that had just risen in her gut. "That's fine. Bring his blanket in case he falls asleep in the car?" As soon as the words came out of her mouth, she felt stupid. She was worried about a blanket when she should have been worried about getting the serum. Focus Kat, she thought to herself, focus.

Steve nodded. "Of course."

Kat checked her Sig. It was holstered on her side. She pushed an extra magazine in her pocket. Between the two seventeen round mags, she'd have thirty-four shots. If she didn't make it past that, there was no hope.

She looked at Steve, "I gotta go."

"Love you," he said, putting a kiss on her forehead. "Text me as soon as it is over."

"I will," Kat called, walking towards the door. She didn't stop to say goodbye to Jack. She knew she'd never leave the house if she saw his face.

As Kat pulled down the driveway, she noticed there was no cable guy. Maybe they were tired of watching the house, she wondered. Maybe they had what they wanted. She had to follow this through. She shivered a little bit, glad that she had a jacket on. The weather was due to warm up, but it still wasn't warm enough for her to leave a jacket behind.

Kat took the freeway to the part of town where the docks were. The last time she was at the docks wasn't when she was with Steve and Jack, that's was for sure. The docks were industrial and not any kind of place for families. She racked her brain, realizing that the stress of meeting the man in the scrubs again was giving her tunnel vision. She gripped the steering wheel a little tighter. She tried slowing her breathing and thinking about the docks again. The fog seemed to clear a bit. She realized that the last time she had been down at the pier was when she was doing a story on environmental hazards. Not that she was a tree hugger. She wasn't. What she was concerned about was unregulated toxins being dumped into the water. That would be a problem for everyone.

The sun had set and car headlights were drifting across the road. Not as many cars were on the road as she'd expected. People were home with their families. That's where she wanted to be. She fiddled with the knob for the radio and turned it on to a sports talk station. The analyst was talking about the NBA finals. Kat really didn't care about basketball or most sports, for that matter. At least it was something to keep her focused on.

Kat got off the freeway and followed the road that led to the docks. The area around the pier used to be bustling with family-run fishing companies and people selling fish off the side of their boats. In the last ten years, the fishing community had pretty much dried up. Bigger fishing operations that could undercut small local fishermen had taken over. They didn't even dock at the pier anymore.

Kat followed the signs down toward the pier, watching carefully. The murky darkness made it hard to see where to go. Kat pressed on the brake. She took her right hand off the wheel and checked to make sure the Sig was still there. It was. A sign loomed ahead of her announcing her arrival to the pier. Right after it, there was a chain-link fence that bordered a gravel road. She followed it and saw as industrial containers and a warehouse sitting staunchly on the banks. As she rolled down her window, the humid night air filled the car. It wasn't warm yet, but she could feel the moisture cover her and everything around her. She pulled as close to dock three as she could, turning her car around to face the exit. She would have tried to park somewhere else and walk in, but she was pretty sure that the man in the scrubs was watching. At least with her car close, she could make a quick getaway if she needed to.

Before she got out of the car, she sent Steve a quick text. "Here," was all she wrote.

His reply came virtually instantly. "Okay."

Kat was grateful for his short reply. She didn't have time or the energy to reassure him that she was all right. If she got really honest, she didn't know that. What she did know was that she had to see this through if she had any hope of regaining her life and her family.

She shut off the car engine, at the last second deciding to keep the keys in the ignition. The last thing she needed was to be fumbling with her keys, trying to get them in the slot with shaking hands if there was trouble. Better to be prepared, she reasoned.

Kat stepped out of the car, the flash drive in her hand. She took a minute to look around. There was really no one at the docks. Dock three was open. There wasn't even a light nearby. The closest light looked like the bulb had blown out long ago. The front of the warehouse looked nearly abandoned, though she knew that there were a few businesses that worked out of it on a pretty irregular basis -- or at least that's what she had known about it in the past. She left the driver's side door slightly open in case she needed to get in quickly.

Kat scanned the area, watching for movement. She had the feeling that she was being watched. Maybe it was just paranoia. She tried to keep herself occupied by thinking about where she'd hide if she was the man in the scrubs. Would she enter the warehouse or slip between stacks of industrial shipping containers? The containers seemed like the most logical place. The shadows there were dark and inky. It would be hard to see anyone hidden there.

Kat shifted her feet, the lumps of gravel pushing up below her shoes. She debated about getting the burner phone out and sending the man in the scrubs a text but decided against it. She wanted to be focused on what was around her. Getting distracted by the phone could be a problem. She had learned that lesson when she was in the Middle East. Distraction could equal death.

Beyond the docks on both sides were tall grasses and acres of undeveloped land. The grasses rustled a little bit with a nudge from a breeze off the water. Kat could see no movement, just one boat moored at dock three that was completely dark.

Kat looked around and kept her back to the dock. She didn't think that the man in the scrubs would come from that direction. She wanted the widest view possible. If he did come from the docks, he'd have to be on a dinghy, approach the dock and crawl up to get to her. She didn't think he'd do that. She scanned the area again, her stomach tightening. Kat looked farther down the dock. There was no movement there except for a boat bobbing slightly down at the other end of the docks. Kat walked over to dock three. Looking down over the edge, she saw nothing but murky water and old tires that had been mounted to the dock walls to keep boats from getting damaged.

It felt like a half-hour had passed, but thinking about it, Kat knew it had been just a couple of minutes. She walked the few feet back from the dock wondering if the man in the scrubs would show up. She saw movement from near the storage containers. A figure approached out of the shadows. How long he had been standing there, she had no idea. In the darkness, he would have blended in perfectly.

As he walked toward her, Kat felt her hands clench. She moved out in front of her car so that she had somewhere to run if she needed it. She didn't want to be pinned to her car. Not that she could outrun him, though, or that anyone would hear her screams if he did attack. The docks were nothing short of desolate. She could only rely on herself.

Kat looked at the man that approached her. He was of average size and average build. There was nothing really notable about him. She couldn't see any of his face. He was wearing what looked to be navy blue scrub pants with black shoes and a black hoodie. The hood was up over his hair. She could only see a black fringe hanging out in a few places. Over his face, he wore a surgical mask. Other than his eyes, which were hard to see in the darkness, there would be no way to identify him.

Kat didn't say anything as he approached. Edgar broke the silence, "Do you have what I need?"

Kat opened her clenched palm to show him the flash drive. "This is it."

"Give it to me," Edgar said.

Kat started to object, but she saw him pull a small tablet out of his pocket, his hands covered by black surgical gloves. She handed the drive to him without saying a word.

Kat watched as Edgar inserted the flash drive into the tablet. He pushed a button on the side. The screen glowed blue. She saw the document load. "This is all of it?" he asked.

Kat nodded.

"Not a big talker, huh?" Edgar snickered a little bit. Kat didn't answer, not wanting to give him any more information than she needed to.

Kat waited as Edgar pulled the flash drive out. He tapped a few more screens and shut the screen off, handing Kat the drive back. "I'm done with this. You can keep it as a souvenir." His gloves touched her hand. She felt goosebumps crawl up her arm.

She waited, still silent. Edgar reached into the pocket of his hoodie and pulled out a vial that had a blue liquid in it. "Here's my end of the deal. It's only good for an hour so go straight to the hospital. And, if you decide you want to do anything funny, just know that after the hour, any chemical analysis will show that it is blue food coloring and water." He made eye contact with her and nodded. "Good luck," he said, the corners of his eyes crinkling as though he was smiling. Maybe he was sneering. Kat couldn't tell because of the mask.

Without another word, she saw Edgar walk away, only the noise from his black work shoes leaving any trace that he was there. As he disappeared back into the shadows, Kat felt her heart beating in her throat. It felt like all of the blood was rushing to her head. She whispered to herself, "Kat, get in the car."

Adrenaline and a good dose of relief running through her veins, she pulled open the car door, climbed in and started the engine, locking the doors and rolling up the windows before doing anything else. She put the vial of serum in the cup holder of her car and put it into drive. Pulling away, not caring how fast she was going or was supposed to go, she left a dust storm behind her car leaving the docks.

She glanced down at her phone and hit redial for Steve.

"Are you okay?" he asked before she could even say hello.

"Yes," she managed to say, wishing her voice sounded more confident and stronger.

"Where are you?"

"I'm leaving the docks."

"Did you get it?"

"Yes."

She heard Steve sigh with relief. "I'm so glad you are okay. Are you headed to Mercy?"

"Yes. He told me that the serum is only good for an hour. I've got to get someone to give this to your mom." All of a sudden, Kat felt like her head cleared. "Can you get Jack packed up and meet me there?"

"I'm on my way. I took Jack to Angela's. He's going to spend the night."

Knowing that Jack was having fun helped. "Okay. I should be there in about twenty minutes. I'll meet you on the floor."

"No," Steve said. Meet me at the gas station. The one right before the hospital entrance. You can jump in with me. I don't want you to go into the hospital alone. Not after what you've been through."

The next twenty minutes were a blur. The radio in Kat's car was still tuned to the local sports station. She didn't hear a word. Kat's mind wandered as she tried to calm down. Memories of the Middle East tried to filter down into her body, but she blocked them. She didn't have the strength to have a meltdown now. They were too close to saving Laura and having everything back to as normal. Kat rolled the windows down, her mind wandering to what it might be like if the serum in the cup holder next to her actually worked. The fresh air prickled at her skin and she drew in long, deep breaths.

Time seemed to slow. Kat felt the wind, heard the radio and felt her Sig on her side. She felt the slight pressure of the seatbelt across her chest. There was more traffic as she got closer to the hospital and the center of the city. For some reason it was comforting, as though there might be someone who'd be willing to help her if she needed it. As she was driving, she looked down at the vial of serum, making sure it was still there and sealed tightly. It only jostled a bit in as she drove.

She made the turn that would take her to the gas station. She hoped Steve was already there. Her mind wandered. Did she really need to go to the meet by herself? She gripped the steering wheel a little bit tighter and realized that she could have included Steve. She knew she preferred to take on challenges by herself, knowing that if she failed it would only be on her. The gas station sign glowed up ahead. At least if something had happened, Jack would have still had his dad. She relaxed a bit, realizing that maybe her instincts weren't too far off.

Ever since she got back from the Middle East, she had second-guessed herself. She did it in her work and in her relationships. Her need for being alone wasn't so much that she didn't like people. It was because she didn't necessarily trust herself. After the Humvee exploded, she always wondered if her own curiosity had gotten people killed. Everyone on the mission, including General Barton, had assured her that what happened wasn't her responsibility, but she had a hard time shaking the thought. Whether it was true or not didn't keep it from weighing on her heart.

Even when she met Steve, she was hesitant. He pursued her gently and patiently and eventually, she let him in. But it took time. Really, the only one she could be truly herself with was Jack. Jack had no expectations, though Kat knew over time that might change. Jack just wanted to be with her as she was. He wouldn't -- he couldn't -- ask the hard questions that she didn't want to face. The most difficult part of Jack's life was which color truck to play with before breakfast. Although she wasn't like other women who had aspired to be a mom her whole life, she was happy when she found out she was pregnant. Jack had been a blessing in her life.

The lights at the gas station grew closer. She turned the wheel into the station and saw Steve there, out of his truck, waiting. She pulled up right next to him. He pointed, "Park right over there. I told the guy inside that your car would be here for a bit."

"Okay." Kat pulled the car into the parking spot, shut off the lights and the engine and rolled up the windows. The cold hit her as soon as she got out of the car. She felt cold to the bones. She leaned back in for the vial that contained the blue serum, handing it to Steve.

"This is it?" he said.

"Yes," she stifled a shiver.

She felt his warm arm around her shoulders. "Come on. I've got a blanket for you in the truck. I thought you might be cold." He followed her around the side of the truck, and she let him open the door and wait for her to get inside. She saw him walk around the other side of the truck. The door opened with a click and he got in, putting the vial down between them. "Let's go do this, okay?"

Kat nodded. She pulled the blanket up over her legs and tucked it around her. She saw Steve glance over to her as he started the truck down the long driveway to Mercy Memorial. "Feel warmer?"

"Yes, thank you."

"Are you okay?"

Kat didn't answer for a minute. It was hard to know what to say. "Yeah. I mean, I guess. I'm not sure what to think." She let the thought sit out in the open, not sure what else to say.

Steve's warm hand covered hers. "I know. We are just about done."

He sounded so certain to Kat. "I hope you are right," she said. Even as the words came out of her mouth, Kat wasn't sure that she believed them. Could getting Laura the cure be as simple as handing over the information? What happened if the Army figured out that she had passed off classified information? What if the cure didn't work? What if they had been tricked? Kat's mind ran ahead of her like a horse free from a pasture. She didn't know what would happen. Her chest clutched with the uncertainty.

They drove down the driveway to the hospital, Steve pulling the truck right under a well-lit parking spot in an area that had virtually no cars. Neither of them were taking any chances. Kat still had her Sig on her side. Hospitals didn't like firearms -- they didn't even generally allow anyone except law enforcement to carry them -- but she didn't care. If she needed her Sig, and God-forbid she had to use it, she'd deal with the consequences later. She just wanted to be safe. She wanted all of them to be safe. Kat picked up the vial of serum and handed it to Steve.

She followed Steve as he walked briskly across the parking lot into the front doors of the hospital. She saw him nod to the security guard that was at the front door. Her jacket hid the bulge from the butt of her gun and she walked right past, managing a weak smile. Kat and Steve went down a series of hallways. Hospitals were always a tangle of different departments and specialties. They found the elevators that would take them up to Laura's fourth-floor room. Kat kept staring at the lighted numbers above the elevator watching them cycle up, then down, then up and then finally landing the elevator car so that she and Steve could get on.

Stepping into the elevator, Kat saw Steve push the button for the fourth floor. The elevator smelled faintly of latex, as though someone had been transporting bandages or gloves to another part of the hospital. As the elevator doors closed, Kat found herself wondering if the people that worked in the hospital ever got used to the smell. It seemed to permeate everything including her clothes and hair. It even stuck to her skin. The elevator glided silently up to the fourth floor, the doors opening with a slight whoosh.

Steve and Kat walked through the anteroom to get to the floor for visitors, washing their hands and walking on floors that were covered with disinfectant paper. They walked quickly, Kat checking her phone to make sure they were still within the hour window the man in the scrubs had told her about. They got to Laura's room. She was asleep, propped up on pillows, the television showing a wildlife program about geese. Kat was sure Laura wasn't watching. She saw Steve reach out to Laura, grasping her hand and giving it a squeeze, "Mom? Mom?" he whispered.

Laura stirred, her eyes opening just a bit. "Hi, honey."

"Mom, we got some medication that is supposed to cure you. Kat's going to give it to you."

Kat watched, waiting. She had learned how to give a basic injection when she was doing a story on critical care. There was a long pause. Laura didn't let go of Steve's hand. She just stared ahead, as if she was watching something at the foot of her bed. "No."

Kat saw Steve stand straight up. "Mom? What?"

"Honey, I've had a good life," she stopped to cough and push herself up in the bed a little bit. "I don't know what you have, but there's someone who needs it more than I do."

Kat, suddenly feeling weak, sat down in a chair across the room. She desperately needed to be away from all of this. They were so close to having this done. The smoke was rising and her stomach clenched. She took a deep breath and closed her eyes. What did Laura mean that she didn't want the treatment?

"Mom, I don't understand. What you are saying?" Steve asked.

"There is a young man down the hall -- three doors down. He has colon cancer. He's got no family except for his daughter."

Kat could tell that Steve was getting angry, his voice rising, speaking sternly to Laura. "Mom, we went to a lot of trouble to get this for you." Kat saw him glance back at her. "Kat went to a lot of trouble to get this for you. You don't understand how much trouble."

Kat saw Laura's eyes track over to her. "Kat, thank you." Laura looked back at Steve. "Lawrence needs it more than I do. He's young. He has a daughter. She will be all alone if he dies. You have each other and Jack."

Steve's voice cracked. "Mom, this is for you. It will make you better. I'll get more for Lawrence."

Kat stared directly at Steve's back. Get more? Kat hoped that Steve was just saying that to get his mom to cooperate

"If you can get more, then I'll take some from the next batch." Laura patted Steve's hand. "I'll be okay. I just need to sleep a little bit." She turned her head to the side. "Wake me up when you give it to Lawrence. Remember, three doors down." With that Laura seemed to go to sleep.

Steve looked at Kat. "I'm just gonna give it to her. She's out of her mind." Kat didn't say a word. She didn't move. She wasn't even sure how to respond. All of the risks they had taken, and Laura didn't want the drug? That didn't make any sense.

Less than a minute later, Steve returned with a syringe. "I grabbed this off a cart. Think it will work?" Steve pulled the vial out of his pocket, stuck the needle in and drew back on the serum. It filled the syringe. "I don't actually know what to do here," he said. Kat could see his frustration. She took the syringe from his hands, tapped it with her finger to get the air bubbles out and was ready to insert it into Laura's IV port when

Laura woke up and stared right at them. "I told you no. Give that to Lawrence."

Kat pulled her hands back and recapped the syringe. Anger rose in her chest. She had risked everything -- her career, her family and even her freedom to get the serum. Now Laura wouldn't take it. She and Steve stayed in her room, but they stepped away from her bed.

Her eyes wide, she looked at Steve. "What do we do now?"

He frowned. "I guess we give it to Lawrence." He stopped for a moment and looked down at his boots. It was a look that Kat knew well. It was the one that he gave when he had a hard question and wasn't sure he wanted to ask it. "Do you think we can get more?"

Kat felt like she had been punched in the chest. "Are you kidding me? After what I had to risk just to get this?" Kat was so angry and tired that she could hardly speak.

A few moments passed. Steve looked at her and said, "What do you want to do? Didn't the man that gave it to you say it is only good for an hour?"

Kat checked her cell phone. She had set an alarm so she'd be sure of how much time they had. Five minutes left. That was all. She walked over to Laura's bed and put her hand on her shoulder. "Gramma, I have the serum right here. It will cure you. Please let me give it to you."

Laura stared right at her. "No, honey. I know you want to. I do want to get better, but I don't feel right about Lawrence. He's young. I'm not. If you can get more, fine. If you can't, I'm okay with that."

Kat stepped away from Laura's bed, realizing that the steeliness that Laura had was what had attracted her to Steve and his family in the first place. Laura was tough. There was no doubt about it. She saw by the look on his face that Steve was crushed. He was pale and his eyes were watering. Kat didn't ask the question, but Steve answered her anyway, nodding, "Go give it to Lawrence. That's what she wants. I'll stay here."

Kat nodded. This was not the outcome she had planned for. Giving up on Laura was going to be tough, but she was running out of time. Kat put the syringe in the pocket of her hoodie and walked down the hallway, looking for Lawrence's room. She just hoped she didn't get caught by a nurse or a family member. She had no idea if Lawrence's daughter was staying in his room or not. What if he was awake?

As Laura had described, his room was three down from hers. She found his name on the doorway. The curtain was drawn. She ducked under the corner, letting it settle gently back into place so no one would know she was in the room. She approached his bed tentatively. He didn't know her. She had no idea how he would react. The light in the room was dim. His monitor beeped and there were six IV bags set up on pumps next to his bed. Many of them were painkillers, Kat was sure.

Lawrence looked to be in his thirties. He was sleeping, covered up to his shoulders with a blanket. He was clearly in the late stages of his disease. His color was pallid and his face was drawn and hollow. He looked like a skeleton in his bed. Kat felt her breath draw sharply. It was hard to look at him. She wondered how much pain he was in. Steeling herself, she stepped closer to his bed, spotting his IV port. It was now or never. She pulled the syringe out of the pocket of her hoodie, uncapped it and made sure there were no air bubbles. She was no medic, but she had seen nurses and doctors on the base do the same process every single time. She squeezed out a single drop to make sure that there was no air in the needle, watching the blue liquid hit the floor. It immediately turned clear. She wondered if she was too late. There was no way to know except to give him the cure and see what happened. Gently picking up the IV line, she pushed the needle into the port and squeezed the blue liquid in. It disappeared into his vein. He never woke up.

Just as she was pulling the needle out, she heard a noise from behind her. She quickly put the spent needle in her pocket, praying she didn't stick herself with it. "Hello?" Turning behind her, she saw a nurse.

"Oh, hi," Kat whispered. "I'm Laura's daughter-in-law from down the hall. She asked me to look in on Lawrence for her."

The nurse smiled. "That's nice. Sorry -- I didn't know who you were."

"That's no problem. I'm going back to her room now. Didn't mean to cause a problem."

"You didn't."

Kat turned to walk out of the room and saw the nurse reach down to pick something off of the floor. The syringe cap had fallen under the edge of the bed. Kat kept moving and went back to Laura's room.

As soon as she got back down the hall, she drew the curtain and put the spent syringe in the hazardous materials box on the wall. Laura was sleeping soundly. It didn't look like anything could wake her up. Steve was sitting by her side, his hands in his head. He stirred when Kat came into the room. "Did you do it?"

"Yeah. I almost got caught."

"What happened?" he asked.

"A nurse came in the room just as I finished."

"But you did it, right?"

Kat shook her head yes. She put her hand on his neck, running her fingers through the back of his hair. "Do you want to stay here tonight?"

"No, she's just gonna sleep. It's depressing."

Kat knew what he was feeling. She was feeling it too. Steve stood up, kissed his mom on her cheek and turned off the television. He and Kat walked out of the room together and took the elevator back down to the maze of hallways that let out of the hospital. The night was pitch black by the time they got out of the hospital.

Sitting in the truck, Kat and Steve were silent until they got to the gas station. "I'll follow you home," Steve said, "just in case you need anything."

Kat opened the door, "Thanks." She slid out of the truck and got into her own car, "See you at home."

32

Parked on the edge of the outdoor lot was the gray car. Edgar had watched Kat and Steve get out of the truck and walk into the hospital. Normally, he would have been the one to administer the serum. If the Apex bosses found out that he hadn't, he would be in trouble. He was sure of that. How serious the trouble would be, he wasn't sure. He was their best closer. His hope was that they would administer the serum and forget about him. If they didn't, he just hoped he'd survive.

At least Edgar got to rest in the fact that he knew they had been to the hospital. What was curious to him was the way they had come out. He liked watching his patients and their families after their ordeal was over. They usually talked a lot and waved their hands around with big smiles on their faces, their animation belying their excitement even if he couldn't hear what they were saying.

It wasn't that way with the Beckman's. They had come out of the hospital looking sullen and not talking at all. They didn't have the faces of people who were relieved or happy. In fact, they looked the opposite. Maybe they didn't believe that the cure wouldn't work. Boy, were they in for a surprise, he thought.

But nothing about this case had gone the way he expected it. From how long it took them to respond to Kat's demand to get the serum from him directly to their long faces at the hospital, it was a mystery.

Edgar watched them drive away. He waited five minutes before he started the car after Steve and Kat pulled away in their truck. He knew they had parked a car at the gas station. He wanted to give them time to drive away before he headed back to the industrial park.

He flipped on the radio, humming to himself. A strange case, he thought. He shook his head slowly. Very strange. A few more minutes passed. He started the car, circling the lot once and then pulling out onto the road that led away from the hospital.

33

K at pulled into the garage just ahead of Steve after collecting her car from the gas station, his headlights washing over the back hood. Still no cable truck in front of their house. She figured that as far as the man in the scrubs was concerned, the transaction was settled. Kat's gut didn't agree. Laura was still sick. The man in the scrubs had more of the cure. They needed at least one more dose. She put the car into park and shut it off, heading into the house.

All of the kitchen lights were on. Steve must have left it lit when he raced off to the hospital. A few seconds later, Steve came into the house, his face drawn and pale.

"I'm sorry," Kat said. "I thought your mom would take the treatment."

Steve sat down on one of the kitchen chairs and started to pull off his boots. "I did, too. I don't know what happened."

"She said it was for her friend."

"I get that, but what about us? She is choosing to die. I want Jack to have his grandma."

"I know. I do too." Kat slid down to the floor, resting her back on the cabinets. As much as the rest of the house was nice, it seemed like everything happened in the kitchen. Kat scooted her feet under the edge of the round rug that covered the wood floor, watching the wool flop over her toes. "It just seems so sad to me. About your mom, I mean."

Steve nodded. "I don't know what to do." He walked away. Kat knew he needed time. She did too.

34

Major Jerry Javorek was sitting at his desk, buried in paperwork. He thought when he came back stateside it would be more relaxing than combat in Iraq. He never anticipated the number of emails, documents and reports that had to be filed. It was almost worse than being deployed.

He looked up from his desk, hoping to see his assistant, Jennifer, who could take some of the paper off of his desk now that he was done signing it, but she wasn't there. He remembered that she had taken lunch. He checked his watch. It was thirteen hundred hours. No wonder his own stomach was growling. Just as he closed the folder in front of him, a list of supplies being used at a site in California that needed to be approved, his phone rang.

"Javorek," he answered.

"Major, I'm sorry to bother you," the other voice on the line said.

Jerry recognized the voice as Hannah Carter, their contractor liaison that ran the site in Aldham. It was early there. He was surprised Hannah was calling.

"I think we might have a problem," Hannah said.

Jerry leaned back in his desk chair. He didn't like problems. "What kind of problem?"

"We might have had a data breach. I'm not totally sure yet, but I wanted to make you aware of it. This just hit my desk minutes ago. We are already working on it."

The one thing that Jerry liked about Hannah was that she handled problems as soon as they came up. He didn't need to tell her to handle it. He wished more military personnel had that work ethic.

"Give me the basics," Jerry said.

"We have someone accessing a file from a mission in Afghanistan. Normally, we wouldn't worry about this. The mission was well over the five-year limit. The thing that caught our attention was who accessed it."

Jerry's attention was piqued now. "Who do you think got the information?"

"One of our journalists, Kat Beckman."

"Are you sure it is her?"

"Not for sure, sir. We are just starting our investigation."

The name didn't sound familiar to him. "Do you know her?"

"Yeah. Aldham is a pretty small site. I'm here all the time so I know everyone. Kat's really squared away. She was part of our journalism team in Afghanistan."

"She was deployed?"

"Yeah, with General Barton."

"Do you know which mission information was opened?"

"Bluebird."

"Why do you think it is this Beckman woman?" Jerry waited for Hannah to answer. There was a pause before she did.

"As I said, we don't know for sure, but based on the time logs, it would make sense it was her."

Off the cuff, Jerry didn't know anything about that mission.

That wasn't surprising since there were literally thousands of missions around the world each and every year. That said, the leak of any mission information was serious. Very serious. It required a lot of self-discipline to not jump to conclusions, but Jerry didn't like to assume anything. Assuming stuff was what got you called into the higher-up's offices and got you in trouble. He wanted all the facts before he acted. "What can you tell me that you know for sure?" He heard Hannah sigh on the phone.

"We don't have a lot nailed down yet. That's what we are working on. The Bluebird mission information was opened by someone in this office during a period of time where there weren't many people here."

"And Beckman is your prime suspect?"

"That's the working theory, but it isn't confirmed."

"Do we know what information was opened?"

"It looks like the mission roster, sir."

Jerry stopped to think about this. Who would want just the names of the people that were on a mission five years ago? More importantly, why did Beckman want the information?

"Were security protocols breached?"

"Not that we can see. I have the security and tech teams meeting right now to vet the information access and surveillance video."

"Okay. Thanks for the update. Call me back when you have something concrete. I'll need an update before the end of the day. I don't want to make any rash moves on this."

"Will do, sir."

"And Hannah?"

"Yes, sir?"

"Call my personal cell with the updates, okay? I don't want to leave a paper trail on this until we have a better sense of what we are working with."

"Of course."

Jerry hung up his office phone and tapped the end of his pencil on the desk. Problems like these were better solved before he reported them. Knowing exactly what had happened and having a solution in place kept him away from the firing line with his brass. He'd have to tell them sooner rather than later, but he needed to buy a little time.

There was nothing else to do other than wait for Hannah and her team to do their work. Jerry stood up and decided to get lunch. He texted a note to his assistant, Jennifer, letting her know that he'd be at lunch until fourteen hundred.

All he could do now was wait.

35

Edgar hummed along with the radio on the drive from the hospital to the warehouse but found himself stopping mid-song to wonder what was going on with the Beckman's. They certainly hadn't reacted the same way that other clients had. Usually, they were just so happy to be able to save their loved ones that it didn't matter what kind of information the Apex bosses wanted. Maybe they just weren't convinced that the cure would work. They were in for a surprise, that was for sure, he thought.

His mind trailed back to Apex. The interesting thing about the organization, Edgar realized, was that they never asked for money from the people they cured. They only wanted information. Why Kat Beckman had been so slow to respond, he didn't know. Maybe it was because she was a journalist?

Edgar pushed the whole situation out of his mind. He was done with Aldham. The team would be packing up pretty soon and heading off to a new city. Edgar smiled to himself thinking about the month off that was coming. He had booked a cabin in Utah under the name John Johnson. It was a name just preposterous enough that no one would ever ask questions about who he was. The pictures of the cabin showed plenty of places to fish and hike, small lakes, boat rentals and places for people to camp. There was even a town nearby that had a few bars and casinos. It was perfect. He could hide there for a month and be back at work when the bosses were ready.

He pulled up to the warehouse. Edgar got out, closed the car door and took the steps up to the backdoor two at a time. As soon as he opened it, a happy Woof came trotting over, his tail wagging. Edgar closed the door and bent over, rubbing Woof behind his ears. Woof immediately flopped over on his belly and waited for Edgar to kneel down to give him a good rub, his mouth hanging open. That was one thing about dogs, Edgar thought, they really didn't care what you did as long as you had treats and time for them.

"Come on, boy." Woof hopped up and followed him back into the office. On a shelf were Woof's favorite bacon flavored treats. Woof sat patiently on the floor, watching Edgar until Edgar reached up and retrieved one. Woof took the treat from Edgar and trotted off, his tail wagging.

"Oh, to be a dog," Edgar said out loud, just as the other nurse came in. Mary, Meredith -- it didn't matter. "What's going on?" he asked.

Mary, or Meredith, was dressed in scrubs, just like he was. She had a tablet in her hand. She was reasonably attractive, but the permanent scowl on her face made her hard to look at. "The bosses called. We are out of here soon."

Edgar smiled. "That's good news."

"Just a few things to wrap up. They've authorized pay."

Edgar and the other Apex employees got paid after they completed a city. While they were at work, all of their expenses were covered. It was really a good deal, as far as Edgar was concerned. The fact that they trafficked in information didn't really bother them. After all, if it helped someone...

On the back wall of the office were pictures of the targets from this trip. Edgar knew exactly what had happened to all of them, except Laura Beckman. He stared at them for a minute. Some of them were blacked out, but on most of them, he had drawn a green box around their picture. The nurse that had tried to expose them, Sarah, was marked up with black ink. Roger, the husband of the real estate CEO, had a green box around his picture. Laura Beckman's picture was still blank. She was the last person for this trip.

Edgar walked into the office where his tablet was charging on the counter next to a box of peanut butter cookies. Woof trailed along. As Edgar opened it and powered up, he tossed half the cookie to Woof. He logged into Mercy Memorial's hospital records. Somehow, the Apex bosses always got them doctor level access to every medical record they needed. Undoubtedly, someone had paid for the cure with that access. Edgar chuckled quietly thinking of the hospital attorneys if they ever found out. That would most definitely be a HIPPA violation.

He tapped on the screen and searched Laura's name. One of the things that he liked most about the program they had is that he could see the diagnosis and medications and live streaming stats. If a patient was on a blood pressure cuff, oxygen, oxygen level monitor or a heart monitor, they could see it. It showed the whole floor on one display page. While he waited for there to be a change in Laura's condition, he decided to get a few hours of sleep.

When Edgar woke again, he stretched and refreshed the page that showed Laura's monitors. He frowned, checked her name and zoomed back in again. For some reason, her heart rate was really slow and her oxygen level had dropped to ninety-two. If she had gotten the treatment, her heart rate and oxygen levels should have returned to normal by now.

Edgar scratched his head and rubbed his beard. Maybe that

Kat woman hadn't given her the dose in time? Maybe it had degraded too much to use?

Edgar started to pace. That shouldn't have been the case. The cure should have worked already. While Edgar told her that it was only good for an hour out of the cooler, that wasn't exactly true. In reality, the serum was viable for at least four hours out of the cooler. It had been tested. Even if it was out of the cooler for six hours, Laura should have shown some improvement.

Edgar looked at Mary/Meredith and said, "I have to run over to Mercy. I'll be back in a little bit."

Mary/Meredith looked at him and squinted the lines around her eyes creating crevices, "Are you sure?"

"I know. I'll be alright."

Too many trips to a hospital were dangerous for Apex workers. Too many doctors and nurses buzzing around. The chance that Edgar or a team member could get caught rose exponentially the more times they visited, but he just had to see what was happening.

He went into the bathroom, changed into a suit and added glasses. The advance team had left him with a briefcase that he could use as well. It was filled with brochures on drugs that he could use to backstop his fake identity, plus an ID card. He knew his story was established, so even someone asked, he'd have credentials he'd need. He picked up the briefcase and nodded at Mary/Meredith, who just scowled at him. It was as if she said, if you get in trouble, it's not on me.

She was right about that. If he got in trouble, it would be on him. No one would come to his rescue unless the Apex bosses determined that they absolutely needed him and no one else would suffice. He knew that the odds of being irreplaceable were slim to none. He had to be careful.

The drive to Mercy Memorial took a little bit longer than usual. The traffic clotted the roads with impatient people wanting to get to their shopping, banking and back to work. By the time Edgar turned down the long, manicured driveway to the hospital, he was annoyed. He wasn't used to dealing with traffic. Up ahead, there was a dark blue security car circling the lot. Edgar knew who they were looking for -- people locked out, with a flat tire or domestic issues. Everything tended to happen at hospitals, that was for sure. He turned the wheel and pulled the grey sedan in a parking spot marked "visitors only." He smoothed his suit coat and slinging the briefcase strap over his shoulder. "I look like a perfectly respectable salesman," he muttered.

Now that morning had broken, the daytime temperature in Aldham was starting to rise. Edgar had started to sweat under the suit jacket. The front doors to the hospital whooshed open, welcoming him with a blast of cool air. He walked slowly to the elevators, checking his phone whenever someone tried to catch his eye. He rode up the elevator with a doctor. The doctor never looked his way, spending the whole time scrolling through something on his phone. Two respiratory therapists who must have been on their break joined them. They were whispering about the doctor that was on his phone. Edgar couldn't make out what they were saying. He tried not to laugh out loud. It always surprised him how clueless people were. Here he was, right in front of them. He was wanted in more states and countries than he could count and they had no idea. Talk about hiding in plain sight.

The elevator stopped on the third floor and the doctor and therapists got off, the doctor still looking at his phone, the therapists still talking about him. The doors closed and Edgar was alone. He set down his briefcase and tightened his tie. Ties were not his thing, but he knew he needed to look the part. He picked up the briefcase just in time for the doors to open on the oncology floor. Every other trip to the hospital meant that he went through the staff doors. This time, he had to go through the visitor's doors, washing his hands and walking on the sticky disinfecting paper. He wondered if it actually did anything to help the patients.

Out in the hallway, he watched and waited, moving towards a wall behind a cart that he had seen there for the last few weeks. He pretended to look at his phone and opened his brief-case. Every now and again, he glanced down the hallway trying to see where the doctors and nurses were positioned. Nurses and aides darted from room to room, pushing laptops on rolling carts, their pockets full of the morning doses. He watched them crisscross the hallway for a few minutes and then saw a pack of doctors head towards one room. They were talking excitedly, smiles smeared across every face. Edgar over-heard one of them saying, "We have seen a couple of patients like this recently. Our new immunotherapy seems to be working on even stage four cases."

The staccato muttering kept on for a few seconds until a small woman with her hair pulled back in a severe bun at the nape of her neck and a navy dress quieted them. He assumed she was the Chief of Oncology for Mercy Memorial, "Let's keep it down when we go into the room. No talking unless you are spoken to. No reason to overwhelm the patient."

The gaggle of doctors followed the click-clack of the woman's high heels into the room. Edgar was too far away to hear what they were saying, but he knew that the men's room was just past the room they had entered. He decided to pretend to make a trip to use the bathroom to get closer. He couldn't stand next to the cart for much longer without questions. He walked past Laura Beckham's room and glanced inside. He could barely see her, but what he did see was a small figure curled up, facing away from the door. She looked tiny and tired. Her vitals weren't good. Edgar frowned. He hadn't realized how far she had slipped until he passed her room. Unfortunately, the yellow serum was doing its job.

Edgar furrowed his brow, but kept walking, not wanting to draw attention to himself. He passed the room where all of the doctors had entered. The blinds on the window were fully open and the lights were on. Edgar paused for one second, pretending to look at something on his phone. Inside, the doctors had gathered around a man's bed, his young daughter sitting on the bed next to him. His legs were dangling off the side of the bed, his feet still in hospital socks. Nearby was a tray of food that was empty. The doctor in the navy-blue dress was talking to the patient and to the other physicians in the room, her face ablaze with a smile.

A nurse startled Edgar, "Crazy what happened, right?"

"I was kind of wondering. I saw all the doctors go in. What's going on?" Edgar noticed that she was young and fit, her blonde hair pulled back into a ponytail. She had on navy blue scrubs and a pair of colorful tennis shoes. Her badge said her name was Katie.

"The docs aren't exactly sure. Lawrence has been getting immunotherapy. All of a sudden, it seems to have worked. He woke up this morning famished. The guy ate four eggs and four pieces of toast, plus bacon and sausage."

"Wow," Edgar commented. "That's a lot of food. What kind of cancer did he have."

Katie squinted her eyes. "I'm not sure I'm supposed to really say..."

Edgar leaned over, pretending to read her badge, "Oh, it's okay, Katie, I'm Paul Johnson. I'm with Medicus Pharmaceuticals. We provide a whole suite of the treatments you use." He patted his pockets. "Geez, I forgot my badge in the car. I'll have to run down to get it."

He watched Katie's face relax. "That happens to me all the time." She took a step in a little closer to him. He could smell her body spray. Sweet and floral. She clutched the tablet she was holding to her chest as she spoke, "Lawrence had stage four colon cancer. We didn't think that he'd make it past this week. The doctors were out of options. It's a sad case really. He's a single dad. Wife killed in a car accident a year ago, just before he was diagnosed." She nodded toward Lawrence's room. "That's Allie with him. She's six. Just a joyful little kid."

"So, what happened, Lawrence -- that's his name, right?" Edgar was putting on a show. Katie nodded, "He just woke up this morning feeling better?"

Edgar saw Katie's eyes get really big, "Yeah. It was the craziest thing. Yesterday, he was on all sorts of pain meds. We couldn't get him to eat or drink anything. The docs were at the end of their rope. Then this morning, I come in and he's buzzing me before I even put my bag down. He wants a big breakfast and coffee. We drew a blood sample and there are no cancer markers in his results. None at all. It's really a miracle." Katie's pager went off, "Sorry, I have to go. Nice to meet you, Paul," she chirped as she walked away.

Edgar took one more look in Lawrence's room and walked toward the bathroom, keeping his head down. He went into a stall, pretended he was using the bathroom and then flushed, washing his hands as he left. He walked back the way he came, pretending to be absorbed by his phone again.

On the way out of the hospital, he didn't know what to think. There was no doubt in his mind that Lawrence had gotten the dose instead of Laura. That was clear. Did he care, he wondered? Not that much. The bosses had the information they needed. Who the Beckman's chose to give it to really didn't matter except that he'd have to have Mary/Meredith go in and wipe out Lawrence's records as soon as he left the hospital. It was time to head out of town. Time to go back into the shadows. The cabin in Utah was waiting for him.

36

The glow of morning came. Kat wasn't sure if either she or Steve had slept at all. At one point, Steve got up and went out of their bedroom. Kat didn't know where. She felt the bed move and saw Steve's broad back facing away from her as he sat on the edge of the bed. When they were first married, she would have reached for him. They weren't in that same spot now. Steve had left the bedroom right after that. He didn't come back. Kat didn't know what time it was. She didn't care. She turned over and pulled the blankets up close to her face.

The next thing she remembered was hearing Jack's feet pattering down the hallway. She heard the creak of their bedroom door open. Jack's head appeared as she opened her eyes, his hair mussed from sleep. Not surprisingly, he was wearing his favorite truck pajamas.

"When did you get home, little man?" she asked, her voice creaking with exhaustion.

"Just now, mama. Daddy came to get me."

Kat sat up in bed, feeling disoriented, pushing her hair behind her ears. "I'm glad to see you. Did you have fun?"

"Yup," Jack left, the noise of his little feet growing dim as he trotted down the steps to the first floor.

Kat looked out the window. It was a cloudy day. Rain must be in the forecast, she thought. She tilted her head from side to side, trying to get the stiffness out when she realized that she didn't know what time it was. She swung her legs to the side of the bed, letting them hang down. She reached for her phone. The display read just after eight o'clock.

Kat used the bathroom, brushed her teeth and splashed cold water on her face. She needed a shower, but she wanted to see what was going on with her family first. At the bottom of the stairs, she turned into the kitchen. Steve was staring out of the window into the backyard. He was dressed in his running clothes and had a cup of coffee in his hand. There was a partially full sports drink on the counter next to his phone and earbuds.

"Hey," Kat said.

Steve didn't turn around. "Morning."

Steve's body language told Kat everything she needed to know. He was mad. "Did you go out for a run," she asked, hoping that she was reading him wrong.

"Yeah. I was up early. I stopped to get Jack when I got back."

There was no eye contact. She watched him put the coffee cup in the sink, pick up his cell phone and earbuds and start to walk toward the stairs. "What's going on?" she asked. "You weren't there when I woke up."

"I told you that I went for a run," he said and walked away.

The steps creaked as he went upstairs. She followed. Normally, she would just have let him go, but too much had happened. She had sacrificed too much for him to be angry. He was in their bedroom by the time she caught up. "What's going on? Why are you acting like you are mad at me?"

"I am mad." Steve's eyes flashed at her for just a second.

"What are you mad about?"

"Are you kidding me? You gave that dose to some guy named Lawrence. That was for mom. It wasn't for him."

"What did you want me to do, just throw it away? She didn't want it. You couldn't even get her to take it! What was I supposed to do?" Kat closed their bedroom door. This wasn't a conversation that Jack needed to hear.

"I wanted you to give it to her anyway. What was she gonna do, fight you?"

"Then you should have done it yourself. I tried. I got it for her, at what may end up being a great deal of personal expense, and all you can do is yell at me because she didn't want it?"

Kat watched Steve. He said nothing. He turned and walked into the bathroom, slamming the door. A well of confusion and sadness forced its way up into her throat. She felt tears form but wiped them away with the sleeve of her nightshirt before they could fall. She was not going to lose it because Steve couldn't see the forest for the trees, that's for sure. He was being completely unreasonable. At that moment, she just had to get away.

Kat changed her clothes, putting on black running tights, a green tank top and covering it with a grey quarter zip windbreaker. She put her hair up into a headband, getting her bangs off of her face. She sent Steve a quick text. "Going running. Please watch Jack."

She picked up her running shoes from the corner of their bedroom and went down the stairs. Jack was in the family room, still in his pajamas, rolling his trucks on the floor. "Hey, buddy?" Jack didn't say anything, he just looked up at her. "I'm going to go for a run. Dad is in the shower. He will be right down. If you are hungry, just tell Dad and he will make you something. Okay?"

"Yup," Jack said, looking right back at his trucks.

· · ·

THE MORNING WAS STILL COOL when Kat left the house. She did a couple of quick stretches in the driveway and put her cell phone into her armband so her hands would be free while she ran. Earbuds in, music starting to run in her ears, she began to jog down the street.

All of the houses in their neighborhood looked so placid. There were a few homes that had papers on their front walks. Some had garage doors open. Some didn't. She passed two people out for their morning walk with their dogs. A man a few doors down had pulled his mower out of his garage, probably trying to beat the rain.

She and Steve had chosen this neighborhood because of the nice lots and cute homes. They weren't the biggest homes in the city, and they weren't the newest, but she and Steve had fallen in love with the way that people took care of their homes. Almost every home had a big tree in the front yard. Shade blanketed the sidewalk as she ran. There were plenty of families in the area, with plenty of kids Jack's age for him to get to know. The local public schools were good, which would save them money on private school tuition. Kat wasn't sure she and Steve would ever be able to afford private school for Jack unless either she won a Pulitzer or Steve's consulting business grew.

Step after step, Kat felt the tension evaporate. That was the thing about running, she knew. It wasn't comfortable when she started. She was always achy, her muscles complaining about the pounding and her lungs trying to adjust to the need for more air. A mile or so into her run, she always started to feel better. Her legs loosened and her body adjusted to having to breathe faster.

This run was no different. Her normal route took her out of their neighborhood and past the local park. Today, she decided to go around the park a few times. She wasn't eager to go home. She didn't know why Steve was blaming her, but what happened wasn't her fault. She ran the trail around the edge of the park once and then decided to walk a lap before starting her run home. They had been at this park just a day or so ago, where they met Van. At that time, they had hope. Now, she wasn't sure.

Slowing down, she waited for her breathing to return to normal. She looked around and saw some geese on the lawn, searching for bugs to eat for breakfast, as she continued to walk around the park. On the far side of the park, she decided to do some lunges and pushups. More than anything, she wanted to work the edge off. Maybe the exertion would get the rest of it out of her system. At least that's what she hoped.

Kat stretched again just before she was ready to start for home. She pulled the phone out of the pouch on her arm and checked to see if Steve had texted back. He hadn't.

They had suffered through fights before, but lately, Steve had become more and more distant. She thought it was Laura and the stress of trying to build a business while she was sick. But Steve had this uncanny knack for taking it out on her instead of focusing on the problem at hand.

Getting out by herself was nice. Kat drew in a deep breath. The morning couldn't have been nicer and yet there was a hollowness to it. She had felt like this in the past when there were stories that seemed to be finished, but she knew in her gut that there was more research to do. She did one more quad stretch and was getting ready to head for home when her phone beeped with an incoming text. Feeling hopeful, she looked at the screen. It wasn't Steve. It was Van.

"You around?"

"Yup," she replied. Kat waited for a second to see if he would reply. She pulled her arm across her body, hugging it with the other arm. The stretch across her back removed an ache she didn't even realize was there.

Just as she let go of the stretch, she heard her phone ring through her earbuds. Van. "What's going on?" she asked.

"You at home?"

"Nope. I'm out for a run at the park."

"Are you okay? What happened? Did you get the serum? You didn't text me last night."

"I'm sorry. I should have. Yeah, we are all fine. It didn't turn out the way that we thought it would."

"What does that mean?"

"Getting the serum wasn't too bad. But Laura wouldn't take it. She wanted us to give it to her friend."

"Did you?"

"Yes."

Kat could hear Van catch his breath, "Did the friend want it?"

"He was asleep."

It occurred to Kat just at that moment that she had never asked Lawrence if he wanted the serum. She didn't know if it worked, didn't work or killed him. She just did it without thinking through the consequences. She shook it off. There was nothing she could do now. If he was cured, he'd never know how it happened. He'd just be grateful, she imagined.

There was a pause before Van continued. "So, Laura is still sick."

"Yeah. Steve is blaming me." Kat started walking around the park, her own anger at being blamed for something completely outside of her control burning inside her. "He thinks I should have done it anyway."

Van didn't reply. Kat wondered if he realized that she and Steve went through rough patches occasionally. Van was always respectful. If he did know, he never said anything about it. Kat had to give him that.

"If Laura didn't want it, what were you supposed to do?" Van asked.

"He thought I should have forced it on her."

"Not a good plan. What does Steve want you to do now?"

"I think he wants me to text that guy again and see if we can get more." Kat looked around the park to see if anyone was close by, "But, I can't go back and get more information to trade with him. There's no way."

"What if I told you I think you should try?"

"What? Get more information?"

"Whatever it takes to get more of that serum, Kat. More people need access to it. A cure to cancer that these thugs refuse to share? You've got to be kidding me." She could hear the disgust in Van's voice.

"You can't tell me that you are okay with Laura dying."

"I'm not."

"Then you need to do something."

"Do what, Van? Get myself in even hotter water with the Army? Get myself killed? These guys mean business. I've never seen anything so well coordinated."

"Doing nothing means that you have to live with that. Doing nothing is a consequence in itself."

"Now you are trying guilt? You are just as bad as Steve. This isn't on my shoulders. I did what Steve wanted and his mom didn't want the treatment. It's over."

"You've never given up this easily before, Kat. I'm not sure what's up with you, but you have some thinking to do." Van paused, "I've got another call. Give me a shout later."

Kat was so angry that she didn't even say goodbye. Van had a lot of nerve lecturing her. All he had done was to look up some batch numbers and determine the fentanyl wasn't from Mercy. They didn't even know if Sarah's death was connected.

Kat stuffed her phone back in the pouch and started running toward home, pounding the pavement harder than she needed to. The strain in her lungs was what she needed. She needed to stop thinking. She needed to not be responsible for everyone all the time. She turned up the music and ran right across a street in front of an oncoming car. She didn't care. The car honked and she waved, never even looking in the driver's direction.

It was rare that Kat felt that kind of blind fury. The same thoughts kept racing through her mind. Why was she was being blamed and held responsible for what happened? It was over. Couldn't Steve see that?

Turning onto their street, Kat slowed her pace. She walked around the block to slow her heart rate again and checked her time on the way home. It was a full minute faster than her best time. It was amazing what anger could do. She walked up the driveway. The garage door was open. She needed to go into the house. She didn't want to go in the house. Sweat was running down the sides of her face and down her back. She opened the door and went in, hoping to get a better reception than before her run. The cooler air in the house felt good. She could smell pancakes cooking. Steve must have made breakfast for Jack.

These moments of unease were challenging for Kat. She weighed whether to go upstairs and shower or face Steve in the kitchen. There was always some reason he couldn't come and find her. It was infuriating. She just wanted him to make everything better. Why did she have to chase him?

"Hey," she said, deciding to go into the kitchen. Might as well get it over with. Jack was positioned at the table, sitting on his knees on one of the chairs. He was still a little too short for the chairs, but he refused to use a booster seat. He complained that he wasn't a little kid anymore. In front of him was a big stack of pancakes. Jack was eating the cut-up pancakes one piece at a time, the squares disappearing into his mouth. While he was eating, he had two trucks on the table. They were small ones, lined up neck and neck, each with a piece of pancake in front of them. It appeared that Jack was ready for a demolition derby.

"Mama!" Jack jumped off of his chair and hugged Kat's legs. "Did you run?" he asked. Kat nodded. "Did you go fast?" Kat nodded again, putting on a friendly face. She didn't want Jack to know how upset she was. When Laura died, they would all have plenty to be upset about. That didn't have to happen now. "Okay." He sniffed the air. "You need a bath. Pee yew!" With that, Jack went back to his food.

It was always so easy for little kids, Kat thought, a little bit of guilt and jealousy nipping at her heels. She turned to Steve, "You made breakfast."

"Yeah."

Jack slid down off of the chair he was sitting on, his trucks in hand, "I'm done!" he announced and ran off to go play. Kat was just about to remind him to help clean up, but she decided not to. She and Steve needed to get on the same page.

"How was your run?" Steve asked.

"Fine. Beat my time home but almost got hit by a car."

"Oh."

That wasn't exactly the response that Kat was hoping for. Your wife almost gets hit by a car and all you can say is oh? Kat started to walk back toward the stairs so she could take a shower. Passing Steve, she felt him catch her arm. "Wait," he said. "Can we go outside?"

"Okay." Kat bit her lip. She didn't want to. She didn't want to be anywhere near him right now. He had made it clear where he stood.

The door to the patio creaked as they opened it. She followed him outside without saying a word. She had mastered the silence game and was going to use it now.

Kat sat down on a chair and waited. Steve finally started to talk. "I called the floor this morning. Mom isn't good. Lawrence is going home."

It didn't take many words for the reality to hit home. She felt like she had been punched in the stomach. The serum did work. She didn't kill Lawrence by administering it, but Laura was still dying.

Before Kat could say a word, Steve said, "We need to get more. We need to. We have to save mom."

37

Hannah Carter had been pouring over surveillance feeds all morning. A breach at her site wasn't acceptable either personally or professionally. Just thinking about it made her stomach turn. Major Javorek had trusted her to manage the space and the data. It looked like Kat Beckman had gotten ahead of them. Hannah still wasn't sure how. What made her stomach churn even more was that she didn't know why. No one would pull a stunt like that without a good reason.

Hannah had parked herself in her office at the back of the facility since she'd found out about the breach. She'd been there all night, although she had taken a quick break to grab some coffee, tie her long hair into a tight bun and put on another coat of her favorite brownish lipstick. On the computer screen in front of her were the images of the cubicles and the front entrance. She rolled the film forward and back, trying to see what she had missed. She twirled a pencil in the fingers of her right hand, stopping occasionally to tap it on the desk.

The video didn't show much. She could see Kat come in. She could see her working at one of the cubicles. She could see her go through security on the way out. Could she just have accessed the information and not taken it with her, Hannah wondered? Why would she do that? What did she need the Bluebird roster for? Hannah's mind spun with questions. She set the pencil on the desk and pushed a button, "Thomas, could you come in here?"

"Of course," Thomas replied.

Hannah watched him lumber down the hallway, leaving his post at the security stand by the door. Hannah took off her glasses and rubbed her eyes. No sleep was beginning to take its toll on her. Thomas walked into her office, the size of his frame pretty much filling the whole doorway.

"How are you?" Hannah asked, trying hard to avoid the urge to pounce on him with a ton of questions.

"Good, thank you. You?"

One of the things that Hannah had always appreciated about Thomas was his good manners. It was hard to find people like that these days. She had been raised that "please" and "thank you" weren't optional words. He had apparently had the same upbringing.

"Listen, we've got a problem."

"I wondered why I didn't see you log out last night..." Thomas answered.

At least he's paying attention to what is going on, Hannah thought. Their last security man hadn't. That's why he wasn't there anymore. She had heard he was working at a local grocery store. "Yeah, I've been here all night."

"Well, you look very nice for someone working that hard."

Hannah smiled. Thomas was pleasant. Everyone in the office liked him. "Could you come over here and take a look at this video with me. I feel like I'm missing something."

For all of his size, she knew Thomas was as smart and as experienced as he was big and pleasant. He was former FBI. He had retired and needed a job to keep him busy. Keeping the site secure was a perfect job for him. Thomas moved in behind her desk. "What are we looking at?"

"I'm concerned that Kat Beckman accessed some information and took it with her." She saw Thomas frown. "Look at this." She started the video, which showed Kat waving to Thomas as she came in and going to a cubicle. Hannah slowed the video down when she got to the part where Kat was working on the computer. "She seems to be accessing something and it almost looks like she inserts a flash drive, but I can't tell from the screen."

"Did you ask the tech guys to look at the terminals? We'd have a record of that, right?" Thomas asked.

Hannah sighed, leaning back in her chair, back to twirling the pencil. "Yeah, I have the tech team looking at it right now. I should know pretty soon. They just got into the office. Can you tell me anything about Kat's visit?"

"She seemed fine when she came in and when she left. If I remember right, she wasn't here very long. I figured she was just reviewing a report or something."

"That's what she is supposed to be doing." Hannah looked out the window of her office and saw the tech team at the workstation Kat had used. There were three of them crammed into the cubicle, one guy sitting at the terminal and two hovering over his shoulder. Whether that was a good or bad sign, she didn't know. Hannah took a sip of her now lukewarm coffee. "Tell me about when she left. Anything seem off to you?"

Thomas pointed at the chair in front of Hannah's desk. "Okay for me to sit?"

"I'm sorry, of course."

"No nothing. We talked about her son. I asked after him. She seemed herself -- maybe in a hurry -- but nothing really out of the ordinary."

Hannah took a moment to fast forward to Thomas and Kat's interaction on the surveillance camera. She pivoted the screen so they could both watch it at the same time. "I see you search her bag here. Did you ask her about her encryption key?"

Thomas watched the video for a moment, leaning forward in his chair, and pointing suddenly. "Right there. I had her bag in my hand and asked her if she had it. It was in the pocket of her bag."

"I see you wanded her. Anything go off, seem different?" Hannah forwarded the video to the part where Thomas was using the wand on Kat so Thomas could refresh his memory.

Thomas leaned forward. Hannah watched his eyes focus on the video. There was no doubt in her mind that Thomas had been doing his job. At least she hoped that was the case.

"There. I wanded her pocket and her keys went off. Kinda strange, come to think of it. Most people keep their keys in their bag or put them on the stand. Anyone who has been in here more than once would know that we use a wand and metal sets it off."

Hannah rewound the video and played the security scene a few more times. She wished she was able to zoom in, but their current system wouldn't allow that unless it was happening in real-time. The recorded video was all from one angle and one distance. Frustrating.

Thomas interrupted her thinking, "What do you think she took?"

"Actually, we aren't sure she took anything at all. She wasn't the only person in the office. If it was her, she may have accessed some mission files." Normally, Hannah wouldn't have told their security guy anything, but with Thomas' background, he came with his own clearance. That had been a bonus when they hired him.

"Was it a recent mission or one of those that were out of top-secret status?"

"This one was from quite a while ago."

"So not top secret."

"No, it doesn't look that way. I just can't figure out why she'd be looking in those files anyway."

"Was the mission in Afghanistan by chance?" Thomas asked.

Hannah furrowed her brow, "Why do you ask?"

"I know you are pretty new here. Not sure if you know that Kat was deployed there as an embedded journalist. Saw some bad stuff. Humvee in her group got blown up. She almost lost her hand. Her wrist, to this day, is messed up. She was pretty messed up in the head, too, from what I've heard. PTSD." Thomas leaned back in his chair.

"I knew that she had been overseas, but didn't know it was Afghanistan. That's interesting."

She watched Thomas stand up. "If that's all?" he asked.

"Yep. I know you gotta get back."

"Yes, ma'am. If you need anything else, let me know."

"Thanks, Thomas. I will. You can leave the door open."

Before Hannah had a chance to even process Thomas' comments, one of the tech guys, Ben, came into her office. "Hannah?" Ben was pale and dark-haired with glasses. He always wore the same thing, dark pants and a plaid shirt. Long sleeve in the winter, short-sleeved in the summer.

"Yes?"

"I've got a little information on the file that you asked about. Kat Beckman's encryption key was used to access a file on a mission called Bluebird. It is an old mission. There's something strange, though."

"What's that?" Hannah asked, hoping that Ben would have information that would put this to rest.

"The only thing that she accessed was the mission roster."

"That's it?"

"She might have looked at the other pages in the file, but if she did, it was really quick, like she was looking for something in specific. The only page that she stayed on for any time at all was just the list of the mission personnel. That's it. She didn't seem interested in targeting or outcomes. I thought you should know that."

"Yeah, that's helpful." Hannah used both of her hands to smooth her pants down her thighs. All of the sitting was too much. She stood up.

"One more thing," Ben said, "Here a download of what she saw. Thought that might help. There is one bit of bad news. It looks like she might have copied it to an external flash drive."

Any calm that Hannah had left evaporated. The idea that Kat could have copied sensitive information and carried it out of her office put her over the edge. "Are you kidding me? How does that happen? I thought those encryption keys were the only thing that fit into the external drives?"

"Well..." Ben started. Hannah could tell by the look on his face he had bad news. "Remember a few weeks ago when I told you we had a new tech company come in to service the machines? They were working on upgrading the external drives. They said they would be more secure. Apparently, you can now fit any flash drive into the same drive as the encryption key. It was supposed to have special coding on it that would only work if the correct encryption key was used. The idea was that changing the code was more cost-effective than changing the hardware."

"What?" Hannah caught herself as her voice started to rise. She sat down in her chair, trying to compose herself. "Close the door."

She waited until Ben closed the door and she pointed at the chair in front of her desk, a silent ask to sit. "I'm sorry. This is alarming."

"I know. I'm really sorry. We just didn't catch it until now."

Hannah could feel a slow burn inside of her. She knew that she'd have not only a lot of explaining to do to Major Javorek, but an uphill battle to keep her job. "Let me go over this one more time. So, some company gets the contract to come in and do tech upgrades on the encryption key hardware and they don't understand that we can't use traditional flash drives?"

"Sort of. Not totally. The only cubicle with the bad drive was the one Kat used."

Hannah leaned back in her chair. Things were getting more complicated by the minute. Fury started to rise within her. She'd had a problem with anger. She'd even had been court-mandated to go to an anger management class. She felt the heat rising, but she tamped it back down for the moment. "There was only one cubicle that had the bad drive?"

"Yep. The tech ran out of the ones that we needed and just put that one in temporarily. He only needed a day to get the new one in. It was supposed to be installed yesterday."

"Why didn't he just close that terminal off?"

Ben looked down at his lap, clearly not enjoying being on the hot seat. "I guess his work order required him to get all of the terminals operational. I wanted to talk to him, but the tech called in sick. I called the company, but they can't seem to find him."

Hannah abruptly stood up from her desk. "I need to take a walk. When I get back, I want a report on my desk with all of those details." Hannah didn't wait for Ben to respond. She grabbed her ID, phone and wallet and walked out. She almost walked right past Thomas without a security scan. He gave her a cursory check and she went out the door. She pushed open the door that led to the hallway and the one that led out to the steps without breaking stride. Taking the steps two by two, she burst out into the bright sunlight of the parking lot. She leaned over and put her hands on her knees, catching her breath. It wasn't that she was out of shape. If anything, Hannah was in peak condition. She did cardio boxing and lifted weights on a regular basis. She had even started taking Muay Thai for self-defense. The anger did it to her. It sucked the oxygen out of her system. The memories of being with her therapist flooded back in her mind. "Hannah, your system can't take the adrenaline rush. You are going to hurt yourself. You have to control the anger."

Her anger was a beast. It had always been, even from a young age. Days like today brought it out into the open. Unchained it and let it loose. Her therapist thought it had something to do with perfectionism. Hannah wasn't so sure. She walked over to her car, a newer model Audi coupe and opened the trunk. She pulled out some tennis shoes and changed into them, putting her dress shoes into the back. She closed the lid and started to walk. Major Javorek knew about her issues. The way anger pushed her. To run a site like the one she did, the Army knew everything, down to the name of her Tabby cat, Scotch. Hannah started to walk. She forced herself to slow her pace of walking. There was a small park nearby. When the stress in the office was too much, she walked there. Today was one of those days.

On most days, just outside the park there was a street vendor that sold water and snacks. She bought a bottle of cold water and a small package of crackers. She crossed the street and entered the park, heading for the shade of the duck pond. Today had been too much to take, she thought, feeling her anger slide back down into her chest. The walking helped. Her therapist had told her to think of her feet as leaving puddles of anger with every step she took as if it was leaking out of her shoes. The image was a little strange, Hannah remembered thinking when she heard it. Today she was grateful she had something to concentrate on that might quell the rage.

Hannah found a bench at the edge of the duck pond that was under the shelter of a tree. With her fair skin, sun without sunscreen wasn't a good fit. She didn't really care at the moment. She sat down and opened the package of crackers. A duck must have heard the rustling of the package because it swam right over to the edge of the pond. Hannah crushed the cracker between her fingers, tossing small crumbs onto the surface of the water. Watching the ducks feed -- it hadn't taken more than a moment for a whole group of them to gather -- calmed her nerves. She watched for details, another trick her therapist had told her. She looked for the way a cracker floated on top of the water, the particular coloring of the ducks that passed her, the noises their wings made when they flapped. These were things she could focus on instead of the drama at work.

Which brought her back to the problem at hand. She had so many pieces all contributing to one mess. The wrong encryption hardware brought in by a guy the new company couldn't even find who was supposed to replace it but never came back. Now they couldn't find him. She tossed another cracker piece into the water. Who was this new company and what happened to the old company? Why didn't Ben tell her there was a change? She started to feel suspicious of Ben. She put the package of crackers down and quickly texted him, "What happened to our old tech company?"

Her phone pinged about three seconds later. That was the good thing about tech guys. They always had their tech with them. "Apparently they were bought out. The new guys were from their headquarters. I just found out last week."

Hannah set her phone down on the bench and kept tossing crackers to the ducks. At least Ben had an explanation. Why he didn't tell her, she didn't know. She refocused on the ducks. There was a mama duck that came by with five ducklings. They couldn't have been more than a few weeks old, but they managed to scurry through the grass and make their way into the water. The babies were cute. Hannah tossed most of the rest of her crackers to them. They needed to eat. They were babies.

The ducks hung around for a few minutes after she had no more crackers to feed them, waiting. Once they figured out she was done, they paddled their way across the pond to a mom and her young daughter that were standing on the edge of the bank across the pond. The child had long dark hair, not much different than Hannah's, although she didn't have Hannah's porcelain skin. The mom had a bag of what looked to be pieces of bread. The daughter, who was probably three, threw the pieces of bread in the water the best she could with her short little arms. Hannah realized that the little girl was probably close in age to Kat's son.

Hannah had read Kat's file last night. The part about her being deployed hadn't been in it. She was sure that Javorek knew all about that though. There was little the Army didn't know if they didn't want to find out.

In Kat's file, it described her husband as being a consultant with a growing business. There was no conflict there. There was a picture of the family at a park not unlike the one that she was at now, playing on the swings. There had been a picture of Kat in the file. The one they used for her ID. The family picture was from the firm they used to do the background checks. Hannah knew about Kat's journalism degree, that she had basically no family and where she and Steve lived. There had been no real red flags until today.

Kat shifted on the bench, turning away from the mother and daughter and looking down the trail that led into the woods. She picked at the wood on the bench with one of her fingernails. A little piece of wood came off of the bench and she flicked it into the grass. The whole scenario bothered her. Why was Kat looking at mission files from Afghanistan? Did she know someone on the mission? Was it for a story she was doing? Why wasn't she more interested in the objectives or outcomes? Why was it only the mission roster?

Hannah stood up and started walking back to the office, crinkling the cracker bag and her water bottle, now empty, before tossing them into a trash can. Even more bothersome was that even though Thomas had tried to do his job the tech guys seemed to have made the access possible. She looked at her cell phone screen and pulled up Major Javorek's personal cell number. She pushed send to call him.

It didn't even ring before he picked up, "Javorek," he said at the other end of the line.

"Major, it's Hannah."

"Hello. How are things?"

"I have a bit of an update for you."

"Go ahead with that."

Hannah had noticed that although the Major was in the Army, he tried to talk in a non-military tone to her. She saw him treat other civilians the same way. It was a nice touch. Maybe she'd figure out a way to tell him that someday. "I don't have anything definitive for you yet. I'm walking back to the office now."

"You left?"

"Ah, yes. I did." Hannah paused. "I was on the verge of an episode. Thought it was better to take a walk than create a scene."

"Copy that. Go on."

"I had Thomas, our security guy -- he's former FBI if you remember, look at the video with me. There is nothing obvious about it. If she managed to get information out of the building, it would be a miracle."

"Did she?"

"We are still studying that, sir. What I can tell you is that we had a tech glitch."

"What kind of a tech glitch?"

"Apparently our normal IT maintenance group was bought out by another firm. The guy they sent to work on our encryption hardware last week managed to do the job correctly, except for one terminal. That would be the one that Kat used."

"What did he do wrong on that terminal?"

"He installed a common flash drive instead of the ones that we normally use."

"What kind do you normally use?"

Hannah passed a few people walking down the street as she talked to the Major. They looked calm. She probably did, too. The roiling in her stomach would need a good dose of antacids at some point.

"Hannah, are you there?"

Hannah's attention went back to the Major. "Sorry sir, just dealing with a bit of stomach upset. I got distracted."

"No problem. What were you saying about the flash drives?"

The Major was so forgiving of her idiosyncrasies -- her need to leave the office for a walk, her almost-addiction to antacids, particularly the cherry ones, and her pencil twirling. It made her wonder if he had interesting habits of his own. "Yes, I'm sorry. The flash drives. The ones that we usually use -- they were recommended by the tech company and were approved by your office -- are the only ones that fit the encryption key. No regular flash drive can fit in it. And, they don't allow any files to be copied. They are read-only. They read the encryption key, identify the user and then open the terminal to them."

"What did this joker install?"

Hannah could hear the impatience forming in the Major's voice. "Sir, he installed a common flash drive reader. Any flash drive from any drug store could read the files and make copies."

"And somehow, the encryption key worked, too?"

Hannah thought back to what Ben had told her as she walked past the snack stand. The man working there was whistling a tune as he turned hot dogs that were simmering in water. The smell was intoxicating. If she wasn't so concerned about her stomach, she probably would have bought one. The little girl and her mom that Hannah had seen at the duck pond had stopped and Hannah saw the man hand the little girl a foot-long hot dog in a bun. It was sitting in a little paper boat. The little girl, her ponytail waving, was grinning from ear to ear. Hannah stopped for a moment to watch, trying to pay attention to Major Javorek and enjoy the peace of watching the mom and daughter.

The mom had whipped out her cell phone and was having the little girl pose with her giant hot dog as Hannah walked by. Hannah refocused on Major Javorek. "The drive he put in had both an encryption port and one for the flash drive. The information that Ben has indicated that it was supposed to be an overnight fix while they got the new drive-in. The thing is..."

"Is there more?" Major Javorek asked, the edge to his voice increasing every single time Hannah relayed more information.

"Well, sir, the company that hired the tech can't seem to find him. He called in sick yesterday and now he's not answering his phone. He never showed up for work."

"Not acceptable. Get this under control."

"I know, sir, but..." Hannah didn't have a chance to finish her sentence. The Major had already hung up. Hannah sighed as she walked along, wondering if this would be the end of her job at the site. A breach like this is such a problem, she thought. Her career could be on the line. Thinking about it made her heart pound.

Hannah made it back to her car and put her work shoes back on. She went back down to the office to see if Ben had made any progress in finding the technician. It was going to be a long day.

38

After her shower Kat went back into the kitchen, her hair still damp, the waves curling around her ears. She grabbed a peanut butter protein bar from the cabinet and put on a pot of coffee to brew. She never felt like eating much after working out, but she knew she'd be ravenous later if she didn't. There was no telling what the day would bring.

Steve came into the kitchen, his feet padding as he moved from the wood floor to the rugs. "I think we need to talk," he said.

"Really," Kat said, her mouth half full of a bite of the peanut butter bar. "What would you like to talk about?" She knew it came out sarcastically, but she didn't care.

"I need to tell you that I'm sorry."

"That's a start," Kat turned away from him to pour herself a cup of coffee.

"But I think we need to try to save mom."

Kat stopped pouring and put the carafe back in the machine. She stared at the curling steam coming out of the cup, trying not to raise her voice. She didn't want Jack to hear her.

She didn't want to lose her cool. "How, exactly, do you think we are going to accomplish that? We had our chance. For all I know, the Army could be sending MPs here at any minute to take me away to question me." She balled her hands into fists, the anger surging through her. "Your mom had her chance. She didn't want it. Didn't matter what I did or the risks I took. She didn't want it." She tried to move away, but he didn't give her a choice.

Steve put his hands on her shoulders. "Kat, this isn't just about you. This is about me and Jack and our family, too. I know you have sacrificed. I appreciate it." He leaned over. She didn't have any choice but to look at him. "There is a bigger picture here. There are people that have a cure for cancer that are blackmailing families for information. That much we know is true. And it isn't right."

With that, Steve let go of her. She stared at his back as he walked to the other end of the kitchen. "What is that you want me to do? I've done everything I could. Why is this my problem?" Even as the words came out of her mouth, she knew they were wrong. Sure, she was a journalist. That much was true. Her job was to report the facts. But she was also a human. A broken one with baggage, but a human nonetheless. Steve was right. There was no excuse for what the man in the scrubs and the so-called Apex Solutions people had come up with. A cure for cancer should be public domain, not the privilege of the few who had information to trade once they had been chosen. None of it was acceptable.

Kat sighed. "What do you have in mind?"

Steve sat down at the table. She hadn't noticed, but he had found the burner in her bag. "You found the burner."

He nodded. He had it between his two hands, resting his elbows on the table. "I think we should ask for another dose."

Kat sat down at the kitchen table. "We already gave them what they wanted. They aren't going to just give us more of the medicine because we are nice. We'd have to have something to trade."

"Maybe we do?"

Kat furrowed her brow and started playing with a stray thread that was coming off the edge of the placemat. "What are you talking about? I am not going to get more information from the secure site. That's a no-go. Not happening."

"I'm not suggesting that. What I am suggesting is that we ask. I mean, what's the worst they could do? Tell us no?"

Kat continued to fidget with the thread. It was coming off of the corner. She pulled at it slightly and watched the stitch next to it tighten. She coiled the thread around her index finger and pushed it off with her thumb, creating a little knot. It wouldn't hold. She just kept fidgeting with it. She looked at Steve, wanting to be cooperative, but a surge of anxiety rose, the bile catching in her throat. She swallowed it. "Tell me how you think this plays out."

"It's simple. We send a text asking if we can get more. He might ask why, but I'm thinking he already knows mom didn't get the dose."

"Why would you think that?"

"Remember the cable guy out front?" Kat didn't even realize that Steve had noticed him. "No one needs that much cable work. He was there for days. I think he was watching us."

Kat nodded, "I think you are right."

"They are probably watching the hospital too. So, we send a text. That's all. We ask if we can get more. Maybe they need something from me? Depending on what they say, we either say yes or no. If they ask you for anything, it will be up to you to decide whether or not you are willing."

"What if they want more classified information? What do we do then? I'm not going to jail." As soon as she said it, she realized that ship had already sailed. She might be going to jail anyway.

"It will be up to you. Either way, I promise I won't get mad."

Kat didn't believe him. He would get mad. That was, if the text even went through and if he even responded. Those were two big ifs.

Kat needed time to think, but she wasn't sure that Steve would give it to her. She saw him passing the phone from hand to hand, barely moving. She rolled her wrist. She felt him watching her.

"If you don't want to do this, it's okay," he said.

Kat didn't that either. She knew his mind was made up. "You are sure that if he asks me to do something, to get more information, and I don't want to, you are going to be okay with that?" She saw him nod. "You understand, that means your mom might die."

"By the time we get the dose, she might be dead anyway. I feel like I've got to do something, though. I can't just sit by her bedside knowing there is something I could do and not do it. I couldn't live with myself. She doesn't have anyone else to help her."

Kat put her hands on the arms of the chair and stood up, folding them over her chest. "I don't like any of this. The whole thing makes me nervous but go ahead."

She barely got the sentence out before Steve had the phone open and was typing a text.

"What are you saying," Kat said, leaning over him.

"Not much," he answered. "Just, 'we need another dose.'" The text had gone out before Kat could even reply.

39

The phone in Edgar's pocket vibrated as he walked out of the warehouse with Woof wagging behind him. It was time to head to Utah. The teardown group would be here in twenty-four hours. By the time they were done, no one would know they were ever in Aldham. Their work was over.

Edgar set down his briefcase so he could reach into his pocket for the burner phone. There was a safe house about twenty miles out of town where he would pick up a new phone and a new car -- that was the plan. He opened the phone, expecting it to be one of the bosses with instructions for him. It wasn't. The text read, "We need another dose." He checked the number and let out a low whistle. It was the Beckman's. He stared at the phone for a minute and then started to nod to himself, "Woof, it looks like we might not be quite done. C'mon boy."

Edgar headed back up the steps into the warehouse, Woof right behind him. The door slammed shut as he went in. He almost bumped into Mary/Meredith. She had let her hair down and had a duffle bag over her shoulder. Out of her work clothes, she was actually pretty and younger than Edgar had realized. "Hold your horses, Kemosabe," he said to her. "We might not be done."

She didn't reply, just stared at him and set her bag down. He headed into the office and placed a call. A woman's voice answered. "Yes?"

"We have a development," he said.

"Go on."

"I need another soccer ball for the game."

Each client was assigned a theme. Beckman's, since their name was so close to David Beckham, the British soccer star, had been assigned a soccer theme. It was the way they could talk without risk.

The woman on the other end of the phone, one of the bosses, paused. "I thought the game was over?"

"Apparently, they'd like to get back on the field."

"I'll see..." The line went dead. He'd have to wait to see what the bosses wanted to do.

40

The woman turned to her assistant, a small, bald man with thick glasses who smelled like old clothes. "Can you pull up the Beckman's file?" With a couple of clicks, their file was displayed on the monitor.

The woman, neatly dressed in a long-sleeved shirt, down vest and pants sat with her assistant in the library of an estate in England, hours away from anything that even looked like civilization. The room had high ceilings with books floor to ceiling. The books had been there when the woman bought the property. She still didn't really know what most of the books were, never really taking the time to pull many off the shelves. The land agent had just mentioned that they were valuable. The room was quite dark, the windows covered with velvet curtains and sheers. The afternoon light could hardly penetrate them.

The woman liked it that way. Being in the shadows was part of her identity. She never could understand people who wanted to put their names all over social media or on billboards or even worse, be on television. Even when they had delivery people come to the estate, she always went upstairs or stood under a stand of trees far enough away that no one would ever notice her. Anonymity gave her complete freedom and she liked it that way.

The Beckman file displaced neatly on the screen. Photos of Laura's family -- Steve, Kat and Jack -- as well as Laura's home, and Kat and Steve's home were part of the file. Financial information, their daily routines, who their friends were -- these were all pieces of information that Apex kept on their clients.

There was medical information on Laura as well. Though she hadn't practiced medicine for decades, the woman's background as a doctor helped her to understand where a client was in the disease process. All of this was meant to give them leverage.

Edgar's notes were in the system as well. Contacts made, serum given, trips to the hospital. They had him document it all on their secure servers. You never knew when the information could become important. Now was one of those times.

The woman congratulated herself on her impeccable planning as she clicked through the file. As she stared at the screen, she could feel her assistant hovering behind her. Normally, she would have sent him away, as she preferred working alone. Today, she kept him close by in case she needed action. It was feeling like a day for a windfall. She would need him to do his job if that was the case.

"Here," she said, pointing a finger at the screen. "This is who we want."

The man clicked through a few more files and brought up a bio, complete with pictures, vehicle information, height, approximate weight and a complete work history. The woman interrupted again, "Wait. We have a buyer for information on that."

Her work now wasn't much different than when she was a doctor. As a physician, she diagnosed a problem, a lack in someone's health, and matched the correct treatment. In her work now, she diagnosed a lack of information and found someone who could fill it. The person whose health had been compromised was restored. The person who needed information was given what they needed. In turn, she and her teams were compensated generously for the solutions they provided. They were at the top of their field. That was what being part of Apex Solutions was all about.

The woman reached into her shirt pocket and pulled a single sheet of yellow legal paper out. There were two columns of information. One had names, one had needs. Straight lines were drawn between some of the names and needs making a perfect spiderweb on the page. She unfolded it and looked carefully at the list and the file on the screen. "Let's match these two."

"For Beckman?"

"Yes."

The woman said no more. She took the piece of paper and refolded it, putting it back in her pocket and left the room. Her assistant would take care of the rest. She would update the paper later once the match was completed with a new, perfectly straight line. All she could do was wait. She took quick steps out of the room, through the back hallway and out into the yard, starting one of her many daily walks.

41

E dgar had been waiting by the door to the warehouse. He had just let Woof out to do some digging in the abandoned yard after feeding him. His phone rang. "Apparently, we've been able to schedule another match," the male voice said on the other end of the line.

"Really?" Edgar answered, hoping he didn't sound too surprised by the information that they had more work for him in Aldham.

The male voice continued, "You will be compensated for your time on the field, of course. You and the rest of the team."

"Thank you." Edgar had learned when dealing with the bosses that less talking was better. They didn't want to know anything about him. They just wanted him to listen.

"We've sent the information." With that, there was a click at the other end of the line. Calls with them were always short and very rare. They preferred their online portal for communications.

Edgar leaned a little farther out the door, the warmth of the sun hitting his back. Utah would have to wait for a few days. He whistled for Woof, who picked up his head and trotted right over to him, his ears flopping as he ran. Edgar bent over and scratched Woof's head, "You are a good boy," he said, as Woof tilted his head left and right trying to get the most out of the scratch. "Come on in. We've got work to do."

The metal door clanked against the doorframe as soon as Edgar shut it. He knew the next steps to take. They were the same as every other client they had. Edgar walked through the warehouse to the office and opened his laptop. He used the fingerprint identifier to boot up the machine and waited for it to warm up. There were only a couple of icons on the page. He clicked on the one that said, "client portal" and waited. Another round of fingerprints, a retinal scan and a thirteen-digit passcode got him into the site.

Apex had not only developed a system for getting information, but they had also developed a system for protecting it. Information was their business and Edgar, though he knew he wasn't an expert in cybersecurity, figured that all of the steps just to get to the portal would keep them safe enough.

Edgar opened the file. There was only one in the portal. The bosses tended to only send them a few at a time in case they were compromised. To say they were a little paranoid would be an understatement, but Edgar didn't mind. It was less work for him to think about at one time. He clicked the pages in the file. There were only two. A photo of a man and a one-liner on the information they wanted. Edgar grunted.

He was startled by Mary/Meredith's voice behind him and nearly jumped up out of his seat.

"What's that?" she asked.

"Geez, you need to scare me like that?" Edgar settled back into his chair and looked again at the file. "Looks like we have another go-round with our soccer team."

"Really? We never do that. I thought we were leaving."

"Me too. I guess not just yet."

With that, Edgar reached for his phone and found the text string between he and Kat. His reply was short. "Okay. Let's play. Tell the editor we need to make a delivery to Harbor Canyon. You have twenty-four hours."

42

Kat looked at the burner phone, chewing her bottom lip. She was alone in the kitchen. Steve had gone into the backyard with Jack for a little fresh air. Steve's laptop screen had gone black. She closed it as she walked by.

"Steve?" She looked outside and saw Steve chasing Jack. They each had a truck in their hands, both of them making loud vrooming noises that normally would have earned them a chastening from Kat for bothering the neighbors, but she didn't care. She watched him stop in his tracks, hand Jack the truck and trot over to her.

"What's going on?"

Kat didn't say anything. She just handed Steve the phone. He opened it and looked at the message. "Does this mean...?" He didn't finish his sentence.

"I think so," Kat said. Feelings rushed at Kat faster than she could process them. Fear, anger, frustration. They washed over her in a series of waves.

"The editor? Do they mean Van?"

Kat's eyebrows raised, "I guess so."

Steve opened the phone again, "Any idea what Harbor Canyon is?"

"Nope."

Steve closed the phone. "We've got one more day. I hope Mom can last that long."

Kat started to walk back towards the house, ignoring Steve's comment about his mom. They were all moving as fast as they could. "I need to call Van."

She walked back into the kitchen and pulled a burner phone out of the drawer. It was the same one she used to get in touch with TJ. He hadn't been of any help, but maybe Van would be willing, especially now that they had heard back from the man in the scrubs. She pulled his number from her phone and typed it in the display. He picked up on the first ring.

"This is Van."

"I need you to come over."

"Kat? I didn't recognize the number."

"I know. Can you come over now?"

"Is everything okay?"

"I'll tell you when you get here. Can you come over now?"

"Yes."

Kat put the phone down on the counter and looked out the window into the backyard. Steve and Jack were back at it, running and laughing. How Steve could act like he was with all of the stress they were going through was a mystery to her. So many things had become a mystery over the last few years. Maybe when this was all over, no matter what happened to Laura, she'd have time to figure things out. Kat folded her arms across her chest, still watching them. If she was arrested for treason, she'd have a lifetime in jail to do exactly that.

43

Van's head swam with questions. He had been in his office when Kat called. She had sounded some combination of afraid and determined. He didn't want her to feel that way. Her tone worried him. He stood up from his desk, pushing the papers he'd been working on in a file folder that he stuffed under his arm. He picked up his keys, wallet and cell phone. Something about her voice hadn't seemed right. The fact that she had called from a number that he didn't recognize worried him even more.

He leaned over and opened the bottom right drawer of his desk. There was a locked compartment. Van keyed in the code, opened it and pulled out a small semi-automatic pistol that he attached to his ankle with an ankle holster.

He walked out of the office and saw Alyssa at her desk. "Do me a favor?" he asked.

"Sure," Alyssa grunted, not looking up. She was working on a piece. She never liked to be disturbed.

"Let me take your car." It was more of a statement than a question. She picked up the keys and handed them towards him, not really at him, still not looking up.

He took the keys from her, "Thanks." He left his own keys on her desk. "Drive the truck for the next couple of hours."

"As if I'm going anywhere," Alyssa muttered.

Van used the back entrance of the office building to leave. Normally, he went out the front, but something in Kat's voice made him a bit leery of using the front entrance.

He went out to the parking lot and found Alyssa's car parked in the same spot it always was. He got into the white Toyota two-door and pulled out of the lot, taking the back streets until he had to merge into busier traffic to get to Kat's house. The whole way there, Van kept his eyes on the vehicles behind him. The people Kat was tangling with looked to be much better organized and dangerous than he originally thought. He was anxious to see why Kat called and why they needed to meet in person.

When he got onto Kat's street, he circled the neighborhood a couple of times, making sure he hadn't been followed. The only person on the street was a cable repair guy that appeared to be taking an early lunch. The guy gave him a little wave right before Van pulled into Kat's driveway.

Van parked the car off to the side of the driveway. He got out, grabbing the file folder, his phone, wallet and Alyssa's keys before closing the door and locking it. The door opened before he could ring the bell. Kat smiled at him. She looked pretty.

"Hey," he said following her into the house, trying not to look at her for too long. "I came as fast as I could."

He saw Kat motion for him to stay quiet and followed her out the back door into the yard.

It was a nice day. The rain from the day before had greened everything up, but it hadn't rained enough to make it muddy. It just dampened the dust down to a manageable level. Out of the corner of his eye, he saw movement. It was Jack.

Jack came running at Van, his fine hair flapping on the top of his head. In his hands, he had a red truck and a yellow truck.

He screeched to a stop before he ran right into Van. "Hi Van," Jack said.

All of a sudden, Van saw a smile peel onto Jack's face. "You have a funny name. Why is your name Van?"

"It's a family name, buddy."

Jack nodded and ran off.

Steve walked up from the back edge of the yard, trailing Jack. Van reached out his hand. Steve shook it. "How's your mom?" Van asked Steve.

"Not great."

Van looked at both Steve and Kat. "I'm guessing that's why I'm here?"

Van saw Kat nod. "Yes."

"Did something happen?" Van asked. "I thought you got the serum for your mom already?"

"We did," Kat said. She stared at Steve.

Steve pursed his lips, "Kat got the serum, but mom refused to take it."

"What?" Van asked. "What do you mean?"

Steve nodded and told the story. "Mom has a friend named Lawrence. A single dad with a young daughter. She thought he needed it more than she did. She wouldn't take it. She told Kat to give it to Lawrence."

Van paused. "Wait, you did that?"

He saw Kat press her lips together and nod. "The guy told us it was only good for an hour. We had no choice. I tried. I even had the syringe ready to put in her IV. She got really mad."

"What did you do?"

"I went down the hall and gave it to Lawrence."

"So, it works."

Van watched as both Kat and Steve nodded. The serum the man that drugged Kat had actually worked. "Do you know what kind of cancer the guy had?"

Steve looked at Van, "Yeah. Colon. Stage 4."

"And he's home?"

"So far as we know."

"Is that why you called me?"

Kat shook her head no. "Steve wants us to try to get more so we can save his mom. She agreed to take another dose if we could get it. We texted the man in the scrubs and he replied right before I called you." Kat extended a burner phone to him. "Seems they want something from you."

Van opened the phone and looked at the text. "Harbor Canyon? How do they?" Van quickly stopped talking and reread the text a couple of times, shutting the phone when he was done. He rubbed his hand through his hair and turned away from Kat and Steve.

"Van, what it is?" Kat asked. "What is Harbor Canyon?"

"Where are your phones?" Van asked, not answering Kat's question.

He saw Kat reach for her back pocket. "Here's mine."

Steve shook his head, "Mine is in the kitchen by my computer, I think."

Van took the burner, his own phone and Kat's and walked over to the backdoor, putting them all inside on the kitchen table. He couldn't take any chances that the phones had been compromised. Even semi-sophisticated hackers could turn a phone into a microphone. They could listen in to whatever you might say.

Van closed the door to the house, making sure that it was firmly closed. He brought the folder with him. "I'm not sure I can help. I love you guys, but this is a really big ask."

"What are you talking about?" Kat asked.

"You aren't the only one that still does a little work here and there for the government."

He saw Kat squint her eyes a little bit, ever so slightly. She turned and looked at Steve. "We can't risk Van getting into trouble, too. It's enough that I gave them that information already."

Van saw Steve hold up his hand to stop her from talking. "How serious is this information that they want?"

"It has national security implications."

"Serious ones?"

Van shook his head yes. "Guys, I want to help. I really do. I'm just not sure that this is a good idea."

Kat looked at him, "I get it. I really do. I wasn't sure what to do either, but what about what you told me? They have a cure for cancer that they are holding hostage. Millions of people could be saved."

"You've got no argument from me, but what they are asking for, I'm just not sure I can give."

Kat folded her arms over her chest, "How can we understand what they are asking if you won't tell us?"

Steve nodded, "I'm a consultant, man. I don't have anyone to tell."

Van snorted, "That's a no go. Everyone can be compromised. You never thought you'd be put in this position until this week, did you? That's why this information has to be kept secret." He felt a sigh escape out of his chest. "I can't tell you what Harbor Canyon is. There's no way." A thought formed in his head. "But there might be a way to get what everyone wants. Tell the guy that he has a deal, but we need two doses."

Steve threw his hands in the air, "Two? Do you really think he's gonna go for that?"

"I have no idea, but that's the deal."

Steve frowned, "Why do you want two doses? We just need one for my mom."

Van looked at Steve with an expression that he had perfected in the military. It never failed to back someone down. "I just do. Two doses or no deal. Text him now."

Steve shrugged and went into the house. He imagined that Steve was sending the text. While he and Kat were waiting, he pulled the folder out that he had been carrying. "You need to look at this," Van said.

"What is it?" Kat asked, leaning close to him to see.

"Remember Sarah, our OD victim?"

"Yes."

"I did a bit more digging. She's clean. She's never even had a parking ticket. Attends church every weekend she isn't working. There is no reason for her to OD."

"That part we knew already."

"There's more."

Van pulled a map out of the file folder. It had small red marks all over North America. "Remember how the vial of fentanyl looked suspicious? Like it was from Medicus, but we couldn't find matching lot numbers?

"Yes, of course. You said that the branding was almost identical."

Van nodded, pointing to the map, "Yup, that's the case. The branding looks the same, but the lot numbers were way off. It's like someone took the time to recreate the logo but didn't bother to really track their numbering system in a way that would hide it."

"Where did you get this?"

"I know the Security Chief at Mercy and I've got an FDA source. They helped me with this."

"Okay, so what does this mean?"

"There have been other OD's throughout the country at hospitals. They all involve Medicus fentanyl. The thing is that none of the lot numbers match ones that were delivered or even manufactured by Medicus. It's all a fake."

He saw Kat look closely at the map. He handed it to her so she could take in all of the information. "So, all of these dots represent OD's at hospitals using fake Medicus fentanyl." She looked up from the map, "There are probably twenty of them here."

"Twenty-three, to be exact," Van said. "And, they are not all in the US. He pointed to a couple that had been marked in Toronto, Vancouver and even Tijuana. "These have all happened over the last ten years."

"Wait, I don't understand how this ties to the serum that we have been chasing our tails with?"

Van started to get excited. He knew they were onto something. "In each of these instances, the person either worked at a hospital or was tied to a hospital somehow. And, in every case, someone on the oncology floor was healed on or about that time."

"What? You are kidding." Van saw Kat blink a couple of times, taking the information in. "So, what you are saying is that these people were eliminated -- Sarah was eliminated -- because they noticed that someone had been given the serum? You think the overdoses and the cures are connected."

Van waited a minute for the information to sink in. It was just a hypothesis, but the data was pretty strong. In each case, there had been a cure close to the time of the overdose. It wasn't a perfect link, but it was pretty darn close.

He watched as Kat sat down on the closest patio chair, folding her legs underneath her, her blonde hair escaping from behind her ear. She looked out at the backyard where Jack was happily playing.

Van looked the same direction. "He doesn't have a care in the world, does he?"

He heard Kat sigh, "That would be right. I'd love to be him right now."

Van saw her refocus on the papers in her hands. "So, you think this is evidence that the cures and the OD's are connected."

"That's what I think. Listen, it makes total sense. They target a family like yours with a loved one that has cancer. You don't want to see anyone die, right?"

"Right."

"They figure out if you have any information to trade that they can sell. If anyone gets in the way, they overdose them on their own brand of fentanyl. Really, the only moving part is whether the families cooperate. I'd guess they all do. Who wouldn't do anything for their loved one if they were sick?" Van shook his head as he looked at the paperwork again. It was simple and it was brilliant. Many of the most cunning plots throughout history had the same characteristics.

Van watched Kat as she processed the information. She absentmindedly pushed the lock of stray blonde hair that had escaped back behind her ear. He'd never seen her look so tired. Even when she came to work for the paper and was in the middle of sorting out what had happened to her in Afghanistan, she hadn't looked as tired as she did now. He saw her roll her wrist without even looking up from the papers.

"Wrist bothering you again?"

Kat looked up at him and then looked at her wrist, a weak smile forming on her lips, "Not too much. Sometimes I think I just do that out of habit."

"Old habits die hard."

The door to the backyard opened and Steve came out, holding the burner phone. "I texted them and was waiting to see what they said. I haven't heard back yet."

Van took the phone and opened it up. The text that Steve had sent said, "Deal, but two doses." Van closed the phone and handed it back to Steve. "Guess we just gotta wait."

44

E dgar had been waiting in the office from a reply from the Beckman's. Why they were always so slow to respond, he had no idea. While he was waiting, he had grabbed his tablet and was watching a replay of a soccer game. He had never been much into it until he did a stint in South America for the Apex bosses. It was all people could talk about there. The people there were so poor many of them didn't have food, but if they had soccer to watch, life was good.

Impatient for an answer, he texted Victor who had come back from set up on another job to sit at the Beckman's. "Any movement?"

The text came back almost immediately, "A guy pulled in driving a white car. He's been there for about a half-hour."

"A white car? No truck?"

"No."

Edgar was wondering who that might be. He expected that Kat and Steve would reach out to Van -- after all, that's who had the information they needed to get their next dose. But someone in a white car?

Edgar sent Victor another text, "Send me a picture of the car."

Within a few seconds, an image of the front of the house with a white Toyota came back. Edgar zoomed in and pulled out his laptop, using one of the portal's functions to enter new data in the file. It even had the ability to run a license plate. He saved the data to the file. The bosses liked updates.

"Aren't you trying to be sneaky," Edgar muttered. He picked up his cell phone again and sent another text to Victor. "It's registered to Van's assistant. Are you sure a guy got out of the car?"

"Yep."

That was all that Victor wrote. Edgar put his phone down and watched another minute or two of the game before his phone beeped with an incoming text. "Finally," he said out loud when he saw it was from the Beckman's. "The question is: do you want to play ball?"

Edgar opened the text and read it. His initial elation at being able to make a new deal with the same people turned on its side when he saw that they wanted two doses. "Two? For what?" he said, talking to no one in particular.

He got up and started to pace in the office. He'd have to ask permission to give them more than one dose. That could take time. He wanted to get out of Aldham. Utah was waiting. He wanted a break. He needed a break. He started to think through the possibilities. Could he give them more than one dose? What would happen to him? Would the bosses find out? Could he split a dose and make it look like it was two doses?

Edgar's instinct took over. He picked up the phone and sent a message back. "Ok. Get it quick. I'll text with details." He hoped they would get this done soon. He wanted out of Aldham. If they wanted two doses, that's what he'd give them.

45

As soon as they got the text from the man in the scrubs with the shortened timeline, Van said goodbye to Kat and Steve and waved at Jack, who was covered in sand with his trucks in the sandbox. He had work to do. The fact they could get two doses was good news. The bad news was that he was trying to figure out how to get the information they wanted, or at least seem to, without getting his own butt in a sling.

Van drove Alyssa's car back to the office. His truck was still parked in the lot. She must not have left at all while he was gone. He locked her car and went back up to the office, taking the steps two at a time. He nodded at Alyssa who was still scowling at her screen and put her keys on the corner of her desk. She didn't even acknowledge him. He could have been offended, but he knew how she was. Sometimes it worked to his advantage. She did her work, he did his. She occasionally helped him with his work. That was all that he needed to know.

Once in his office, he closed the door. In the corner of his office, there was a small refrigerator where Van kept his water and creamer for his coffee. He pushed the fridge out of the way.

He leaned over and pulled up the corner of the carpet, revealing a small hatch in the floor. He had put it in when he first rented the office for the paper. He lifted the lid and looked down inside, pulling out a small black duffel bag. He set the bag on top of the refrigerator and unzipped it. In it was a change of clothes, a stack of cash in small bills banded together, three passports with new names from Canada, Germany and Argentina and a full-sized CZ pistol with two magazines, already loaded. At the bottom of the bag was a small zippered pouch. Out of it, he pulled a flash drive and a key that were both on a chain. Van slipped the chain over his neck.

He replaced the bag and the hatch, recovering the floor with the carpet and putting the refrigerator back where it had been. He smoothed the lines in the carpet with his boot. No one would ever know the refrigerator had been moved.

He stood up, grabbed his keys off of the desk and headed out. He had work to do.

46

Hannah Carter still didn't have all of the answers that she wanted. She still didn't know whether Kat Beckman had taken intel or not. And, they still couldn't find the technician that put in the unsecured drive into the site. There were too many loose ends. Hannah didn't like loose ends. They didn't make her look good. They didn't make the Major look good.

Hannah was sitting in her office, twirling a pencil between her fingers. It was a new day. She had finally gone home after spending nearly a full day at the site trying to determine what happened. Late the night before, she had sent Ben and his tech crew home to rest. No good answers would come from a team that was exhausted. Hannah herself had finally gone home about an hour after her tech team. She took a shower, ate some food and collapsed into bed. After some sleep, she had gotten up, taken an early morning cycling class and taken another shower. She picked up coffee on the way to the office.

Hannah clicked on her email and found one from Ben that was time-stamped about four o'clock in the morning. It read, "Do you see what I see?" There was a link to a video file that

Ben had attached. She sat up in her chair and clicked the link. Once the video loaded, she hit play and saw the feed once again of Kat being searched. She didn't see anything new until she saw a shot where Ben had zoomed in on Kat's keys. There seemed to be something behind them. Hannah flipped back to the reports and saw that when she had been wanded by Thomas. The wand had alerted, and he found her keys in her pocket. Hannah ran the video back and forth a few more times, blowing up Ben's image even more than it had been. Kat did have the keys in her hand, that was for sure. She also had what looked to be a small flash drive attached to the key ring. Squinting at the screen, Hannah couldn't tell if it was attached, but it looked like it was behind her keys. Thomas would have never seen it unless he was looking for it. Hannah leaned back in her chair and groaned loudly. She pulled her email back up and told Ben that he and his team should take the day off. It was good work.

It wasn't definitive proof, but it was at least something. Hannah punched a button on the phone on her desk and paged Thomas to her office. She saw him approaching, coffee in hand, dressed in his suit and tie for the day. FBI guys and their suits, she thought.

"Yes, ma'am?" Thomas asked, bringing his bulk through the door.

"Morning. I've got something for you to look at." Hannah turned the screen toward him and hit play, she could see what was going on and gauge his reaction.

Thomas' face wasn't one that hid a secret well. The crags and wrinkles immediately showed his reaction. "What? Is that?" Thomas looked right at her. "Can you play that again?"

Hannah reset the video that Ben sent and pushed slow play. It ran along at half speed, giving Thomas a chance to see the images that Ben had put together slowly and close up.

"Son of a gun," Thomas whispered under his breath. He

looked right at Hannah, "Does she have some sort of a flash drive hidden behind her keys?"

"Looks that way to me. Ben found it."

"I'm sorry about that. I never would have..."

Hannah cut him off with a wave of her hand. "Don't worry about it. This was a comedy of errors. You'll know to look next time. I'll be on the watch too if I'm still here." She was serious about the comedy of errors. She wasn't serious about not worrying about it. She was worried.

"You don't think you'd get fired over this, do you?" Thomas asked, slumping down into one of the chairs in front of her desk. By the look on his face, Hannah could tell that he was not only devastated that he had missed the flash drive but devastated that she might lose her job. "That wasn't your fault. If anything, I should get fired."

"They will hold me responsible. It was a bunch of errors. Kat could never have gotten a flash drive into the system to copy anything if the tech company hadn't installed that unsecured drive."

"Yeah, I didn't know anything about it."

"That's what I mean. I don't know what they will do."

"Did they ever find the tech that did the install?"

Hannah shook her head no, "Not that I know of."

There was a knock on the open door of Hannah's office. It was Ben. "What are you doing here?" she asked. "I gave you the day off."

"I got a call and thought I should come in," Ben said.

Hannah looked at him closely. He was pale and his hair wasn't combed as neatly as usual. "Are you okay? Is something wrong?"

"The tech company just called. Actually, the president of the company just called me."

"What did he want?" he asked, having turned halfway to see Ben.

"Remember the tech they couldn't find?"

Hannah answered, "Yes?"

"He's dead. They just found his body in the park. Blew his brains out. From the looks of it, he did it right after we had the breach."

Hannah stayed quiet, not sure what to say. Thomas' face compressed into a new set of wrinkles, "Why would he do that? What exactly is going on here?"

Hannah looked at them and said, "I don't know, but I need to make a call."

BEN AND THOMAS got up and left her office. She watched Thomas lumber back to his position by the door, his head hanging. She knew he would take this hard. She turned and saw Ben sitting at his desk. He wasn't moving. He was just sitting, his hands knotted together. She would have to make a point to talk to him later to reassure him. For now, she had to tell the Major what was going on.

Hannah got up and closed the door to her office. Her employees knew that if the door was closed it would have to be a near disaster to interrupt her, and there was nothing more important now than calling Major Javorek. Her only hope to keep her job was to tell the truth, under control, without exploding in anger. She picked up her cell phone to make the call. The anger rose in her, her mind screaming that she had done her job and that they couldn't blame her. She shouldn't lose her job because other people had screwed up. But she knew that wouldn't be the case. She pushed the torrent back down so that she could speak clearly and hopefully calmly.

"Javorek." The Major answered his phone before it even rang.

"Good morning, Major."

"Hi, Hannah. How are things?"

"Well, sir, I have a bit of an update. Two updates, actually."

"Good. Information is always helpful."

"We think that Kat Beckman did have a flash drive with her. She concealed it behind her keys during her physical search. Our security guy just never saw it."

"You've got to be kidding me. How is that possible?"

"I'm sending you the file right now." Hannah clicked on the email that Ben had sent her and forwarded it to Major Javorek's email.

"Okay, I've got it. What am I looking at?"

Hannah pulled up the file on her computer and hit play so she could describe to the Major what he was seeing. "What you'll see first is a section of the security video where Thomas is wanding Kat. You'll first see him go through her bag. He identifies her encryption key in her bag and then runs the wand over her. Next, you'll see the wand go off near her pocket. Thomas asks her to pull whatever is in her pants pocket out. It was her keys. Then you will see the zoomed-in shots that Ben made."

"Yep, I see that. It's just a picture of her keys in her hand?"

"Look a little closer. What you'll see is a small black rectangular object behind one of her keys. If you'll go to the next image, you'll see Ben has highlighted it for you."

"And you think that is a flash drive?"

"That's what we are thinking, sir. We wouldn't know for sure without recovering the drive, but that's what it looks like to us."

There was a pause. Hannah wasn't sure what was coming next, but her gut told her to stay quiet. She twirled the pencil in her fingers.

"Hannah?"

"Yes, sir?"

"What are the next steps?"

"I'm not sure, sir. We don't have anything specific on Kat. The data hasn't resurfaced yet."

"I need to know what you are planning on doing next."

"There's one other thing, sir."

"I'm hoping it's good news."

"I'm not sure it is."

"I don't like the sound of that."

"I'm sorry sir, but the tech that installed the unsecured drive, remember him?"

"Yes."

"His body was just found. He killed himself. Park police found him."

Hannah could hear the Major hiss through his teeth. "That can't be good. Are we sure it is a suicide?"

"Sir, I'm not sure. I just talked to Ben. The president of the tech company just called him. I'm guessing the police are still investigating."

"Obviously, I've got to run up this up the chain. I'll keep them busy as long as I can, but I need more answers, Hannah. Can you get with the police chief and see what is going on? Have him call me if he holds any information back. This is becoming an issue of national security."

The phone clicked off before Hannah could say goodbye or ask any questions.

Hannah had a lot of work to do. She opened her office door, "Ben," she called from her office.

She saw Ben hop up from his chair like he had been stuck with a hot poker. "Yes, what can I do?"

"I just talked to the Major. We need information about the tech. Do you know what officer is working the scene or where the tech was?"

Ben fumbled with his phone. "Yes. The company president said a guy named Haskins is the one that called him. I'll send you his number. I have it right here."

"Thanks." With that, Hannah's phone chirped with the contact info. "Let me call them and see what is going on."

Ben walked away. "Let me know if you need anything," he said as he returned to his desk.

"Ben, go home. A lot has happened. I'll text if I need you."

"Are you sure? I mean, I can stay."

"No. You were up all night working on this. Go home. I mean it." Hannah furrowed her brow at him so she'd know that she meant what she said.

HANNAH CALLED the number Ben had sent to her. "Haskins," the voice said.

"Officer Haskins?"

"Detective."

"Sorry about that. This is Hannah Carter. I'm a contractor with the Army. I heard you have caught a case that might have national security implications."

"Which one might that be?"

"There was a suicide in the park."

"Yup, I'm here right now."

"Okay for me to come down to the scene? Major Javorek asked me to take a look."

"I have no idea who that is but bring your ID and we will see you when you get here."

"Thanks."

HANNAH MOVED her Department of the Army credentials from her waistband to dangling around her neck so they would be easy to see when she got to the scene. She picked up her bag and walked out of the office at a quick clip, her heels clicking on the floor. Ben had sent her the address where the body had been found. It wasn't more than a fifteen-minute drive from the office.

When she arrived in the park, the main park road was

closed off by a cruiser, it's lights flashing. She pulled up and the officer approached her car, "I'm sorry, the road is closed."

Hannah showed her Army ID. "Detective Haskins is expecting me."

The officer nodded and waved her through. "The scene is a quarter mile down on the right."

As Hannah got closer, she felt her stomach tie into a tumble of knots. Dead bodies weren't her forte. The idea that someone had shot themselves was even worse. She pulled her car into a parking spot that was just outside of the taped-off perimeter. The yellow tape was blowing in the wind and she could see that uniformed officers were doing everything from talking on their phones to joking with their friends. There was a vehicle, a blue SUV, in the back corner of a parking spot that had detectives surrounding it. There were photographers and other people hovering around. Hannah couldn't tell what they were doing. She unbuckled her seat belt and swallowed hard, getting out of the car.

She walked toward the perimeter and approached one of the officers, "I'm looking for Detective Haskins," she said, lifting her ID so that he could see the Army insignia.

"Over there," he pointed toward the back of the SUV, where an older man with a shock of gray hair was making notes in a notebook.

"Thanks." Hannah put her shoulders back and walked straight toward him.

He looked up just as she approached, tilting his head to the side, his eyebrows meeting in the middle, "Can I help you?"

Hannah extended her hand, "I'm Hannah Carter. We talked on the phone."

Haskins didn't take the time to grasp her hand. She couldn't tell if he was ignoring her or was just busy. He just kept making scrawling notes in his book. After a minute or so of Hannah waiting, he closed the book and looked at her. "You wanna take a look?"

Hannah swallowed hard. She was good at management. Dead bodies, not so much.

Haskins must have noticed her discomfort. "First time at a crime scene?"

"Yeah. Is it that obvious?"

Haskins nodded, his shock of gray hair bobbing up and down. "You look a little green, actually." He fumbled around in his pocket and pulled out a mint, wrapped in a cellophane wrapper. "Take this."

Hannah lifted her hand to decline. Haskins wasn't having it. "It will help. Trust me."

Hannah opened the mint as Haskins pulled another one out of this pocket and put it in his mouth. They walked up to the car where two crime scene investigators were swabbing and taking pictures. Hannah paused, not sure she could handle what she was about to see. "Is it normal to have this many people working a suicide?"

Haskins grunted, sticking his notebook under his arm and pulling a pair of rubber gloves out of the pocket of his jacket. "Yeah. We just got here a little while ago. Took us a couple of days to find him. Finding anything in this park is a problem."

He offered her a pair of rubber gloves. She shook her head no. "I don't think I need to touch anything." Haskins nodded.

Hannah's stomach clenched and she hadn't even looked at the body yet. She was grateful for the mint. "Best way to look at the body is just to look. Don't think. Just look." Hannah took a couple of steps forward, passing the rear of the SUV and then the rear passenger door, getting closer to the driver's side, where the door was open. She saw the driver's foot first and then part of his leg and then his hip and then she had a full view of the scene. His head was cocked to the side and there was a hole where his brain should have been. From the driver's side, it wasn't too bad. The passenger side was filled with bone and blood and brain. The gun was in his lap. Haskins' voice cut through the images that Hannah was trying to process.

"Here's the thing that I'm trying to understand," he said, using his pencil to point to the driver, "These crime scenes are all about understanding the story. You go too fast putting the pieces together, you get it wrong. Make sense?"

Hannah nodded. Haskins handed her another mint. She took it.

"The way that that gun fell is peculiar. In order for the spray to go on the passenger window, he'd need to hold it in his left hand." He stopped for a moment and looked at Hannah, "Do you know if this guy was right or left-handed?"

Hannah swallowed, "I'm not sure. I never met him. We might have some video though..." the thought trailed off. "Let me just send a text."

"That's okay," Haskins interrupted. "You can do that when we are done here. So, if he held the gun in his left hand, we'd expect the muzzle of the gun to be facing to the passenger side." She watched Haskins as he pretended to shoot himself in the head. He flopped his hand down, mimicking how he'd expect the gun to fall. "But we see the gun has landed the other way. Now, I don't know if this is just a gravity thing or it fell funny or if we are looking at something else."

All of a sudden Hannah's vision narrowed and she felt weak. Haskins words trailed off and she could only see the hand of the guy in the car and the gun, blood-spattered on his jeans...

HANNAH AWOKE a few minutes later and found herself on a gurney in the back of an ambulance. A paramedic was sitting next to her. She was sitting up. The world came into focus very slowly. The first thing she saw was Haskins standing at the back of the ambulance, chewing gum. He had some sort of facial expression. Hannah wasn't sure if it was a smile or a sneer.

The paramedic put a hand on her arm, "Welcome back."

Hannah looked around, the smell of latex and bandages filling her nose. She looked down and realized that there was an IV line in her arm and oxygen on her face.

The voice of the paramedic cut through the questions that were swimming in her brain. "You fainted. You've been out for a couple of minutes. This big guy over here," he motioned to Haskins, "caught you when you went down. You didn't hit your head or anything. Your elbow got a little scraped up, but I already put a dressing on that for you."

"Thank you. I feel okay now." Hannah struggled to get up, but the paramedic stopped her again. "Hold on there. I've gotta finish checking you out unless you want to take a ride to the hospital."

She saw Haskins raise his eyebrows. They were just as gray as his hair. "I'd avoid that if I were you. Emergency rooms can suck up a perfectly good day."

Hannah leaned back on the gurney while the paramedic listened to her heart and took her blood pressure again. He stood up and stepped out of the ambulance. "I'm going to do the paperwork. I want you to stay here. Unless you aren't feeling well, you can go once the IV is done." He nodded at Haskins, who took a step closer to the ambulance.

"I'm so sorry," Hannah said.

Haskins waved her off. "Happens to all of us from time to time. First dead body I saw had been sitting for four days before we found her. Walked in, looked at the body, smelled the smell and promptly ran out and yarked my entire pastrami sandwich onto the sidewalk. The guys called me 'Yark' for quite a while."

She saw him pause. "Your color does look better. You up to answering a few questions?"

Hannah's eyes got wide, but she didn't say anything.

Haskins held up his hand, "Don't worry, these aren't hard. I can tell you aren't involved. No one could fake that episode," he chuckled under his breath. "I'm just trying to understand why the Army has their panties in a twist about this guy."

Hannah sighed and shifted on the gurney, the sheets shifting with her. She said, "Some of what is going on requires a clearance."

Haskins nodded, pulling out his notebook, "Just tell me what you can. I'll have our brass reach out if we need more information."

"The guy you have over there," Hannah pointed, trying not to think about what she had seen, "He worked for a tech company. He came in and did a project for us. It was a hardware repair and installation. It didn't go the way that we planned."

"Can you tell me a bit more about that?"

Hannah tried to clear the cobwebs out of her head. Could she tell him? What was off-limits? "I can't be super-specific. What I can say is that the equipment he installed didn't secure our networks up to our usual standards."

"Are you saying there was a data breach?"

Hannah flushed. She wasn't doing a good job of hiding the truth of what had happened. "I can't really say."

Haskins didn't even look up, "But if you could say, would you agree that I'm on the right track?"

Hannah didn't answer. Haskins looked at her, one of his eyes narrowing a bit. She knew that he knew exactly what had happened. He said, "Do you know anything about the victim?"

"Just that he only worked for the company for one day. And, this is probably public record, but the vendor that we usually use was just bought out by the company that he," she pointed to the car, "worked for."

"Did anyone on your staff have contact with this guy?"

"Yes. Some of our IT guys."

"Names, please." Haskins started writing as Hannah gave him the names of her three tech guys.

"I'll have to get clearance for you to talk to them, if that's what you want."

"It is." Haskins looked at her, "And you said you might have some video? You said that right before you fainted."

Hannah instantly regretted saying that. She wasn't sure Major Javorek would ever release that. "I'll have to get an approval to share that."

Haskins nodded. "I understand."

"Just out of curiosity, how did you hear about this apparent suicide?"

Telling the story of the tech made Hannah realize how much of a mess her site was in. "Well, my lead tech..."

"That's the guy you mentioned, Ben?"

"Yes. He got a call from the president of the company that does the tech work. They had been looking for their tech. He hadn't shown up to work and wasn't answering his cell phone. The president of the company told Ben."

"And what did you do then?"

"I called my superior."

"Who is?"

"Major Javorek."

"Spell that?" Hannah did. Haskins continued, stopping for a moment to scratch the back of his head. "So, none of you knew the guy over there other than the one-stop he made to fix your computers?"

"That's right."

"Does the name Tommy Scanlon mean anything to you?"

"No, should it?" Hannah shifted on the gurney. She was ready to get out of the ambulance. She glanced up at the IV. It looked like it was almost done.

"That's what was on the ID in his wallet. For what it is worth, we don't think that is his real name?"

Hannah frowned, "Why do you say that?"

"It's clearly a fake ID. We took his prints. We will run them and let you know what we find. My guess?"

"Sure."

"I bet he's not in the system. If your bosses want copies of his prints to run through their own databases, let me know." Haskins reached into his breast pocket and handed her a card. "Just give me a call. Let me know about the video, too, will you?"

Hannah nodded and watched him walk away, his slumped figure and rumpled suit turning toward the scene. She stayed on the gurney and was reaching for the needle in her arm to take the IV out when the paramedic came back. "Whoa," he said. "Lemme help you with that." He quickly put on some gloves, pulled the needle out of her arm and pressed a gauze dressing on it. "Hold this for a moment," he said, opening a bandage. He took the gauze off of her arm and looked. "Yup, looks good." He put a plastic bandage on it and took off the blood pressure cuff. Pulling the gloves off, he handed her a clipboard with a form on it. "This just says that we treated you at the scene and you don't want to go to the hospital." Hannah quickly signed it and stood up. As she was stepping out of the ambulance, the paramedic said, "Take it easy for the rest of the day and get plenty of liquids. You were pretty dehydrated."

"Will do. Thanks." Part of her was grateful that someone took the time to care for her. Part of her was angry at herself at fainting.

By the time she got out of the ambulance, some of the cruisers had left the scene. The coroner's office had arrived and was removing the body from the car. Hannah looked away, not wanting to repeat her fainting spell. It looked like Haskins had left as well. She was pretty sure she would hear from him again. He wasn't the type to be shy with his questions.

She walked back to her car and started it up, turning the air conditioning on high even though it wasn't that warm out. The cool air made her feel better. On her way back to the office, she ran a drive-through and got a chicken sandwich and a salad. She didn't normally eat drive-through food, but she wanted to get something into her stomach as soon as possible. The last thing she needed was to pass out behind the wheel. That would make things unnecessarily complicated. She ate a few bites of the sandwich on her way, figuring she'd eat the rest of it when she got back to the office.

As soon as she got back to her desk, she called Major Javorek again. "Yes," he answered.

"Sir, it's Hannah." He didn't answer. Hannah felt a pit in her stomach. His tone told her that she had been the subject of conversations that weren't flattering. "I just got back from the scene of the tech. The detectives think that he was using a fake ID."

"Why would he do that?"

"That part I don't know. They also said that the way that the gun fell made the incident suspicious."

"What does that mean?"

"I guess with the direction of the shot they would have expected the gun to fall in the opposite direction. It didn't look right to the detective. And sir, they wanted to know if they could see the video of the tech working at the site."

"That's a hard no."

"That's what I thought. I told him I'd have to check with you. He also asked for the names of the tech team. I provided them, but I thought you should know."

"Tell them not to talk to the police without either you or one of my staff there. Did we find out any more about what Kat Beckman took?"

"No, sir. I just got back from the scene this minute. I'll check with Ben as soon as I get off the phone." As soon as she said it, Hannah remembered that she had sent Ben home. I'll have to interrupt his rest, I guess, she thought.

"Keep me posted," she heard the Major say. That was the end of the conversation.

47

K at paced around the house. There had been no news from Van. He hadn't told them what Harbor Canyon was, but she could tell by the look on his face that the man in the scrubs had requested information that put Van into nearly a panic. What kind of information could be that sensitive? Her training as a journalist kicked into high gear. Unfortunately, the questions she most wanted to ask, she couldn't. She could tell by the look on his face when she mentioned Harbor Canyon that he would never answer her. A sense of sadness crept into her chest and she bit her lip. Whatever the ask was, she was afraid that what the man in the scrubs wanted from Van had damaged her relationship with him. As much as she loved Steve, she and Van had something different. It was something that she didn't necessarily share with Steve. She and Van had been through some similar things. The difference was that Van had the training. She didn't. His reentry had been easier than hers, though it wasn't always for people in his position.

There was nothing to do but wait. She walked over to the kitchen sink and finished up the dishes. Steve had retreated to their home office. The door was closed. She could hear him talking in muffled tones. She didn't know if he was talking to someone or watching something on his computer. Whenever she asked, he was never very specific. He always just said he was on a call with some other consultants. Kat didn't care that much.

After doing the dishes, she couldn't take the uncertainty any longer. She picked up her personal phone, not the burner that the man in the scrubs had given them, and almost sent Van a text to see if he needed anything. She stopped as soon as she opened the text app. Van didn't need anything. Most certainly, he didn't need anything from her. He was more than capable of handling himself.

One other thing was bothering her. She pushed the door open to Steve's office. He was staring at the screen as someone said the word, "projection." He looked at her. "I'm going to have to call you back," he said, ending the call. "What's going on?" he asked.

'Is this a bad time?"

'No, it's fine." He took off his glasses and looked at her. "What's going on?"

It seemed to Kat that he seemed strangely unconcerned about what had been going on. "I'm just worried that we are putting too much pressure on Van."

Steve's face softened, which made Kat feel better, "It is a lot of pressure. Did he say something? Does he not want to get the information?"

"He didn't. I haven't even heard from him. She sat down on the chair that was in front of Steve's desk. He closed his laptop. "It just doesn't seem fair. He doesn't have anything to do with us, really. It's not his responsibility."

Steve stood up, looking out the window, his back to her. "Well, if he doesn't want to do it, that's on him. He just needs to know that my mom won't make it. That will be on him."

"That's what I'm saying. It's not really his responsibility. Laura isn't part of his family." Anger started to rise in Kat's throat.

"Yeah, but he's been a part of ours." Steve was getting mad. His moods had been really erratic over the last few weeks. She had chalked it up to worries about his mom. "Maybe Van needs to learn to sacrifice for others."

"Steve..."

"No, I'm serious. When was the last time he did something for you, Kat? All they want is a little information. How hard can it be? Or maybe he's more worried about the story than my mom. Maybe that's it." Kat could see the muscles in Steve's jaw flex. He didn't normally lose his temper, but when he did, his jaw muscles were a sure indication there was trouble brewing.

"Listen, I know you are worried about your mom..."

"Worried? She's dying, Kat. Have you forgotten? If you would have just given her the serum, we would have been fine. This would have all been over."

Kat stood up. She was not going to be Steve's whipping boy. "This is not my fault. I didn't give your mom cancer. I didn't have anything to do with that. And, it's not my fault that your mom wouldn't take the drug. Van has been nothing but good to all of us. Honestly, I couldn't fault him for whatever he chooses to do."

With that, Kat stormed out of the room. She was tired of trying to get through to Steve. If he wanted his mother to have that serum bad enough then he should have just grabbed it from Kat and put it in Laura's IV. Steve's family, for how lovely they had been to Kat, did have a big flaw -- blaming others for things that were clearly their responsibility.

Kat had left the room without as much as a goodbye. She was at the stage where she didn't care. She had put her career and her freedom on the line to help Laura without so much as a thank you from Steve. For all she knew, MPs could be arriving on her doorstep at any minute to take her in for questioning. She knew that the Army would figure out that she had taken some information. Apparently, Steve didn't care. It didn't bother him that she sacrificed. He had done nothing but whine and watch Jack.

The only thing Kat could think to do was to reach out to Van. At least she could show her appreciation by offering to help. She pulled her cell phone out of her pocket and finished sending the text, "Need anything?" There was no answer.

48

V an's phone chirped. He looked at the screen and saw that it was a text from Kat asking if he needed anything. It was a nice thought, but where he had to go and what he had to do he had to do alone. He couldn't rope Kat and her family into acquiring the information on Harbor Canyon.

By the time the text reached him, he was sitting in his truck about fifty miles outside of Aldham. It had been an hour-long drive. The day had heated up and so had the traffic. The normally easy drive required more attention than Van liked, especially given what he was about to do.

He drummed his fingers on the steering wheel, waiting for the traffic light three cars ahead of him to turn green. He was on the outskirts of Mattis, a small city that was known for not too much. There were a couple of nice restaurants, an upscale movie theater where Van had heard they would actually serve you food at your seat, and a small airstrip just on the outskirts of town. That's where he was headed.

The airstrip had originally been used for the businesses that wanted to get their VIPs into Aldham. They would fly them into Mattis and then have a chauffeured limousine ferry them in for their meetings. Since Aldham's economy had taken a drop, the airstrip was mostly used by people who wanted to get their pilot's license, a sky diving school and Harbor Canyon Air.

Van's stomach clenched as he approached the gate to get into the airstrip. There was the typical six-foot-high chain-link fence with barbed wire coiled around the top like a never-ending snake that you'd see on the perimeter of any airfield. One end of the airstrip was directly ahead of him and there were a series of white buildings off to the right. All of the buildings looked exactly the same except for their differences in height. Some of them were short and squat. Some of them had large doors that could accommodate a small plane or a helicopter for service. The fence extended to the edges of the driveway where there was a small checkpoint covered in peeling paint. It wasn't bigger than could hold a single man and a chair for him to sit on. Van pulled the truck up to the guard and stopped.

"Afternoon," the guard said. He was about five-ten and had a full beard. He was dressed in navy pants and black boots with a polo shirt. He could have easily been dressed to work as a salesman as the guard at the gate. Van knew better. Underneath the polo shirt was a full-sized pistol and a K-bar knife -- the kind the military carried. Van glanced up at the overhand from the guard shack. There was a small camera positioned where someone who wasn't looking for it wouldn't see it. The guard and his guard shack were more than they appeared to be. All of the guards at the gate were former operators -- Special Forces. The ramshackle guard shack had been equipped with high tech surveillance equipment, both audio and video. Inside the shack was a fully automatic M4 within reach of the guard. What looked like a series of sewer covers across the breadth of the driveway were actually steel barriers that could be raised by the security staff with the touch of a button. The video feed of

Van arriving had already been clocked and logged by the security staff inside Harbor Canyon Air. That was the disguise of the black site.

"Hi there," Van replied.

"Can I see your ID?" the guard asked. Not that Van would refuse, but he knew if he did, he'd be blocked by the barricades in front of him and a Jeep filled with more ex-Special Forces from behind.

Van reached over onto the seat, where his ID was. He'd been told when he was first brought to Harbor Canyon that it was a good idea to pull out his ID just outside the facility. Digging for anything could require a more thorough search that might prove to be unpleasant. He put the ID near his face, allowing the team inside to take a look. The guard waited for a moment and then extended a tablet to him. Van touched his finger to the tablet, verifying his fingerprint and signed his name using the digital pen. The gate opened. "Have a good day," Van said, putting the truck in gear.

The guard nodded, "Thanks, you too."

Van pulled ahead and watched the guard stroll back into the shack. So much of military work was watching and waiting. People didn't understand that. They thought that you were always heading out on missions, shooting things up or getting shot at. They never grasped that the firefights were mere minutes out of days and months waiting and planning. Unlike many of the missions that Van had gone on himself, this one didn't have much of a plan.

Van pulled the truck around to the back of the third building. Sometimes they flagged his truck inside, sometimes they didn't. It just depended on what they had happening. The higher-ups never wanted the same vehicle to create a pattern that could be identified. While they didn't require him to drive a different vehicle, they did change where he parked from time to time. It wouldn't be a surprise if they started requiring different vehicles to enter the area. With these people, anything was possible.

Van put the truck in park and took a deep breath. While his work in intelligence had given him some special skills, he certainly wasn't of the same ilk as the Special Forces guys that peppered the area. There was no time like the present, he told himself, and got out of the truck. He walked over to a steel door that had been painted white and slid his ID card through the reader to get the door to unlock. He glanced behind him before going in. No one looking at the back of the building would think anything of it. There were untrimmed weeds growing up through cracks in the concrete. Cigarette butts and dead leaves had clustered against the edge of the building's peeling paint. The only interesting thing about the entrance was that there was no door handle on the door. Van's ID badge popped it open. No lock meant no lock to pick.

Inside, Van was immediately greeted by the sound of voices talking softly and the hum of the air conditioning. There was a room in front of him that was kept relatively dark. Its high ceilings were part of the original construction of the hangar. They had been covered by monitors that were bolted to the walls. Most of the monitors were black at the moment, with just two illuminated in the front of the room. They were only used if there was a situation that was being watched by Harbor Canyon.

There were a few offices on the side, their doors closed, the lights off. Nothing was very fancy. On the other side of the wall behind the offices, Van knew that there was a small private plane that the CIA used to ferry people and money in and out of the area. On the other side of the room, there was a separate door off to the right with a guard sitting nearby. Van had only been downstairs once. He had been asked to verify some intelligence that had come in and the prisoner happened to be on site. Harbor Canyon held prisoners like those for days, weeks, even years. The basement, as they called it, was creepy in its own right. It was eerily quiet with empty hallways except for a rotation of guards to move prisoners and bring food and supplies. Those same prisoners could be whisked off in a heartbeat in the plane they had stored next to the offices if they needed to be moved.

He wasn't going into the basement today. There was no need. Van stepped forward onto the grey-blue carpet and walked toward a bank of computers. He wasn't exactly sure what to do next. The text had said that the man in the scrubs wanted to make a delivery to Harbor Canyon. If someone wanted to get into Harbor Canyon, they wouldn't want to go in the front door, that was for sure. They would need the lock types and the codes. The types weren't hard, but the codes were something different. The codes were housed on the terminals. Van didn't have access to them, but using his encryption key, he could update them onto his flash drive. They were usually stored there anyway. The problem was the ID. He couldn't just hand over his ID.

Van sat at the terminal, pretending to get some work done, but thinking about how to go about getting someone access to the site. They'd never get through, he realized, but maybe they wanted the information for something else.

Every few months, they had to get new IDs and flash drives. Van had always felt bad for the woman who ran the ID system. She would get everyone new credentials and then just as she finished, she was back at it again. Creating new credentials was a lot of work. Her office was on the other side of the main office area. Van glanced over at her and saw her moving around in her office. Unlike the other offices, hers was completely open. The only thing that kept her away from the rest of the people in the building was a low counter that blocked her desk off from people just wandering in. Van sighed. You'd think something like ID badges would require a bit more security, he thought.

Just a few desks over from Van was a guy named Arjun. He wasn't military or ex-military. He was some sort of analyst. Van had heard him making fun of some of the former Special Ops guys in the past. Probably not smart and not something that had earned Arjun any respect in Van's eyes. Van had the utmost respect for the guys that could make it through that much training.

Arjun was at his desk, typing away at some computer code. He was slight and always wore the same thing every single time that Van saw him: pressed blue pants, brown shoes, a light blue shirt, and a brown belt.

Van got up from his desk and went into the break room. Once there, Van bought a package of sugar cookies and some peanut butter wafers. On his way back to his desk, Van opened the peanut butter wafers and ate one. He opened the sugar cookies and pulled one out., rubbing just a little bit of the peanut butter from the wafer on the bottom of the cookie. Just as he passed Arjun's desk, he stopped. "Hey, Arjun, what's up?"

"Nothing Van. I'm trying to work."

"Dude, you gotta eat something. You work too hard. Here, have a cookie."

Arjun didn't look up and didn't say thank you. Van handed him the sugar cookie. It was the only kind Van had ever seen him eat. Van went back to his desk, sat down and started typing. He waited. Not more than a minute passed and there was a thump behind him. He turned to see Arjun had flopped out of his chair, his face turning blue.

"Somebody, help!" Van yelled. "There's something wrong."

People were running toward Arjun as Van went the other way, "I'll get the medkit!" he shouted. Even the woman in the ID office had come out of her office to try to help. That's what Van was waiting for. While they were clustered around Arjun, Van slipped behind the counter in the ID office and grabbed a single set of IDs that had been turned in. The flash drive and

ID had been connected. Van slipped it into his pocket and trotted back to Arjun, carrying the medical kit.

Arjun was wheezing and pointing to his desk drawer. Van interrupted, "He's got a peanut allergy. There's an EpiPen in his drawer. Van saw the medic that was attending to him pull the drawer open, quickly prep the pen and jab it into Arjun's leg. Van stood in the background and quietly slipped out while the medics were still attending to Arjun. Van tossed the rest of the cookies into the dumpster just outside the door as he left.

Pulling out of Harbor Canyon, Van gave the guard a little wave as he left. The guard returned the wave. Van shook his head. You couldn't get a reaction out of those guys while they were working to save your life. After work, that was a whole different story. Those guys knew how to blow off steam better than any others Van had ever met.

Van drove the truck back the way he came. He doubted that in the chaos the woman in the ID office would even notice. He had seen her take lumpy bags filled with used IDs to the incinerator. Van flipped on the radio and sang along on the way home. He wasn't gifted in music, but he did enjoy it. For the moment, it was a good distraction.

Van headed back to Kat's house. He had what he hoped would get them more serum, but now what? They needed to create an actual plan, not just improvise like he just did. He picked up his phone and opened the talk to text feature. The text to Kat was simple, "OMW." On my way.

The traffic back to Aldham was better than on the way out. As he drove, he realized he was sweating. The stress of trying to figure out how to get in and out of the black site had sent his body into overdrive. He took a couple of deep breaths, letting the swirling air in the truck fill his lungs. He started to relax. At the same time, his mind was working on the problem of the exchange. There were a lot of variables that Van couldn't account for. If he was working this on the intelligence side, he'd have help. When he was overseas, there were whole teams of people working on the planning of a mission before anyone ever left the base. He didn't have that option here. His only option was to rely on Kat and Steve to work with him. Kat was a known quantity. She had been through some hard times, and although she hadn't been through military training, he knew she could handle herself. Steve, on the other hand, represented an unknown. He was a consultant. Not that there was anything wrong with that, but Van didn't know how he'd react under pressure. His gut told him that Kat would be far better in a fight than Steve.

A memory surfaced of a training that he had gone to a few years before. It had been held by a security company that was selling systems to school districts. Van had gone to do research on an article about how schools were trying to better protect their students. The presenter, a former police chief growled at the crowd about how civilians needed to be tested for their reactions before something happened. "We had one school we did an ALICE test in," the chief said, referring to an active shooter drill, "We had a teacher that had a complete meltdown over blanks. She was off work for three days getting herself together. In a real situation, you can't afford that. You have to test your people."

Van knew that was what he was facing with Kat and Steve helping him. He had to work through the problem of getting the doses with them. Backup simply wasn't available. Operational intelligence wasn't available past what Van had discovered about the fentanyl, the string of texts and his own observations.

Van made the final turn down to Kat and Steve's street. The cable van was still sitting there. Van was tired of the games. He pulled up alongside the truck and rolled down his window. "You can stop watching the house now," he said.

"Me? I'm just eating a sandwich on my way to my next gig," the guy in the truck said.

"You'd better be gone when I come out."

The guy in the van didn't respond. He just stared at Van and chewed his sandwich.

Van pulled the truck into the driveway and walked into Kat and Steve's house without ringing the doorbell. The noise of the door must have started Kat. She came charging around the corner, her hand on her hip, ready to draw. "Easy," Van said. "It's just me."

"Sorry. I knew you were coming. I didn't expect you to get here so quick."

Van walked over to the front window. The spot on the street where the cable guy had been was empty. "The truck is gone. I told the guy to get lost."

Kat stepped closer to him so she could look. He was always surprised at how petite she was. Her blonde hair caught a glint of the light, the smooth skin on the back of her neck peeking out from below the fringe of her hair. He stepped away before he got caught up in the moment. "Where's Steve?"

"Working on his computer."

"Can you get him and meet me outside? Remember, no phones."

Kat nodded and walked off. As Van made his way through the house, he spotted Jack playing on the floor. He had two trucks nearby and a book about trucks spread out between his legs. The kid was focused, that was for sure. Van knew he got that from Kat. She was like a dog with a bone on a story. Jack looked like he'd end up the same way. "Hey, buddy, whatcha doing there?"

Jack jumped up, "Van!" The little boy lunged and wrapped his arms around Van's legs. His little hand grabbed Van's larger hand. "Read this with me?" he asked.

"Yes. But let's do it outside, okay? It's a nice day."

Jack furrowed his brow. "Can I bring my trucks? They want to hear too."

Van nodded. "Of course. Trucks are always welcome."

Jack ran ahead of Van and was out the door before Van could even tell him to put on a pair of shoes. With all they had going on, he wasn't sure that it mattered, but he'd find out pretty quick. He could hear Steve and Kat following behind them.

As soon as Jack made it out the door, he abandoned the book on a patio chair and ran with his trucks to the sandbox, his little bare feet tossing up sand with every step.

"Jack! Shoes!" Kat yelled as she stepped out of the back door.

Van smiled. Kat was a good mom. She might have troubles as Jack got older. She'd want to keep him close to home, but Van knew that her intention was good. Steve was right behind her.

"No phones?" Van asked.

They both nodded.

"I have what they want. It's time for us to make a plan."

Van caught Kat glaring at Steve. He wondered what had gone on while he was at Harbor Canyon. Would they pressure him to know what he got? Steve was the first to speak. "Thanks, man. I mean it."

"Don't thank me yet. This thing isn't over." Van sat down on one of the patio chairs, glad they hadn't asked a question he wouldn't answer. Steve and Kat followed his lead. "The next thing to do is to text them and let them know."

Steve jumped up, "I can go do that right now."

Van held up his hand. "Hold your horses. We need a better plan than just giving them what they want."

He saw the idea land for Kat. He had no idea if Steve would realize they needed a plan. He just seemed to want to get the dose and give it to his mom. He wasn't interested or concerned about any type of a bigger picture. He was completely compliant.

The questions had a purpose. Van needed to see where Steve and Kat's mindset was. Clearly, Kat was in the game. She was quiet. Listening. Waiting for more information. That's what he would have liked to see in Steve. He didn't. He just saw a man that didn't know what to do and had an "any port in a storm mentality." Van was surprised by this. After all that Kat had been through, he expected that Steve would have been more engaged or at least more protective of Kat. Something about it didn't seem right. Van chalked it up to Steve's lack of training.

"Here's what I'm thinking. We should let them know that we have the information."

"That's what we did the first time," Kat offered.

"Then they should be happy. Let's see what he comes back with once we let him know."

Van realized that although he wanted a plan, until they knew what the man in the scrubs, as Kat called him, would ask or want. They'd have to wait and craft the plan once they heard back. Like everything in intelligence work, you had to build in for uncertainty.

Steve disappeared into the house and brought the burner phone out to the patio.

Van looked at him, "Don't say much. Just tell him we have it." A shadow of anger passed over Steve's face. Van wasn't even sure that Kat saw it. Clearly, Steve didn't like being ordered around. He'd have to get over it if they were going to get through this, all of them in one piece.

A moment later, Steve looked up. "Okay, it's done. Now what?"

Van squinted his eyes at Steve wondering why he even asked. "We wait."

49

Edgar had been waiting. Just waiting. Victor had texted an hour earlier telling Edgar that he'd been made. Edgar didn't really care. He just wanted one of his people near the house, just in case. Edgar shook his head, sitting with his feet up on the makeshift footrest in the office. The Beckman's had been a lot of trouble. They were pesky clients for sure.

He rolled his neck, hearing the bones and ligaments creak. All of this up all night chasing after people wasn't doing his health any good. His phone chirped.

It was the Beckman's phone. "We have it."

Good, Edgar thought. One step closer to getting to Utah and away from Aldham. He walked around the office. How did he want to get the information from them? There was a post office in the middle of Aldham. Downtown, if you could call it that, wasn't very busy late at night. There were few people that wanted to go out in that area. They were far more likely to populate the old city center with all the restaurants and bars that were a few blocks away. In the dark, there would be few people hanging around the post office.

Edgar took a minute to think and then decided his best option was to just go for it. "There's a mailbox on the corner of 6th and Ridge. Tape the information to the bottom of the box at 10 pm tonight. Use duct tape. A key for a locker in the bus terminal will be waiting."

He wasn't sure if he needed to tell them to use duct tape or not. It wasn't like the Beckman's were career criminals. Better he tell them than they use some other kind of tape and somebody walks off with the information before he could get to it. Get to it, he would. He would be watching. This delivery was his key to get to Utah.

50

Hannah had a headache. She had been at her desk for hours trying to figure out how the tech's apparent suicide and Kat Beckman were connected. She was beginning to wonder if they were.

She got up from her desk and walked back and forth a couple of times. She needed fresh air, but that wasn't going to happen right now. She had to understand what was going on or at least have a good enough command of the situation that she could relay the details to the Major in a way that wouldn't get her fired.

Thinking about it was so frustrating. She collapsed back into her desk chair. Would it be that bad to be fired, she wondered? She could go back to West Virginia and work on their family farm. There would be plenty of sunshine and outdoor work with no one bothering her with national security issues she just couldn't figure out. She pushed herself up in her chair and took a deep breath. She couldn't give up. It wasn't like her. It wasn't who she was.

Just as she was giving herself a pep talk, her cell phone rang. She didn't recognize the number, and it said restricted. It couldn't be the worst thing that happened today, so she decided to answer it. "This is Carter."

"Hannah, this is Detective Haskins." Immediately, Hannah was curious about why he called. He'd probably have more questions that she couldn't answer. She would have to think of a way to deflect those.

"We've had a few developments in the case."

"Okay."

"First, are you feeling better?"

Hannah was surprised such a grizzled old detective would be concerned. Then she wondered if maybe he had family somewhere that he cared about. She pushed the thought out of her head. It wasn't one for the moment they were in.

"Yes, thank you."

"Glad to hear it." She heard him shuffling some papers in the background. "Two things have come up that I thought the Army might be interested in. The first is that our victim has no GSR on his hands. That's..."

"Gunshot residue," Hannah finished his sentence for him.

"That right." Haskins seemed to wait for an explanation of how she knew.

"I grew up on a farm."

"Uh-huh," Haskins continued, "The second thing we found was that he had an injection site on his neck. He tested positive for ketamine. He would have been dizzy, groggy and confused. With the amount in his system, he wouldn't have known that gun from a plastic fork."

"So, you are saying he was murdered."

"That's about the size of it."

DIGESTING the information that Haskins had shared took a full dose of antacids. Hannah was resisting calling Major Javorek until she knew more, but the pieces of the puzzle just weren't coming together.

Hannah had left the office and was back in the park. She had a timer set on her phone. She was giving herself exactly one more hour to piece things together before she called the Major. She was afraid she would make that call basically no answers. Every time she thought about the conversation, she knew she'd have to have with him, her stomach clenched. Surprisingly, she wasn't angry. She was afraid.

Her phone rang. It was Ben. "Ben, what's going on?"

"Hannah, I've been doing a bit more digging."

"Great. Tell me what you've found."

"Well, I've checked the profiles of the people on the Bluebird mission. There's been no strange activity on their social or financial records. I've even checked their emails."

"How did you do that?"

"I reached out to Major Javorek's office to get logins and permissions."

Hannah's stomach clenched even more than it already was. Ben had gone off the reservation by doing it without talking to her. That wasn't good.

"Hannah, are you still there?"

"Yes, sorry." She'd have to deal with the fallout from that later. "Did you find anything?"

"No, nothing. Apparently, if Beckman took anything, it didn't go anywhere." Ben paused. "Are you sure you don't want to just ask her about it?"

"Not yet. I need to update the Major first."

"Did something happen?"

"Yep. The tech that killed himself? It was a murder."

"What?" Ben sounded startled.

Hannah probably should have thought through telling him before she blurted it out. Ben didn't have the strongest constitution. It was out now. "Yeah. The detective just called. He was drugged."

"Wow. Do you think the murder and the Beckman thing are connected?"

"That I don't know, Ben. We have to try to figure that part out."

With that, Hannah told Ben she had to go. The timer on her phone was about to go off. She didn't have much of a choice. It was time to update the Major. She could avoid it no longer. She stood up from the bench she was sitting on and started walking back to the office. She called the Major's cell phone on the way back.

"Javorek," the Major answered when the call connected.

"It's Hannah."

"Do you have news for me?"

Clearly, he was upset with her. Anything that represented a breach would be an embarrassment for his command. Hannah didn't know how to fix it. All she knew how to do was to give him the information that she had. "I do. The tech that disappeared? He was murdered."

"Are you on a secure line?"

"No, sir."

"When you get to one, call my office."

"Of course."

The call ended as abruptly as it started. Hannah picked up the pace walking back to the office, cleared through security where Thomas was standing and went to her office. Using the landline, she called him back.

"Major, it's me." Hannah heard him sigh on the other end of the phone. She knew that he was near retirement. She was sure he didn't want to go out because of a problem on his record.

"Good. Now, what's going on?"

"The tech that we thought committed suicide -- Tommy Scanlon -- was murdered."

"What?"

"Detective Haskins called me a couple of hours ago. I wanted to take some time to try to put the pieces together, but I have to be honest, Major, I'm not making any headway." Telling him the truth made her feel better. She might not be able to solve the riddle, but at least she was honest about it. She hoped he would respect that.

"What do we know?"

"Apparently there was no GSR on Tommy's hands and the ME found an injection site on his neck. His system was full of ketamine. That's a tranquilizer."

"A pretty powerful one," Javorek offered. "We don't know if this is linked to the Beckman breach or not?"

"No. That's what is so frustrating. Kat couldn't have gotten the information if Tommy hadn't messed up the drives. But Ben looked and there is no evidence of any tampering or outside communications that look sketchy in regard to the Bluebird team. It just doesn't make sense."

"Okay. This is good work, Hannah. I appreciate you bringing all of the chess pieces to the board. That helps. Let me get some of my people working on it. You keep going on your end."

Hannah breathed a sigh of relief. "Of course, sir. I appreciate your patience."

"Yup, just keep working the problem."

Hannah hung up the phone and realized that she wasn't going to lose her job immediately at least. She would live to fight another day.

51

The sun had started to set. Kat had arranged for a sitter to come and watch Jack while they dealt with the drop and the serum. Jack was happily nibbling on pieces of a hot dog with his sitter, a girl named Anna from down the street. Anna was patient and kind, or at least seemed to be whenever she came over to be with Jack. Her older brother was going to come and stay with them as soon as he got home from work. There would only be a small window of time where Anna and Jack were alone.

Steve had just come home from work. He and Kat hadn't talked about his eruption from before. Kat didn't know that they would ever talk about it. It might just be one of those potholes in the road of their marriage they had to deal with down the line.

Kat was ready to go. She was too nervous to eat dinner. She sipped on a bottle of orange sports drink and checked her Sig to make sure that it was ready. She had on jeans and boots and a t-shirt that just covered her gun. A loose jacket helped her to cover it. No one would know that she was carrying unless they looked closely. She doubted anyone would. She twisted her hair into a low ponytail. It was all she could manage.

Kat didn't know a lot about Van's plan. All she knew was that he had left a few hours earlier and told them he'd be back before it was time to go. He said that he would take care of placing the package. They just needed to be ready a couple of hours before the drop was due.

Kat knew Van well enough to know that there was more going on than met the eye. He had seemed focused when he had left them, but a little distracted at the same time, as though a thought he couldn't talk about was in the back of his head. It was probably nothing, she thought.

Steve came down dressed in jeans and a polo shirt. He rarely wore t-shirts, only when he was running or laying on the couch at the end of a long day. He had on an old pair of jeans and dropped a pair of work boots by the door. "I'm ready," he said.

"Did you want to borrow one of my guns?" Kat asked.

Steve looked at her with a question on his face. "Why would I? These people are not the threat you and Van have made them out to be."

All she could do was nod. It wasn't worth arguing about. "Do you want something to eat before we go? There are a couple of hot dogs left from what Anna made for Jack."

Steve nodded and ate the hot dogs standing up. They were both nervous, but there was nothing to do now except wait for Van to arrive.

52

V an started up the truck. He had just left his house where he had put together the ID in a manila packing envelope that he had found. It was sealed. He had a roll of duct tape next to him on the seat. He adjusted his pistol on his hip. He didn't know what to expect, so it was better to be prepared.

His next stop would be Kat and Steve's house. He wanted them to head out at the same time. He wanted to be sure they were ready. In the last few hours, he had formulated a plan that would likely get all of them what they needed, but it would take some cooperation on their part. Kat he was sure of, Steve not so much. He had formulated the part of the plan that Steve could play that wouldn't require quite so much trust on Van's part. Trust wasn't part of Van's personality. He'd been burned far too many times.

The part that Van couldn't calculate was the threat level. He had no idea how dangerous these people were. Clearly, they were well organized. Clearly, they had resources. But were they violent? That he didn't know. What he did know was that there would be no way to tell until they got there. None of them had the backup intelligence or assets they needed to make good decisions. Van knew he'd have to trust his gut, Kat's steely nature and Steve.

Pulling into Kat and Steve's house, he saw the front curtain move. Kat must be ready. It was just about go time...

53

Edgar left the warehouse after nighttime had settled on Aldham. The nice thing about night drops was that the darkness provided a shroud for his movements. He had so many fake IDs that even if he did get picked up, there would be no warrants out. The Apex lawyers would see the ping on his fake record and show up within the hour.

He drove the gray Honda on a street that was parallel to Ridge Road where the mailbox was located. He turned up Seventh Street and eased the car down an alleyway pointing towards Sixth. He pulled the car up behind a dumpster that was right on the corner of the alley and Sixth. It provided good cover. He could watch the mailbox and be there to get the information as soon as they dropped it off.

On the way to the pickup, he had stopped and gotten two chicken tacos and a beef burrito. Waiting for the Beckman's, he sat in the car and ate. These events used to make him nervous, but after the first couple of times, he discovered that there was no reason to worry. The clients weren't hardened criminals. They were just average, everyday people that had access to information that could buy them a cure for cancer. It was a simple proposition. It was no different than paying for a bottle of aspirin. They just had to pay a different way.

Edgar hummed to himself, crumpling up the wrapper from the burrito. He looked at his cell phone. There was an hour to go before the drop was due. Time to get out of the car to watch.

He left the keys in the ignition, got out of the car and closed the door quietly, checking above him. He pulled a black base-ball hat down low over his forehead and kept his glasses on. Everything he wore was black. There were only windows to office buildings above him. There were no fire escapes, just a dotting of dumpsters and trash along the alley. As Edgar stepped closer to the rusted dumpster on the corner, he real-ized it smelled like spoiled milk.

Time to watch and wait.

54

K at was by the door when Van arrived. "It's time to go," he said.

"Do you have a plan?" Kat asked.

"Sort of. It's hard to plan without all the intel."

Kat saw Steve roll his eyes. "Guys, this isn't a military mission. We are just gonna go get some serum for my mom. These people just want to make a buck. That's all."

Kat saw Van raise his eyebrows. For someone like Van, the threat was real. Kat thought he was smart to take the situation seriously. She almost reminded Steve about how the Apex people killed Sarah but getting into a fight wouldn't be smart right now. She was pretty sure it would just erupt into something ugly. "Tell us what you need us to do," Kat said.

"We are going to have to divide and conquer. Steve, I want you to retrieve the key and go to the bus terminal and get the serum. There should be two doses. Get one right over to your mom and hold onto the other one for me. Have the nurses put it in a refrigerator."

Steve nodded.

"Kat, you and I are going to tail this guy when he picks up

the information. We need to see where he goes. We've got to try to get the information back that I gave him. If we can figure out where they are keeping the serum, we might be able to get even more and expose their operation."

"You are kidding, right?" Steve said. "Listen, all I want is a dose for my mom. You think you are going to take my wife and go on some commando mission?" Steve's face was filled with fury. "That's just not going to happen."

Van looked like he was going to reply, but Kat spoke first, "Steve, we are just going to see where he goes. We will call the police and let them handle it." She laid a hand on his arm, trying to calm him down. "You just get the serum and get it over to your mom."

Kat wasn't sure he believed her, but he seemed to calm down knowing that at least the idea was they were going to just follow the man in the scrubs.

With the group's tasks setting in, Van said, "Kat, you come with me in the truck. Steve, you drive separately so you can go to the bus terminal and the hospital. The man in the scrubs said he'd text the burner when he places the key. You take that phone and head over as soon as he texts you. Everyone have your burners? No regular phones, right?"

Kat and Steve nodded. Kat followed Steve and Van outside. She gave Steve a weak smile and got in the truck with Van. There was an envelope on the seat between them. She didn't ask what was in it.

The drive to the location downtown near the post office only took about twenty minutes. Kat felt small in the truck next to Van. The fear was eating away at her, the smell of smoke in her nose and the ache in her wrist were chasing her. She felt Van's eyes on her, "You okay?"

"Yeah."

"This is going to be okay."

"I hope so." Kat's gut feeling didn't match with Van's words or her own, for that matter. She wasn't sure that she believed Van. She could tell by the set of his jaw that he was preoccupied thinking about what they were about to do.

"Once we get to the site, I'm going to stop right in front of the mailbox and do the drop. If they are watching, they will see me do it."

"How are we going to watch them?"

"That's where you come in. I'm going to drop you about a block away. Think you can find a spot to watch the mailbox for me while I leave the envelope for them?"

Kat felt better knowing there was a job she could focus on. "Sure."

"Once I drop off the information, I'll leave. I'll drive down the street and circle around. There is a parking lot just down the street that has a lot of heavy bushes, but you can see the mailbox and down the side street pretty well. I'll leave you there and pick you back up in the same lot. Just find a good spot to hide, okay?"

"Okay." Kat sat for a moment. "How do you know about the parking lot?"

"I did a little recon."

Kat smiled. It was just like Van to do the extra work for them. They were quiet for the rest of the drive. The streets in downtown Aldham were deserted except for a few people going into an all-night diner that was lit up a block or so away. The rest of the after-work crew would be seven or eight blocks over at the restaurants and bars. Van took the side streets to the parking lot and turned off the headlights as he pulled into the back of the lot, where there was no way that he could be seen. The truck stopped. As Kat opened the door, Van pointed, "There's the stand of bushes. There's also a building with a couple of side door entrances that are dark. I'm going to go out the back of the lot and circle around. You should see me in about two minutes at the mailbox. I'll make a big show of leaving and then circle right back here to meet you."

Kat nodded, the knot in her stomach growing. She closed the truck door as quietly as possible and watched as Van pulled away. She moved quickly to the trees that bordered the parking lot. It must have been Aldham's way of beautifying a concrete mess in the middle of the city. Tonight, the mature trees and overgrown shrubs were welcome cover for her.

The darkness covered her. She moved toward a hiding place and waited.

55

Van didn't like leaving Kat in the middle of the city alone. He knew that she was armed, but he'd heard someone say, "The day you have to draw your weapon is the worst day of your life." While that didn't apply to the military, Kat wasn't exactly military. Van pushed his worry for Kat out of his mind for the moment. He needed to concentrate.

As soon as he got out of the parking lot, he put on his headlights. The last thing he needed was some cop pulling him over for something stupid like that. There were already too many variables. He didn't like it, but that was what they had to deal with.

As much as he wanted to get a dose of the cure for Steve's mom, he wanted to get the story and some of it to the lab for analysis. Van's innate sense of justice and fairness made him think that the cure should be available to everyone whether they had information to sell or not. The current cancer treatments were just placeholders that made pharmaceutical companies a lot of money. Sure, some people were cured, but not as many as should be, given the advancement of medicine.

At some level, Van wondered if it was a racket just meant to make money.

Van drove slowly and made the turn onto Ridge Road. He had chosen to approach the mailbox on the same side of the street, which meant he had to make a couple of other turns to get the truck turned around that way. What he didn't want was to have to park the truck across the street, run with the package, place it and then cross the street again. That was too many steps. Too much exposure. If something went south, at least he'd have the opportunity to dive into the truck for cover.

Van wasn't sure that these guys would use a sniper or over-watch. While they were dangerous enough to kill Sarah, and he was pretty sure that Apex was behind the Medicus fentanyl scam, he wasn't sure they were the bullets type of people. All in all, their game was pretty passive. Time would tell.

Van pulled down Ridge Road and stopped at the mailbox. He had already put strips of tape on the envelope that had the IDs and codes in it. He didn't want to be standing on the corner fussing with it. He wanted to get out of the truck, place the envelope and get out to pick up Kat. He stopped to look quickly around him, trying not to seem obvious about evaluating the area. He was relatively sure they would have at least one scout or pickup person already in place. At least that's what he would have done.

Getting out of the truck, there didn't seem to be anyone on the other side of the street. The lights were brighter there, anyhow. Down the street a little further, he could see a small, inky spot in the middle of a bush. That was probably Kat, having taken up a low position where she could see the mail-box, waiting for him to get back. He turned his head quickly, not wanting anyone to follow his attention. Down Sixth Street, it was dark. He couldn't see anything beyond the edges of the buildings.

Van moved around the front of his vehicle, the package in

his right hand, the sticky part of the tape facing up. There was no reason to pretend to be doing anything other than what he was doing. He crouched down and pressed the tape into the metal bottom of the mailbox. There had been no rain for the last few hours and although the post office wasn't known for their efficiency, Van was happy to see that the bottom wasn't rusted through. The package stuck to the bottom of the mailbox like glue. It wasn't going to come off unless someone pulled it off. At least that part had gone well. The first step was complete.

Van stepped off the curb and walked back to the driver's side of the truck. Anyone watching him would have likely thought he had just dropped something. His movements were that fast. He started up the truck, revved the engine for good measure, turned the headlights on and drove down the street, away from the drop site. He even turned the radio up loud to attract attention.

Van drove down Ridge Road for about a half a mile, well out of the sight of anyone who might be watching, turned off the radio and circled back to the parking lot where Kat was waiting. As soon as he got to the back entrance, he turned off the headlights, pulling the truck into a spot that was hidden by the overgrown shrubs.

When he got out of the truck, he saw that Kat had positioned herself at the base of one of the shrubs. From far away, her dark figure just looked like a tangle of branches. Someone would have to look closely to see that it was actually a figure.

"Kat," he whispered. He saw her turn towards him and nod. "Anything?"

She shook her head no. "What do we do now?"

"Watch and wait."

A few minutes went by. Van started to wonder if the man in the scrubs would actually show up. A couple had walked by and a man walking his dog, but no one had approached the mailbox. Van checked his watch. They still had a few minutes before the ten o'clock deadline. Most likely, they had been watching Van do the drop and wanted to give him plenty of time to leave.

At five until ten, a hooded figure came walking down the street, his hands in his pocket. He dropped an envelope in the mailbox and then bent over, pretending to tie his shoe. Van saw him reach up and pull the envelope from under the mailbox, stuffing it in his pocket. Van couldn't be sure, but it looked like he replaced it with something else.

"That's it," he heard Kat whisper. "Let's go."

"Wait for one second. Let's see which way he goes from here."

They waited, not moving in their concealed location behind the shrub, watching. The man in the scrubs went down Sixth Street avoiding the main drag of Ridge Road altogether.

Kat and Van moved quietly to the truck, getting in to follow. Van had turned off the interior light so there was nothing that would attract any attention, even if the man in the scrubs had turned around to look. Van pulled out of the parking lot, using the side entrance on Sixth Street this time, watching and waiting.

"There," Kat said, pointing down the side street. There's a car leaving now.

Van had seen it too. A compact car in a non-descript color had emerged from what looked to be an alleyway. It moved with no headlights on until it was well on Sixth Street.

"That has to be him," Kat said, shifting in her seat.

Van focused on the car ahead of him. He didn't want to follow too closely behind. These people, although they hadn't been violent in the past, had been clever. He drove slowly and let another car merge between them.

The car drove through the city and moved over into the

right lane to take the highway. "Where do you think he's going?" Kat asked.

"I've got no idea, but we will see."

Once on the highway, Van eased the truck back, keeping an eye on the compact car, but not getting to close. They'd have to watch and wait and hope not to lose him to see where he was going. If they lost him, they'd have no way to find him again.

56

Steve didn't wait to leave until the text came through. He gave Van and Kat a ten-minute head start and then told Anna, their sitter, that he needed to go. Jack was so absorbed in watching a video that he didn't even look up. "One of us will be back by eleven." Anna nodded and turned her attention back to Jack and her phone.

He got in his truck and headed toward downtown Aldham. He had the burner phone with him on the seat. He felt ridiculous wearing work boots. He could easily have worn his running shoes, but there wasn't time to worry about that now.

The traffic was light and Steve got through it easily. Why Van and Kat were so worked up about this, he wasn't sure. Then again, he wasn't the one that had been drugged and had to do the initial trade. Maybe that was why Kat had been so edgy. Once this was over, maybe she should go see that trauma therapist again, he thought. She definitely needed more help.

When he had met Kat, she had been home from the Middle East for a few years. From their first date, despite how beautiful and smart she was, he could see that there was trouble underneath. By the time he understood how deep the trouble ran, he was already in love with her.

At one point, they had seen her counselor together. It was for only one session. Kat had asked him to come so that the therapist could tell him more about what Kat was going through. Kat, herself, had a hard time describing it.

The therapist, a sweet woman, told Steve, "It's like being caught in an ocean tide that you can't get out of. Kat has all the smells and thoughts and experiences from that day. Some days, there is less tide. Other days, the sea is angry and there are a lot of waves. We can't remove the tide. What we can do, and what we have been doing, is to give Kat the skills to keep herself from drowning."

Steve had asked about drugs to help her stay calm. He remembered how violently she had reacted, "I'm not going to be beholden to a pill every single day for the rest of my life. I will get through this," he remembered her shouting. The therapist simply looked at him and said, "It seems her mind is made up." He still thought their life would be easier if she would have agreed to medication.

Driving into Aldham, Steve hoped that Kat could keep it together. Although he would have preferred going with her instead of Kat going with Van, Steve understood why Van had divided the work the way that he did. His dislike of weapons and his lack of training made him more of a target in Van's eyes. He got that. He made a mental note to look into martial arts training when this was all over. It would be good exercise too.

A few miles out of Aldham there was a shopping center with a coffee shop drive-through attached. Since Steve had some time to wait before the burner would go off, he pulled in and got a black coffee with two creams and a sugar. He pulled the truck around to a parking spot and sat, sipping his coffee.

All he could do now was wait.

. . .

STEVE THUMBED through his phone and drank his coffee while he was waiting. For all of Van's good intentions, he brought his own phone with him. At least he could keep up with his emails while he was waiting. He knew that Van was just being paranoid. That's how those ex-military types are, he thought to himself. On the seat next to him was the burner phone that had been delivered in the box. He read an email from a potential client who was asking a few questions about a proposal he had submitted and sent a text to the nurse on duty at the hospital to check on his mom. He was partway through the response when the burner vibrated on the seat. Steve abandoned the email he was writing on his own phone and looked at the burner. The text read, "Delivery made."

Steve already knew the location for the key, so he put the truck into gear and started driving. At about twenty after ten, he started down Ridge Road and found the box at Sixth Street. He did a U-turn to get across the street, not really worried about getting pulled over. Stopping at the box, he stepped out of the truck and leaned over. Underneath, there was a key taped to the bottom. He pulled it off and went back to his truck. At least the man in the scrubs had provided the key. He was close to getting the cure for his mom.

He pulled out into traffic and drove two blocks to the bus terminal. The man in the scrubs hadn't needed to tell him which bus terminal. There was only one in Aldham. He parked in the public lot to one side of the station, the smell of diesel engines idling filling his lungs. As he walked into the station, the bright lights forced his eyes into adjusting. There was a ticket counter off to the left and a series of metal benches in the center. Off to the right were the loading doors where passengers went out to catch their ride. Along the back wall, there were two aisles of lockers. Steve made his way across the waiting area, nearly stepping on the hand of a homeless man that had fallen asleep under one of the benches. Steve muttered, "Any port in a storm, buddy," and kept going.

Once he got to the locker area, he looked at the key. It was marked with a 213. Steve found the locker -- it was at the end of the row, as far away from the public side of the terminal as possible. The back of the bus station smelled like a combination of fumes, body odor and urine. There is a reason I don't travel by bus, Steve thought.

He fit the key into the lock and turned it. The red-painted door swung open. There was nothing there. There was no bag, no box. Steve looked at the key again and checked the number. He had the right box. He felt around on the top and sides, wondering if there was something there he just couldn't see. There wasn't. Nor was there anything in the corners. There simply was nothing there.

Steve relocked the box. He wasn't sure what else to do. He was sure that by now Van had dropped off the information that the man in the scrubs wanted. Bus lockers only had one set of keys. A feeling of nausea filled Steve's chest and he choked back the coffee that was threatening to come up on him. They had been tricked. There would be no cure for his mom. This was her death sentence.

He quickly walked out of the bus station, wanting to text Kat, but realizing that he didn't have her number. She had one of the burners and not her own phone. There was no way to reach her.

57

Ben stopped by Hannah's office. "I've got news," he said.

"Come on in." Hannah took off her glasses and looked at Ben. He seemed excited. He stopped to close the door.

Hannah watched him as he plopped down in the chair in front of her desk.

"The file has been accessed."

"The Bluebird file?"

"Yes."

For a moment, Hannah thought her heart stopped. "Was there another breach? Did it happen here?"

"No, that's not what I mean. I wrote a little program that would search for the names of the people listed anywhere on the Internet -- even the dark web."

Now he had Hannah's attention, "And...?"

"It's been accessed."

Hannah leaned forward in her chair, "By who? Where?"

"I don't know the who yet, but the where is Iran."

Hannah leaned back in her chair, letting the information sink in. Iran? "Tell me what your next step is."

"I'm going to keep working on tracking it. I just have to warn you, we might not ever be able to find out who has it though. It's not as easy to find out who has information on the dark web."

Hannah nodded. She knew that Ben would do everything he could, but there were places on the dark web that even the most sophisticated military tech and the best minds couldn't figure out. Unfortunately, this might be one of those cases. Hannah's mind ran ahead. She knew that Major Javorek had the list of names. She wasn't sure what the protocol was to notify them and what the next steps might be. She had no idea if they were in danger, would have to be moved or even given new identities. For a moment, she imagined that they had children and families. This was nothing short of a total disaster. Lives were clearly on the line. "Okay, I have to call this one in. I'm sure they are going to want to talk to you directly."

Ben smiled for the first time in days, "I know. I have to use my best techno-babble."

Hannah returned his smile, knowing right away that he was referring to a running joke they had about him talking in English and not in tech. "That's right. You are going to be here?"

"Yup. I'll let you know if I need to go anywhere."

Hannah nodded and Ben left the room. Not only did she now know that Kat Beckman had taken the information out of the site, but that she had sold it and it had somehow ended up in Iran. "Gotcha," she muttered under her breath, picking up the phone to call the Major. He'd need to hear about this right away. With this level of information, she thought, Ben might just have saved her job. She'd have to buy him dinner after all of this was over.

58

K at and Van followed the car they believed had the man in the scrubs in it. They had been on the highway for only about ten minutes, going straight north out of the city, when they saw the small gray car, veer off onto an exit lane. Another car came speeding off, cutting off Kat and Van, but at least it provided some distance between them and their target.

Kat was hoping that by now Steve was on his way to the hospital with the serum for his mom. She felt choked up a little bit. Van said, "You doing okay over there?"

"Yeah, just watching the car."

"That's it?"

"I was thinking a little bit about Laura. I hope she's okay. I hope Steve got the serum."

She felt his hand cover hers just for a moment, giving it a squeeze. "Me too." Van pointed, "He's turning."

The car turned down a side road that had a sign at the entrance, announcing an industrial park. Next to it was a sign from a commercial real estate agent who was apparently trying to sell the land. The sign itself had seen better days.

"The industrial park," Van said. "That's a good cover. I don't think there are many businesses left in there, are there?"

"Not that I know of," Kat said.

The industrial park had two manufacturing companies left in it. They were both close to the main road at the front of the development. Toward the back of the park, there were quite a few other buildings that had for sale signs in front of them or had simply been abandoned. As Kat and Van drove further and further back into the park, there was less traffic and a blanket of darkness.

"I'm going to pull in here just for a minute so he doesn't see us," Van said, turning into a driveway. "You keep watch. We'll follow again in a second."

Kat leaned forward on the seat so that she could see better. She pushed her bag out of the way. It had been sitting on the floor and she needed the legroom. She watched as the little car went up another quarter mile and turned into a building on the left side of the road. "There," she pointed, as the car disappeared around the back. "He pulled in there."

Van gave the man in the scrubs a minute to get himself into the building and then looked at Kat. "I think we should go in for a closer look." Van had the truck started and was rolling forward before Kat had a chance to answer.

"Wait!" Kat stopped him before he put the truck into gear. "Look." Out from behind the side of the building came the car again, this time heading the other direction. Kat quickly looked up their location on a map, "It looks like the road goes in a circle. He must be heading out the other way."

"Where are you going?" Van whispered. Kat realized he was talking to himself. "It looks like he left. Let's go get a closer look."

Before she could answer, the truck was rolling slowly forward, across the street and onto the driveway of the building.

Knowing that the man in the scrubs had left gave them a

chance to get a better look at the building. The building itself looked abandoned, although some of the details were hard to see with the headlights off. The truck tires crunched on what was left of the gravel that surrounded the building.

"The front looks like it used to be offices, but it looks dark," Kat said, rolling down her window. "Are we sure that he came in here?"

"I thought so," Van said. Kat felt him let his foot off the gas. The truck eased forward around the far side of the building. The grass had grown long and tall against the building and in the field next to it. On that side of the building, there was only one door. It was solid, so there was no way to tell if there was light coming out of the building. As the truck pulled around the back of the building, there was no other noise except the truck's engine. In the moonless night, it was hard to see, but what they could make out was that there were a couple of loading docks, three to be exact, two positioned up higher and one a little lower. There was also a dumpster in the back that looked like the waste management company had forgotten to collect it. The lid had flopped back and had broken off of one hinge. On one side of the loading dock were a set of concrete steps that led to a landing area and a door.

"Do you see that?" Van said.

"What?" Kat strained to see what he was looking at.

"It looks like there is light coming out from under the door."

"Really?" Kat sat back in her seat. "You think this is the place?"

"Might be. Maybe we should go have a look."

A knot started to form in Kat's stomach. This is not Afghanistan, she told herself. Van must have caught the look on her face, "You can stay in the truck if you want."

"No, I'm okay."

"Are you sure?"

"Yes," Kat hissed a little more intensely than she meant. "How did you know?"

"You roll your wrist. Lotsa guys have something similar. It's okay. You're okay." Van smiled at her. "Let's go have a quick look."

From behind the seat, Van produced a short crowbar. "Just in case," he said. They both got out of the truck. Kat closed her door with a click, checking to make sure her Sig was still in place. She pulled her t-shirt up over the butt of the gun in case she needed to access it.

Van walked toward the steps by the loading dock. There was no noise at all, save for a few crickets chirping or peeper frogs making noise. Kat couldn't tell which. It seemed even darker outside of the truck with no dashboard lights offering their glow. Out of his belt, Van pulled a small flashlight. He clicked it on, the beam of light cutting through the darkness around the building. Van didn't say anything, but Kat knew by the way he glanced back at her that he wanted her to follow.

They made their way up the steps and to the door. Van used the flashlight to look at the frame. There was a security pad next to the door. "Haven't seen one of these before," he whispered. "Looks like overkill for an abandoned building, don't you think?"

Kat nodded, not wanting to make any noise. They had seen the man leave, but there was no reason to attract any attention just in case.

"If there's an alarm system, won't we set it off?"

"We might..." Before Kat could stop him, Van took the crowbar and wedged it between the door and the frame and with one move, he popped the door open. There was no sound inside.

The interior of the building was even darker than outside. Kat watched as Van stepped inside, sweeping the flashlight from left to right, trying to determine the space they were in. In front of them were manufacturing machines. It looked like some of them had been taken out of the building and others just left behind. Some were covered and some weren't. A thin film of dust seemed to cover everything, although Kat thought she saw footprints in a few areas. Across the main workspace was a wall with a door in it. To the right, there was a glassed-in office area.

"Let's see if they left any of that serum in here," Van said, making his way across the floor. He shined the light at the office and then again at the door. "Let's try this door over here." Van walked over to the door. It was a double door with another keypad that matched the one that was outside. Van used his crowbar and he wedged the door open.

Lights went on as soon as the doors opened. It took a second for their eyes to adjust. Immediately to the left, there was a desk with a chair. There was nothing on the desk except for an empty coffee cup. In the center of the room, there were two long stainless-steel tables filled with scientific equipment.

Kat stepped forward to look at the tables. She ran her hand along the edge of the table. It was cool to the touch. "Do you know what all of these things are?" she asked Van. She realized she was whispering, but she wasn't sure she needed to.

Van was off in the corner checking the desk drawers. He walked over, "I'm not sure." He pointed to one of the pieces of equipment on the table, a white cube-shaped item. "That looks like a centrifuge."

Kat made a face. What did they need a centrifuge for, she wondered? Two large refrigerators caught her eye. They were stationed against the wall and were humming softly. "What do you think is in there?" she asked Van.

"Don't know. Let's take a look." Van said. He walked over to the doors and pulled gently. The interior lit up. Inside the refrigerator on the right were vials held in racks. Some of them were blue, some of them were yellow. In the other refrigerator, there were red vials and clear vials on the bottom. Van reached in and pulled one of the clear vials out. "Look at this," he said, handing it to Kat. She could clearly see the Medicus labeling on the side. "Is this the fentanyl that they found with Sarah?" she asked.

"Looks like it to me," Van said, putting it in his pocket.

Kat reached into the refrigerator and pulled out two vials of blue and yellow serum. She knew the blue serum was the cure. That was what she had injected into Laura's friend. What the yellow serum was, she wasn't sure. "Can you give me some of that red stuff," Kat asked. Van handed her a couple of vials. All of a sudden, Kat started to feel really nervous. "I think we should get out of here before he gets back, don't you?"

"Yeah, probably."

They left the room where the serum was and closed the doors. Van's flashlight hit the wall on the other side of the lab and Kat saw something on it, but she wasn't sure what. "Shine your light over there," she said. Van nodded.

In the darkness, she saw a board with pictures stapled to a piece of plywood. Immediately, she recognized a Senator, two CEOs of pharmaceutical firms and a police chief. In the lower right-hand corner was a picture of Laura. She had an X through her in wide magic marker ink.

Van whispered, "Isn't that Laura?"

Kat nodded. Anger filled her system. She realized at that moment that the man in the scrubs, whatever his name was, never had any intention of healing Laura. He just wanted what he wanted. "We need to get out of here," Kat said, feeling pulled between fear and fury. "Let's get this over to the hospital. Maybe we can beat Steve there."

59

Major Javorek hung up the phone with Hannah, sitting in his office. He should have been home to his wife hours ago, but the call he just received confirmed the breach was real. The threat was now more urgent than ever with the discovery that the Bluebird roster had been accessed by someone in Iran. The Major popped a handful of antacids in his mouth, the chalky taste sticking to his tongue. He washed it down with a gulp of lukewarm black coffee. When this was over, he knew he needed to switch to tea.

He pressed a button and his administrative assistant picked up, "Sir? How can I help?"

"Get me through to OPS."

"Yes, sir."

A momentary silence was replaced by a deep voice, "OPS. This is Baker."

"This is Javorek. Secure the assets and bring her in. I'll be down in a minute. I want things moving by the time I hit the head and walk in the door."

"Roger that."

60

L eaving sounded like a good idea. Kat just wanted to get out of the warehouse. They hadn't heard an alarm go off, but she wondered if there was some sort of silent alert going off somewhere. She hoped that Steve had made it to the hospital. "Let's go," she said. Van nodded and they both walked toward the door. As they walked to the door, she heard a click and then the overhead lights went on.

The man in the scrubs stood right in front of them, blocking the door. "You found my home away from home, did you?"

Kat froze in place. The man in the scrubs must have seen them follow him after the drop. Out of the corner of her eye, she saw Van try to reach for his gun. From a shadow, another man stepped out, took the gun from Van and smashed the butt of the gun into the side of Van's head. Van crumpled, unconscious.

"No!" Kat yelled. She felt strong arms pull her wrists behind her, the gun pulled from her holster before she could reach for it. She had no way to defend herself.

"You just couldn't leave well enough alone, could you?" the

man said. "I guess I should introduce myself. My name is Edgar. Don't bother introducing yourself. It's nice to see you again, Kat." The man that was holding Kat searched her pockets and pulled out the vials. "So, you were doing a bit of stealing here with your friend, Van, huh?" Edgar held the vials in his hand, rolling them over each other almost unconsciously. "It's not nice to take other people's things," he sneered. "You know, we don't like people nosing around in our business. It's not the way that we do things." Edgar looked at Van, who had been trussed with cable ties on both his wrists and his ankles. "We have quite a mess to clean up here. And, since you have violated our agreement, we did the same. Show her," Edgar said, nodding at the office.

From behind the glass, the lights went on. There was a man standing in the window holding onto something. "Say hello to your little boy, Kat." Edgar yelled toward the office, "Jack, say hello to your mama. Oh, you can't, can you? What a shame..." Edgar walked toward her. "When you left to go to the drop, we decided we needed a little insurance policy on you. Here he is."

From where Kat was standing, she could see Jack. It was as if a knife had been stabbed through her heart. She could see that his wrists were taped together and there was a band of duct tape over his mouth. The lights above caught the glint of tears falling down his face.

A feeling of desperation came over Kat. She looked down at Van, who wasn't moving. A trickle of blood was rolling down the back of his head from where the butt of the pistol had hit him. She couldn't even tell he was breathing. He couldn't save them.

Her eyes moved over to Jack. He was pale. All she wanted to do was to run over to him and hold him in her arms, stroking his hair. It tore her to the core to see him terrified like that.

Nausea swept her. The smell of smoke filled her lungs in a way that she couldn't begin to imagine was possible from a memory. She started to cough and choke, going down to her knees. She couldn't breathe. Breathe, Kat, breathe, she tried telling herself. Nothing was working. Through the memory of the Humvee window, Jack's tears were the last thing that she saw.

61

K at had no idea how long it had been since she passed out. She didn't know where Jack was. She opened her eyes slowly, not sure if the men were standing over her. As she started to get her bearings, she saw the men over in a corner talking. Jack was still sitting on the chair in the window, his eyes staring at her.

The men in the corner weren't paying any attention to her or Van, she noticed. They were talking intently about something, the subject of which she couldn't make out. She moved her head slightly to see if Van had woken up. He hadn't. She looked to see if he was breathing. He seemed to be, but she couldn't tell.

The cold of the concrete floor was soaking into her body. She tried to move her arms, but they were secured with duct tape. Her hands were on the opposite side from the men. She pretended to still be out cold and started working on the tape that held her hands. Within a couple of minutes, her fingernail pushed through the adhesive and fibers of the duct tape, setting her hands free. She kept them behind her back, pretending until she figured out what to do.

She had to get to Jack. It didn't matter what else happened. She had to get to him. She took a deep breath. She had a moment to think. The men were still talking, now pointing to the room where the serum was. At that moment, she knew she was Jack's only option. No one else was coming. No one else could save her child.

She knew that Van carried a backup gun in his ankle holster. The question was whether it was still there. From how her body had fallen, she could reach his ankle without them seeing. His foot was near her face. She eased her arm around and felt for it. It was still there. She quickly pulled it back behind her, pretending that her hands were still taped in place.

The office where Jack was being held had an entrance door at each end. The far end was where the guards were standing. On the end that was closest to her, she could see the door was ajar. If she ran as fast as she could, she might have a chance to get to Jack before they got to her.

Her heart started to pound. It was now or never. At some point, Edgar would decide they needed to do something with her, Van and Jack. Better for her to act first.

She rolled to her feet and sprinted across the shop room floor to the office door. As she started to move, she heard what sounded like an explosion behind her. She had no idea if she actually hearing it or dreaming it. It didn't matter, she had to get to Jack. She punched the door open mid-stride, turning the corner.

Yelling and gunshots had filled the shop floor. Kat had no idea what was going on. It didn't matter. Only Jack mattered. She saw his small form turn towards her as she rounded the corner. Then he was on his feet before she could get to him.

"No, you don't!" Edgar yelled, pulling Jack in front of him. He pulled a hunting knife out of his belt loop at held it to Jack's throat. "You think I won't! Try me!"

Kat stopped about ten feet from them. The look of pure

terror on Jack's face was too much to take, a drop of blood rolling down his neck from the pressure of the knife. "Let him go now!" she yelled. Behind her, she could hear more shouting and gunshots, but she didn't take the time to look.

"No. I won't." Edgar sneered at her.

Something inside of Kat snapped. She raised the gun, centering the sights on Edgar's head.

"You won't do anything. What if you hit poor little Jack?" Another trickle of blood slipped down Jack's neck. Tears poured from his eyes.

Kat didn't respond. Her finger was on the trigger. She pulled it.

Edgar's body slumped and she ran to Jack, dragging him away from Edgar's body and under a desk. She pulled the tape off of his mouth and held him tight.

"You are okay. We will be okay."

Sobs were wracking Jack's body. "Dad, Dad, Dad..."

"He's not here."

"Keep him away from me!"

Before Kat could ask what Jack meant, she heard voices, "Clear. Clear." And then another, "I think she's in here."

Kat pushed Jack further back under the desk, putting Jack behind her, the gun pointed and ready to shoot.

A man in full tactical gear with an American flag on his helmet kneeled down, "Easy Kat. You are okay. We are here to help."

"TJ?"

TJ took his helmet off and keyed his radio. "I've got them. We need a medic in here ASAP." He looked at Kat, "Yup, came to save you again."

"How?"

"Major Javorek called me in. They know about the breach, Kat. They thought if I talked to you it might be easier. But now I see that there might be more to the story?"

Kat slumped back, putting Van's gun on the floor next to her. TJ quickly picked it up, cleared it and stuck it in his vest. "There is. Is Van okay?"

"The medics are looking at him now. Let's get you and Jack out of here."

As they stood up, Kat looked over at Edgar's body. By the way he fell, she assumed he was dead. TJ put his hand on her arm, "He's dead, Kat."

Kat could barely take a step. She felt weak and confused. She saw TJ lean over and help Jack out from under the desk. TJ picked him up. Jack buried his face in TJ's neck. Kat didn't move until the nudge from a medic helped her to take a step forward.

THE NEXT FEW minutes were a blur. Flashing lights greeted her at the door of the building. She and Jack were taken to a waiting ambulance where they were treated. TJ stayed with them the entire time. "Where's Van?" Kat asked again.

"They just took him to the hospital. He was awake and asking about you. Looks like he will be okay. Probably a concussion. He's got a hard head though. The docs will check him out."

Kat couldn't concentrate. She knew she was in shock. She looked back in the ambulance from where she was sitting on the bumper. Jack was on the gurney, covered in a blanket. The medic had given him a stuffed animal, a purple alligator, and was checking his blood pressure. They had already started an IV on him. She turned to TJ, who was standing by the ambulance doors.

"How did you find us? No one knew where we were."

"Your bag was in Van's truck."

"My bag?"

"Your encryption key has a tracking device."

She didn't know that, but it made sense. "Where's Steve? Is someone bringing him here? Did he make it to the hospital?"

TJ looked at her, a combination of sadness and anger crossing his face. "We picked him up, Kat."

"Why?"

"He was part of this."

Thoughts of their life together flashed through her mind. How was he part of Apex? How could she not know? "What are you saying? How is that possible?"

"We aren't exactly sure, but apparently the serum these guys have can cure cancer but can cause it too. He had been hired to marry you because they knew you had access to intel. You didn't have any family, so they used Laura as bait. I think he was hoping to be able to get the cure before the cancer killed her. He gave his own mother cancer and put you and Jack at risk to make a buck."

Kat's head spun with more questions than answers as the medic asked her to sit on the bench next to Jack on the way to the hospital. TJ stepped into the ambulance, his tactical gear off. "I know you have questions. You are going to be okay. You and Jack will be okay."

That was the last she heard before she passed out.

EPILOGUE

The chains from the swing creaked a little bit as Jack kicked his heels. He'd gotten heavier in the last few months after a few weeks of not wanting to eat or sleep. The psychologist said that it was normal after the trauma of having a knife held to his throat.

It was a beautiful day. The sun was shining and the first cool fall breeze had started to form. Kat pulled her jacket closer and looked to her right, "You okay there, Mom?"

Laura looked back at her. "You bet."

Jack squealed. "No, don't do that!" he yelled as a big dog nipped at his heels as he swung past.

Kat smiled, "Woof, be good," she said. The dog they had found at the industrial park had been their constant companion since that night. She hadn't been sure she wanted to have a reminder of that night in her house, but Woof was innocent and he loved Jack. Kat was learning to live with reminders of her past, both the good and the bad.

She felt a tap on her shoulder. She looked at Laura, who leaned in close and whispered, "Who's that?"

Laura had been staring across the street at a man who was standing next to his parked car watching them.

"I have no idea..."

THE END

ABOUT THE AUTHOR

K.J. Kalis is a writer who specializes in thrillers and Christian non-fiction. Currently living in the Midwest, when she's not working, K. J. spends her time chasing her two dogs, traveling and trying to get her husband to pick up his socks.

For more information on books written by K. J. Kalis, visit www.kjkalis.com. You can find her on Facebook (Karen Kalis) and Instagram (karen.kalis). Thanks for reading!

Lightning Source UK Ltd.
Milton Keynes UK
UKHW021153150621
385550UK00008B/1795